I0831423

PINOT NOIR

Blood, Wine, Magic

Book 1

JUSTIN GODEY

This is a work of fiction. Names, characters, places, and incidents either are products of the author's imagination or are used fictitiously. Any resemblance to actual events or locales or persons, living or dead, is entirely coincidental.

Pinot Noir – Blood, Wine, Magic: Book 1 by Justin Godey

Written and Published by Justin Godey

http://www.justingodey.com/

justin@justingodey.com

Cover by Jacqueline Sweet.

I would like to dedicate this book to my family. To my wife, Katherine, who supported and encouraged me when I said I wanted to become a novelist. To my children, Kairi and Cassidy, who have inspired me to be myself and pursue my creativity.

I would also like to thank:

Elizabeth Alton for being my mentor and sponsor and for letting me text and call her when I was freaking out or unclear on my next step. Her insights and feedback got me to the end.

Gerry Valle for being my first, harshest, and most insightful critic. His high standards have pushed me to improve my material far beyond my imagination.

Sativa January for offering to edit and bring a literary eye to my work. She helped me identify themes and ideas I had put into the book that I wasn't even aware of!

"Any sufficiently advanced technology is indistinguishable from magic" – Arthur C. Clarke.

"Once magic has been documented, categorized, and explained, it becomes just another principle of science. It can then be applied, recreated, systematized and turned into technology" – Genevieve Gale

Prologue

At some point, everyone finds themselves having been forever changed by some trauma, some bad decision, or regret that haunts them for the rest of their days. At least I do. It took one year for my view of the world, of life, right and wrong, and truth to change forever.

What is truth? What is a lie? Who determines which is which, and what proof can be provided as concrete? In school, I was taught many "facts" that were later revealed as lies. "Facts" about history. "Facts" about science. "Facts" about how people think and learn. The people who taught me those facts were, for the most part, not intentionally deceiving me. They truly felt as though they were bestowing the truth upon me. Does ignorant complicity in a greater lie make one a liar? Or does one's conviction or one's intention make it true?

Our perceptions are, at best, incomplete. One might argue they are, in fact, critically flawed. There is so much around us that we don't perceive, even on the best of days.

Physically, our vision can only perceive a tiny band of the light spectrum. Our hearing senses only a tiny fraction of the vibrations in the world around us. Taste, smell, touch: all flawed in their own ways, when considering the grand scheme of things.

Psychologically, even the most empathic are all but blind to the thoughts and feelings of others. Our attempts to communicate those thoughts to others often end with us finding ourselves lonely in a crowded room. Even our endeavors to understand our feelings and motivations are clouded and obscured by our egos.

Our perceptions are flawed. Our senses lie to us.

Regardless, we continuously base our decisions, our actions, and our entire lives on these flawed perceptions. We accept our senses; we are ignorantly complicit in the lies they tell us. Does that make life a lie?

It's been said: "The greatest lies are the lies that we tell ourselves." Those little things we say and do that help us get through our days. If we saw ourselves from the outside, most of us would just stay in bed and wither away from despair. Maybe at their inception, we see these lies we tell ourselves. Maybe we don't. Maybe we never did and never will; but we repeat them over and over again until they are true, at least to us.

Does this make truth subjective? Relative? Is truth contextual?

These are the questions I ask myself when I reflect on my first year of college. I was an angsty, emo eighteen year old. I read supernatural horror in the quad. I wore a black trench coat, even when it was 90 degrees out. I wore black combat boots and a black turtleneck and black jeans. Always. My hair was shaggy and hung down to cover my eyes. I didn't wear jewelry or anything with logos or branding. I had personal beliefs, a perceived truth about a stark aesthetic, and strong morals on not advertising other people's shit. I was, for the large part, miserable, lonely, and outcast.

I met Hale during that first year. I was perusing the stacks of the library for a paper I was going to write. All these years later, I don't even remember what the paper was about. Hale was there explaining the nuances of reading auras to a few other kids when I came across him.

He was tall, dark-haired, and a few years older than me. I took immediate notice of the leather jacket and tattered jeans he wore, accompanied by a punk band t-shirt. He even had a chain on his wallet. I think back on him now and laugh at what a poser he was, but back then I thought he was shockingly cool—especially compared to all the uptight grade-seekers I'd met up to that point.

I didn't know much about much back then. However, thanks to my incense burning, sweat-lodge sweating, crystal-rubbing, new-age parents, I knew a bit about hippy-dippy stuff. I knew about auras, astrology, and tarot. So, I inserted myself into Hale's lecture. He was not too happy about someone taking part of his spotlight. But he quickly warmed up to me, and after the others left, we kept talking. He was a senior majoring in anthropology and minoring in classics. He tended bar on weekends at a club nearby and was very, very into the occult.

I bumped into him a few more times on campus and even went to the bar where he worked. He served me, even though he knew I was underage. That should have tipped me off about the kind of person he was. But I was young, impressionable, and naïve.

And I was very impressed by Hale.

We became friends in the weeks that followed. In hindsight, friends is probably the wrong word. I fell into his circle and became a part of his little cult of personality. He'd ask me favors, and I'd do them without hesitation. The relationship was mostly one-sided, but I found myself seeking validation from him time and time again.

A few months after we met, Hale invited me to join a "club" of his. Hale had found a handful of other students interested in the supernatural and occult. They got together once a week or so to perform "magical" rituals and rites. I was amused at first. It was like cosplay, where we would dress up in robes and put on ritual makeup. We would go out into the woods where Hale had built an altar on a stump. We'd make circles and chant and burn candles. Then when we were done, we'd have a few beers, tell stories, and laugh. It was the first time I felt like I belonged. I never thought anything bad of the group, to me it was a place to call home.

There was a revolving door of names for our group. It seemed like every week we dubbed ourselves with a new moniker. They were all childish and my ears still redden when I think of them—The Eldritch Circle, The Brothers and Sisters of Night, that sort of thing. We weren't a real coven doing real magic. It was just a bunch of emo kids messing around after class.

I don't know if Hale always planned it that way, or if he found a book of some kind, or what. Things started changing. Slowly at first…until things became a little more serious and a lot darker.

Hale started having us use blood—pigs' blood at first that he got from a butcher. Then he started showing up with live chickens and such to sacrifice. A few kids dropped out of the "club' at that point, but the majority of us stayed. I can't tell you why. Hale had a way of making it seem like this shift was nothing to worry about. He had the sort of charisma that fuels a cult leader's success, I suppose.

Then he started asking us to cut ourselves.

I began to get wary. Or is that true…? Did I ever question Hale? Or is it simply in hindsight that I wish I had? How ignorantly complicit was I in what was happening? What is the truth?

I'm still not sure I know.

Shelly was different than the other girls in the club, being interested in the magic and the implications of mastering such occult and supernatural arts. She wasn't interested in Hale for anything other than getting his knowledge from him. For his part, Hale—like most people who are used to being the center of attention—was therefore infatuated with Shelly.

Slowly, ritual by ritual, Shelly resisted him less and listened to him more. One day Hale and Shelly showed up to our meeting holding hands. I didn't think much of it at the time… of anything. While I questioned the bloodletting in the back of my mind, I still felt a strong need to impress Hale. It just seemed obvious that Shelly would come around too.

But then I started to notice Shelly acting differently. She spoke less. She had fewer opinions. I became concerned, as did a few of the others. But Hale wasn't concerned. In fact, now that Shelly seemed to dote on him, he didn't seem to care about her at all. Something wasn't right, but I didn't know what to do about it.

One day I was playing with a crystal and decided to read everyone's auras. Really read them, not the smooth-talking pickup line version that Hale always tried on people.

"I can tell from the azure of your aura that you are a very creative person," he'd say, using the opportunity to touch or caress the girl he was talking to. It was always a girl. As he rubbed their arm, he'd say something like, "But these red lines here tell me you have an intense passion in your soul."

Blah, blah, barf. That's not what it is like at all.

When I looked at Shelly's aura, I knew something was very, very wrong. Shelly didn't have a vibrant, colorful, changing aura like a regular person. She had a dull, flat, gray aura and a thin thread attaching her to Hale. The grey sheet of Shelly's aura was a tattered mess. Hale used constant and persistent power but lacked finesse. Little coherence remained in the wreckage of Shelly's essence.

This prompted me to look at Hale's aura. Similar threads were attached to everyone else in the group myself included. The color was leaking out of the edges of the others' auras, and they were slowly being drained of what made them unique. It's impossible to see your own aura, but I assume that this was true for me as well.

At that moment, I realized what Hale was doing. What we were doing with our magic rituals. We were all slowly, unwittingly sacrificing ourselves to Hale.

He was doing this intentionally.

I felt sick, angry, and scared. I sought help. I went to the school health center and talked to the school psychologist. I told the administration about the blood and the chickens, but of course, it wasn't taken seriously. Not seriously enough anyway.

Hale and I got pulled into a few conflict resolution sessions with a school counselor. Questions were asked, but ultimately the response was a boys-will-be-boys, laissez-fair shrug. The only way I was going to be able to stop this was with magic.

I took a deep dive and read what I could in the school library. When I found little useful information there, I went to larger universities and studied everything. I found people on the internet with theories and ideas on magic and how to stop it. People who claimed they could do all sorts of improbable and supernatural things, but most of that was fiction.

Eventually, I cobbled together enough knowledge to protect myself and the others and sever our connection to Hale. My present-day self could do this quickly and easily. Back then it was a real struggle. None of the wards or counter spells I tried on Shelly helped. I could sever her connection to Hale for a short time, and she would wander around like a lost sleepwalker until he reasserted his control. Hale figured out what I was doing fairly quickly. Our relationship degraded to outright passive-aggressive hostility. But he never confronted me.

Everyone from the group stopped hanging out over time, except for Hale and Shelly. And then Hale graduated. He went to grad school on the other side of the country, and I never saw him again.

Shelly continued to be a husk of the person she once was. She rarely spoke, didn't do her work, and barely managed to feed herself. I tried everything I could to help, but nothing worked. Not long after he left, her family came from Colorado to get her.

I later heard she was diagnosed as schizophrenic and was

institutionalized. Any further attempts I might have made to help her were gone.

It took a long time for the horror of that year to fade, but when it did, I came to a resolution. If no one else could stop people like Hale, that I would have to do it. After graduation, I threw myself into this life and never looked back. Rarely looked back.

That isn't true though, is it?

I always look back, always wonder if it was all my fault. Was I so busy lying to myself about my own trauma that I couldn't see the trauma I was helping inflict on someone else? A trauma that I could have prevented, if only I had been more aware.

Chapter One

My life has fallen into a bland routine after graduating from college.

Picking up corporate contracts, I spend a few weeks drawing sigils. These ritual symbols help to shape and redirect the flow of magical energies benignly back into the energy of the universe. It pays well when I get work…but more often, it pays nothing because I don't.

I'll pick up a side job here or there just to pay the bills, often unrelated to magic. Once I spent a week trying to convince a client that it was rats, not ghosts, causing the lights to flicker in their home.

At a certain point, chaos began to seep in around the edges of the dull monotony that I slowly sank within. It is hard to say when. Change often begins subtly. It sneaks up on you, one tiny ninja step at a time. By the time you realize things are changing, they already have. If I had to choose one moment when I heard the first faint whisper of change skulking in the shadows at the edge of my perceptions, it would be the day I met Chris Benson.

. . .

IT STARTED last year with a phone call. It usually starts with a phone call, so this was nothing new. Since I suffer from an overabundance of caution and work-from-home syndrome, I almost never give out my physical address.

"MILES WARD, Private Mystic Security Consultant, speaking. If you've been cursed, call me first!" I answered the phone.

I kept coming up with new catchphrases every time I took a call and regretting them immediately. Like most of my odious personal habits, I blamed my father. I needed to start workshopping my catchphrases before blurting them out.

"Um. Hello. My name is Chris, Chris Benson," a soothing but hesitant tenor tone said.

"Hello, Chris. What can I do for you today?"

"Um. Well, I think.... God, this is crazy. Like, I don't believe this stuff, but I think I might be cursed or something," he said.

"That's something I can help you with," I replied, trying to sound business-like. "Could you be more specific about what you're experiencing?"

"Um. Well. Can we meet somewhere in person? I don't really feel comfortable talking about this over the phone. This is...well, this could get me fired," he said.

"Yeah. Yeah. Of course. Where would you like to meet?"

"Do you know the Oxbow Preserve?"

"I'm familiar with the preserve, yes."

The Oxbow Preserve is one of those notable geographic features that, everything nearby gets named after. It's just a little man-made bend in the Napa River that loops around and around. I'd only lived here for a couple of years then, but I'd invested a lot of free time in finding out about the area. If you know where you are, stepping into a trap is much harder.

"Can you meet me there, say, this afternoon? One o'clock?" Chris asked.

"In the parking lot, one o'clock, it is," I responded. I'd had more than a couple of potential clients want to meet privately. My line of work is starting to gain more acceptance in society, but a lot of people still think it's hokum. There can be a stigma, and many don't feel comfortable talking seriously about magic where they might be overheard.

I got to the preserve about half an hour early. I try to be early to these things when I can to scope things out and get a lay of the land. The Oxbow Preserve was an interesting choice of location, out of anywhere in the city. There might have been a few people walking dogs, fishing, or picnicking, but it wasn't heavily trafficked. There was enough traffic that being there wasn't suspicious. The entrance is off of Silverado trail and hidden between an apartment building and a little shop, I think sells wood-burning stoves.

The preserve is where you can find privacy, but you aren't so far away from civilization that you can't find help easily. It means this Chris guy has more than a passing knowledge of the city.

I WAS SITTING on the hood of my Wrangler, playing a silly game on my phone, when a man walked up to me. He was a little shorter than me and very muscular. He had the demeanor of a Marine—with close-cropped hair, clean-shaven, and focused eyes. My first thought was military, but he may have also been a firefighter or police officer.

"You are Miles," he said. I couldn't tell by his inflection if this was a statement or a question.

"I am indeed." I hopped off my hood and held out my hand to shake.

His grip was strong enough I knew he could have crushed it. However, he managed a squeeze gentle enough not to cause pain, but firm enough to make sure I knew he could.

"You must be Chris Benson," I said

"Yes," he scanned the area over my shoulder. It wasn't a furtive look but the confident and unconscious look of someone used to surveying his surroundings.

"Good to meet you, Chris. What can I do for you?"

He motioned with his head toward the path, and we started to walk. The paved path is a giant loop with little dirt paths leading off into the underbrush. Despite there being two other cars in the lot, there were no other people we could see.

"This is confidential?" he asked tentatively.

"I promise you I will keep our conversation here in confidence as long as it doesn't make me an accessory to any crime or anything like that," I offered.

"I respect that. Okay. I'm an officer with the Napa PD," he said, confirming one of my suspicions. "I'm worried that the guys on the force could get weird if they found out I am going to psychics or whatever."

"Well, I am not a psychic, but I do hear your concern. I want to help out and have no desire to make your personal or professional life more difficult," I assured him.

"Okay. So, about maybe six weeks ago or so, I started having problems—little stuff at first. My drill broke, and I cut my hand. A ladder fell over and almost hit me. It started out as little, you know, like normal stuff."

I nodded and stayed quiet, letting him continue. After he saw I didn't have anything to say, he kept talking.

"But then it started getting worse. Getting more and more…improbable. Like crazy stuff started happening. A wheel came off my patrol car while I was on the freeway. A piano fell out of a window and almost crushed me. A piano! That only happens in cartoons, right? I found a black widow's nest in my bed. In my bed! At first, it seemed like a coincidence, and then it seemed like someone was out to get me. But these things happen so constantly and so randomly that it can't be a coincidence, and I can't see how someone would plan it all. It feels like I must be cursed!"

Not twenty seconds later, as if to prove his point, a branch broke off a tree and came crashing down, forcing the both of us to leap away.

"*See?*" he said as we both got up off the ground and dusted ourselves off.

"I do," I said, brushing dirt and leaves off of my pants. "The good news is that this is probably an entropy curse. I've encountered this before."

"And the bad news?"

"Why does there have to be bad news?"

"If someone clarifies the good news, it always means there is bad news waiting around the corner," Chris said.

"Yeah, that tracks," I responded. "The bad news is that you have an enemy, probably someone close to you."

"Why would it be someone close to me?"

"Because a curse like this has a foci, something that draws chaos to it. Common culprits are jewelry, accessories, and tattoos. Things you would have on you most of the time. Anything new or changed around the time that this started?" I asked.

"No, nothing that I can think of."

"This has been going on for six weeks?"

"Yeah, that's right."

"So going back, say, three months or four months. Anything new? Jewelry? Tattoos? Any big changes in your life? There is a good chance this has been going on longer than you've noticed. Often, it's just that the early stuff was so small that it didn't register. That it wasn't until you had a good number of events that a pattern started to form in your mind."

"Well, two months ago, I broke up with my girlfriend."

"Now that's something. Why'd you break up with her?"

"She thought I was having an affair. She didn't believe me when I said I wasn't. She got kind of crazy about it. I said it wasn't going to work out."

"Were you having an affair?" I asked. "Not that it's my business, but it might be important."

"No," he said hastily, too hastily. "Well, not really, no," he added a moment later. "This other woman was flirting with me. We get it all the time in the uniform. I was flirting back, but just talking, that was it…Angela caught me and accused me of having an affair. I said I wasn't, but I felt a little guilty. I probably didn't sell myself well."

"Do you have anything of Angela's on you now?"

He paused to think.

"Yeah, actually, this necklace was hers. She gave it to me when we broke up to 'remember her by,' she said."

He held up a silver chain around his neck, hidden beneath his shirt. It had a little pendant, an abstract metal blob that gave the impression of a bird without encumbering itself with enough detail even to begin to hint at species. It had two little gemstones for eyes. Later, I confirmed they were sapphires.

"Take it off."

"Really?"

"Yeah," I said, reaching into my courier bag and taking out a small crystal. I never leave home without my courier bag; it's filled with all sorts of useful things in my career—in this case, this small crystal lens.

He removed the chain from around his neck and handed it to me. I gazed at it through the lens. It helps examine the aura of things, an imperfect art that I rarely use. It's little more than a parlor trick, but it can be helpful when you need to see an aura in a clearer light."Here's your problem," I said. I saw magic slowly being drawn into the two little sapphire eyes. Crystals can also be used to store magic if properly prepared. There was a tiny trickle of energy flowing into the sapphires which made up the bird's eyes.

"This gathers up magical energy and then when it's full, I think, then it pulses out entropy. It causes something random to happen. It probably isn't always bad. You also probably get to stoplights at just the right time more often and get more little winning lottery tickets. Stuff like that."

"So, what, I just don't wear it?" he asked.

"Well, the only way to stop the effect would be to destroy it or store it in a special magical protection device that kept it from collecting and storing magic. But if you take it off, weird stuff will just happen sometimes around wherever you leave it."

"Okay," he said, scratching his head.

"I think your Angela might dabble in the craft," I told him. "You could be in more danger."

"No, I think I'm okay. I heard she met a rich wine guy and moved to Italy or something."

"Well, can't be too cautious. I can set wards up around your place if you'd like. Just in case," I told him. Then I held the pendant out for him.

"You can keep that; I don't want to touch it now. I'm not sure why I started wearing it in the first place, I guess I wasn't quite ready to move on. Now I am. And thanks, you know, about the protections. I'll take a rain check, but if anything else comes up, I'll let you know."

"Okay, yeah just let me know."

"What do I owe you?" he asked.

"For this? Nothing, call it a consultation. If you decide to call me to put wards on your place, then we can talk turkey," I said, sliding his necklace into my bag. It had recently activated when the branch almost fell on us, so I had at least a few hours before I needed to worry about another entropic event.

"Great. So…is that it then?" he asked.

I looked him over with my crystal lens again, examining his aura.

"That's it. Call me if something happens," I said.

Chris called me a few days later, saying his problems had vanished completely. Ever since then, he's called me if he runs into anything on the job that defies rational explanation or that standard police work can't crack. I call him if I encounter an issue better dealt with by law enforcement than apotropaism. I don't know that this makes us friends per se, but we certainly have a professional relationship.

That day, I took his little entropy-cursed bird pendant home and destroyed it—both physically and magically. However, from time to time I wonder if a bit of its magic might have rubbed off on me first.

Chapter Two

I'm sitting in the corner of Tonic, the restaurant-bar on the first floor of an upscale hotel that costs as much a night as I gross in an average week. I'm eating a wedge salad, and it's okay…for a wedge salad, which is to say that it is really not okay at all.

It's just a quarter of a head of iceberg lettuce covered in bacon, blue cheese and a creamy dressing. Why am I eating a wedge salad? It was the cheapest thing on the menu. It costs as much as my shoes, but it's still the cheapest thing on the menu. I don't want to even think about how much the burger costs.

Welcome to Napa, California.

The food is really a pretext to sit here and watch the lobby. I had to have a heated debate with the host to get a table with a good view of it. I've been sitting here for a while now, long enough that the waiter keeps giving me the stink eye. I've only finished half of my wedge salad when I see the person I am looking for come into the hotel. He waltzes across the lobby with an air of arrogance surrounding him.

Not literally waltzes. That is a weird expression. As I think about it, he doesn't even figuratively waltz across the lobby.

He stomps across the lobby. He's a big frat-boy-looking twenty-something with blond hair, a perpetual scowl, and a cleft chin. He bypasses the elevator with a look of entitled menace on his face. It's like he's daring anybody to stop him, including the stairwell door which he collides into, throwing it open with a crash.

Interesting.

I wait a moment and then stand and empty my wallet onto the table, including shaking it so that change comes out. I quickly estimate how much there is. It looks like just enough to cover the bill and provide slightly less than a 2% tip to boot. I prefer to be a decent tipper, but I didn't anticipate the high meal prices. I'm improvising here and I don't have time to pay with a card.

Hustling out into the lobby, I duck into the stairwell as quietly as I can. I'm trying not to let the door bang as I open it. There is the echo of a door closing above me. Cautiously I close my door and skulk my way up the stairwell. Each door has a sign indicating that it can't be opened from the stairwell side, only to exit. I check each door handle anyway as I ascend the stairs from one echoing metal landing to another. None of the doors budge.

The building isn't that high. Even pausing to check the door handles, it only takes me a few minutes to climb to the top. The rooftop door, however, is propped open with a folded-up newspaper. Where the hell did he get a newspaper from? Does anywhere even print newspapers anymore? I don't bother looking at what the paper is broadcasting. I'll probably be disappointed or disgusted if I find out. I glance out the small pane in the rooftop door.

It's dark. Why do these things always happen in the dark? Why can't it be bright, sunny, and warm? Why do I always end up on a darkened rooftop confronting some entitled frat-boy who is up to no good? There is no good reason for it. And technically this is neither my first darkened rooftop, nor my first entitled frat-boy up to no good.

It is, however, the first time I am checking all of those boxes at once.

Maybe people who are up to no good feel like if you are going to get up to no good, it should be dark. Like you'd be less likely to be seen or caught. The dark is certainly the standard environment for no good in the media. I'm not sure I agree with the logic, but here I am.

I quietly open the door and peek out. There's no indication he's heard me. I don't hear anything for a moment, then far across the roof I catch the sound of a subdued chanting. I think I am in the clear, so I slowly close the heavy metal fire door.

Very slowly. It's almost comical. I expect it to slam with a loud crash, like in a cartoon, just to spite my effort. It doesn't. I pull my phone out and fire up the voice memo app to start recording. I tuck the phone into my breast pocket with the microphone facing out.

My plan for tonight is mostly showmanship and pageantry. I feel like a proper entrance can make the difference between easy money and a rough night. That's the approach I am banking on. I move through the dark across the rooftop.

MY TARGET IS LEANED over the edge of the rooftop with binoculars, and he's staring out across the street. He's standing in a carefully chalked-out circle. He must have drawn it in advance. He hasn't had time to put something like that together while I made my way up the stairs. Guttering candles sit at the corners of a pentacle inscribed within the circle. Amateur work.

He is chanting in a low, mumbling voice. Almost like he's embarrassed to be standing in a fancy circle painted on a rooftop, in the dark, holding binoculars and chanting an ancient rite he probably doesn't understand.

It's not a good look for him, I'll be honest. Unfortunately I know exactly what he's up to.

Stalker gonna stalk. Sorcerer is gonna...sorcel? Is that right? Hell, I don't know.

His name is Eric Walsh. He was engaged to my client's daughter, Vanessa Schultz, but she broke things off. I don't know why she did, and I don't care. It doesn't matter, it's not my business. Mr. Walsh, however, couldn't take rejection. So now, this part is my business.

He's been going through her garbage, collecting hair and used tampons and other gross stuff. Gross stuff that is useful in curses and hexes and the like.

I get close, but he still doesn't notice me. The trick to not being noticed is belonging. I just let myself be part of the background. Walk like you belong and people don't notice. Even in ridiculous circumstances like this, it can work. Sometimes. But tiptoe and sneak like you don't want to be seen and pretty much anyone who is looking will see you.

It's not magic; it's just human psychology. Our brains are wired to notice the things that break expected patterns. This approach always worked for me in childhood hide-and-seek, so why not now?

"Hey," I say from about ten feet away. I have a policy of not surprising people from within striking distance. He jumps, fumbling with his binoculars. I've put him off guard—step one of "The Plan" is complete. I'm not sure this particular plan deserves to get a proper noun, but it just feels right.

"What the fuck, man!" he exclaims.

I stroll toward him casually. Or at least what, in my head, is casual. Based on his expression, I must look more like a drunken clown trying to find his way back to the circus after a bender.

"Sorry," I say. "I just came up here for a smoke."

I continue to calmly close the distance. It should be noted I don't smoke, but he doesn't know that. I dislike lying in any circumstance. Lying stresses me out, but I find myself doing it with ironic frequency. Usually I lean toward half-truths and misleading honesty, but I can't think of any right now. The goal is to keep him off guard while I close the distance.

"You scared the hell out of me. Do you mind? I am kinda

doing something here," he says, shooing me away. He looks nervous.

"Bird watching?" I ask with a sardonic tone. "Something better?"

I pull out a sealed pint bottle of Goldschlager and hold it out to him, keeping it up level with his eyes.

"Want some?"

"No thanks," he says, looking agitated as he waves a hand at me.

His eyes stay focused on the bottle. His words are polite, but his tone is not. My ruse is working, and he's distracted. I take the opportunity to drag my foot through the chalk circle on the ground around him.

I imagine that I can feel the slight zephyr of energy whisper by me. But of course, I can't. I don't think anyone can. No human can anyway. He doesn't notice my move. This confirms my suspicion: total amateur. There's no way a pro would have let me get a foot on his circle. I mean *I* certainly wouldn't.

Up close, I realize he's bigger than I thought. He's an inch or two taller than me and beefy. Clearly this is a guy who works out more than he reads. He's got a mean face, the face of someone who's always gotten their way and is poised to throw a violent tantrum the instant that changes. I'm less and less excited about my plan as it progresses. Definitely downgrading this from "The Plan" to "a plan".

"Hey man," I say.

I'm just going to come clean. This will put him even further off guard.

"I need to be honest with you. I'm recording this. I was hired by Vanessa's parents to get you to stop following her. It's over, and you need to accept that."

There is a long, quiet pause as he stares at me, and I stare at him.

"Fuck you," he finally breaks the awkward silence. Not the quickest on the uptake, it seems.

"A wordsmith," I respond. "So here's what's what. You and Vanessa had a thing at some point for some time. Maybe you think it's still a thing and haven't moved on. But she has. I am going to propose that you and I go down to the hotel bar. I buy you a drink, I get you a cab, you go back to your hotel, and you head home tomorrow morning. Go on, live your life, and forget about Vanessa."

In general, I prefer reasonable. I rarely get it, but it is my honest preference. Eric's face changes, it contorts in an expression of barely controlled rage. He's all but frothing at the mouth.

Looks like I don't get reasonable tonight.

"She'll love me again! I can fix this. You'll see. They'll all see," he says.

I realize at this moment that he's high on something. I don't know what, but his pupils are tiny pinpricks in his irises and his demeanor unhinged. I downgrade 'a plan' to 'a bad plan'.

"You mean that 'love' spell you've been casting on her?" I ask. "Yeah, that's not gonna work. She didn't drink the complimentary 'cocktail' you sent her. Come on, who'd fall for that? And I broke your magic circle. Doesn't matter how much blood you spill. The spell you were casting isn't gonna work."

"How'd you know about that?" he sputters.

"Come on, Eric," I say. "You made a video about your entire plan, and the video is not flattering. It explains why you only have six followers."

His face is now bright red.

"Fuck off," he says, inching toward the expected tantrum.

"Never record a magic ritual. It looks stupid. There you are in a white robe, with a circle of chalk and glitter on the ground. You're burning herbs and saying made-up gibberish while smearing...what was it? Was it chicken blood on your forehead? It looks like a scene from an 80s satanic panic movie. Seriously, it's like bad cosplay," I say with a cartoon version of a South Boston accent, swallowing all my Rs and elongating all my As.

My mouth runs on autopilot when I feel stressed. As I often do, I instantly regret it.

"I don't think your 'spell' was ever going to work. You're an amateur who ordered his magical grimoire on Amazon. Do you think real magic comes with free shipping? Well, maybe it does, if you have Prime..." I hold up my phone, recording our conversation. "I, on the other hand, am a professional."

Once again, my mouth and my face seem to disagree on how comfortable they are with getting hit.

I watch him look down; he sees where I breached his circle. He looks up at me and sees the phone. His eyes move slowly, taking in the scene. I can see the gears in his head turning until they finally click into place. It gives me far too much time to rethink this plan and regret it. It sounded good on paper.

Disrupt ritual, piss stalker off.

This isn't the kind of consulting I usually do. This is more like magical PI work. But the Schultz family had somehow heard about me and apparently felt that I was the man for the job. The pay is very generous, and I am very broke. To be fair, I would have taken the job even if it wasn't.

I am particularly sensitive when it comes to people being enchanted, ensorcelled, or otherwise controlled after what I saw happen to Shelly. It's the most horrible and evil magic there is, in my opinion. Taking other people's free will away; it's abominable, unacceptable, and always pisses me off. The whole point of his "love" spell is to make a feeble attempt at taking away another's capacity for self-determination.

He lunges at me. This was part of 'the bad plan', so I'm expecting it. I twist away at the last second and run for the exit. Running is my go-to in situations like this, but he's bigger and faster than me. Between self-entitlement and drugs, he's fearless, painless, and absolutely self-certain. He has no fear of tripping or falling or running into a wall. All of which I am keenly worried about. When it comes to decision-making and snark, I have the advantage. When it comes to inflicting bodily harm though, it seems the advantage is his.

Stopping to open the door is too slow by measures. As I get it open, he hits me like a defensive back, and we go careening down the first flight of stairs and land hard on the steel landing. It echoes like a car hitting the building. His weight is on top of me, pressing my face into the cold hard metal floor.

Will I ever come up with an actual good plan?

He's heavy. The wind is knocked out of me, and he's got me pinned face down on the floor. It's only an instant's delay before his fists are pummeling me. I get my arms up around my head. I only take a couple of shots, mostly cushioned by my arms, before he is lifted bodily off of me and into the air. Another day free of traumatic brain injury.

Barely.

I hear him slam into the ground with a deflating grunt. As I shake the stars from my eyes, I can hear Officer Chris Benson rattling off something. Maybe it's the guy's Miranda rights? The sharp metallic click of handcuffs punctuates each phrase as he ratchets them down slowly. I can imagine this as the start of a rap song. I start to beatbox a little, but Chris stops to stare incredulously at me. I sheepishly bring my beats to an end.

Okay, maybe a little traumatic brain injury.

Chris to the rescue! Man am I glad I called that guy.

Chris offers me a hand and helps me to my feet. He's a little shorter than me, but he's a fireplug and has a handshake like a pneumatic vise. He's in uniform and gives me a goofy grin that doesn't fit with his overall severe demeanor and aesthetic.

"Thanks," I say, one hand over a bruise rapidly raising on the back of my head. "You arrived just after the cosmetic damage, and before the actual concussions began. Your timing is impeccable."

Chris laughs.

I shake my phone at him.

"He pretty much confessed to stalking her and trying to make her love him again before he attacked me," I say.

Chris nods.

"I witnessed the whole thing. You're an idiot. But this should at least get your client a proper restraining order and him out of the way for the time being. I like your style, Miles—a magical bodyguard whose plan is to get himself beat up so the perp gets arrested," he says, still laughing.

He thinks I'm an idiot. It might be the head injury talking but he might be right. In hindsight, I'm not sure that was the sharpest approach to the problem.

"I'm not a bodyguard," I protest. "I'm a private security consultant."

"To-may-toe, To-mah-toe," he says as he starts to put Eric on his feet and guide him down the stairs. For his part, Eric seems to have lost the wind in his sails and is now sullenly compliant.

I reach over and tuck my business card into the little decorative breast pocket of Eric's polo shirt. He'll probably never look at it, but I think I am hilarious. It reads:

Miles Ward

Private Mystic Security Consultant

Apotropaism, Wards, Charms, and Abjurations

email: miles@ward.magic

PHONE: *707-555-2552*

Chapter Three

I wake up late, which is not normal for me.

I've hit snooze on my alarm four times already. I'm awake enough now to debate just turning the alarm off. An ingrained feeling of guilt washes over me for sleeping in. A little voice in my head says get up and get started with the day.

It sounds like my dad. Bastard's still making my life hell, even from beyond the grave.

I roll out of bed and instantly regret it. I'm sore all over. Getting slammed into that metal staircase last night bruised me up good.

I gingerly reach up and touch the large goose egg on the back of my head. It is huge and tender. The skin is swollen, warm, and sensitive. Note to self: no more jobs that involve pissing off angry, muscle-bound stalkers.

Groaning loudly, I walk down the short hallway to my bathroom. It could be cleaner, but I live in a one-bedroom apartment by myself. I've had no romantic interests to scare off with my slovenly nature, so things have become a bit more grubby than usual. I silently decide to clean it tomorrow as I look the mirror.

With only a superficial look, you wouldn't know I got

pounded into a stairwell last night. I splash water on my face and brush my teeth, going about my day as normal.

A quick, warm shower loosens up my bruised muscles, and I am no longer groaning and shambling as I walk back to the bedroom. I get dressed carefully. Then I carefully dress Hank and form a bruised goose egg with makeup on the back of his head.

Hank is my simulacrum. He's a mannequin based on a body mold—as close a copy of myself as I can manage. He's got the same ritual tattoos on his forearms, calves, and chest, and I dress him every day in an exact copy of my outfit. A lot of people think this is a weird habit, but it's a precaution really. An expensive precaution.

A simulacrum is used to confuse and redirect malicious magic. It's expensive and requires constant upkeep. The simulacrum must have as many possible physical and symbolic links to its creator as possible to remain effective.In theory, I would be able to redirect the magic to Hank.

I've never actually had to use him though, for which I am thankful. One might ask, if you haven't had to use your simulacrum and it might only work theoretically and even then, maybe not completely, is it really worth it?

From a different perspective, by the time a sympathetic effigy created by a malign sorcerer pierces my heart and I die, it would be far too late to concoct theoretical protections.

A sympathetic effigy is what used to be called a 'voodoo doll', but that seems like a culturally offensive phrase. It is also a highly inaccurate phrase as the practice is fairly universal and not unique to any one religion or culture. A simulacrum is, in effect, a sympathetic effigy, but with the directional flow of magic reversed. A sympathetic effigy is used to redirect mystic energy from the effigy to the victim. The simulacrum redirects mystic energy from the victim to the effigy. I like to plan for as many scenarios as possible.

I like planning, which isn't that same as being good at it. Hank gets to hear me carry on at length each morning about all my thoughts and plans for the day. I'd like to say that's because it helps build a sympathetic bond, allowing magic to flow freely between us—and not just because I like hearing myself talk.

But I don't like lying…even to myself.

"Do you know what I'm up to for the day?" I ask.

"You're going to go get coffee and perv on women?" Hank replies.

"Jerk," I say. "No, I was going to go shopping for a new mannequin."

"You can't afford to replace me," he says. *"You already spent practically all our rent money on coffee this month. Good news though, perving is free."*

"Why do I talk to you again?"

"Cause you don't have any friends."

"That's not true. I have Jeff." I stick my tongue out at him.

"Okay, you have one friend."

"And Alistair."

"You play poker with him once a week. That's an acquaintance."

"And Mike."

"You play poker with him once a week, and he hates you," Hank says. If he had a working tongue, he'd probably stick it out at me.

I flip Hank off and start to get ready for my day. I eat a bowl of cornflakes while watching cartoons; it turns out being a bachelor does have its perks. I throw my bowl into the dishwasher, grab my bag and I'm halfway out the door when my phone vibrates in my pocket.

"Hello. Miles Ward, Apotropaist to the stars," I answer. I need to stop with the catchphrases. It's embarrassing.

"Miles Ward?" a perky woman's voice says. She sounds a little confused at first, but without stopping she continues speaking fast. She has a very faint New York accent. "I'm Abigail Klein, personal assistant to Jean-Marie Baptiste. Will you please hold while I get Mr. Baptiste on the line? This might take a few minutes, so please be patient."

Before I can respond in any way, I find myself serenaded

with Muzak appropriated from the last decade. I stand blinking. It takes a minute for my confusion to fade to annoyance. A few more minutes and annoyance grows to anger. A few more and anger shifts to curiosity. Nobody puts me on hold without my consent. But who am I angry at?

John Marie Batist, I think she said.

I put my phone on speaker and open the web browser. I search for John Marie Batist. It wasn't the right name, but it's close enough that whatever sorcery they have going on over at Google figures it out.

Jean-Marie Baptiste is a wealthy winery owner, sixty-three years old, a French national but lives in the Napa Valley—winery, French oak, ninety points, yadda-yadda.

My search is interrupted by a sudden question from my phone.

"Mr. Miles Ward, Apotropaist…to the Stars? Was it?" the voice is deep and rumbling, with an almost indecipherable French accent. It takes me a moment to process the question.

"Yes! Miles! Ward! Consulting! Apotropaist! Speaking!" I say. I realize I am speaking loudly and slowly like a lost American tourist. I rein myself in.

"Hello, Mr. Ward," the voice continues, and I strain to follow his words, between his very low timbre voice and his thick accent. "My name is Jean-Marie Baptiste, I am the owner of JMBaptiste Winery. You may have heard of me. I, sir, have certainly heard about you. Very good things about you, Mr. Ward. I have heard you have a way of dealing with things of dark and mystical natures."

"That's what my card says. I've been operating as a consulting Apotropaist for three years now. It's a fairly new industry, but I like to think I'm at the head of it," I say. I always feel awkward talking myself up, but I'm told it is required for a small business owner like myself.

"Yes, Mr. Ward.As I said, I have heard great things. Mr. Walt Carmichael gave you glowing recommendations. A name like that carries some weight, no?" he continues jovially in his hearty baritone.

So that's the kind of circles Jean-Marie Baptiste runs in.

Walt Carmichael is the billionaire owner of Syzmek Industries. I never met the man, and I'm not sure that I have ever met with anyone who's met the man. But I did work with architects designing the new Syzmek Building in San Francisco.

Everyone said Walt Carmichael was a big believer in the occult, and apparently he requested the building be designed with magical wards intrinsic to its infrastructure. The whole building is a giant network of magical conduits designed to redirect magic harmlessly back into the ambient background of the universe—the Ley.

The Syzmek Building was an impressive job. The job that made my career. It got me paid. It got me mentioned in a couple of articles in business magazines. It got me fleeting nicknames on the internet like quack, charlatan, grifter, and a few more colorful ones. So yes, I know who Walt Carmichael is, and I remember the job.

However, I'm very shocked to hear that Walt Carmichael not only knows my name but personally recommends my work to others. I realize that I am sitting silently thinking and haven't responded yet, so I clear my throat.

"Yes, of course, that name carries quite a bit of weight, a seismic amount I'd say." I laugh at my own pun. My stunning wit is met with nothing but silence.

Awkward.

"What can I do for you, Mr. Baptiste?" I say, trying to talk over myself.

"Yes. Thank you. I have come to believe that I myself or my winery have come under a sort of curse or magical attack. We have been plagued with strange events of late. Grapes dying on the vine. Wine turning into vinegar in the bottle. That sort of thing. I have exhausted the tools available to the viticultural and enological sciences. The authorities have been useless, like the keystone cops in the old movies, you see? It has been suggested to me that perhaps more occult avenues might provide answers."

"I see. Well, I am certain I can help you with that," I say. Actually, I have no idea what the problem is, so that certainly isn't exactly true. I will certainly try to help him with whatever might be going on, however.

"Excellent."

"When and where should we meet for a free assessment?" I say, trying to sound up-speaky and business-forward. Worrying I come off serial-killer-perky, I add, "I can get you a proposal by next week."

"Of course. Spare no expense. You will need to arrange the details with Mr. Whitman, my production manager. Abigail will give you his contact information. Thank you, Mr. Ward, I hope you have a most excellent day." Suddenly Abigail the personal assistant is launching enthusiastically into the details of how to contact this Mr. Whitman.

It is only a couple of hours later and a short drive up-valley before I am pulling off the road and up the way to JMBaptiste Winery.

JMBaptiste Winery is relatively new, just outside town on the Silverado Trail. A right turn up a short, paved drive leads to a small parking lot. Beyond is the winery itself, a huge, beautiful, and sprawling sight to behold.

It was designed to look like a Mediterranean villa, as imagined by a coked-up Los Angeles architect. One large central building has a tasting room and a small cafe. The building has a terra-cotta tiled roof with sand-colored, stippled stucco. A large open garden stands in front with stone pathways leading to sitting areas among the trees and plants, where tiled tables and benches invite wine drinkers to sit in relative seclusion.

The main building contains the tasting room. It is the front bastion of a circle of other buildings: The winery, a large barrel house, and other buildings that are probably storage. In between them all is a large grassy plaza that I assume is used for outdoor parties and events.

Olive trees have been planted exactly twenty feet apart across the whole compound line nicely. Their wide swaying branches create a sort of barrier between the winery and the rest of the world.

Behind the winery, climbing up the hill and spreading out on either side for a half mile in either direction are the terraced vineyards. Rows and rows of vitis vinifera cut the landscape into strange flowing, verdant lines.

I park and walk up the short path, between the olive trees to the front of the winery's tasting room. A man stands there, clearly awaiting my arrival. He seems to recognize me; I realize I probably don't look like the other customers here at the winery. I may have shown up a little underdressed for the occasion.

He's standing a few feet to the side of the front door, back straight, hands behind his back. He wears a suit, black and modern—it's lose cut, skinny legs, tight at the wrists. Expensive, I assume. My clients are lucky if I button up my shirt all the way. This man clearly spent forty minutes this morning putting product in his hair. He's grown out just enough scruff on his face to make it clear to everyone that he's laid back and casual, without being long enough to look unkempt. The kind of guy who spends tons of energy trying to look nonchalant, to hide the fact that he's as uptight as they come.

"Hello, Mr. Ward. You are five minutes late. I'm Charles Whitman. That's Charles, not Chuck, not Charlie, not Chase, Chip, Chaz, Char, Chaddy-O, or Kyrie. You may call me Mr. Whitman. Let's keep it on a Mister-Mister level, pun not intended," he pipes out in a nasally voice.

"Mr. Ward was my grandfather. It's Miles, please just Miles. I apologize for being tardy, I got caught at a couple of lights," I say as I hold out my hand to shake.

When that is refused, I close for a fist bump. When that's

ignored, I go for the elbow tap. I chuckle awkwardly and put my unshaken, unbumped, and untapped limb back at my side.

"I don't know you, Mr. Ward. I don't like you, Mr.Ward. You, sir, are a charlatan. You know it, I know it, but my boss doesn't know it. A fool and his money are soon parted, Mr. Ward. I do not begrudge you your entrepreneurial spirit. I ask simply that you get to your chicanery quickly, and quietly conclude your business without disturbing any of our customers, employees, or events. Having executed your hocus-pocus, I ask that you be gone," he says in a locomotive-like fashion, plowing forward and refusing to be derailed.

"Understood," I say, giving him a sarcastic salute. "Please show me to my chicanery!" Whitman groans. He takes a folder off the counter and slaps it into my hands. I glance at it; it looks like a quarterly report for JMBaptiste Winery.

"Mr. Baptiste asked me to give you that. I suppose you'll be wanting to see the cellar," he says as he turns without waiting for an acknowledgement. All of the winery's employees seem to be very brusque and hurried.

I follow him across the yard into the main winery building and down a corridor. Iron girders have been added inside the infrastructure to make it earthquake tolerant. I had assumed the building was new construction, but the earthquake retrofit makes me adjust my thinking. It was likely built in the '60s.

We come to a large wooden door, bound in metal. It is designed to look old, sturdy, and imposing. Mr. Whitman leads me through. Inside, it is climate controlled and filled with pallet upon pallet of cases of wine.

"The cellar. All vinegar." He looks ready to sob. "This is an unprecedented loss. Millions of dollars in wine. Worthless."

"When Mr. Baptiste said that some of your wine had turned to vinegar…I had no idea," I say, looking at row after row of shelved wine bottles.

"Mr. Baptiste is being very stoic about it, but this may well ruin us. We have rented a refrigerator truck that we have parked in the parking lot as a temporary cellar. If we leave any wine around the winery for more than a few hours, it goes bad. I can't imagine why, in the face of financial ruin, Mr. Baptiste has turned to a palm reader to fix the problem! But he has, so please do your business," he says petulantly.

"Let me have a look around. Where can I find you if I have any questions?"

"Oh, I'll be right here. I'm not letting you out of my sight," he says, glowering and crossing his arms on his chest. He probably thinks that he looks intimidating, but with his slight build, primped suit, and generally snotty expression he looks like a spoiled child.

I shrug and get to searching.

Wherever I look—high and low, the front and back of each wine rack, wall, electrical conduit, seismic reinforcements, everything—I don't find anything inside the cellar.

Nothing in the winery or tasting room either. I make my way between the various buildings. There are little gardens dotting the landscape, taking up corners and spaces. They provide soft barriers to guide visitors to 'stay on the path' walking between buildings. These gardens have a mix of edible and ornamental plants growing together. They are probably all edible, but certainly some were chosen for their ornamentation.

Laying in one of these small gardens is a rock that catches my eye because it has a shape drawn on it. I stop and pick the rock up and look it over carefully. It's a river rock, almost flat, about the size of my palm. Someone has written a sigil on it in black marker. I look at where the rock was sitting in the garden.

It was touching the very corner of the Cellar.

"Hmm," I murmur, and I walk around the building until I find another such garden. A brief search reveals another rock, also a river rock, a little rounder, a little smaller circumference, and another rune in black marker. These sigils look hastily drawn, inexpert.

After a thorough search around the building I find five

such rocks, all river rocks, with similar sigils. One at each corner of the building. One is sitting on the ground behind a small hedge next to the rear of the building.

Down the hill a couple of hundred yards from the winery I can see a green cluster of trees. I know the area well enough to know that these trees are clustered around the trickle of a small creek, a tributary to the Napa River. I'd put money that these rocks came from there.

This is starting to feel like MystiCon all over again.

I carry the rocks over to Whitman and hold one up.

"I'm not going to make accusations here, Mr. Whitman. But these sigils are totally bogus. Someone has concocted these to…I don't know, throw me off the scent? Have a laugh at my expense? Whoever did these wasn't a sorcerer. These sigils look like they are taken from a video game. Their location around the building seems arbitrary and this sedimentary rock doesn't have enough crystal in it to have any ritual significance. These are bogus, Mr. Whitman," I conclude. "A red herring if you will."

Whitman looks a little surprised by my revelation. He shrugs and says, "You are the expert, Mr. Ward."

These stones have no magical significance or power. I can't imagine a real practitioner ever making such shoddy and useless fakes. I can't help but think of Whitman; he looks a little guilty to me but confronting him further doesn't seem worth it. This was probably meant as a practical joke.

But I do think something real and magical *is* going on, and I want to get to the bottom of it.

"Mr. Whitman," I begin.

"Yes, Mr. Ward?" he says, raising an eyebrow. He is expecting me to give up and is waiting to savor the moment.

"Mr. Whitman," I repeat. See, I am not a douche. I address people how they want to be addressed, even when I find them unpleasant. "Where's the blood?"

He looks alarmed for a moment.

"What do you mean? I never mentioned that to Mr. Baptiste," he sputters.

"There's always blood, Mr. Whitman. There's always blood."

It's true. In magic, there are symbols and chants and hand signs and wands and all of that. Those are all tools to channel the magical energy, to shape it, and give it form and direction.

But there is only one thing, to my knowledge, that catalyzes the magic. Only one thing to make it go from symbols and shapes to something more.

Blood. This is the secret that most people don't know, the thing that amateurs misunderstand. So, if I cannot find what is shaping a spell, I try to find where the spell was triggered and catalyzed. I try to find the blood.

He suddenly looks a little pale, and his shoulders slump. He gives a long, heaving sigh.

"Follow me," he says, shuffling off.

He leads me past the cellar and tasting room, out past a little outbuilding, and into the open grass leading toward the vineyard. The only thing between us and the vines is the standing circle of olive trees. I glance down as we walk and see a flat piece of volcanic rock in the grass with a smudge of something on top of it.

I stop and kneel to examine it. There is a dried red-black splatter of blood on the rock. It's a large splatter, probably an ounce of fluid before it dried. This isn't someone just cutting their hand or getting a nosebleed, but it also doesn't seem to have any sigils or other indicators of a magical ritual.

"That's not it, Mr. Ward. That's just what remains from the cleanup," Whitman says bluntly.

I look up at him. He looks a little pale, as he indicates the ring of olive trees with a motion of his head.

"This way," Whitman says.

He continues forward. I stand and follow him, quietly girding myself for the horror show I am about to see.

I don't have any particularly strong feelings towards rats. I don't think they are particularly cute, nor am I scared of them or worried about them or phobic of them. Don't get me wrong: I wouldn't want to wake up with one crawling on my face, but I'm generally blasé about them. That said, what someone did to the rats at JMBaptiste Winery I wouldn't wish that on any living creature.

I'm not sure if I hear the flies or if the odor hits my nose first. The combination alone is enough to make my stomach churn. The smell starts with a hint of the metallic tang of blood, but over that, the horrible, nauseating odor of rotting flesh. The sound and smell both intensify as we approach an olive tree on the edge of the property.

I see the first rat, flayed out, body-wide and flat like a frisbee, tacked to the side of the olive tree. Its entrails dangle down, covered in oozing black blood and a cloud of charnel flies. The smell is so strong when we get close that I have to pull my shirt up over my nose, but it doesn't really help. I feel a little bile in the back of my throat. Sigils carved into the tree trunk are painted-in with the rats' blood.

Intricate, complicated runes. Combinations I am not familiar with.

This is just one of twelve such rats nailed to twelve such trees. Mr. Whitman shows me all twelve of the sites. The twelve rats flayed out in the same fashion. I snap pictures of them all from different angles. I jot down notes about each of them, including where on the site they are located.

Four putrescent rat carcasses were placed at the cardinal points: the north, south, east and west of the property. Four more are at the inter-cardinal points. The last four are placed in no discernible direction or pattern. A symbol of near order, an order twisted awry. A symbol of hidden chaos.

I examine the runes closely, the precision and detail with which they were carved. It would be difficult to render these in a well-lit studio with a full array of woodworking tools.

But in a darkened grove at night? With hand tools?

I start to get worried, a hint of anxiety creeping into my

brain. This is the work of a professional. Up to this point, my personal experiences in the magical world have been the work of hedge wizards, and for most even that moniker was generous. Bumbling amateurs. If I'm honest with myself, I'm only a little better.

I hope I'm not getting in over my head here.

I stare at the last tree, feeling a tiny bit woozy. I don't often deal with this kind of magic. It's nauseating.

"Did you go to the police about this?" I ask. "This is alarming."

"No, by the time we found this, it was clear that the police would not be any help. Mr. Baptiste asked me not to bother," Whitman says.

I sigh. Mr. Whitman said earlier that he didn't tell Baptiste, but now he's saying he did. Why is he lying? What version of the narrative is true? I'm not sure that the answers really matter for my purposes.

"Mr. Whitman," I tell him. "Get a chainsaw."

"Excuse me?" Whitman says, raising both eyebrows to look at me incredulously.

"Sorry for being melodramatic. But yeah, we are going to have to cut these trees down. All twelve of them. Do you have somewhere on the property where you can burn them?"

"You have got to be kidding me," Whitman says, throwing his hands up in the air.

"No. Not kidding. The sooner the better. It must happen or this won't stop." I pause for a moment, letting the words sit with him, before saying, "But first, tell me something."

He puts his hands on his hips, staring at the tree with a dark look of gloom on his face. After a moment of silence, he impatiently motions for me to continue.

"How long have these been here?"

"Well, I don't know about the original ones. They'd been there a while before the landscaping crew discovered them."

"Original ones?"

"Yes, we had them taken down a couple of weeks ago, but more showed up."

"More showed up…what does that mean?"

"Yeah. The landscapers used arboreal paint or something of the like to seal the holes and keep anything from growing in the wounds and killing the trees. A week or so after that was done, someone noticed another was up. We checked and the rats had all been replaced, the paint carved back out. We cleaned it, resealed it, and got rid of the bodies. A few days later we noticed new ones. We started checking daily, and they get replaced every night," he says.

"I see."

"We have tried to catch whoever does this. But the rats and the gore, it keeps reappearing. Finally, I decided that it wasn't worth it, and we stopped bothering. The locations are all off the beaten path, so we just discourage guests from coming out here."

"Off the beaten path, hard to notice. Yes," I say. "Rats…. The rat is probably symbolic. Betrayal maybe? This is personal."

I scratch my chin and look around.

"Personal against the wine or maybe the winery? Or to a person?" I mutter.

Mr. Whitman is about to respond to my questions, but they were rhetorical, so I preempt him.

"Cut the trees down."

Whitman looks miffed.

"You cannot expect me to cut down a dozen established olive trees to accommodate for your hoodoo, Mr. Ward," he sputters.

"The sigils are carved into the trees. The blood is in them...this is just going to keep happening. You could try washing the trees, you could try carving out the sigils, but the only way to destroy this for sure is to cut down these trees and burn them."

Mister Whitman looks angry and very upset.

"I am afraid I cannot do that."

"I will advise Mr. Baptiste of my recommendation," I say calmly. "For the sake of the winery, this is essential." He makes eye contact and stares me down for a while.

"Fine," he blusters. "I'll get someone to cut these trees down today. Anything else? Would you like me to burn the cellar building down too?"

"No, I think this will be fine. I'm going to take pictures of the sigils. I will come up with a plan for wards we can place around the winery to help manage whatever else is going on. I will come back tomorrow morning."

Mr. Whitman turns to stalk off, muttering darkly to himself.

"Oh, anything thing, Mr. Whitman?"

He turns and looks at me expectantly.

"How did you try to stop whoever kept doing this?"

"We put up surveillance and hired overnight guards. The cameras always got unplugged or something and the security guards never saw anything. It was like…" he stops.

"Like magic?" I ask.

He turns without a word and leaves.

Chapter Four

These jobs never start interesting. It's always a weird little complaint, a superstitious suspicion. Most never get interesting. Most of them aren't even magical. Honestly, most of them are just paranoid people seeing malice in coincidence. Apophenia is a more powerful magic than any spell or ritual. No one wants to pay to hear that their mind is playing tricks on them.

But the jobs that do go somewhere are the ones I find interesting. They pull me in because a question comes up. A nagging question that I don't know the answer to, but I can see the beginning of how to find it. Like a little string sticking out the bottom of a sweater: if you can pull it, the whole thing will unravel.

At least, I hope that the worst it will unravel is a sweater. What if I've stumbled into something that is out of my league?

Today I have nothing but questions that ultimately all boil down to just one: Why? Why this winery? Why the elaborate spell that seems to only be spoiling wine? Why now? Why?

I jump into my Wrangler. I've had it for years, and it's a little beat up. Not because I go off-roading, I don't. In theory, I am going to take it off-roading. It's just that every time I say, "I am going to take my Jeep out off-roading today," I always come up with a reason to not do it.

No, my Wrangler is beaten up because I, like so many others in this world, do not know how to parallel park. I'll admit it. I have many strengths: parallel parking is not one of them. I've hit a light pole, one of those old newspaper machines, curbs, so many curbs, jersey barriers, trees, buildings, and another car once. And the rest of the world has given it as well as they got it.

To be fair, I've found more dents and scratches on the Wrangler that I was not responsible for. I feel strangely loyal to the beat-up old piece of junk. It costs more to maintain each year than it is worth, but I keep driving it.

It's only ten minutes or so before I am pulling into my designated parking space in front of my apartment. Thankfully no parallel parking here, and I avoid any more scratches or dings. I rush upstairs to my apartment and go into my "office".

The space other people would call their living room is my office. My apartment is not big, so I have my TV and video game console in my bedroom. There I can sit in bed and watch TV and play video games by myself. Not at all like a single loser, but like an empowered and independent man! Since the only other three rooms are the kitchen, a bathroom, and the 'large' living room, that last room is where I set up my home office.

I have a desk and laptop in one corner. I have a printer on a stand next to it. I can't remember the last time I used the printer, and I am not certain it even works. I have a decent-sized bookshelf filled with books ranging from language, history, and occult texts to cheap paperback thrillers. In the center of the room, I have a large, solid, wooden table. I spent two days carefully etching and inscribing an inclusive circle on the table—a single ring, with a series of glyphs around it.

An exclusive circle keeps energy out while allowing the energy inside to escape. Think of this as your standard magical defense. My inclusive circle, however, keeps energy in, while allowing more energy to flow in. The remaining type of circle is a conclusive circle, a complete barrier, no energy in, no energy out.

The inclusive circle I've drawn will allow the ambient magic in the world around to flow in, but then it gets trapped and pools there. This is usually a requirement for any spell of significant power. Spells, like anything, need power. That power comes from the Ley—a term for the ambient magical energy of the universe. Before doing almost anything magical, one first needs to gather and contain power from the Ley. An inclusive circle is the quickest and easiest, but certainly not only way to do this.

The Ley is just one name for magical energy. It has lots of names, more than I know. Ylem. Mana. Cosmic Radiation to name a few.

I prefer to use Ley, an Old English word meaning "field".

In the early 20th century, Ley Lines became a popular theory on the flow of magic in the world. The idea is that ancient landmarks and structures (for example, Stonehenge) form points of lines denoting the flow of "Earth Energies" around the world. The ancient world had a better understanding of this and built these structures to help channel those energies.

Ley Line theory was an attempt to map, clarify, and measure magical energies, but it was a little off base. The energy is neither entirely terrestrial nor does it flow linearly. So many in the Eurocentric magical world now just call it the Ley; to acknowledge that magic itself is more of a field than a network of lines. The enormous inclusive circle at the winery seems to collect massive amounts of energy from the Ley, like a huge cistern or pool.

The term circle is also misleading. It gets called a circle because most practitioners use a circular-shaped boundary as it makes things easy. But it doesn't have to be. It can describe any area or shape and the lines can be implied or conceptual, so long as the manner in which the runes are crafted implies the boundaries. This is how a series of runes painted in rats' blood on trees surrounding a winery could be used as an inclusive circle to pool magic in the winery.

The sigils were placed on the outsides of the trees with the trees acting as the implied boundary, which is ultimately what makes it inclusive. If the sigils had been placed on the interior face of the trees, it would be an exclusive circle. A conclusive circle is harder to create with implied boundaries because it requires dual boundaries, with sigils in between.

I toss the JMBaptiste quarterly report on the counter and dig a bottle of wine out of a cabinet in my kitchen. I don't drink wine usually, but somehow, I still always seem to have a bottle in the cabinet. It's kind of a Napa thing. Then I go to my refrigerator and get a bag out of the crisper drawer. I go into my office and set the bottle of wine in the middle of my inclusive circle.

I'm not a sorcerer. I try to avoid actual magic. Magic is icky, it's gross and it causes more problems than it solves. Magic is distasteful at its best and evil at its worst. But in order to fight a fire, you must know how things burn. Sometimes you must light a fire to stop a fire. I bring up the bag I got from my fridge, a Ziplock full of a thick, viscous, blackish-red fluid.

Blood.

What I am about to do is called hedge magic, though it is barely even that. At least I call it hedge magic, there is not to my knowledge a set of standard classifications. In my mind, I classify magic by category to help me identify the level of power I may be dealing with. I categorize by the type of blood sacrifice since as I said, blood is involved in basically all magic. A lot of people think that human blood is more powerful than animal blood, but that isn't true—strictly speaking. Animals cannot, or perhaps rarely do, willingly part with their blood and willingness does factor into the equation.

Hedge magic uses Dead Blood, which is blood drained from an already dead creature. Dead Blood is the least powerful by far and it requires a lot of it to do anything of particular impact. I get mine from a local butcher who sells me a couple of pints every month and doesn't ask questions. A cup of Dead Blood is plenty to activate a two-foot-wide circle like this, and it will last until the blood dries.

Sorcery, on the other hand, uses Live Blood—blood from a creature still living.

This is a more powerful way of catalyzing a magical reaction. More powerful still is Live Blood that is freely given. If the donor of the blood willingly gives it for the spell, it is considerably more powerful. This makes sorcerers dangerous because they can get willingly granted blood from their own bodies pretty easily. To me, this seems like a dangerous and desperate act. It doesn't take a lot of blood to start a magical event, but the bigger the event, the higher quantity or quality of blood is required.

The last category I call Necromancy. This is using Heart's Blood to initiate a magical event. Heart's Blood is the last blood drawn from a living creature before it stops being a living creature. It requires a creature to die to power the ritual. A living sacrifice. It is very powerful.

No doubt the ritual with the twelve rats was a Necromantic ritual, one that required life to end to empower. Twelve lives in fact. Heart's Blood willingly given is the most powerful of all, but something I have thankfully only read about and never encountered.

I carefully fill the troughs of the runes on my table with blood—pig's blood if I recall; I wasn't paying much attention when the butcher was telling me. As I meticulously pour it in, I chant an old rite. As I said, this is barely magic. Blood and chanting are needed to activate the circle, to bring the barrier up if you will. A real spell would then have a method of channeling the energy it was capturing, of giving it shape.

For the purposes of my experiment, I just want the wine sitting in a pool of magical energy created by the inclusive circle to confirm or disprove my hypothesis. There is no need to direct the magic to do anything.

I wash my hands and put my half-empty sack of blood away. While that experiment is cooking, I need to do research. I spend fifteen minutes skimming through the quarterly report on JMBaptiste Winery. It is very thorough. Mr. Baptiste must believe there is a financial motivation, but I find nothing compelling in the report.

When I finish that, I toss it back down onto my kitchen counter. I go into my office, grab a few books from the bookshelves, and sit down at my desk. As I thumb through them, I look at rows of symbols and compare them to those carved into the tree.

The primary book I am using is called *Traditions of Magic* by Beatrice C. Arthur. It's a dull text about magical beliefs and traditions in different cultures across the world, both a high-level conceptual analysis of what they believe magic is and how each approaches practical application. The author describes all kinds of rituals, sigils, and symbols used by different cultures. The last half of the book is page upon page of runes and glyphs from cultures around the globe and an explanation of their nuanced meaning. It's a huge book.

I got *Traditions* from some mega-chain bookstore almost a decade ago. Usually, books you get in the New Age section of a chain bookstore are complete hokum. Sometimes a little nugget of truth is hidden in them. *Traditions* was a real find. As far as I can tell, it's a book documenting real magic which is sitting right out in the public eye and hiding in plain sight. The only real omission in *Traditions* and probably its saving grace; there is no mention of blood sacrifice anywhere in it, making it effectively useless to those who don't know the intricacies of the craft.

There are many magical traditions. Many ways to shape or direct magical energy. There don't seem to be any hard and fast rules so far as I can tell. You can mix and match, but not just any symbols will work. There are countless different variations and combinations that exist in every culture of man.

While they all contain similar concepts and structures, there are nuanced differences between the different traditions, sigils, and symbols. These variations can make all the difference when it comes to trying to undo them. A sigil or symbol from one culture, say, an ancient Saxon symbol might channel energy into heat that will heat the metal in an object. Whereas a Māori symbol to channel energy into heat will, say, cause wood to burn. Similar symbols, and similar ideas, but one might work situationally better than another.

Do you use a metal knife to scrape away the symbol or a wooden scraper? Knowing the difference in your heating sigils is important if you don't want to get burned.

An analogy I use for what different sigils do: you could put a sprayer on the end of a garden hose, or you could put a sprinkler. They fulfill fundamentally the same purpose, but if you put one on expecting the other, you'd probably be surprised by the results. Thus, knowing the tradition of magic that you are dealing with is very important if you want a reliable outcome.

It doesn't take me long looking at my reference books to see that this is going to be complicated. The sigils and runes that make up this spell are from at least three different traditions. Some sigils I recognize, but there are a few more mixed in there that I don't. I am going to need help, but unfortunately, it is getting late in the evening. I don't have too many resources to draw upon when I come across something I don't know. One of them closes at 8 PM and the other I won't visit after dark.

I bring my reference books and phone into my room and sit on the bed with TV mindlessly playing in the background while I skim through page after page, trying to identify runes. I wouldn't admit this to anyone else, but it is the most complex magical thing I've ever seen. I don't even have a clue why, since all it seems to be doing is gathering energy.

Some of the spell is designed to manage the energy inside, a kind of pressure valve so that the circle doesn't blow itself out if too much energy builds up. Other portions seem to be a sort of reinforcement, so that it can contain more magical energy. But all this alone doesn't explain the complexity; there is more at work here.

I wake up the next morning, still sitting in my bed, TV still running with a book in my lap. I'm uncertain when I went to sleep. The sinister complexity of this spell has me paranoid, and I check all my wards and precautions to make sure nothing has changed.

Everything seems fine.

A quick shower and shave and I'm ready for the day. I dress Hank and eat an untoasted, uncream-cheesed bagel from my breadbox.

Yum. Then I go to examine my experiment with the wine. The blood has dried. Theoretically, this bottle of wine should be the same as it was yesterday because it's just sitting sealed on the table. I take the bottle open it and give it a whiff. Vinegar. Just a hint. Not the overwhelming smell that the bottles at the winery had, but a bit. I pour a bit and taste it. It's not good. I put the open bottle back in the middle of the circle.

Even open, it shouldn't have turned that fast. I don't know a lot, but it should have taken much longer. I would assume weeks if it was open. Years, even *decades* sealed. I suspect this wine will turn to vinegar pretty quickly sitting open in this circle. I hypothesize that I have discovered a new property of magic I didn't know before. One that obviously, someone else must have.

Wine stops magic.

Okay, well, that isn't quite true. For some reason, it seems that wine, or maybe it is alcohol in general, absorbs magic when exposed. The magical energy causes it to change state from alcohol to vinegar. However, I know that changing the state of anything requires energy. This is true of anything. Turning water to steam? It takes energy. if you have enough wine changing state, it in theory should use a great deal of magical energy to do so. That energy then can't be used for another purpose.

And I theorize that knowing this, someone set up a spell specifically to ruin all of that wine. I think this circle is a giant spoilage spell.

But why?

It could be that the wine was the target all along. It seems like there are far easier ways to target the wine. I sit staring at the open wine bottle for a while.

Or maybe if there is that much wine, the wine was blocking another spell. Maybe destroying the wine was more about eliminating it from the magical context of the winery, so that another spell could work correctly. When dealing with magic, you always have to look for the blood and consider the context.

Magical rules are all contextual.

Chapter Five

As I drive downtown, I call Mr. Whitman. It goes to voicemail after two rings. Seems like someone is screening his calls.

"You have reached Charles Whitman. Please leave me a message at the tone," he says in a nasally voice which sounds eerily like a snobby butler in a cartoon. Everything about this guy is like sand in my underwear.

I leave a brief message telling him I won't make it by until the afternoon. I try to use as business-like a manner as I can muster.

I park in front of Soothsayers, my favorite coffee shop and walk to the front door. The earthy, roasted smell of coffee greets me at the door. I sigh a little, the smell embracing me like a warm blanket.

Today, like most days, Jesse is working behind the counter. I don't really know Jesse other than that on Thursday through Monday, he serves me an excellent cup of coffee. Older than me, Jesse is one of those guys that screams "barista for life". He's probably been doing this for twenty-five years. He's got that old-school barista look, full sleeve tattoos, flesh tunnels, and eyebrow piercings. I imagine when he was younger, he probably had a mohawk and wore a leather vest with no shirt or something. Middle age has mellowed him out and he has a very nondescript short haircut and wears a plain t-shirt and jeans every day.

Where Jesse makes me think of '90s coffee shops, Soothsayers is not a '90s coffee shop. It is styled much more modernly than the coffee shops of Jesse's youth were. Soothsayer sports crisp clean counters of stainless steel and glass, and smooth grey ceramic tile floors. All are easily and regularly cleaned. The art is a rotating display of tasteful pieces by local artists and photographers. However, like everything in town, the art is more focused on grapes and wine than I care for. The tables are clean, white, laminated wood with stainless steel legs and matching chairs. It overall has a fairly clinical look. The decor alone though is not a draw for me.

The coffee and pastries? Perfection. The only thing I dislike about Soothsayers is that it closes Tuesdays and Wednesdays. On those days, I have to go to Roast! all the way on the other side of town.

"Miles!" Jesse greets me from behind the counter. "How's the magic business?" He has a jovial tone, but I can never tell if he is genuinely interested in my work, or if he's having a secret laugh at my expense.

"Bumpin'," I say. "How's the coffee business?"

"Bumpin'," he says with a smirk on his face. I can't tell if he's questioning my awkward attempt at slang or if he's answering my question. "How bumpin' are we talking?"

"I just picked up a contract with JMBaptiste Winery," I say nonchalantly.

Jesse whistles. "Big money there…if the price of their wine is any indication," he says.

"I'm not complaining," I say. He hands me my triple espresso and a cranberry walnut scone that I haven't ordered yet. What can I say? I am a creature of habit.

"Oh! Hey. Actually, Miles," Jesse says. "Karen, she owns Soothsayer—"

"Yeah," I say. "We've met a couple of times."

"She just saw an article about protecting your businesses…

you know, magically. I mentioned that one of our regulars did that sort of thing," he says.

I guess there is my answer on if he's just having a laugh at my expense or not. It seems Jesse the barista is not as skeptical as I thought.

"Here, pass my card along to her," I say, handing him one. "I'd be happy to have a consultation with her," I chuckle. "But really, who would curse this place? It's the best cup of Joe in town!"

"I appreciate that," he says, taking my card and waving it. "I'll pass this on to her."

"Thanks," I say and sip my espresso before adding too much sugar to it. "Well, I'm late! See you next time Jesse."

"See you in an hour!" Jesse says, laughing.

"I might be back in fifteen minutes, the way the day is going," I reply, smiling. If I am being honest with myself, I drink more coffee than one might consider in the strictest sense to be healthy.

When I walk outside, I see a couple of men coming out of the liquor store up the street. They are both wearing camouflage and trucker caps. One of them sees me and raises a hand to tip his hat. I notice both men's hats have a stylized image of a man impaling a dragon with a lance or spear. The Knights of Saint George.

I've run into them once before. They are a bunch of militant fundamentalist types who hunt monsters. They're more like a club than an organization that hires or has employees. It seems weird to me that a group of gun-toting monster hunters advertises and is so public with their business, but that's the modern world for you.

There are lots of unpleasant things in this world of men and monsters, as they say. Okay maybe only I say that.

However, in my experience, some of the worst monsters are men, and some of the best men are monsters. I learned that the hard way when I was young. How do you keep from stopping the good and supporting the bad? An ounce of prevention is worth a pound of cure. So, I got into the magical protection business.

These guys, the Knights of Saint George, espouse to take the exact opposite approach. They have a "human first" policy and a single solution to any problem.

Violence.

I watch them get into their truck and drive away. As they pass, the guy who tipped his hat at me waves. That's weird. I've never seen people walking around town sporting their logo before, and I can't help but wonder what has called a bunch of monster hunters down on our town. I'm sure these guys are everywhere, but I will always associate them with Reno. I first encountered the Knights of Saint George at the MagicCon conference in Reno last year.

My hands are full between my coffee and scone, so I pop open the door to my Jeep with a hooked thumb and a foot and slide into the driver's seat. I shove the scone in my mouth to hold it there while I start the car and then put the rest down on its paper bag on top of my center console. The old, familiar, awkward, coffee-scone-car-key juggle. I take a gulp of espresso to wash down the bite of scone. They are, as expected, both perfectly executed. Best in town.

I zip across town and stop in front of Grape Reads. It's a quaint little used bookstore, hidden in the fringe between the busy downtown and a residential neighborhood. It is flanked on one side by a wine bar on the other side a restaurant with an aging Michelin recognition sticker in the window. Across the street is Roast! my backup coffee shop. Grape Reads is one of only two bookstores left in town. The other, Coopertown Books, is large and sells only new books.

Coopertown caters mostly to tourists and sells best sellers, books on wine tasting, wine tours, and Napa Valley history. Grape Reads, on the other hand, has an extensive used selection and covers any topic you can imagine. Including, in the far back of the store, works of magic.

Sergei, the never-present and possibly fictional owner,

keeps a small, secret, reference library of more obscure, not-for-sale books in the back room that certain distinguished regulars are allowed to use. I am happy to be counted among those distinguished few.

I wolf down the rest of my scone and coffee in the car. No food or drink allowed in the bookstore, for obvious reasons. Then I bound inside. I'm always excited to visit Grape Reads.

"Miles!" Emily says in her usual chipper tone. I am a big fan of books, and the books are the main reason I come to Grape Reads.

But if I were being honest with myself, getting a chance to chat with Emily is why I am excited to come to Grape Reads.

Emily is about my age, give or take. She's smart and funny, and she knows everything about...well everything. She has read more and has more knowledge and trivia floating around in her head than anyone I've ever met. She has a style I'd describe as librarian chic. Glasses, clothing selected for comfort not style and an overall un-made-up look that works perfectly for her. I like Emily, and seeing her is always a highlight of any trip to Grape Reads.

I can never exactly tell if she's flirting with me or just being nice. I'm just not good with reading cues of romantic interest. I never really have been. When I say that I like her, I mean I have a huge crush on her. Really though, I'm always too awkward and weird to do more than talk shop. I'd rather stay friends with her than ask her out and make it awkward when she says no. I show up here, talk about books and tell jokes and laugh and that's good enough for me.

While seeing Emily is a highlight of coming to Grape Reads, I am here in the pursuit of knowledge. It is an amazing bookstore, and I could spend hours just wandering the rows of shelves and looking at titles. But the private collection in the back, and the fact that Emily lets me reference it, is the real professional value of me coming here today.

"What sort of weird topic are you looking for today?" She seems excited. That's another thing I like about Emily. She takes what I do seriously and thinks the stuff I research is interesting. I never feel judged or mocked by her, which is not something I can say about a lot of people.

I pull out the papers that I've transcribed the sigils from the winery onto.

"I am trying to figure out what these sigils and runes are," I say.

"You write those yourself? Your handwriting is terrible," she says.

"That is true. I have photos of the originals, but they are kinda gruesome. Bloody"

"Can I see them?"

"I mean, yeah, but it's bad. I wouldn't want to surprise you with them."

"Not like…human…stuff, is it?" she says, squinting her eyes and gritting her teeth.

"No, not like that…well, yes like that but not humans. It's rats."

"Lay it on me tough guy," she says, perking up. Apparently, vivisected rats don't phase her. I've been trying not to barf in my mouth every time I think about the scene back at the winery.

I show her the photographs. She spends time examining them carefully. She's very intense and focused. I'm sure there is something she sees that I am missing. She gets to a particularly gruesome photo and makes a hissing sound through her teeth.

"Yup, that is a nasty business. What kind of horror movie are you getting yourself into Miles?" she asks. Without waiting for an answer she adds, "Those runes are weird, I recognize some of them, but not all. You've referenced *Traditions* already I assume?"

"Yes," I say with a little pride. I introduced her to *Traditions of Magic*.

Emily looks at the pictures for another moment in silence.

"Hmmm," she ponders. "It's all Greek to me!"

She laughs. She pauses when I don't reciprocate and then awkwardly continues. "A bunch of the sigils are Greek," she says.

I feel dense.

"But you are in luck, I might have another reference that could help. It's in Greek though, as you might expect, so that could be a challenge," she says and smiles jovially over her shoulder as she starts toward the back room.

I feel like there is an opportunity to flirt here, but I'm pretty much guaranteed to say something stupid, if I say anything at all. I learned long ago that keeping my mouth shut is usually the best plan in cases like this. I rarely take my own advice, but today I do. Silently I follow Emily into the backroom.

The worst thing about Grape Reads is the name of the store, though I've never mentioned anything to any of the employees. It's really one of the worst trends in The Valley to make everything a grape or wine pun; it drives me nuts. But that's really the only flaw the store has, in my very humble opinion.

The best thing about Grape Reads, however, is the backroom. Past the tiny door labeled "Employees Only" lies a room. Only it doesn't look like a room. It looks more like a maze, a maze of books. Shelves, stacks, tables, piles of books. Some are books they've just recently gotten into stock, and they are working on getting priced and on the shelves. Some are special orders or reserves.

Some are a collection of works for a more selective clientele. That is, some of them are their books on magic. While Sergei's special collection is only a couple of bookshelves worth, it is an impressive collection. Rare and one-of-a-kind works, industry staples, all the good stuff.

You can find works on magic online. You can find them in the new age and occult sections of big chain bookstores. You can find them in the public library. You can find them in all sorts of places.

However, most of the books you find in those places are absolute works of fiction. The best of them are half-informed or watered-down translations of other, more archaic works. The worst are the self-aggrandizing ranting of egomaniacs and cult leaders. But in Sergei's special collection, you find none of that. It has been carefully hand-selected and pruned. Sometimes it does make me wonder about the mysterious Sergei. And someday I will probably have to find out more. But today isn't that day.

Emily points me to a table and pulls down a few books from their reserve shelves.

"Here," she says. "I think these ones might have useful stuff in them. These are from Sergei's collection, not for sale, but it'd be fine if you look at them."

Emily always clarifies any time she's letting me look at books from the special collection, they are Sergei's. Though at this point, I'd be pretty dense not to have picked up on that. It has always struck me as a little odd how all the staff feel the need to mention Sergei every time I come in.

"Thanks," I say, smiling at her. She smiles back. I'm certain I am grinning like a goofy idiot at her, but she doesn't seem fazed by it.

"I need to get back up front. But keep me in the loop, that dead rat business is going to get interesting! I can feel it!" she says and then breezes away to the front of the store, leaving me in the cool and silent backroom.

After she's gone, I realize it's probably a good thing; I'm not sure I'd get much studying done if she'd stayed.

This is not my first time rifling through Sergei's collection in the back room, I've been here a dozen times before. I'm as impressed by the collection now as I was the first time that I came in. I like it in the back room. It's crowded with books and not people, as it should be. Crowded though it be, it is cozy, not claustrophobic. It smells like old books and musty paper. It's calming. I start looking through the books.

Emily always amazes me. She only had a minute or two to

look at the glyphs, but she's found exactly the right books. Both are large and bound in dark paper. Neither has a title and both are written in cramped handwriting. Not the same handwriting, I note; they clearly have different authors.

One is a treatise on Greek mysticism, written as promised, in Greek. The other is more of an anthropological work, studying the rites and practices of several South American tribes, it thankfully is in English. I begin skimming, jotting notes, and cross referencing. I need to get a book on Greek and lean heavily on a translation app since I don't read, write, or speak Greek. I quickly lose track of time, and it seems like only a few moments later when Emily comes in. She sets down a double espresso in front of me.

"Ren is working the counter. I grabbed you another coffee and thought I'd see how you were doing," she says.

"Thank you!" I say enthusiastically, sipping the coffee. "Intriguing stuff!"

"I didn't have time to swing over to Soothsayers. I know that's your favorite. This is from across the street."

"No, no! Thank you. It's perfect," I say, still engrossed in the books.

"Have you figured anything out yet?" Emily sits down next to me. I immediately start feeling warm all over my body. Did I remember to put deodorant on?

"I haven't finished deciphering all of the symbols yet, but yeah, I think so. These sigils are all gathering sigils," I say, "used to constantly draw energy in and pool it up. But I don't think it does anything specific. It has no direction or shape that I can see."

She looks over my notes and glances back at the photos. She twirls her hair on her finger while she thinks. It occurs to me, though I don't say it, that these runes are the opposite of how normal wards work. Normally one would funnel magical energy away from what you are protecting, these are designed to constantly funnel energy from the Ley into the winery. This could be used to empower a huge and persistent magical effect, but all it seems to do is act as a huge magical cistern.

"I see what you mean, energy with no purpose. That is unusual. Why do you think that is?" Emily says.

"I have a couple of theories, but I need more information before I commit to anything. There is a lot here, and these are so complicated."

"Yes, it's an amazing amount of detail. I've never seen anything like it."

"Especially for one person to do unseen in the dark," I say.

"Why do you think this is the work of one person?"

She makes a fair point. I've been operating under the assumption that this was done by one person. But it is a lot of work for even a few people in the timeline as Whitman described it.

"I guess I was thinking it was one person because…well it feels like one person? It's like writing styles. Two people can contribute to the same paper, but they have their own writing styles, so usually, you can kind of tell when the primary author switches."

"Interesting," is all she says. I can't tell if my reasoning is interesting, or if it is interesting what a big doofus I am.

"Yeah."

"I have my lunch break in a bit. Do you want to go grab something? We could talk it through, I've been wanting to try—" she begins, but I interrupt.

"Wait. What time is it?" Something is nagging at the edge of my memory, a little voice calling to me through the fog of my focus.

"Oh…it's twelve fifty."

"Shit. I lost track of time. I need to run. I'm late! My client's representative, this guy *Mister* Whitman," I say emphasizing the Mister, "he's a real hard-ass, looking for any excuse to try to get me let off the job."

I hate being late. I hate when other people are late. I hate when buses are late. I hate when airplanes are late. I even hate words that rhyme with late. I hate hate hate late.

I'm never late and I pride myself on that. When I have a moment like this, where I have let myself get distracted from the world around me...well, I kind of freak out.

"I should be there. Thank you so much for the coffee! And the books! Is it okay if I come back later and look more?" I say, gathering my things all in a rush.

"Of course. No problem. You're welcome," Emily says. Her tone doesn't match the words she is saying. She sounds annoyed, and I'm not sure why.

I carefully put Sergei's books back on the shelf, shake Emily's hand awkwardly, and rush out the door. Emily stands by the door with her arms crossed, looking a little put off. But I don't register this till I'm on the sidewalk. I furrow my brow, confused at her sudden change of mood.

Moments later I am gunning it down Soscol Way.

"Wait," I say. "Did she...?"

"Yeah, jackass, she just asked you to lunch," I can imagine Hank's voice in my head.

Even violating several traffic laws, I'm three minutes late to the winery. I'm cranky with myself for a couple of reasons.

I stand in the corner of the main tasting room. Whitman is speaking to a small group of people in the opposite corner, sipping red wine from long-stemmed glasses and talking quietly. He seems to be intentionally ignoring me. While part of me wants to go over and flash dead rat pictures just to irritate him as much as he is irritating me, that wouldn't be professional. Instead, I wait patiently for a while. When it seems obvious that he's in no rush to see me, I decide to check on things by myself.

I slip out the back door and do a tour of the grounds. True to his word, all the suspect trees have been cut down, which frankly surprises me. I look to see if any new sigils have been erected. There are none, but I am not surprised.

Magic is contextual. Cutting down the trees has changed

the context of the winery. There are no longer trees at the cardinal and inter-cardinal points, and the circle has been broken. New sigils, if they worked at all, would not work in exactly the same way. Now, they would be in different locations on the circle. With these trees gone, the entire spell would need to be reworked, replanned. Even for a professional, this would take time.

I poke around a bit more, wander the grounds and examine the buildings. I head back into the wine cellar. I try every door I come across and peek inside. All of this is to say, I get nosy, which is much easier now that I don't have Whitman hovering over my shoulder the whole time.

A half hour of poking around and I am satisfied that nothing new has cropped up overnight. The attacker has either achieved their goals or changed the direction of their attack. So, I return to the tasting room.

Whitman and his drinking buddies aren't here anymore. I ask one of the tasting room attendants where I can find Mr. Whitman. They inform me that he's gone to an important meeting and won't be back for a couple hours. I leave a note for him that just says I will be back tomorrow.

Back in my Wrangler, I sit in the driver's seat for a minute to think. What's the next step? I've delayed the one most obvious problem for the time being. But something tells me this isn't the end, that I haven't even scratched the surface of what is going on here. I need to come up with a plan to ward the winery. There is something at play here, something I don't understand. A gathering of power, for no clear purpose. To what end has this rather extensive pool of magic been built?

Most people who use magic do it for petty reasons. To gain a sense of personal power is probably the most common motivation I've encountered. But in my experience, these people tend to be sloppy and magic is a means to an end and not an art to be mastered. The level of detail and complexity I've seen in the spells here at the winery implies a pursuit of the artistry of magic.

Perfectionism.

The other motive that causes one to turn to magic is jealousy or revenge. Like that jerk Eric Walsh that I met on the rooftop a few nights ago. Magic is used in petty attempts to lash out in a way that is difficult to trace or prove. The motive is fundamentally irrational. Irrational people are sloppy and hurried.

What I am dealing with here feels clinical. Detached. Unemotional. It's just a sense I get, but it feels professional.

What do I have to work with? Professional. Magical. Attack.

That is not a combination I am super comfortable with; that means the person doing the magic may well be a contractor. The client's motivation could be anything, but we know one thing about the client if they did hire a contractor of this caliber. They have money.

The most obvious motivation for someone with money to attack is money. It could be industrial sabotage. Yes, destroying the cellar of wine would be a significant financial hit to JMBaptiste Winery. However, based on what I read in the financial report, this isn't going to break Jean-Marie's bank. The same level of effort could be so much more devastating focused elsewhere.

Like on their vines. Also, their actual barrel room wasn't inside the circle. The barrel room at the winery is just for show. The real one is in an industrial building out near the airport. It didn't get affected. The only wine that was destroyed was the wine they store for their tasting room and wine club efforts. While this was an inconvenient blow for the winery, it could have been much worse, their retail pipeline is their biggest revenue source. I can't shake the feeling that the wine was destroyed as a distraction or a step in a bigger plan. My gut says this was an elaborate way of removing the wine from the context of the winery.

I drive back to Grape Reads thinking about all of this. When I arrive, Emily isn't there. Another employee, Ren, tells me that she clocked out for the day. I ask if they mind if I go into the back room for a bit. I don't know Ren as well as I know Emily, but they usher me back anyway.

Apparently, I'm on the list.

Ren makes sure to emphasize that the books are all Sergei's. I sit back down to study the volumes from his collection as I had been earlier, trying to figure out if there is something I am missing in the intricacies of this spell.

I'm bleary-eyed from staring at handwritten scripts when I'm interrupted by Ren coming to tell me that the store is closing.

"Last call! It's 8 PM. You don't have to go home, but you can't stay here," they say humorously.

"Right. Sorry," I reply, standing and rubbing my eyes. I put the books back and gather all of my notes. "Thanks for letting me stay this long. I totally lost track of time."

"No problem. Have a good one. Good night!" Ren ushers me to the door, turning lights out behind us.

As I climb into my car I realize that tonight is poker night and I'm already late. I hate being late.

Hank wasn't entirely wrong when he was making fun of me for my lack of friends. I have people who I know around town. But in most of those cases, I am a regular customer at their place of business. Jeff is the only real friend I have in this town, so I don't want to disappoint him. I am off my game today, cutting it close twice in a row.

I tear off down the street to Jeff's house for our weekly poker night.

Chapter Six

Jeff's house is surprisingly large for what you might expect a single man would want. It's a two-story house off of Wine Country Avenue that was built in the '90's. Like a lot of California homes from that era, it sort of defies a single-word description. It has a stucco and tile roof that looks like it wants to be modern and wants to be Mediterranean and wants to look stately, but not too stately, all while still having been inexpensive to build. The intersection of all those desires means it just looks like a big house.

Jeff gave me the tour once when I was visiting. I don't remember the most of the rooms, other than the fact that there were a lot of them, and they were all shockingly clean and well-decorated for a bachelor pad.

The room we mostly hang out in is his game room. It's done up with vintage mid-century furniture and casino memorabilia. The overall vibe is 1950s Las Vegas with posters of Marilyn Monroe, Elvis Presley, and Frank Sinatra on the walls. He has a couple of old slot machines on one side next to a mahogany and brass bar. In the center of the room is a large octagonal card table. It's larger than my bed and more sturdily constructed. The chairs are comfortable, and it's a great place to spend a couple of hours feeling social and normal.

Once again, I am the only one of the four of us drinking beer—mainly because Jeff only serves Holtzhom wines that retail for at least one hundred and fifty dollars a bottle. The beer, however, is just his home brew.

I never really cared for wine to begin with, but since I moved to The Valley it appeals to me even less. Jeff's home brew, however, is good. When one says home-brew, it usually brings to mind overly watery funky liquid with the faint taste of alcohol and a silt of yeast at the bottom. But Jeff's an educated man, Masters of Fermentation Science and all that. While oenologist might be his job title, turning stuff into alcohol is his job, and his passion.

When I was a kid, I had to sneak TV in when my father wasn't around. He'd tell me how television would rot my brain, but we still had one so that he could watch football every Sunday night. There was a little over an hour each evening between when I got home from school and my father got home from "work."

It was just enough time to sneak in a rerun of *Cheers*, a story about a bunch of regulars at a bar. I always thought that when I grew up, I'd be a regular at a bar like that. Then I grew up and realized that while being a barfly might have been funny in a show, in reality, it's just kind of sad. And bars make me uncomfortable.

There are too many people, doing too many things, and alcohol makes their behavior erratic and unpredictable. I get anxious and nervous. Sitting at Jeff's and sipping a beer, however, reminds me of that magic hour from my youth. I feel like a normal person who has normal friends and does normal stuff. The beer is probably my number one reason for coming to poker night at Jeff's. The company is the other reason.

It's malty, a little hoppy, and pleasant…just like the beer.

Poker is not a reason I come here. I look down at a pair of twos, nine high.

"Mike is stacking the deck," I mutter and sip my beer.

"Hah," Alistair says.

Alistair is tall and kind of gangly and his hair is jet black, but he is fairly up-front that he dyes it. "Kids make you grey," he always says. He always wears a short-sleeved button-up shirt and khaki pants. He has a rotation of shirt colors, but it's always pretty much the same outfit. He has a little paunch that he didn't have when I met him. Again, he blames the kids.

"You always think someone is stacking the deck. You're just bad at poker," Alistair retorts.

Everyone at the table laughs, including me. I know he's trying to be funny, but I am a little sensitive about it. I get destroyed week after week, and I don't understand why. Maybe I have a lot of tells.

The guys played a much higher-stakes game before I joined. After the first time I got fleeced, we lowered it to a penny-ante. It's not about the money for this group. It's about the social time. Mike and Alistair both have families and kids and are always looking forward to an evening away. Jeff's a workaholic who only takes breaks if he's got a firm commitment to drag himself away too. And me? I just don't have any other friends.

Mike, in strong contradiction to Alistair, is short and stocky with curly red hair and a pointy nose. He's always smiling and outgoing. People just generally like Mike. He works in hospitality, serving wine, running events, and the like. He currently works at a big winery; I can't remember which one. It seems like he works for a different place every week, which I am led to believe is standard for hospitality workers in these parts. I worked to remember the first few he went through after I met him. At a point, I found myself perpetually two wineries behind and so I quit. It rarely comes up in conversation anyway.

I grab a handful of lightly sweetened cashews from one of the many snack bowls Jeff always leaves out. They are addictive. I know I should stop, but I can't. I pop one into my mouth, wondering who Jeff's dealer is.

"Call. Aren't you the one who does magic, Miles?" Mike

asks me, his eyes give a slightly sarcastic eye-roll and he curls his top lip slightly. He has always seemed offended by my occupation. This 'covert eye-roll' is the expression he usually gets when the whole magic thing comes up. He plays three of a kind.

"Not today," I respond while laying my hand down on the table.

"Looks like magic to me," Alistair says, playing a full house.

"How does he do that? If anyone's cheating, it's Alistair. The probability of a full house is..." Jeff says.

Jeff's one of those guys who is a few years older than me but looks a few years younger. He's a sort of nondescript handsome that seems to get him a lot of comments like "You have kind eyes" from women. Jeff is that friend who seems like he's good at everything, and if he was conceited about it, you'd hate him. But he's kind and humble and so instead of hating him, you are just glad he's on your side.

"About six hundred and ninety-three to one. It's a little more, but I know how you hate it when I get all technical," Alistair says. He's a therapist now, but he hustled poker in his youth. He gets crazy about statistics and keeps a log of his every hand so he can track his actual averages on cards, hands, wins, losses and compare them to statistical averages.

"Speaking of magic," Jeff says, suddenly sounding serious. "I was wondering if I could talk shop with you for a minute, Miles?"

"On that note," Mike says. "I'm gonna hit the head."

Mike doesn't believe in magic which is fine, not a lot of people do. I don't blame him. Some days I wish I didn't. However, he gets uncomfortable when I talk about this stuff, which honestly I try to avoid. He blames his Catholic upbringing but gets defensive when I point out how much mysticism there is in Catholicism. He wanders out the door whistling to himself, there might be a tune there, but I don't recognize it.

"I'm going to step out back," Alistair says. "Give you two a minute to talk."

That's code. He's going to vape. Jeff doesn't like it in his house and Alistair's husband, Jon, won't let him do it at home or in front of the kids. Alistair lectured me one night when I caught him in Jeff's backyard. If Jon asks, Alistair doesn't do that anymore.

The other two depart and Jeff and I are left in the game room.

"If I can ask your professional opinion…" Jeff begins.

"Sure." I'm not happy about this. Poker night is my break, my chance to be normal. This is like asking if you can dip your pickles in my ice cream. But like I said, Jeff is my only real friend in town.

"What do you make of this?" Jeff asks, pulling his shirt up and showing a small intricate-looking tattoo on his stomach, just to the left of his belly button. It's long and narrow, the bottom poking down below his pant line. The tattoo is so new that it's still puffy and red. The sigils I see, at first glance… well, it doesn't look good.

"Do you mind if I look close?" I ask, my annoyance fading like the sun behind a cloud of concern.

"Yeah, knock yourself out. Do I need to pull my pants down?"

"Not right now," I say, skipping over any obvious crude jokes I might make. I want to keep this serious because I worry it is, in fact, serious. I get closer. The top is about three inches wide, narrowing as it goes down his abdomen. If the two outside lines continue on the trajectory I can see, it would be about eight inches long.

I recognize one sigil, The Evil Eye—at least that's what I call it. It is a sort of rough eye shaped oval with a flame in the pupil, depicted at the top. Below it are rows of runes of descending sizes so that as the outer shape gets more narrow, the runes get smaller and smaller. I ponder in silence for a moment. Its presence signifies destructive intent.

"Yeah, let me see if you don't mind," I mutter. He carefully pulls the top of his pants down, revealing just the upper part of his pelvis, where, as I expected the two lines meet about 8 inches below the top, creating a sort of arrowhead like triangle pointing toward his genitals.

"How did you get this?"

"Well, I didn't ask to have it done."

"I should hope not," I interrupt him, but then motion him to continue.

"I was at this mixer thing over at the Culinary Institute. A bunch of winemakers, chefs, and sommeliers. It was like, you know, a networking thing done by the Vintner's Association. These sorts of things are usually one of the perks of the job, a free five-star meal and some nice wine. But not that day. I went to the bathroom and woke up in the vineyard behind the institute, with this tattooed on me."

"When was this?"

"Yesterday. It was probably one o'clock when I went to the bathroom, probably about four when I woke up."

"Did this happen to anyone else?" I ask while continuing to look at the runes.

"Not that I have heard about, but honestly I didn't mention it to anyone, I was kind of freaked out."

"You reported it to the police, I hope?"

"I…uh," he stammers. "Well, no, I kind of wanted to talk to you about it. It seemed like more your thing than the police's thing."

"Magic or no, someone still drugged you and inked you against your will. You should report it," I tell him. "Besides, it might be a way to get more information. Ask if anyone else has reported something like this."

"Okay," he says. "I'll go in tomorrow."

"Ask for Officer Chris Benson and tell him I sent you. He will understand," I say.

I look him in the eye, and he quickly turns his eyes away. I get the sense that he's being cagey. There is something he's not telling me.

"Jeff, I have no desire to dig into your personal business, but what are you not telling me? I might not be able to help if there is something I don't know."

"I—" he sighs. "Yeah. No. That's fair. Okay."

He seems very uncomfortable, thinking about his words for a moment.

"There was a woman," he says. "I bumped into her on the way to the bathroom. We were flirting, and then I woke up outside with this tattoo."

"A woman? Why were you hiding that?"

"I don't know, it just makes me feel stupid. She was so… aggressive, you know. It was suspicious, but I didn't think anything of it. Well, at least not until I woke up in the bushes with a tattoo on my junk," he says sheepishly. "I feel like an idiot."

"No. It could happen to anyone…you know, who was drugged heavily enough," I say to console him. It's a lie. This sort of thing doesn't happen to just anyone, but I'm just trying to be nice. It's not dishonest when you are trying to avoid rubbing salt in a wound. Right?

"Wouldn't have happened to you," he says. "You are too paranoid."

"Careful. I'm careful," I say.

"I've heard it both ways."

"Okay, so there was a woman. What did she look like?"

"She was pretty…."

"That is not much of a description."

"Honestly, I don't remember much else. I think she drugged me before we started talking or something, thinking back on it. It was all kind of hazy, and I just remember she was tall and attractive and…" he finishes with a shrug.

We sit in silence for a couple of minutes, me rubbing my stubble, something I do while I am thinking. He's sitting in front of me in uncomfortable silence with his shirt pulled up and his pants pulled down. I realize the awkwardness of the situation after a moment and motion him to put his clothes back together.

"I'm all set," I tell him. "Do you want the good news or the bad news?"

"There's good news?" he asks.

"Sort of. The good news is I don't think it's going to be fatal."

"Well, that is good," he sighs. "But what's the bad news?"

"Okay, here is what I think this is. I think this is a sympathetic curse. You're not the target, you're just the…power source? I guess that is the best way of stating it," I tell him.

"Power source? What does that mean? That doesn't sound good at all," he says with a worried look on his face.

"Permission to get pedantic and over-explain?"

"Permission granted?"

"A lot of people don't like it when I ramble on about 'mumbo-jumbo' so I figured I would ask."

"Ramble on," he responds.

"By the look of this, it is a sympathetic curse. Magic is like in a video game, you know, where you find places where the physics model doesn't work and you can exploit it?"

"Like rocket jumping?"

"Yeah, like rocket jumping or whatever, all those hacks and easter eggs. Well, that's magic. It's just knowing the places where the universe wasn't put together right or the rules sort of leave a loophole. A loophole in the fabric of reality. A place where the corners don't quite line up, where there is a space between two planes where the game builders never intended you to go. Magic is just finding a way to exploit them. Some people figure it out on their own, and then there are people who go get a book of cheats and easter eggs and do it by the numbers. That book of cheats is a grimoire or a spell book."

"Okay, and why is this important?"

"I am getting there. So, this is what you'd call sympathetic magic, where one symbolically creates a link between two or more like things. Then one channels energy between them. This is the core principle of magic: define a relationship with symbols and maybe an incantations and then release energy into the relationship. The good news is that whoever did this was a professional. This work is stunningly executed. This wasn't just someone who picked up a book and started trying to muddle their way through it, this was done by one of the people that wrote the book."

"And how is that good news?" he asks, eyes looking like they're pop out of his head.

"Here is what I think this spell does. I think it channels a little bit of heat energy out of your body and into someone else's body, or probably more like into a magical reservoir that someone else who is also marked by the spell is carrying. When enough energy is in the reservoir, then the spell triggers and dumps all the energy into the target. They burn from the inside out. Spontaneous combustion," I explain.

"Basically, stealing heat from me to burn another person to death?" he asks.

"Exactly. I think it will just make you kind of sick, but ultimately, you'll live. The other man, however, I'm pretty sure isn't going to."

"How do you know it's a man?"

"Right. That's where the law of sympathy comes in; it's easier to channel energy between like things. If two things are too dissimilar, it is impossible to channel energy between them, at least not reliably. It would be very hard and unreliable to channel energy directly from fire into a person, for example. It's much easier to transfer energy between two people."

I take a breath and collect my thoughts.

"You have that tattoo. The victim will have a similar tattoo only upside down, backward, reversed, something, denoting that yours is an outgoing conduit and his is an inbound conduit. Also, I suspect there are probably several other men with the same tattoo you have, or there will be depending on how aggressively the spell is being pursued. If I were to guess, you are all winemakers, you all are roughly the same height, and probably all wear glasses. The more similar, the better, for the purposes of the spell. Tall, fancy dark hair, cleft chin, five o'clock shadow, all likely," I say.

My voice fades off a little as I realize I've just described Whitman, the manager at JMBaptiste Winery. Jeff and Whitman look a lot alike, now that I think about it. You wouldn't see them and think they were related or anything. But when described in bullet points, it is uncanny. The details of the glyphs at the winery and Jeff's tattoo....

"How again?" he asks simply.

"How what?" I ask, I've lost my train of thought.

"How is that good news?" Jeff's eyes go wide, and his bottom lip quivers a little. The expression on his face is not one I've ever seen him use before. He looks terrified.

"Because of the quality of this spell, this necromancer is a professional and wouldn't leave anything to chance. They'd pick a lot of different people to siphon the energy out of, because that way they don't kill any extra people, drawing more attention. Finally, the level of detail in the sigil they put on you, they don't want to lose any energy to coincidental sympathy."

Jeff furrows his brow at me questioningly.

"Magic requires balance and it requires a connection. People are all intrinsically similar. In fact, we're alike in more ways than not. One could easily make a ritual to transfer heat energy between everyone in, say a specific room.

However, it would transfer evenly between all the people, drawing as much as it returned. Making for essentially a zero-sum game. If you want to change that you have to create directionality and specificity. If I were trying to channel energy between Alistair and Mike, I wouldn't want to risk sending some or all of the energy to some other guy, that happened to kind of look like Mike and was also named Mike, or whatever, you get my point."

Based on the look on Jeff's face, he does not. I take a deep breath before continuing.

"This is an oversimplification, but it does happen. So, sorcerers and the like use symbolism and ritual to specify, and clarify to the universe the connection they are making. And this necromancer was not going to make any mistakes. An amateur would have probably just drawn their sigil on with a pen or a stamp, which could be washed off. This person took the time to tattoo it. This isn't someone who leaves things to chance."

"I guess that kind of makes sense," he says. "What do we do about it? Should I just have the tattoo removed?"

"If this were a dime store curse, done by an amateur with a book, that's what I would recommend doing. But it isn't, and the person that did this may have built in fail safes or secondary effects. Who knows. I've never seen anything like it honestly. It's like stories of the Hizarin," I say.

"Hizarin?"

"Yeah, they are like a kind of guild or cult or whatever of magical assassins. I've never encountered them myself. Honestly, I kind of thought they were a myth, something you read about or people tell spooky stories about. I don't know much about them. But from the stories I've heard, this sounds like their MO."

"This seems like a lot of work just to kill someone."

"It is," I say, and ponder. "Killing him is probably not the point. It's the message it sends. He's going to immolate from the inside out starting with…well you see where the tattoo is pointing," I explain, nodding toward his lower abdomen.

"You mean he's going to burn junk first?" he says, eyes widening and his posture closing in an unconscious defense of his groin.

"Pretty sure. I mean, normally it'd take weeks to figure out all those runes and unravel the context and ritual of the spell. But I think this is related to a case I am already working on; I recognize a few of them from that. And that is an advantage."

"Really? That's a weird coincidence."

"I was thinking that too," I narrow my eyes in concentration.

"So what do we do?"

"For now we play poker, and you make your police report tomorrow. If you can, find out if there have been any other reports like this. I will dig into it and see what I can figure out. My gut says this isn't going to be fatal for you, but it might get uncomfortable. Either way, I'll try to figure out a way to get you out of this. If you remember anything else, let me know," I finish as Mike and Alistair return from outside where they've been waiting for a while.

"Everyone decent?" Mike asks as he comes in. Were they eavesdropping or did they already knew something about what was going on? Or maybe knowing Mike, it could just be his attempt at cajoling us.

"Yeah, we're fine," Jeff responds.

"Is our local wizard here going to be able to help you more than, say, the police?" Alistair asks with a faint hint of judgment in his voice.

Maybe Alistair *was* eavesdropping.

"He should go to the police. But yes, I think I can help," I say. "And also, not a wizard. I'm an apotropaist."

What even is apotropaism? People often ask me what the word means. By the book, it's any rituals, incantations, or formulas whose function is to avert evil or undo dark magic. The apotropaist is one who practices apotropaism. In the world of modern fringe magic, my profession is also called a warder, a break spell, or a number of less flattering monikers.

Undoing magic is more about reinforcing reality than it is about exploiting the weird things in the corners and edges of it. It's more eraser work than pencil work.

Magic is inherently dangerous; magic always comes with a price. Want to burn one man? You have to cool another. Do you want to heal a broken arm? Guess what? You are going to have to break one to make that happen, at least symbolically.

The Greats, the superb sorcerers, can create a facsimile that meets so many of the universe's requirements that they can have an inanimate surrogate such as a a simulacrum like Hank, pay this price for them. They could heal an arm by breaking the arm of the surrogate. But that's in the skill set of maybe a handful of practitioners in the world. Certainly beyond my talents and the talents of basically anyone I've ever met.

The price, in truth, is paid in more than blood and sacrifice. The price is larger still. It taxes the mind, the body, and, if you believe in its existence (I am not sure that I do), the soul. Sorcerers are rarely healthy and never completely sane. The very best sorcerers are the kind of people who don't care whom they hurt or the consequences of their actions. In fact, it's one of the most common traits for sorcerers, or wizards or witches, or whatever you want to call them. A complete lack of empathy. The words change but the idea is the same. It helps because you always have to sacrifice and being able to do that without a conscience, well it is a handy tool in the world of magic.

"Hey, Miles," Jeff's voice interrupts my reverie. Jeff's brow is sweaty, and it might be the light, but he looks a little pale. He gives me a weak half-smile, that doesn't make it up to his downcast eyes. "You going to ante up or what, man?"

Chapter Seven

"Hey, Jeff," I say, spraying crumbs as I speak into the phone. He answered quicker than I expected. I should probably not stuff a scone in my mouth as I am dialing. In my defense, I haven't yet finished my first coffee of the day. I wash down the huge bite of scone with the rest of my coffee. *Now* I have finished my first coffee.

"Good morning, Miles," Jeff says. "What's up?"

"I was wondering if you could get away from work this morning. I was thinking about it and there is a guy I wanted to see, who might have answers about your…uh, problem," I tell him.

"I can get away in…" he pauses, and his voice gets quieter, he's looking through his calendar. "Can you give me forty-five minutes?"

"I'll pick you up at the winery in forty-five?" I ask. Jeff works at Holtzhom Winery, which is about half an hour up valley.

"Sounds good," Jeff replies. "See you then."

We get off the phone. I've got fifteen minutes to kill, and I could use more coffee. I turn around and walk back into Soothsayer.

"Give me a bucket of coffee, Jesse. I'm going to need it."

"Coming right up, Miles!" he responds, laughing. "I'm a barista and I am telling you, you drink too much coffee."

"You sound like my doctor," I tell him. They are both right. I do drink too much coffee, but it's okay. I can quit any time that I want.

Armed with java, I head out the door toward my Wrangler. I glance up the block and see the liquor store. I pat the pocket on the outside of my messenger bag where I keep a pint of Goldschlager. It's only a pint, so I detour into the liquor store and buy a bigger bottle.

I don't know a lot of supernatural beings. But I know that bringing an offering is important and crucial. Gold and alcohol are both almost always good offerings in my experience, but the offerings are more symbolic than about actual value. Goldschlager fits the bill in many cases, so I always carry a pint around with me, just in case.

The liquor store is empty; I guess not a lot of people buy booze this early in the morning on a weekday. I go up to the counter and point up to the bottle on the shelf, the guy at the counter scans the bottle and charges me. We exchange all of about three words, and I rush out.

I'm moving so quickly that I almost run into a woman on her way in. She wears a long, form-fitting black dress, a wide-brimmed black hat, and enormous black sunglasses. She's young and full-figured with more than a little cleavage showing.

"Sorry about that!" I say as I step to the side.

"Excuse me," she says, she has a hint of an accent. Swedish maybe?

"I am trying to find this place," she says, holding up a brochure.

I look at the little pamphlet. It is for a winery up valley that is built into a castle. I went there once when I first moved to Napa. It's expensive, but the old castle is pretty interesting.

"This is in Calistoga, it's a pretty long way away," I say.

"Oh. I do not have a car," she says, her English is a little clunky.

"You might be able to take the bus…getting a car would be pretty pricey."

"I can take car then." She smiles and then reaches out and rubs my arm in a way that is a little more intimate than I am comfortable with from a stranger. I flinch away, but a sense of politeness keeps me from dodging completely.

"Okay," I say. "Good luck then."

"You have the good luck as well," she says as she steps back to the curb and takes out her phone.

That was weird. I start speed walking to my car. My caffeine and alcohol acquisition consumes just the right amount of time so that by the time I get to Holtzhom Winery, Jeff is just about wrapping up and meets me in the parking lot.

"Do you want me to drive?" he asks, looking dubiously at my Wrangler.

"No, we are going to need the four-wheel drive where we are going," I say.

"Okay," he says, his brow raising. He is growing more dubious of this morning's outing.

"How's the investigation?" Jeff asks as he climbs in and slams the door. It's loud. One of my least favorite things about the Wrangler is how loud the doors are when you close them.

"Nothing new since last night, so, honestly, it's a little intimidating," I say.

"What do you mean?"

"I'm worried I might be a little in over my head. That tattoo work, the other stuff I'm dealing with. It's well done, the best I've ever seen. Immaculate."

"Not instilling me with confidence," he says through gritted teeth.

"No, no, you're going to be fine. I am pretty certain of that. This person we are going to see. He can almost certainly help," I tell him. "Oh, that reminds me."

I reach around behind the seat, grab a round-bellied bottle of Goldschlager and put it in his lap.

"You are going to need this as a gift to give to Goldsmith," I tell him.

"Goldschlager for Goldsmith?"

"It's a long story, just trust me."

A dozen miles up Valley we turn off the road and onto a dirt side road—another reason I drive a Wrangler. We are pretty well developed here, but even so, there are little bumpy lanes that go off the beaten path and into the "wild."

The road is windy and rutted with potholes and places where rivulets of water have carved their way through the red clay. Clumps of scrub and weeds fight their way up from the dry cracked earth and my Jeep bounces and jolts in a teeth-rattling march up the hillside. We wind our way through a maze of green-leafed valley oaks, red-barked manzanita, dead yellow grass, and the huge grey granite boulders that dot the brown hillside. We turn left at a fork, straight through a cross-roads, and then we pass below a huge distinctive stone cliff.

That's how I know I didn't make a wrong turn.

After twenty-five or thirty minutes—which seem like five times that—we pull up in front of Goldsmith's house. It's large, and it might once have been nice, even extravagant. However, it has since fallen into disrepair. Rows of rusted cars, trucks, old dryers, broken toilets, and rusting street signs stand like a walled fortification around the house. The vine-choked front door can barely be seen through the labyrinth of junk.

"You brought me to a hoarder's house," Jeff states as he starts to open the door.

"No, stay in the car," I warn him. "We wait till he greets us."

There is an alarm in my voice that I am trying unsuccessfully to cover. Jeff furrows his brow in concern but closes the door and settles back into his seat.

We sit in silence for a few moments, then the door creaks open, and out shuffles Goldsmith. He looks like a little old man, with wild hair, missing a couple of front teeth. He wears an old black corduroy jacket, worn jeans, and a beaten Panama-style straw hat. He hunches slightly and walks with a cane. He eyes my Wrangler for a bit, then recognizes me. He beckons us in with a shouted grunt. Goldsmith doesn't wait for us to get out, he just turns and starts shuffling back inside.

"Okay," I say, and we hop out.

"What are we doing here exactly?"

"Just trust me, I'll explain later."

"Why didn't you just explain in the car? Why all the mystery?" Jeff continues to press me.

"Honestly, because either you wouldn't believe me, or if you did, you wouldn't want to come. Just trust me, okay?"

Jeff grunts and shrugs. He's not a fan of being kept in the dark. I lead him to the front door, which stands open now. The inside of the house is more cluttered than the outside. There's tacks of newspapers and bookshelves piled with books stacked on furniture that's stacked on furniture. The rooms are filled so that only a narrow path traverses the house, winding its way from room to room.

Jeff trips on something, and we look down. On the floor lies an ornate helmet, gilded scrollwork covering it. It looks old and expensive, not a cheap replica you'd buy online. Jeff gives me a quizzical look. I just shrug. We turn a corner and pass by an old Aladdin-style lamp sitting on a faded purple silk pillow surrounded by old coffee cans full of screws, nails, and the like.

"I expected it to smell worse," Jeff mutters.

"We can have this conversation, but not now. Trust me," I tell Jeff, and he follows me in silence.

We finally wind our way into Goldsmith's "sitting room." He sits in a high-backed wooden chair, painted gold on top of a wooden platform. There are about eight feet of space cleared in this room around the platform. Ringed around Goldsmith's perch are numerous buffets, dressing tables, hutches, and cupboards, all provide drawers and shelf space that can be easily accessed from the chair.

While the place is cluttered beyond comprehension, it is not dirty. As Jeff observed, it doesn't smell bad; there is no food waste or refuse, and everything is well organized. There is not a sign of rats or vermin anywhere.

"Let me do the talking," I whisper to Jeff, and then turn to Goldsmith.

"Goldsmith!" I say cheerfully.

I step forward.

"I bring you an offering," I say and I hand him my pint of Goldschlager.

Goldsmith looks at it, swirls the gold flakes in it around admiringly, and then sets it on a shelf next to him, nodding and looking me over.

"I have brought my friend Jeffery. He is a winemaker," I say, trying to be as formal as I can. Goldsmith is mercurial, and the tiniest misstep can buy his silence. But also, if I am honest, I am terrified of him. I motion Jeff to follow suit.

Jeff walks up.

"I bring you an offering," he says and holds the larger bottle of Goldschlager out to Goldsmith. Goldsmith's hand snaps it up, with surprising speed for such an old man, and he clutches Jeff's wrist.

Jeff looks back at me with fear in his eyes. I shrug noncommittally. This is not Goldsmith's usual behavior. Goldsmith looks at Jeff's hand and follows it, up his arm, to his face, and stares into his eyes for a moment. Then he takes the bottle of Goldschlager from Jeff and releases Jeff's wrist.

"Jeffery, maker of wine, master of your craft, I thank you for your offering," Goldsmith says, falling to his knees in front of Jeff and holding the bottle up. He opens the bottle and sips it, then bows his head to the floor.

This is not Goldsmith's usual behavior at all. I try to hide my growing alarm. I have come to visit Goldsmith a few times a year since I moved to Napa. He is usually abrupt, taciturn, and patronizing. Polite, deferential, and grateful do not seem like words in Goldsmith's vocabulary.

"Warder, why do you bring the Anointed to my lair? Why am I blessed by the presence of the Blethspa Amah?" Goldsmith asks, a look of almost sadness in his eyes.

Jeff turns and looks back at me, his eyes wide, and he mouths an incredulous "What. The. Fuck?" at me. I can only shrug, as I'm as confused as he is and slightly more alarmed.

"Um," I say. "He has been made a part of a curse and I was hoping you could help me with some information."

"A curse upon the Blethspa Amah? This cannot be. Let me see," Goldsmith says, standing back up.

"Go ahead," I say to Jeff.

Jeff hesitates. Apparently, coming to a hermit's house, being called the Anointed, and dropping his pants wasn't what he'd planned on doing before lunch today. After a moment, he sighs and reveals the tattoo.

"Hmm. Ancient. But. Modern," Goldsmith says. "No one respects the old ways anymore. Pidgin-tongued magus, blending symbols to hide his intent."

Goldsmith begins to reach a finger out toward Jeff's stomach, but Jeff jumps back.

"We ask for consent these days before we touch," I try to remind Goldsmith without sounding too judgmental.

Goldsmith grunts, sounding irritated.

"May I touch the curs-ed mark, Blethspa Amah?" Goldsmith asks; he seems grumpy and put off by this.

Jeff looks at me and I nod at him, trying to hide my absolute confusion behind an encouraging look. Probably I just end up looking constipated.

"Sure," Jeff says, sounding anything but.

Goldsmith reaches his finger out and touches the mark. The mark glows, first yellow, then orange, and finally a brilliant red. Jeff screams. He screams a lot. I plug my ears and force myself to keep watching.

Then it's over; the mark is gone, Jeff stops screaming and looks down, blinking incredulously.

"What more can I do for the Blethspa Amah?" Goldsmith asks.

"Well, I would kind of like to know what Blethspa Amah means," Jeff stammers.

"The Blethspa Amah is the Anointed, who will free the Hom and burn away the indignities of the past. The most sacred figure to my kind," Goldsmith says, misty-eyed. "I had begun to think you were but legend, that prophecy was but gilded despair. Now I see it was hope tarnished all along."

I don't know what he means by any of this. This is truer to my usual interactions with Goldsmith, where he gives a complicated answer that effectively has no meaning because I lack the context to understand it.

"Thank you? Great to meet you…Mr. Goldsmith," Jeff says. He starts toward the door, trying to remain polite, while also trying to hustle out.

"Please," Goldsmith interrupts. He sounds concerned, something I didn't think was possible. "Take this. My favor."

Goldsmith reaches into one of the drawers near him and pulls out a piece of gold-leafed paper. His slender, aged hands quickly and deftly fold it, and he hands it to Jeff. He takes it and nods.

"Thank you," Jeff says, looking at the little gold origami in his hands.

"You are welcome," Goldsmith replies.

Jeff turns and starts to depart once more, the little paper shape cradled in his hands.

"Blethspa Amah, before you depart, is there anything else I can do for you?" Goldsmith interrupts our departure once more. This is not his usual taciturn behavior, and it's making me feel a little insulted. He doesn't seem to want Jeff to leave.

Jeff looks around. I know him well enough I can tell by his expression that he feels like he should ask something but doesn't know what. Finally, he points to a sword that hangs on the wall behind Goldsmith. It's very simply made and nondescript, with no ornamentation or gilt of any sort. It hangs on a large and equally unremarkable wooden plaque. I've never noticed it before.

"What is that?"

"You have a keen eye, Blethspa Amah. That is Durendal, the unbreakable blade of the Paladin Roland, peer of Charlemagne. I would gift it to you, if you wish it, Blethspa Amah."

"Um, thank you, but no. I'm all set for unbreakable blades. I went through a little 'As Seen on TV' phase a while back. But thank you for your help, Mr. Goldsmith," Jeff says a slight tone of distress in his voice.

"As you wish, Blethspa Amah. If there is nothing else, go in peace," Goldsmith says and bows to Jeff again.

Jeff half bows and hustles out past me.

"Goldsmith, I was hoping you could give me information," I say.

"A mark lifted, questions answered. My patience grows thin. Now you must depart young warder," Goldsmith says. "You may return as always, in a year and a day."

I nod. There's no sense arguing with Goldsmith, and a great deal of sense in not arguing with him.

"Thank you, Great One," I say and bow my way out of the room. Then I trot back out of Goldsmith's lair and to my Wrangler once more. Jeff is waiting for me.

"What. The. Fuck. Was. That?" Jeff asks as we get into the car.

"That was not how these things usually go. I didn't tell you, because I didn't want you to get spooked, but Goldsmith is a dragon," I tell Jeff, his mouth and nose wrinkle like he's about to laugh. He sees the expression on my face and he opens his mouth and quirks one eye into an expression of confusion and disbelief.

"A *dragon*?" he asks incredulously.

"Yeah," I say simply. I didn't expect he was going to take it at face value. I wasn't planning on telling him at all. If we had just gone, asked questions, received answers, and left, Goldsmith might as well have just been a cooky old hermit. But that's not what happened.

"Is this something I should Urban Dictionary?" he asks as I start the car.

"No, I mean it literally," I told him. "He's a literal dragon."

"I have so many questions," Jeff says. I'm sure he does.

"I am afraid that I only have a few answers," I tell him.

We begin our bumping, jolting, tooth-jarring journey back down into The Valley. I can see a plume of dust thrown up by my car in the rearview mirror. Maybe it is my imagination, but it billows out, framing Goldsmith's house like smoke.

"Okay. So first, aren't dragons make-believe?"

"I don't know. It might be that Goldsmith is just a little old man that knows things he shouldn't know and can remove a magic curse tattoo with Reiki. But he says he is a dragon and based on the things I've learned from him; I have no good reason to doubt that."

"Question two, isn't a dragon supposed to be a giant reptilian monster?" Jeff asks.

"Supposed to be, yes. But as I understand it, they can be pretty much whatever they want. The stereotypical giant reptile form was just like…a way of intimidating people? Goldsmith has never looked like anything but an old man when I've met him."

"Then how do you know he's a dragon?"

"Well, that's what he told me when I asked."

"But that isn't evidence, is it?"

"He touched your cursed mark and it vanished. Actually, I think the whole thing, the whole spell, went poof like the whole thing never happened. Even if you don't accept that as a spell, he erased a tattoo with a touch. Dragon's Breath, they call it. Dragons can destroy almost anything, people, buildings, even magic…time itself if you believe a few of the stories. 'As if with a breath,' to quote a book I read," I tell him, "I've seen him do things. Know things. Things he shouldn't be able to do or know. So yeah, I accept him as a dragon."

"Okay. Okay. So let's say he *is* a dragon. Why does he live in that crappy house, surrounded by garbage?" Jeff asks.

"Fair question, this is where my knowledge gets a little questionable. I have an idea of the story from books and things people have told me and little hints Goldsmith himself has dropped here and there," I say.

"How long have you known him? I mean if you can only ask him a question every year and a day…like how many times have you gotten to talk to him?" Jeff asks.

"Oh, yeah, the year and a day thing. I think he just says that to be dramatic. Either that or dragons don't tell time the way we do, or he's getting senile. Or all of the above. Either way, as long as I give him a couple of weeks, he doesn't seem to care if I come back," I say.

"Oh," Jeff says, clearly not knowing what else to say. "So…what's with the hoarding?"

Staying on the winding dirt road is taking so much concentration that my train of thought is wandering to compensate.

"Sorry, I needed to focus. Here is everything that I have pieced together about dragons. One. They are older than humanity by quite a bit. Two. They are very powerful; some claim they were the first to introduce magic to humankind. A couple of things that Goldsmith said today supports that supposition. Three. Most people who know that they existed believe them now to be extinct. They used to be much more prevalent, the young ones were impetuous and impulsive and would go do rash things, attacking villages, kidnapping princesses, or whatever. The older ones advised kings, controlled nations from behind the scenes, etc.," I explain.

"What does this have to do with the hoarding?" Jeff asks.

"I'm getting there. Then along comes this guy, St. George. He might have been one guy. Or it might have been a whole series of 'em, like the Dread Pirate Roberts. Or it might have been an organization of people, I don't know. There are lots of stories. George, whoever he was or they were, whatever, had a hate-on for dragons. Some of the stories say it was because his wife and family were slain by a dragon, and he set out with a Batman-like vendetta against dragons. Others say he just wanted to slay the most dangerous prey he could. Like all these stories, there is a lot of spin on his motivation, whether he is being portrayed as a hero, a villain, or just a bumbling idiot," I say.

"St. George and the Dragon is a pretty well-known myth," Jeff says.

"Yes. But probably misleading. St. George raised an army and they set off to wage war on Dragon-kind. It wasn't a war; it wasn't even a fight. It was a slaughter. Dragons can change into whatever they want, including impersonating specific people. They are masters of magic. They are all but unkillable. St. George's army didn't have a chance," I explain.

"But he did win? Right?" Jeff asks.

"Depending on your definition of win. St. George realized he had no chance of winning. He surrendered, threw up the white flag, and called for a truce. The dragons accepted. St. George said he wished them all to come to a feast, where he could properly make amends for his wicked ways," I tell him.

"A Trojan Horse gambit?"

"Yeah, basically. Dragons were…are to a lesser degree, arrogant beyond human comprehension. Also, dragons don't lie. I don't know if it is a 'can't lie' or a 'won't lie'." Either way, they don't. To this day. Goldsmith has never told me a lie."

"Never?" Jeff asks.

"Never. He just doesn't answer a lot. If he doesn't want to answer, he just doesn't. I've never known him to lie. He'll just sit and stare at me stone-faced or tell me it is time to leave if we get to something he doesn't want to say. And until St. George, I understand, dragons didn't believe others would lie either. Lying was so far out of their process, that they didn't expect or look for it from others"

"I can see where this is going," Jeff says.

"I suspect you can. It turns out that when you are an immortal, unstoppable, innately honest creature, who does not need protection or deception...well, the dragons didn't see the real threat coming. St. George had searched long and hard, high and low, and interviewed every magical expert. Had combed every magical tome, for a way to kill a dragon. He found one...eventually...somehow. Then he used a poison. A magical poison. He invited all of the dragons to a great feast and poisoned them. And the dragons, being what they were, never suspected it. Now, the ones that survived rarely trust humans. End of story."

"So," Jeff says, scratching his chin. "If he poisoned all the dragons, how come Goldsmith is alive? And what does that have to do with Goldsmith's home?"

"Right, right, getting there. So, when St. George's poison took effect, all the youngest dragons died almost on the spot, foaming at the mouth and screaming—if you believe the more dramatic accounts. The more mature ones lingered and suffered for a long time. It was only the oldest, the strongest, and the most ancient wyrms that survived. They survived, but they were not intact. The poison took a lot away from them and it each was affected differently. All suffered damage to their bodies. It is said the poison affected their minds and their magical prowess. Others say it was the grief of losing almost all of their kind that drove them all a little mad. Only a dozen or so survived, and they went into hiding for centuries," I explain.

"You're saying the poison made Goldsmith a hoarder?" Jeff asks.

"Um...yes...but also no. All dragons are hoarders. In fact, they are well known for it. Gold and treasure are typical. It was just exacerbated by the poison, redirected. I think Goldsmith's mind was broken by George's poison, just like the rest. But where some of the dragons went to create massive multinational conglomerates, intent on guiding humanity into its own destruction, Goldsmith became a hoarding hermit living on the fringes of society. Talking to Goldsmith, I think a lot of his eccentricities come as much from the grief and trauma of losing literally everyone and everything he loved in one ill-fated meal."

"That makes sense. I guess. I have a few more questions. Is Goldsmith his real name? What happened to St. George and his army? How powerful are dragons, if the poison took away part of their magic?" he asks these questions rapid-fire, and I have to mentally catalog them.

"No, Goldsmith is almost certainly not his real name, I don't know what his real name is, and I suspect he would never tell anyone…well, he might tell *you*. There is a group that calls themselves the Knights of St. George. They are a club of monster hunters, semi-underground, but not that underground. I saw they had a table at MystiCon last year. They might be the successors of St. George, or they might just be using his name. Finally, I can't tell you how powerful the remaining dragons are, I couldn't even guess what Goldsmith is capable of. Diminished from near godlike power doesn't mean weak."

"Why do you think he might tell me his real name?" Jeff asks incredulously.

"Because you are, apparently, the Blethspa Amah. That seemed very important to him. Significant. I've never seen him prostrate himself. That seemed very out of character."

I pull up in front of the winery where Jeff works and turn the engine off and we sit in silence for a moment, each of us thinking.

"Do you know what that was all about? What's Blethspa Amah mean?" he asks.

"Not a clue. I can try to figure it out, but he's a looney old dragon, so it might just be that."

"What do I do with this?" he says, holding up the little origami figure that Goldsmith had given to him. I see for the first time that the origami is a dragon.

“I’d hang onto that. A looney old dragon is still a dragon, and a dragon’s favor could come in handy.”

“What’s a dragon's favor for exactly?”

“I couldn’t tell you,” I say, chuckling. “I’ve never had it.”

“Alright, I should get back to work. I’m going to call you when I get home though. I feel like there is still more I need to understand here. It’s a big leap of faith to buy all this. Honestly, I would say you were both crazy, but he burned a tattoo away by waving his hands at me. And that defies explanation,” Jeff says, opening the door and climbing out of my Wrangler.

“I’m not sure how much more I can elucidate,” I say and give him a little salute.

In my mind the salute is funny, but it just seems to confuse Jeff. He waves and walks into the winery. Jeff more than most of my other acquaintances around town has always been more accepting when I talk about the supernatural aspects of my life.

He’s less skeptical. I think this is because he has a very analytical mind and believes that anything and everything has an explanation. His mind is not plagued by a series of beliefs that can be shattered by skepticism. He takes what is put before him and starts looking for evidence to confirm or refute it before coming to judgment.

Now I need to find Mr. Whitman.

Chapter Eight

I tear off down the road toward JMBaptiste Winery, traveling just a little faster than the law would allow. I find a good parking spot right next to the tasting room entrance and hop out with a little spring in my step.

I waltz in through the front doors like I own the place and stroll right up to the tasting room counter.

"I'm looking for Mr. Charles Whitman please," I say, putting on a really bad British accent.

Two young women at the end of the bar glower at me. They turn to mutter to each other, I can't pick out what they are saying, but they do have actual British accents. Looks like I'm on a roll.

"Sorry," I murmur. "Meant to be a joke."

"Goddamn hi-lar-ee-us," one of the Brits down the bar drawls in an attempt at a bad American accent.

She's light-skinned with dark hair. She strikes me because she has the palest blue eyes I've ever seen, and she is now putting on one of the worst southern accents I've ever heard. I have no attachment to the southern accent, so this isn't the sick burn she thinks it is, but I nod at her anyway.

"Touché," I say and turn back to the attendant who shakes her head at me, disappointed.

"I think he's in his office. Just through the door over there and on the left. Can't miss it." She points "You're good to go on in, Mr. Ward"

"Oh, so you know who I am?" I say, smiling.

"It'd be tough to work here the last few days and not know about the…as Mr. Whitman puts it, 'Conniving, rat-faced, money-grubbing charlatan.' His words, not mine." She smiles an insincere smile at me.

The ladies down the bar giggle loudly.

"All right then, I'll just go see Whitman now, shall I?" I say sheepishly and slouch my way through the door toward Whitman's office.

I see the door. I couldn't have missed it, just like she said. It reads 'Charles Whitman – Operations Manager' on a little faux wood-grained vinyl plaque. I knock.

A terse voice says, "Come in."

I open the door and step inside the office, which is pretty large. Whitman has an immense oak desk with a laptop on it. The walls are lined with framed wine labels. Not all of them, I note immediately, are JMBaptiste labels.

"Oh. It's you," Whitman says, sounding disappointed.

"Yes. Me," I say as he motions me toward a seat.

I sit down, still scanning the framed labels on the walls. One frame holds three labels from Whitman Cellars.

Interesting.

"You make wine yourself?" I ask, indicating his wine label on the wall.

"Yes. Well…I used to. I got hired here as a winemaker, but as I got more involved in the operations, I was promoted. Now I don't have time to make any wine, professionally or recreationally," he says, looking the least grumpy at me he ever has.

"Do you miss it?"

"Yes, it was why I got into this industry. What I do now… it's just a paycheck."

"Ever considered starting your own winery?" I ask. I am

guessing from the labels, he certainly has considered it, if not actually done it.

"Yes. I actually had my own winery, but…well, let's just say I trusted the wrong people and we didn't make it. My name was dirt in The Valley for a while. Lost my investors and a lot of money. Lost friends who had decided to invest. I was young and foolish," he says.

I nod. "I'm familiar with young and foolish," I say.

"I can see that," he quips. I ignore him and carry on.

"If you don't mind, how much money are we talking about?" I ask.

"Why are you so interested?" Mr. Whitman asks.

"Just thinking about the motive for this whole curse thing," I say, waving a finger around indicating the whole winery.

"Bankruptcy money in a few cases, including in my case. But I digress, Mr. Ward. What can I do for you? Certainly, you didn't come in to ask me about my resume. You have other nonsense to waste Mr. Baptiste's money on, I presume?"

"Well, yes, now that you mention it," I say. "My approach here is two-pronged. I think before we build wards and defenses, we need to acknowledge that your winery, and perhaps you personally, are under direct attack. We need to determine if that is going to be ongoing and if so, what we can do about it. Once we've dealt with the immediate problem, we focus on general mystical security measures."

"What do you mean *I* might be under direct attack?"

I take a deep breath to center myself and think. I have some suspicions here. I suspect that Whitman is the target of the spell Jeff was embroiled in. I suspect that when Goldsmith burned away Jeff's tattoo it would have burned away all of the others linked to it magically. I have no real way of confirming either of these suspicions, so I will take a shot in the dark and see what I hit.

"Let me ask you something directly, if you don't mind," I say. He starts to answer, but I was being rhetorical, so I interrupt him. "Did you recently get a mysterious tattoo on your pelvis, and did it then mysteriously vanish? Probably very painfully?"

He stares at me slack-jawed. His lips quiver a bit.

"Yes...how did you..." he stammers.

"I thought that might be the case," I say. "I don't think Mr. Baptiste or the winery or any of your guests are the targets of this magical assault. I think you are."

"That's preposterous! Even if all this magic nonsense were real, why would someone want to attack me?" he stammers. His pupils are dilated, and his eyes have the deep purple rings of someone who hasn't slept well in days. There is a quavering to his voice. If I were to guess, this is the face of a man kept awake night after night by paroxysms of anxiety.

"It was me that made that tattoo vanish. I would think that alone should dispel your skepticism about me. If you want things to go more smoothly, please set aside your bullshit for the moment at least."

I, of course, didn't make the tattoo vanish, but I need his cooperation. Though, it's kind of true, from a certain perspective. Sure, Goldsmith removed the curse that linked Jeff and Mr. Whitman and who knows how many other people, but I brought the Blethspa Amah to Goldsmith. So, by transitive logic, it was my doing...right?

"Yes. I...how exactly did you do that?" he asks, his face contorted with justifiable incredulity.

"That's not important right now. Right now, the important thing is I need to know how you got it and why someone might want you dead. Not just dead, but brutally, humiliatingly, and inexplicably dead."

"Honestly, I don't know," he says. He's far too casual in his response. He doesn't pause to consider for an instant.

He knows exactly why.

"Okay, when did the tattoo appear?" I ask, sighing.

"I got it about five days ago." His ears turn a little red. "It's kind of embarrassing."

"Oh?"

"There was this woman…this lady," he says emphatically. "She was beautiful. Stunning. Amazing really. She came in to taste some wine, we started chatting. She invited me to her hotel room after a few glasses…."

"And of course, you went."

"Yes. I mean, I don't normally do that sort of thing. But she was very alluring," he says, looking sheepish.

"And you had a glass of wine with her…and you fell asleep and woke up with a tattoo," I guess out loud.

"In a nutshell, yes. She was gone. Room empty. I couldn't get a name from the hotel staff. She just vanished."

"What was her name?"

He turns a deeper shade of red.

"You never got her name?" I try to keep my voice professional, and I don't physically slap my head with my hand. But in my mind's eye, I just broke my nose with my overenthusiastic facepalm.

"No. Honestly, it was like I had been drugged from the instant I met her like my brain was just turned off."

"Okay, so why would someone target you?"

"I don't know. I'd never met her before in my life, I'd never even seen her."

"I think she's just a contractor. A sort of assassin."

He gets a series of weird expressions on his face. I think he's considering telling me something, but then his stoic, condescending expression returns, and his face becomes placid once more.

"Magic. Curses. Assassins…that's insane. Who would want to assassinate me?" he asks.

"I think for whoever set this up, it's very personal. I think they wanted you to go in a way that was going to make the news. Painful. Horrible. Humiliating. A death that was going to be a warning for others."

I pause dramatically before continuing. His eyes have grown wide, but he refuses to give me anything.

"Bankruptcy money sounds like a motive, especially for friends who've lost money. Tell me about these investors."

"I've made amends and reparations to basically everyone at this point. In some manner or another," he says. I am suspicious of the vagueness of his answer and catch a slight shifting on his arms which gives me pause.

"Basically everyone isn't exactly everyone though."

"No. There's Phil. Phillip Harmon, we went to school together. He was my business partner at the winery. We started it right after college. I was the winemaker, and he had the business sense. We were young, and it was poorly planned. There were insurance and assets that we liquidated to pay off all the investors, eventually. But Phil and I both lost our shirts. We walked away with nothing, and most of the investment capital was his…" Whitman says, trailing off.

"I see. So, you both had to pull yourselves back up by your bootstraps then?"

"Yeah, that's one way of putting it. It took me time and hard work, but I have taken this opportunity Mr. Baptiste has given me and worked with it."

"And Phil?"

"Well. It was worse for him honestly. When the winery failed, it came out that he had been doing a little creative investing on the side," Whitman says. "He did soft time, and he works at the market up at Belle Aire now. He never really came back."

"Ah," I say, furrowing my brow in thought.

"I've tried to make amends. But he won't even look at me, let alone talk to me."

"Hiring someone of this caliber…it would cost money. A lot, I'd imagine. It doesn't sound like he has that kind of cash. Motive yes, but means…maybe not."

"Probably not."

"Anyone else who might have that kind of motive?"

He thinks for a long, quiet moment and then shakes his

head no. I crane my neck to see if, behind his desk, his pants are secretly on fire. He glowers at me.

"That's the best I can come up with," he says finally.

Whitman looks guilty. He is slightly pale and his eyes dart around, trying to focus on anything other than making eye contact with me. There is something he's not telling me, but I get the sense nothing I say is going to change that.

"Alright," I say, thinking aloud. "I'm going to go talk to this Phil…"

"Harmon," he says. "Phillip Harmon."

"Which market at Bel Air?"

"The TJs. That's where he was working the last time I saw him. He lives with his uncle. I tracked him down to try to patch things up a while back, I have his address here somewhere," he says, pulling out his phone.

"Great."

"Here, it's off of East Pueblo, near the hospital."

"You should call the police too. Ask for Officer Chris Benson," I say. I honestly don't imagine there is anything the Napa PD can do for him. This is more of a trawling for information tactic on my part.

"I'll do that," he says. I can tell by his downcast eyes and tone that this is a lie. He has no intention of talking to the authorities. He knows exactly what's going on, and he has something to lose by going to the authorities.

"Okay. I'm going to construct a magic circle here in your office that should deflect any magical attacks. You will want to sit in it for…well basically till I tell you it's safe." I stand up and start getting salt and chalk out of my bag. "Oh, and here."

I put my salt and chalk down on his desk and take off my necklace. I hand it to him.

"Wear that for now. I will want that back, but it's a powerful ward. If the ruby breaks—"

"That's too big to be a ruby," he interrupts me.

"As I said, I am going to want that back. Anyway, if it breaks, that means it's just stopped something very powerful. You should get into the circle and call me if that happens. It won't happen. Well, I hope it won't happen. It shouldn't happen," I get lost in a series of doomsday thoughts about worst-case scenarios. "Anyway, it probably won't happen. But if it does, get in the circle and call me."

He nods. Looking at the ruby, I can see him reconsidering his assessment of the situation. Somehow my handing him very expensive jewelry gives more weight to my argument in his mind.

I begin drawing an exclusive circle around his desk. I try to go as quickly as possible, while still paying attention to detail. I don't have any pig's blood, so I have to nick the back of my arm for blood to activate the circle. Thankfully I carry Band-Aids in my courier bag.

I stop and look at the necklace I've given him—a gift given to me on Walt Carmichael's behalf by a Syzmek executive. A generous thank you for all the work I'd done. It is old, very old, and with all of the protective sigils etched into its facets it is probably considered priceless. I don't like Whitman, but my mother raised me to believe that a life is a life, and they are all more valuable than objects. Hopefully, I get it back.

Having finished that, I bid Mr. Whitman ta ta for now. I head back out through the tasting room. My fan club from the other side of the pond has gone, thankfully. I return to the parking lot and jump back in my Wrangler.

The Phil Harmon lead is probably a dead end, but I don't have any other avenues to pursue unless he's willing to give me more information. I head over to the address that Whitman gave me. It looks like a nice enough house, but it's been left unmanaged for a while. The grass is overgrown in the front yard, vines creep up on the corners of the house, and the magnolia trees around it have gone wild, all but blocking the view of the house from the street. The windows are dark, but I approach the door anyway and ring the doorbell.

Nothing. I wait a few minutes, humming to myself. After a few moments, I have the self-conscious realization that I am humming "Be Our Guest" from Disney's *Beauty and the Beast*. Why? I stop. I walk back to my Jeep and hop in.

I spend time debating with myself. Do I try the market? Do I walk the aisles looking for someone with a name tag that reads "Phil"? Do I go to the customer service desk?

Cornering someone at their place of work hardly seems like a productive approach. But getting an idea of what shift he is on might be helpful.

Time to go shopping!

The market isn't large, but there are a surprising number of employees on the floor. I wander the aisles and grab a six-pack of beer—likely not as good as Jeff's, but it'll do in a pinch. I grab canned cold brew coffee; you never can be too careful. I grab another pint of Goldschlager. Hey, I never know when I might need another offer.

I stop in the freezer aisle. On the shelf in front of me above the freezer troughs is a box of chocolates. It's pretty. The box is all wrapped in a linen material that seems somewhere halfway between paper and cloth. It looks simple and elegant. It has chocolates from seven different sources—Peru, Brazil, Ecuador, Côte d'Ivoire, Ghana, Nigeria, and Cameroon. I don't know chocolate like I know coffee, but it's interesting to me that they have a lot of the same regions in common.

"It's fascinating that coffee is indigenous to northern Africa, but some of the best coffees are grown in South America. Yet cacao is indigenous to South America, and the best chocolates are sourced in Africa."

I realize that I have been vocalizing this out loud and people are moving away from me in the aisle. Embarrassed, I grab the chocolates.

I have a weird fantasy that I will give these to Emily as a romantic gesture or something—to make up for not picking up on her cues the other day.

Just then I spot Phil Harmon. He is about the same age as Whitman, probably forty or so, but he looks much older somehow and more tired. He is skinny; I might even go so far as to say emaciated. His oily skin and thinning hair further the overall sickly feel I get from him.

He's stocking shelves. I watch him for a minute, taking him in. He doesn't strike me as particularly threatening, if anything I feel a flash of sympathy watching him. He looks up at me and we make eye contact. There's a moment of connection there. His eyes look sad and tired. I glance to see what he is doing. He's stocking pickles.

"Do you have any gherkins there?" I ask, trying to cover up my creepy spying.

"Yeah," he says. He sounds as exhausted as he looks. He hands me a jar of gherkins. I guess I'm having snacking pickles this evening.

"Are these any good?"

"I'm more of a bread-and-butter guy myself," he says. He visibly stares at my shopping basket. "Big night planned?"

I look into my basket: booze, coffee, chocolate, pickles.

"Breakfast of champions," I say, raising the basket. "Have a good one."

He chuckles a little and shakes his head.

"You too," he says.

I go to the checkout line and buy all of my items. I brought my own bag; I had a bunch printed up as marketing swag,but nobody ever wants a reusable bag with my name on it, so I always have a couple handy.

I stroll across the parking lot to where my Wrangler is parked, a cloth bag of groceries swaying in one hand as I walk. I open the passenger's side door and I am about to toss my groceries on the passenger's seat, when I realize with a start, that someone is sitting in it. Somewhere very nearby someone makes a little high-pitched squeal of surprise and terror, but it's definitely not me.

"Hello there," a sultry female voice says.

I jump back.

The gherkins slip out of the bag and the bottle smashes on the ground.

Chapter Nine

"So sorry to startle you," the woman in the passenger seat says, swinging her legs out of the car and placing both feet on the running board in a very suggestive posture.

She's six feet tall if she's an inch. She has smooth dark skin and dark hair. Her eyes are a yellow-brown color, almost orange. They remind me of fox eyes—narrow, sly, and predatory.

In any room, in any city in the world, she would turn heads and stand out as mysterious and foreign. She looks at me and smiles with full lips painted red. She's wearing a black dress; it's slinky, but I also note that it has a practical cut that would let her run in it. She's wearing flats, not heels. Of course, she doesn't seem to need the extra height. Her shoes, like her dress, are fashionable and functional. I don't need an introduction to feel certain that this is the woman both Whitman and Jeff mentioned.

"Mr. Miles Ward," she says. It is a statement, not a question. Her accent is difficult to place.

"Yes," I say. "And you are?"

"I'm your dream girl," she says in a tone that sounds like a cheap come-on but somehow makes me feel more threatened than anything.

"Uh. Okay. But what should I call you?" I ask.

"You can call me Circe," she says, smiling wryly as she does.

"Of course," I say. "It's a little on the nose, isn't it?"

She laughs, high and melodious, like the chime of bells.

"You are as clever as I hoped."

"I never disappoint," I say, trying to bring a little swagger and bravado. I doubt I succeeded, but she gets a flirtatiously surprised look.

"Oh, I'm sure that's true," she says in a way that makes my cheeks warm.

"How can I help you, Circe? If you don't mind me asking, why are you in my Jeep?" I say, trying to sound cool and collected, which I am not.

"I just wanted to meet you," she says. "You are an interesting man."

Her eyes are taking me in like a wolf taking in a lamb. It's both flattering and terrifying at the same time.

"You seem like a very interesting lady, but I am afraid you have me at a loss," I say. "How do you know me exactly?"

"Oh, come on, Mr. Ward. Or do you prefer Miles?" she says in a way that makes me flustered.

"Mr. Ward was my grandfather," I say out of reflex. "Do you mind if I put these groceries in the back of my car?"

I don't wait for an answer, and I hustle around the back and open the tailgate. I set the groceries in the back. I stop momentarily, taking a deep breath, and center myself, one hand resting on the opened tailgate. When I close the tailgate to walk back to the front of the car, I am startled. She's slid out of the car and is standing right next to me, somehow moving to my side without making a noise or me noticing anything in my peripheral vision. My car doors are the noisiest things on the planet. They don't open or close silently.

She's standing before me, not sitting in a darkened car. She's considerably taller than me, well above my estimated six feet. She has a beautiful look and bearing that is slightly unconventional. The whole image is betrayed by the predatory look of a jungle cat in her eyes. She's even more intimidating standing up. I get the feeling that every move, every word, and every action she takes is carefully planned and executed to evoke this ambivalence.

"I think, Miles, we can stop playing all these games. Don't you?"

"I'm pretty sure that even if we do, one of us is still playing to win."

I'm not even sure what games we are playing.

"You undid my curse, Miles. That's impressive. Please tell me how you did that," she says, her sultry tone underlying a sharp threat. I have to play my cards right here.

"The Hizarin aren't used to encountering resistance?" I inquire.

I'm fishing for answers, but this is the best opportunity to gather real information.

"It's been a long time since I've felt challenged. It's exhilarating," she says in a breathy tone. The Hizarin is a mythical order of magical assassins. Whether they exist or not is a matter of debate. That she isn't denying membership tells me something about her. Either it is real, and she is a member, or she's suicidally reckless. Though it occurs to me, the two are not mutually exclusive.

"So, what now?"

"Well," she says. "Normally, I'd just kill you. But I think you are sweet. Delectable. Like a fine pastry."

She licks her lips.

"Um," I say, my feeling of unease growing. She's talking about killing or not killing me like she's deciding if she wants the red or the white wine with dinner, with the afterthought of if she wants to sleep with it first.

"You could come back to my hotel with me. You would like that, I'm sure."

"I am busy tonight. I have to...wash...my...hair," I stammer out the first thing that comes to mind. It's a lie, but it's a flimsy lie. We both know it's a lie, so it's basically not lying.

She laughs, and whatever game we are playing, she is winning. While she is very attractive, every fiber of my being tells me to run.

"I am not going away empty-handed, Miles."

"Oh, here, I got these for you," I blurt out and reach back into my vehicle. I give her the chocolates I bought. I don't know if she counts as a supernatural being, but regardless, offerings never hurt in my experience.

She takes them and smiles.

"Not the sweet treat I was hoping for, but these will do," she says, clearly enjoying my discomfort.

"Great to meet you, Circe, but I have an appointment I am running late for."

"Your hair?"

"Yeah, I need to get it washed and permed," I say, running my fingers through my very short hair.

She laughs again. It's the exact same laugh as before, rehearsed.

I'm about to jump in my Jeep and roar away, but I realize I should try to gain something more from this experience. Since I now have identified my suspect, knowing how to find her again would be helpful.

"How can I get in touch with you?" I ask.

"Oh, you don't find me. I find you," she says.

As an afterthought, I hand her my card and jump into the Jeep. She kisses it and slips it into the top of her dress suggestively. I slam the door, suddenly feeling as embarrassed as a Puritan caught skinny-dipping. When I glance back out the passenger side window, she's gone. I look around and can't see her anywhere. She's just vanished.

That's creepy.

I get out of the parking lot as quickly as I can. But a couple of hundred feet later, I am stopped at a stop light. I take the moment to think. What am I going to do? It's late afternoon, I could still get a bit more work done, but I'm feeling pretty shaken right now.

Home. I want to go home, somewhere I feel protected and safe.

I can't help wondering what her intentions are…I brush the thought of her sultry voice from my mind.

"She's nothing but bad news, Miles," I warn myself out loud, then turn the volume up on the car stereo and drive home.

I park and bound up the stairs to my apartment. I unlock the door, rush in, slam the door and lock it behind me. I go around the house checking all my wards. Finally, I sit down on my bed and look up at the mannequin standing against the wall opposite me. I look into the glass eyes that I paid to have made in the same hazel color as mine. His emotionless unmoving face stares blankly back at me.

"Ugh! Today is stressing me out!" I rant at Hank.

"Oh, what's up buddy? You get a parking ticket?"

"No, it's just this job, it's snowballing on me."

"Oh, come on, Miles, how bad can it be? You draw some pictures on winery walls, you glue crystals to their doorframe. Maybe if you're feeling a little plucky, you hide little bags of chicken bones in the vents, get paid, and call it a day."

"No, it's just that there is this guy who is being targeted with curses, and it might be the work of the Hizarin."

"That's not your job, Miles. Do the job, get paid, and get out."

"You sound like Dad."

"Being an asshole and being right aren't mutually exclusive."

"Then there was this woman, Circe…she was like all over me. There was something off about her. She was like a pastiche of sexy cliches."

"What's the problem, Miles? A beautiful woman hit on you, and you fell to pieces?"

"Yes, but I think she was a member of the Hizarin. She's a professional killer!"

"Yeah, maybe, but she was hot, and she was into you. You are always

complaining you can't tell if women are interested or just being nice! Well, she wasn't being nice!"

"She's probably a vampire, Hank!"

"Well then, at least you know she likes to—"

"You suck, Hank!" I interrupt and throw myself on my bed and put my pillow over my ears. "Not listening to you anymore!"

Movies, stories, comics, fiction, all have vampires wrong.

For the sake of argument, let's define monsters as creatures with potentially malevolent intentions toward humans that have not been taxonomically and scientifically categorized. That is, you might say that a hungry tiger stalking you in the jungle is a monster. But that isn't what we are talking about, we are talking about the things that go bump in the night. I see them as being categorized into three groups.

First, there are the creatures that pre-existed humanity. Like dragons. I don't know much about these sorts of creatures, but I assume like dragons they are all very powerful and mysterious. Other than dragons, I am not even sure what might exist in this category. Maybe everything from every myth, fairy tale, legend, and story, but maybe not.

The second category is creatures from the Dreamtime. That's what I call it, anyways. It isn't really a place, it's the world, but different. Maybe it's time but it's different. When you sleep you glimpse into the Dreamtime, but it cannot hurt you. A few people can gain agency in the Dreamtime, Lucid Dreamers, Dream-walkers, whatever you want to call them. It is also possible to enter the Dreamtime using psychoactive drugs, but that's very dangerous as I understand it because you can get stuck there. There are things that live there which we've all encountered in our dreams, though they are harmless in that context. I've read that under the right circumstances and in the right locations, a Lucid Dreamer can open a physical passage into the Dreamtime. Sometimes when this happens, things come through. It is rare, but it happens. I've never really dealt with something from the Dreamtime, but I've heard stories, and they are truly the stuff of nightmares.

The last category of monsters is those that man created. Often, things that man turned himself into. One example I know something about is vampires. A vampire is a sorcerer, possibly a necromancer, that has prolonged their life through the ritual consumption of human blood. When they start, they are human. As the decades turn to centuries, they consume enough blood to start magically changing themselves more and more. They usually make themselves very attractive, fast, strong, and immortal, all with magic. At a point, they stop being completely human and start being something else. A vampire. They aren't undead per se. They have a pulse, they eat and drink and sleep. No two are exactly the same; they use magic to change themselves in different ways. Some of them are hundreds of years old. And all of them, every single one, is a powerful sorcerer.

Vampires don't create other vampires through biting either, as fiction suggests. They create other vampires by teaching them the rituals to accompany the drinking of blood to make the changes take effect. So, in a sense, the stories are true: vampires create other vampires, but it is through education, not murder.

I met a vampire named William Morris a few years ago. "Billy-M" as he preferred to go by. Billy-M was looking for feeding partners, people willing to give him their blood. He was very polite and cordial and would only feed on willing participants—which I respect because it is not vampire standard operating procedure. I didn't give Billy-M any of my blood, but I did enjoy the opportunity of asking more about his kind. He was the kindest and most polite abomination I have ever met, and I learned quite a bit from him.

Everything about Circe screams vampire. The unusual, unplaceable beauty. The perfect flawless skin—not a blemish, freckle or mole to be seen. The lilting voice. Drugging and tattooing people without consent. Everything about her, sculpted to complete a perfect image to lure people in.

"Lure people in, Miles? Or lure you in specifically? It feels like she's checking a lot of your specific boxes there, amigo."

While it isn't welcome, Hank makes a fair point. Maybe she's using magic to influence me. The more I think about it, the more convinced I am that Circe is one of those dark sorcerers whose obsession with power had lured them down the vile path of drinking human blood to fuel their immortality.

"My brain is numb. Hank! Couch potato time."

"Can we watch the show where they get all those hot women to compete for the one guy's attention and then get all drunk and tear each other's clothes off?"

"No reality TV, Hank. You know the rule!"

I get a beer from the fridge and sit down on my bed to watch a little trash television. At some point, I fall asleep. It sort of sneaks up on me, so I'm not certain when. It really is the best way to go into oblivion.

Chapter Ten

I'm running. Being pursued. Whatever it is, it's toying with me. So much faster, so much stronger. But every time I can hear it close in and I turn to look, there is nothing there.

I'm on a street that's dark and empty. Dark windows stare at me like haunted black eyes. A paper wrapper blows through the street. It hits my ankle and I kick it off. The breeze blows it down the street like a tumbleweed, and I see it catch on a branch. I'm so fixated on the rippling, tumbling scrap of paper that I don't hear my stalker until it's right behind me. I can feel breath on my neck, but it isn't hot. It's like a blast of arctic air. I turn quickly, wheeling my arms.

There's nothing there. I trip and fall, clumsily I roll myself to my feet.

I run.

I'm in a building, dashing down empty long hallways, over the linoleum tiles and past blank industrial walls. There are faded spots and odd stains everywhere. Once there were posters and decor on these walls, but they are now blank, bare, a mottled, industrial, eggshell white.

It's still here, behind me. I run down the hall and slam through the door at the end. The room on the other end is a giant, old-fashioned apothecary. Glass jars and things line the tops of shelves, and the shelves below contain more jars. In the jars are herbs and crystals and other odder things.

In one jar I see a floating eye; I observe it from up close. I can see the pupil focusing on me. I start back and bump something cold and hard and animate. Wheeling around, there is nothing there. Glancing around frantically, I see a giant red door in the back of the room. I charge toward it and through.

I'm in a black room, where a woman is sitting on a large stool. She's smoking a cigarette through one of those long cigarette holders. She's dressed like a flapper, but not a real flapper. Like a flapper in a high school theater rendition of The Great Gatsby. *I scan her face, but she doesn't look familiar at all. She has light brown hair and soft features. I'd call her pretty, except the look on her face is downright hostile, this is someone who wants me dead.*

Only I realize it isn't me she's looking at. She's looking over my shoulder. I spin around once more, expecting to see the blankness where my stalking monster is. But sitting on the floor on the side of the room, near the door I came in through, is Charles Whitman. He's playing solitaire on the floor, but I see that the cards are all the same suit.

Diamonds.

I turn back around; the woman is gone, but there is a staircase. It is the front stairs to my home. Only it's a building I've never seen before. A part of me just knows somehow, it's home. I run up the stairs and through the familiar door that I've never seen before and into a house. The house is large and white and there is mid-summer sun shining through the windows. Outside the trees are green and the sun feels warm on my face.

I'm happy for a second. Then I feel that cold breath on my neck and I hear a low chuffing sound. Once again I run, through a door, down a hall, turn a corner, another hall, another door. I'm in my bedroom, only now it's really my bedroom. I jump into my bed and hide under the covers.

I wake up. I was dreaming. I relax.

Okay, I'm okay, I tell myself. *Just focus on the day ahead and don't dwell on the nightmare, it's fine.*

I go to roll out of bed, but I realize I can't move.

I'm paralyzed. I feel the cold breath on my neck.

There is something—a heavy, dead weight pinning me face down on my bed. I go to scream.

I wake up. I was dreaming. I relax.

Okay, I'm okay, I tell myself. *Just focus on the day ahead and don't dwell on the nightmare*...oh wait, I'm still paralyzed.

There's a cold breath on my neck, and I try to scream.

I wake up. I was dreaming, I relax.

I'm okay, I tell myself. But I'm not, I'm still paralyzed, I'm still dreaming, there is a cold breath on my neck. I say, "What the—"

"Fuck!" I scream as I sit up in my bed. The TV is still on, the remote is sitting on my lap. I'm still dressed. It's two in the morning, and I had a nightmare. I haven't had a nightmare like that since college.

I don't know much about the Dreamtime. What I do know is that everything you experience in dreams is sort of real. It's how your brain processes the experiences that you have while your spirit, for lack of a better word, travels there. When it returns, your mind has to reconcile your experience with the real world.

You can't always trust the specific images, but usually, the summation, the takeaway, is true.

True-ish. A verisimilitude. Maybe.

Long and short, my takeaway is: Someone or something is stalking me.

Lucid Dreamers can control the dreams, strip away the interpretation and metaphor, change the context and own the dream. At least that's how it was explained to me. That's not something I can do.

Now the advantage of being a normal dreamer, of not having that control is, I can always wake up. It's difficult for anything in the Dreamtime to harm me because I can just leave. Things can try to drag me back in, which I believe was what caused the cycle of me waking up from the nightmare into the nightmare. But they can't keep a normal dreamer there; no one is in danger in the Dreamtime when they are just there as a visitor. It's those who have agency that are at risk. Physically entering the Dreamtime, I am told is possible, but that is where the greatest risk exists. Thankfully that isn't a problem for me.

I get up and change into pajamas and brush my teeth. The nightmare has faded to only a vague memory by the time I get back into bed. It takes me a while to get back to sleep, but my mind keeps racing over all the madness of the last couple of days. I drift off again when I'm not paying attention and sleep dreamlessly for the rest of the night.

I am awakened by my phone ringing a few hours later. It's Jeff calling.

"Hi, Jeff. What's up?" I answer, bleary-eyed.

"Not much, you up? You sound like you were asleep. It's 10 AM, so I didn't think that it would be too early," he says.

"No, it's fine. Is there something wrong? The tattoo's not back?" I ask.

"No, no, everything is just fine. No, I was thinking about it, and I want to help you out," he says.

"What do you mean?" I ask.

"I mean, I kinda had fun, meeting a dragon and stuff. It's thrilling. I'd love to come along and help you out," he says.

"Yeah, I think this is a bad case to help on. It's getting kind of scary," I say.

"All the more reason you should have an assistant. Besides, I'm the chosen one or whatever. Can't hurt to have the chosen one on your side!" he says, chuckling at himself.

"Mmmm. It was Anointed. He said, the 'Anointed'," I groan.

"Anointed. It's settled then, I'll meet you at Soothsayers in a half hour," he says.

"Don't you have to work?" I ask.

"It's pretty slow here. It's not going to be a problem if I skip out on a few hours here or there," he says.

"You should work. I'll be fine."

"No really, it's no problem. I insist," he says, something in his voice sounds eager, excited even.

"Why? You've never shown more than a polite interest in my work before."

"That's not true!" he says. "I don't know. I feel like I should. You ever have something you just felt like you had to do?"

I am quite familiar with that feeling. On one hand, I am not super excited about the idea of Jeff getting involved in all this magic assassin stuff. On the other hand, he's already involved. On the third hand, it would be nice not to feel like I was in this growing shit show by myself. Besides, he is the Blethspa Amah. Whatever that means.

I go to let out a long sigh of exasperation, but I can hear my voice echoing back through the phone and it sounds more like a growl.

"Okay," I grumble. "I'll meet you at the coffee shop in a half hour."

I rush through my morning routine, the dressing of the Hank, the blessing of the wards. The dirtying of my kitchen counters.

I'm eight minutes late getting to Soothsayer. But that doesn't matter much, because Jeff's even later than that. I'm on my second mug of coffee when he arrives. He doesn't drink coffee, so I hand him a (now) cold Earl Grey tea and a scone.

"I took the liberty of ordering for you. I hope you don't mind," I say.

"No, looks perfect. Thank you," he says.

"Of course. Eat and I'll bring you up to speed. There have been developments since we last spoke. The target is Charles Whitman at JMBaptiste. Someone has hired a Hizarin to assassinate him. The Hizarin is a beautiful, murderous, probably-vampire that I think was the one who seduced and tattooed you. She believes that I undid her curse and knows who I am, but hasn't killed me yet. The motive for killing Whitman may be settling a score over a bad investment, but the person most likely to want to do that…well, I don't know how he'd afford a brick to throw through Whitman's window, let alone hire an assassin." I'm panting by the time I finish my hastily delivered summary.

"Great," Jeff says enthusiastically. He sits with pursed lips for a moment, then asks, "So this Hizarin thing is like some kind of vampire death cult?"

"I only know the stories, but vampire assassin death cult? Y'know what, that's close enough."

"Cool."

"Hopefully not," I say with a shiver, remembering the cold breath from my dream last night.

"What's the next step?" he asks, again there is an eager energy to his statement. It's less of something I see or hear, but more just a sense I get from his tone and the speed with which he replies.

"Well, it seems like Goldsmith removed all the tattoos and that spell is stopped, for now. We still need to figure out who hired the assassin and why."

"If I can ask," Jeff says. "Is this your job? I mean shouldn't the police handle this?"

"If I say that a supermodel vampire assassin was hired to kill a winery manager to settle a score for a middle-aged stock-boy at the market down the street…" I start.

"Got it. But is this what you are being paid for? Aren't you being paid to build wards at a winery?" he asks. His point is fair.

"That's what Hank said."

"Who?" he asks, looking confused.

"Never mind. Building the wards isn't going to be useful or effective if the winery is under active magical assault. No, we need to get things quiet and then build the protections. Besides, if I don't do something, Whitman is going to die. He's a douche and I don't like him, but I don't think he deserves to die like that."

"But you said the tattoos are gone, you got that fixed."

"If this is Hizarin, they will try again and again and again until he's dead."

"You're a good guy, Miles."

"Well…thanks," I say, feeling a little embarrassed.

"So, as I said, what's the next step?" he asks.

"Well, we have motive and opportunity, I think we are looking for means," I say. "We need to go talk to Mr. Phil Harmon, stock-boy and once friend of Charles Whitman."

"Sounds good."

I let Jeff drive this time. He has a fancy electric car, it looks like something out of a sci-fi movie, inside and outside, with screens everywhere, and information projected onto the windshield in front of him. Almost silently he drives us across town to Phil Harmon's house.

"Do you have a plan for building these wards on the winery?" he asks, breaking the silence.

"I've done a dozen jobs like this, honestly that part I am not worried about."

"No, I get it, it's this whole vampire assassin thing. That's not what you got hired for though. You asked me why I wanted help, but why do you?"

"You ever watch someone get hurt and weren't able to do anything but stand by and watch?" I ask.

"I mean, sure, I guess."

"I mean, like really hurt?"

"No. I guess maybe not. I take it that you have?"

"A couple of times, yeah."

"So why not go to the police?"

"This is all very fringe still. I've tried to go to the police in the past. They have enough concrete problems to deal with, so this stuff just gets filed with the pranks and hoaxes in my experience."

"Yeah," Jeff says as he pulls up and parks in front of Harmon's house. "I see your point. Though don't you have a friend on the force?"

"I do, but there isn't much he can do. I'm not sure anything that would constitute a serious crime has even happened. Legally, it's at best vandalism. And all the evidence is pretty shaky."

Jeff nods but doesn't look completely satisfied with my answer. I am feeling uncomfortable with the direction of this conversation. It's closing on aspects of my childhood I don't like to think about, let alone say aloud. I open the door and get out of the car before he can follow up.

I walk through Phil Harmon's overgrown yard. Jeff falls in right behind me as quietly as his fancy electric car. I ring the doorbell.

The door opens, Phil Harmon is standing before us. He's wearing a bathrobe over flannel pants and a white t-shirt. He looks older and more tired than he did yesterday at the grocery store if that is possible.

"Yeah," he says. It's much more a statement than a question.

"Mr. Harmon?" I say, trying to sound businesslike.

"Yeah," he says.

"Hello, I'm Miles Ward. I'm a private security consultant, I'm trying to find out more information for a contract I am working on, and I was wondering if I could get a moment of your time," I say.

"I recognize you," he says. "Breakfast of Champions. You're the pickle guy!"

Out of the corner of my eyes, I can see Jeff quirking an eyebrow at me questioningly and silently mouthing "Pickle guy?"

"Yes, that was me. I'm sorry, Mr. Harmon. I was just doing a little preliminary investigation," I say, feeling a little sheepish.

"Uh, huh," he says. "Have a good day, pickle guy."

He starts to close the door.

"I'll give you fifty dollars for five minutes of your time."

The door pauses, then slowly re-opens.

"Cash up front."

I agree and pull out my wallet. I look through it and realize I only have twenty-dollar bills.

"Here is sixty," I say, handing him sixty dollars. However, this has already been enlightening. Nobody that's going to change their mind that quickly over fifty dollars could afford to hire the Hizarin.

He takes the cash.

"Okay, what do you want?"

"You are familiar with Mr. Charles Whitman, yes?"

His already sullen face gets darker, his lips purse, and his nose crinkles into a petulant look.

"Yeah, I know him. Knew him. Why?"

"It seems that there may have been an attempt on Mr. Whitman's life. When asked, the only enemy he could identify was you," I say bluntly. This may not be the "right" tactic, but this isn't my area of expertise.

"Well good on them," he says. "Wait. You don't think I am trying to murder Charles, do you?"

"No," Jeff interrupts. "We're just following up with all parties he may have offended in the past. Due diligence."

"Due diligence, yeah," I say. "We're talking to lots of people, but you were mentioned as someone he'd upset."

"Of all the parties that he's offended," Phil says flatly.

"It's a long list," I agree. "Gonna take us the rest of the week to get through it."

Jeff raises an eyebrow at me. He knows this was a lie. Our list is currently a list with one name on it. But Phil seems placated by the idea that Whitman has pissed off a whole lot of people.

Phil looks at me appraisingly then he turns pointedly toward Jeff.

"Charles and I used to be friends. We had a falling out. We started a winery together. I made a business plan. I got investors. He made crappy wine and put his name on the label. He pissed away a ton of our investment capital gambling, and when it all came crashing down, he left me holding the bag."

"I'm not going to lie to you. I won't cry at his funeral," Phil says, "but I'm not trying to kill him. Shit I barely have time to go grocery shopping, and I work at a grocery store."

"Why is that?" Jeff asks.

Phil motions us inside and takes us into the front room. There, a man sits in a wheelchair in front of the television. He's got oxygen tubes in his nose and a complicated machines hooked up to his arms. He's completely hypnotized watching the television, though I suspect from his glassy-eyed look that he's getting intense medications through the IV.

"I take care of my uncle. I have to work double shifts to make enough money to pay the property taxes and keep food on the table and pay for all his medical bills. We have a caregiver while I'm working, but the rest of the time I'm here," he says.

I nod to Jeff.

"Thank you for your time, Mr. Harmon. I am sorry for the intrusion. If we have any other questions, do you mind if we come back?" Jeff asks.

"Sure. Whatever," Phil says.

He follows us back to the front step.

"Thank you for your time, Mr. Harmon," I say.

"Good day," he says to us and closes his door.

We get back into Jeff's fancy car.

"Well, what do you think?" Jeff asks once the doors have securely closed, ensuring our privacy.

"I think if I ever have to question people again, I'm calling you first," I say.

"Thanks, but no I mean what do you think about Mr. Harmon there?"

"I think he's telling the truth."

"The gambling?"

"Yeah, I think that's our next avenue. But I'm not sure where to start. We might be able to get something from Whitman, but honestly, I doubt it. He's hiding something and I feel like he might rather die than talk about it."

"Alistair, retired gambler, current therapist." Jeff says. "He's who I would go to for questions about gambling or gambling addiction."

"Alistair," I say. It's a good idea but I didn't even think of it. "It seems like a long shot, but if anybody knows about it...."

I text Alistair to see if he's available for lunch. I've never contacted Alistair outside of poker night, because he's always busy between his work schedule, his family, and his hobbies. He just never seems available. So busy he never responds to texts in a timeframe that works for my crazy lifestyle. I wait five minutes with no response. I'm impatient, so I'll have to call.

While Jeff drives, I call Alistair. He answers after a couple of rings.

"Hey, Alistair, Jeff and I are out on the town, and we were wondering if you had lunch plans," I say. I could just ask him over the phone, but I feel like that would come off very mercenary.

"What's up? Is something wrong?" Alistair asks.

"Why would something be wrong? Why can't I just call and see if you want to grab lunch?"

"Because you've literally never done anything like this before? And you're with Jeff. And you sound nervous."

"Okay, I mean we do just want to hang out but...yeah, you're right, there is kind of something wrong. I have a work question for you. If that's cool," I say sheepishly. I was hoping to make this all seem more casual. I don't know Alistair that well. I've been to a couple of backyard parties at his house and played poker with him, but other than that, we don't have much in common.

Alistair is quiet on the other end for a minute.

"I can clear a few things off my calendar. How's 12:40 at Lukas?" Alistair says, sounding a little peeved.

"Okay, sounds good. Lunch is on me."

"I wouldn't have it any other way," Alistair says. "See you then."

Alistair hangs up without another word. What can I say, I am socially very smooth.

"Very smooth," Jeff says to confirm my own inner monologue.

We've got an hour to kill before we meet Alistair.

"What do we do for an hour while we wait for lunch?" I ask Jeff.

"You want to go talk to that Whitman guy to see if we can get anything from him?"

I sit for a moment. Thinking about the question.

"Shit," I finally say. "We should. But I don't like it. I've talked to him more than I care for."

Jeff drives us in his sleek space-aged car over to the JMBaptiste winery. We stroll through the front doors; the tasting room is deserted. I'm not surprised, because it's still before noon on a Tuesday. Whitman is there talking to the staff about something. Jeff and I wait quietly by the door. Eventually, Jeff strolls around looking at the décor and comes back to stand by me.

"I can't stand these guys' wine," Jeff says.

"Oh?" I ask. I'm not really a wine drinker, I don't really care about the quality of their wine, but letting Jeff say his piece gives me something to do while we wait.

"They just make the same basic stuff you get up and down Highway 29. Tourist wine. A big bodied Napa cab, an oakier-than-thou chardonnay, and a sauvignon blanc that tastes like a lawnmower bag in late May," he says. "No envelopes pushed and no risks taken."

"They get scored better than you?" I ask, smirking.

"No!" he retorts. "But they do much better sales. Jean-Marie is a schmoozer."

"Never actually met the man."

"Did you know that he's not even French? He was born

and raised in New Jersey," Jeff adds. "He puts on that whole French accent and looks down his nose at people as a persona. I mean, his parents were from France I guess, but still he rubs me the wrong way."

"I picked up on that. Well, he is paying well, so I am not going to complain," I say and then nod my head to indicate to Jeff that Whitman is crossing the tasting room toward us.

"Mr. Ward," Whitman says, nodding at me.

"Mr. Reba," he says, nodding at Jeff.

"You've met?" I say looking from Whitman to Jeff.

"Yeah," Jeff chimes in. "A few times. He was at that mixer we were talking about. Good to see you again, Charles."

"Mr. Whitman while I'm at work."

"Oh. Sure. Mr. Whitman it is," Jeff says.

"You didn't mention that he was at the mixer with you," I say to Jeff.

"When we first talked about it, it didn't seem relevant. aAnd honestly I forgot about it until I saw Mr. Whitman here," Jeff says. I grunt in Jeff's general direction.

"What can I help you with?" Whitman says.

"It has come to my attention," I say warily, "That you may have outstanding gambling debts."

"Hmph," Whitman says, clearly annoyed. "Where did you hear that?"

"I keep my sources confidential," I say. It's kind of a lie; this is more of a discretionary policy. But I don't feel like telling him anything more than I absolutely must.

"I see," Whitman says, his teeth all but clenched. "It is true, I have made an imprudent bet here or there, but I have reconciled all of my debts."

"Sure, sure. Where do you mostly play?" I ask.

"I don't really anymore, just an irregular weekend game with a select handful of work associates," he says. He won't look me in the eye, he fidgets with his hands, and he has a slight crack in his voice.

He's being dodgy.

"That's it, just a little casual game with work friends?"

"That's right."

"Is it possible to get the names of these friends? Maybe talk to them?"

"You are not a police officer; you are here at my employer's bequest to play Dungeons and Dragons or whatever it is you do professionally. Not to dig into my personal life."

"You're happy to cooperate with me when I'm providing my 'mumbo jumbo' to protect you from a fake magical curse, but if I want more info, you're going to stonewall me?"

"No, I simply don't see how interrogating my friends is going to help. So no, sir. No thank you. If you want your ruby-clad fetish back, please take it," he says, starting to take the necklace off.

"No, you wear that for now. I'll come to get it when I feel it's safe. I think you are a jerk, Mr. Whitman, but I don't want a jerk to die on my watch."

He grunts at me; it is unclear what he means by the sound.

"Is there anything else?" he asks.

"No, actually I think we need to get to lunch."

Whitman doesn't even bother with pleasantries and turns on his heels and walks away. I look at Jeff, who looks amused. In silence, we walk out the door to Jeff's car.

"What a pleasant fellow," Jeff says.

"Is he always like that?" I ask.

"He doesn't usually seem that annoyed. I think that's your influence. But yes, he has always come off as kind of a ponce, that's for sure," Jeff says. "Talks about himself a lot."

"Hey, Jeff?"

"Yeah?"

"So, this winery, all of their wine turned to vinegar, like overnight. Does that happen in your experience?"

"It could," he says. "But it isn't likely. First, wine doesn't turn to vinegar. Vinegar is a very intentionally created product, using a vinegar mother to cultivate a colony of bacteria. Wine forms acetic acid."

"Isn't that just vinegar?"

"In a technical sense, yes, but when wine turns unintentionally…the product. Well, you wouldn't want to put it on your salad is all I am saying."

"Okay, it's a semantic point, but a significant semantic point."

"Yes. Anyway, when wine does form acetic acid, it is a sign of a secondary fermentation. Something that isn't yeast gets into the wine and with enough oxygen and time, it ferments the alcohol in the wine into acetic acid. Eventually, if left unchecked, acetone also forms in the wine. It gets gross. It usually happens because the cork is flawed, and oxygen and bacteria get in there. It can also happen from contamination getting in during bottling or people not using clean tools on their—"

"Have you ever heard of a full cellar of wine bottles going bad like that at once?"

"If people use contaminated equipment, it can happen. But in the modern world, with modern technology…it doesn't really happen in industrial winemaking."

"Overnight?" I ask.

"No, I've never heard of that happening overnight. It takes weeks or usually more for wine to go bad. If the bottles are being opened for tastings or something, I'd imagine they'd notice. It's a gradual change."

"Yeah, this was super quick. I tried it at home and put the wine in an inclusive circle. It turned gross overnight."

"That's interesting. What do you mean by an inclusive circle?"

I explain the intricacies of wards, types of wards and the flow of magic in and out of the Ley.

"But when I just gathered energy around the wine, it spoiled very fast. No spell, no intention or direction for the magical energy, effect with no cause. This defies my understanding of how magic is done," I conclude.

"I'd like to study this phenomenon, as it might help me

make better wine," he says. He has a sort of faraway look in his eye, like he's got an idea. I'm sure he's not the first to try to use magic in the wine-making process.

"After this, let's head to my place. I can show you what I did. You have like a whole enology lab at your disposal, right?" I ask.

He nods. "Yes I do."

"Cool," I say. "Cool."

Chapter Eleven

Luka's delicatessen is popular with a certain demographic in town. I dislike Luka's personally, but I won't mention that to Alistair. The demographic is mostly white and all middle to upper-middle class. The type that can afford a twenty-dollar sandwich. Chips are extra. It has a spartan decor that says, "We could have paid for decorations and atmosphere, but instead we decided to devote that time and energy into marking up the price of an otherwise unremarkable sandwich."

We fit right in.

Alistair is already in line and he greets us with a wave. We all walk and stand in the Soviet-style line. I feel a chill and waves of despair washing over me as we wait to order our mediocre sandwiches. It's about thirty minutes before we have our numbers and sit down.

As I said, it's popular, and I don't understand why.

"To what do I owe the honor of dining with the infamous Miles Ward?" Alistair asks. "And hi, Jeff."

"Infamous or famous?" I ask.

"I've heard it both ways," Jeff says.

"I haven't," Alistair says, quirking an eyebrow goofily. This is supposed to be a joke. No one is laughing though.

"I am working on a project that has become a little more like an investigation," I say, deciding I might as well just get this part over with.

"Because he can't say no," Jeff chimes in. I cast him a dark look and he shrugs.

"No! See, I can too say no," I rebuke Jeff. "Anyway. I'm trying to figure out who wants this guy, Charles Whitman, dead."

"Aside from literally anyone who has ever talked to him," Jeff adds.

"Not helping, Jeff. Anyway, it seems like he might have a gambling problem. We figured if there was anyone we knew, that could tell us where someone would get a gambling problem in this town, Alistair, that'd be you."

"Well, you could get yourself in a lot of trouble anywhere, thanks to the internet," he says.

"Hire a high-priced assassin to burn your private bits off kind of trouble?" I ask.

"Well…that'd be harder. But pretty much any above-board place isn't going to let you get into that sort of trouble these days. Bad for business."

"What about below board places?" I ask.

"With the Rancheria casinos, and the local card rooms cropping up, there isn't much of a market for such things anymore, I mean except on the internet," Alistair says.

"Yeah, this feels more personal than that. So, nothing local?" I ask.

"Nothing?" Jeff says incredulously.

"Well, there is one place in town. The Red Door," he says.

"The Red Door?" I say, flashing back to my dream last night. "Yeah, that might be something. Tell me about that."

"You know The Lantern? That dive bar on the southwest side of town?" Alistair asks.

"Yeah," I say. "I went in there once. It was smokey. I had a beer and left."

"Well in the back there is a literal red door. There's a sort of invite-only card game that goes on in a private room upstairs, behind the door," he says. "I got invited once and went. It was very sketchy. The buy-in was too high, so I bowed out. Never went back. Like I said, sketchy."

"The Red Door huh? How does someone get invited?" I ask.

"Well, I got handed this little…like, token? A little metal coin sort of thing, that got me in through the red door. Like there was a bouncer I had to give it to to get in," Alistair says.

"How'd you get the token?" I ask.

"I was at the Rio Vista card room a couple of years back; I was having a really good run, and someone said I should check out the game at The Red Door. Gave me the token. I don't know who it was. I don't even really remember the person; it was kind of random. Nothing I went looking for," he says.

"Thank you, Alistair. That is very helpful."

"Happy to help."

We chat a bit more, about poker, hobbies, and work. My takeaway is I don't talk to Alistair enough. The whole kid thing is intimidating to me. It makes it hard to associate with his perspective. I'm just not used to, or ready for, that kind of responsibility. I feel responsible enough for that jackass Whitman, who I can't stand. I can't imagine the crushing weight of responsibility of my own offspring.

But that said, Alistair seems more grounded in some ineffable way than I am. He's more certain and, for the lack of a better term, on track than me. It's nice just chatting for a bit. I vow to myself to do this again.

Jeff and I leave Luka's, and he drives me across town to my apartment. He follows me up the flight of stairs to my door and I open it.

"I've never been to your place before," Jeff says as we walk in. "How long have we known each other, and I've never been here?"

"Like what, five years?" I say. "It's small and not set up for entertaining."

"Yeah, I see that," he says as I give him the tour of the apartment, it only takes about thirty seconds. He glances into my bedroom and then half-laughing says, "What is up with the mannequin? And why does it look like you? And why is it dressed exactly like you? That's weird and frankly…it's kinda creepy."

"You're creepy," Hank says.

"Oh. That's Hank" I say, ignoring him.

"Oh, ignore me, huh? What? Worried your friend is going to think you're crazy?"

I give Jeff the short version of Hank's function as a simulacrum.

"That's insane!" Jeff says, with a tone of admiration and humor.

"Not as insane as your buddy Miles here, he talks to a mannequin!"

"Probably," I say, leading Jeff over to my workbench with the bottle of wine still on it.

"A real friend would understand!" I can hear Hank from the bedroom.

"Hey, Jeff, give me a second," I say. I leave Jeff looking at the bottle of wine while I duck back into my bedroom and close the door.

"Will you shut up!" I hiss at Hank.

"Probably not."

I throw a blanket over Hank and walk back out into my front room, closing the bedroom door behind me. Hank's muffled protestations follow me from the other room.

"What was that about?" Jeff asks, his face scrunched up in a look of confusion or maybe concern. Probably both.

"Nothing. Just thought I heard the neighbors playing their TV loudly again."

"I don't hear anything."

"Like I said, it was nothing."

Jeff shrugs then picks the wine up and smells it.

"Ugh. Yeah, that is…that is bad," he says.

I smell it, and I almost gag. It smells even worse than it did before; it's basically nail-polish remover at this point.

"Acetone and…something else. The acetobacter in there are…out. Of. Control!!" Jeff seems more fired up and excited than his usual stoic self.

"Acetoba-what?" I say feeling little foolish like I should know this, but I don't.

"Acetobacter. The other stuff that grows in wine. It's bacteria that digest alcohol and other compounds and make acetic acid, and acetone," he says.

"Oh. Right. Cool."

I take another whiff of the wine.

"Whew! Yeah, that's nasty."

"This is amazing. So cool," he says. "Can you show me how you did it? I can set up a few more experiments, and maybe figure out what's going on."

I spend about ten minutes showing Jeff the process. He produces a small notebook and pen from a pocket somewhere and takes diligent notes in a sort of personal shorthand. He asks questions. Lots of questions.

I remember at this moment that while he might be a winemaker by trade, he's a fermentation scientist by training, and he takes the science part very seriously.

Once we're finished, Jeff glances at his wristwatch.

"As much fun as this is, I need to do a couple of things at work before the end of the day," Jeff says.

"That's fine, I need to figure out how I can get into this Red Door, find out what that is all about."

"Mike," Jeff says succinctly.

"Mike?"

"Yeah, he knows like everyone in town. If anyone knows someone that knows someone who can get you somewhere in this town, it's Mike," Jeff says.

Jeff, Alistair, and I are all transplants; we aren't from Napa originally. But Mike iss a local, born and raised.

He's been working in the hospitality industry in town since high school. There is not a back room, back office, back door, or back of the house in this town that he doesn't know. He has worked in every restaurant, tasting room, and coffee shop Napa has to offer.

The couple of times I've gone out with Mike, it can be the most infuriating thing, because no matter where you go, he gets stopped by an old coworker or acquaintance who wants to catch up and swap stories. Because not only is Mike known around this town, he's funny, he's got charisma, and he's the kind of person that people remember. Jeff's right: if anybody knows someone who knows someone who can get me through The Red Door, it's Mike.

And Hank said my Thursday night poker game was a waste of time.

Jeff gives me a ride back to my jeep and I drive over to the tasting room of the month that Mike is working. It's indistinguishable from all the other wineries on the trail, in my opinion. Unsure if it wants to look modern or or French or Mediterranean, it manages to look like none of them.

However, it is certainly, definitely, and definitively surrounded by olive trees.

Chapter Twelve

I walk through the large glass double doors and sidle up to the bar. A woman comes down and asks if she can help me.

"I'm looking for Mike," I say.

She nods her head down toward him, at the other end of the counter.

"Are you here to taste some wine?" she asks perkily.

"Sure," I say. "Nothing personal, but can he pour it?"

She looks at me brow furrowed, right side of her face twisted upward into a poorly veiled sneer like I'm the biggest asshole on the planet.

"Sure honey," she says in a fake syrupy-sweet voice and goes to swap places with Mike.

"Good day to you, my good sir. How may I be of service to you on this fine day, my illustrious client who is making me enemies at my place of employment?" Mike asks me with a veneer of faux formality.

"Sorry about that. Hi, Mike."

"Hi, Miles," he replies. "What's up, man?"

"I am here to taste wine and maybe ask you a few questions if you don't mind," I say.

"Sure, let's start with the wine," Mike says.

"What's your most egregious flight?"

"Egregious? Do you mean the most expensive? The best? Or like what takes me the longest to pour?"

"Yeah," I say, "egregious."

"The executive tasting, but it's a hundred and twenty. And you only get about six ounces of actual wine and two bites of cheese. But you get all the crackers you can eat," he says matter-of-factly.

"I can expense it!" I say enthusiastically. This is not technically true. I don't actually have a job or a contract yet. But I am confident that I'll get the contract and I can sort the details out later.

"Executive!" he says, putting a large wineglass in front of me. "We will start with our cabernet sauvignon."

"Is it fruit forward, big and bold?"

"Have you been talking to Jeff again?"

"Hints of strawberry?"

"Yup," Mike says. "That's Jeff."

"No, Jeff would say hints of strawberry in a scathing tone and then go on about esters and pyrazines and..." I start, but I can't think of any more of Jeff's science words.

"And terpenes," Mike fills in. "You are right, that's more like Jeff."

"You know, you could skip the upsell. I just want my wine to taste like rotten grapes," I say, chuckling at my sense of humor.

"THEN YOU HAVE COME to the right place. Rotten grapes are all that we have," he says, lining up six wine glasses and pouring out the remaining tastings of wine without comment.

I sip them all, pretending to be a connoisseur. I swirl them around, sniff them, and comment on the bouquet, making up terms as I go.

"Am I picking up a little braised arugula in this? With perhaps a whiff of pork fried rice?" I say. Mike just shakes his head at my stupidity.

I know what I like, but I can only describe what I don't like. I don't like a lot of astringency; I hate the feeling on my tongue. I like a little bit of tannins, but not so much as to make it buttery, I know I don't like that. I like it fruity, and acidic, but not too acidic.

"Yes!" I can hear Hank's voice in my mind. *"You like Welches!"*

I'm not here for the tasting though, the wine drinking is just a pretext to talk to Mike mid-afternoon. I only sip a little from each of the glasses. It's not much, but I'm not much for day drinking. Playtime is over.

"Mike, I was wondering if you know anybody that works at The Lantern, or if you know about The Red Door." I cut straight to the chase. Mike prefers direct.

"Yes, and yes," he says. "Sidney, a girl that used to work here. She got a job 'tending at The Lantern. She hates it, but it pays well. I haven't talked shop with her too much."

"And the Red Door?" I ask.

"High stakes underground gambling?" he answers in a way that is more question than a statement. "I've heard of it, never been there. Has a pretty bad reputation. Lorelei Redbrook owns The Lantern, so you know…"

"Redbrook? Why does that sound familiar?"

"Are you fucking kidding me, Miles?" Mike sounds incredulous.

"Um….no?"

"Miles," he says emphatically. "There are literally signs on half the lawns in town. She's running for mayor."

"Oh. I don't pay attention to local politics I guess," I say, feeling stupid.

"Well, you should, because she's bad news. Wants to round homeless up into camps. Decrease property taxes and increase sales taxes. She pretty much wants all the poor people, the brown people, and the gay people out and to keep this town a bastion for rich, white, straight people," Mike rants.

"And she runs an underground high-stakes gambling hall? That doesn't sound right," I say.

"No, exactly. She gets up to all sorts of unseemly back-room shenanigans while espousing all this moral majority crap. And high-stakes gambling isn't the worst if rumors are to be believed."

"What is the worst of the rumors?"

"The worst I've heard?" he says. "Like weird stuff? Murder, human trafficking, I mean eating babies, crazy stuff. As I said, there are some fugly rumors about her and that bar of hers."

"Really?" I don't doubt the rumors. Knowing the Hizarin are involved, very little seems off the table. But the fact that they might be open enough about it that Mike has heard these things; that is a bit surprising.

We sit in silence for a while.

"How can I get in?" I ask.

He shrugs.

"No clue, no desire to go there. Everything about it creeps me out. You should avoid it too. It's bad news, Miles. Bad news," he says.

"What about your friend…Sidney was it?" I ask.

"She just tends there, I don't think she could get you in the Red Door. She might know how you could, but…" he trails off and sighs. "I don't want to ask her, but I will next time I see her. That might be a bit though. We are 'see you when I see you' friends."

"You don't have her number?"

He shakes his head no.

"Okay, don't sweat it. And thank you, this has been helpful. I learned a few things I didn't know before, but probably should have," I say.

"Anything else?" he asks.

"I mean," I say. "I can't think of anything, is there anything weird I should be asking, but I'm not?"

"No," Mike starts to say, then he interrupts himself. "Well…maybe."

I raise an inquisitive eyebrow but remain quiet.

"Well, it's something that sounds made up to me, but it sounds like something you'd find interesting…I was at a thing and there were people and this other thing…the details aren't important," he says, he seems a little embarrassed. My mind comes up with a bunch of reasons he might be vague about this 'thing'.

A swinger party? Is he a Brony? A Furry? Was he watching a boy band?!?

"Anyway people were talking, swapping stories of all the weird stuff they'd seen and heard, sort of like making it a party game. Who had seen the most Rebobs? Where the scariest ghosts were, urban myth stuff. Anyway, someone said that Lorelei Redbrook eats kids. And I mean, in every debate or interview she does, she goes on about all the kids she has fostered," he says.

After a small shudder, he continues, "She says it in such a creepy way that everyone has made that joke about her. But this guy, he said she was a La Me Ah. Something like that. Sounded French or something. I remember at the time, I didn't know what it was, but I thought 'I wish Miles were here, he would know what the hell this guy is talking about.' Anyway, I thought it was weird."

"Lamia? Like the Greek myth?"

"I guess so?" Mike says, sounding uncertain.

"In myth, Lamia was the queen of Libya. Zeus falls in love with her. Hera, Zeus' wife, is so jealous that she steals Lamia's children to punish her. Wracked with grief, Lamia tears out her own eyes. Zeus then out of pity or…something, transforms her into a monster so that she can exact her revenge by eating children," I explain.

"Why'd he do that? That is an awful story."

"I don't know, most Greek myths are pretty awful. The

logic of the gods is, I think, intentionally erratic and inexplicable. Like life."

"Well, I don't know if that has any significance, but I hope it helps."

"It will. I'm sure," I say and stand up, leaving most of the wine untouched. I won't say it to Mike because I don't want to hurt his feelings, and I won't say it to Jeff because I don't want to stoke his ego, but Jeff's wine is way better.

"Thanks, Mike. I need to get moving," I say, handing him a credit card to pay for the tasting. I leave him a good tip. As I said, I'm going to expense it. Hopefully.

I bid Mike goodbye and tell him I'll see him at poker night on Thursday. He waves goodbye and is already talking with another customer before I make it out the door.

I sit in the parking lot, deciding what to do next. I'm running out of leads and I'm not sure what direction to go next. After a few minutes of consideration, I decide that I will stop by the bookshop.

I start driving back south to the city. I pass a sign that reads 'Lorelei Redbrook for Mayor! Get 'er done Napa!' I pass another. And another. Mike's right, they are everywhere. I really am oblivious.

I arrive back at Grape Reads wondering how many other blatantly obvious things I am missing. Emily is working again; she's standing behind the counter reading a book when I arrive.

"Hi, Emily," I say.

"Oh, hey Miles," she gives me a broad, but brief smile.

"How are things in the book biz?" I ask.

"It's a little quiet today, but fine. How's the warding of the winery?" she asks.

"The warding of the winery?" I say confused.

"Yeah, the JMBaptiste winery that you were doing research for the other day?" she asks, giving me a look like I'm crazy.

"Oh, shit," I say. "I got so caught up in all this murder stuff, I forgot about finishing the proposal."

"Murder stuff?" she asks, sounding more intrigued than horrified, which strikes me as weird for a second, but my mouth starts moving before I can dwell on that.

"Yeah. Rather, intended, but thus far averted murder. It turns out there is this magical assassin, and a crotch-burning curse, and my friend Jeff is…" I start to say, but I decide that Jeff's anointment is his business to share.

"It's been a really weird couple of days," I conclude.

Once more, I talk about my crazy work to Emily, and she doesn't look at me like I am crazy. I don't think she buys all of it. Based on her facial expression, she might be a little skeptical now. She listens to it all and considers it, which is more than I get from most people.

"Is that all?" she says, chuckling to herself.

"Oh, and a Lamia? The Lamia? Maybe?"

"Like the Greek myth?"

"Yes!" I say. "Thank you! Well. I mean maybe. No, I mean definitely thank you, but maybe like the Greek myth. I don't know, that's what I was hoping I could get more info on here."

"Of course," she says. "How can I help you?"

"Right. Oh, quick question before we talk about that. What do you know about Lorelei Redbrook?"

"Redbrook? Ugh, she's awful. She says creepy stuff about her foster kids. She's said horrible anti-LGBTQ things, like on the record, in debate, *and* in interviews. Oh, and she's a Holocaust denier? I mean, what the fuck?" Emily says.

"Yeah, that's what I've heard. I really should follow local politics more."

"Oh! Oh! Is *she* the Lamia? Because that would totally track," Emily says. I can tell from the glee in her voice that she is just trying to be funny.

I don't laugh.

"I don't know. Maybe," I say awkwardly.

Emily looks confused. I think she expected me to laugh. There is an awkward silence.

"Anyway, I am looking to know more about the story of the Lamia or myths or I don't know something about monsters that eat children or run underground casinos or magical assassins. Or. Um. Something."

I feel like this conversation is slipping away from me. I feel bad at talking most of the time. I feel bad at talking when I am flustered, and today I'm feeling very flustered. Maybe it's because I thought Emily asked me out last time I saw her.

Maybe it's because I bought her fancy chocolates as a gift. Maybe it's because I gave those chocolates to an assassin and possibly vampire that I seem to currently be in a magical tête-à-tête with that I have no hope of winning, and could almost certainly end in my horrible, painful death. Maybe it's because I also find the magical assassin very attractive in that same way my brain wonders what it would be like to jump every time I'm on a balcony. Maybe it's because I'm worried that Emily is going to somehow know all those other maybes and judge me for them.

In reality, none of those are maybes.

"Great," she says, looking confused by my verbal fumbling. "We have plenty of books on Greek mythology. Here, let's see if we can find anything that might have useful information."

Emily leads me over to their mythology shelf. I'm always surprised by the array of books they sell here on an insane variety of topics. I don't know how they cram that many books into such a small shop, but somehow, they manage.

Ultimately, I buy three books on Greek mythology and classics. One is a graduate thesis, analyzing Greek myth in terms of what is known of actual history and making suppositions about the anthropological implications. Another is a collection of short stories. Emily says that it gets a surprising number of things right about magic and the supernatural. One of the short stories is about Lamia, making it sound more like a species than an individual. The last is a more traditional mythology book. I pay for them and slide them into my messenger bag.

"Is there any way I could look at more of Sergei's private collection today? You reminded me, I really should get my proposal in," I say.

"Wait, you are just getting your proposal in? Do you get paid for that?"

"Um…technically no, but Mr. Baptiste said 'spare no expense' so I'm going with it."

"But you are busy trying to stop a murder on a job, you haven't technically gotten yet." She has one eyebrow raised and her lips pursed into a judgy face.

"Now you see why I need to get this done. So, the private collection?"

"Yeah. That should be fine," she says. "I have to finish up here before closing, so just head on back. I trust you," she says, winking at me.

"But does Sergei?" I ask.

"Of course. My word holds a lot of weight."

"Thanks." I smile back awkwardly and fumble my way to the back of the store.

As always, when I get started on the bookwork part of this job, I lose track of time quickly. I'm jotting down sequences of runes and glyphs, comparing them to Circe's work, and formulating how to best disengage the energy flow, without leaving loopholes or openings. I'm starting to get into a groove when Emily comes in. She is carrying takeout from the Chinese place a few blocks away.

"I brought dinner, thought you might be hungry. I closed the shop an hour ago but had plenty to finish up, so thought I'd let you work," she says, setting takeout down on the table near me.

"You are amazing," I say. "I lost track of time, but I am starving. Thank you!"

"No problem," she says, smiling. "Anything I can do to help?"

"Actually, I'm looking for stuff on Russian and Eastern European rites and rituals to make sure I make the place Baba Yaga proof."

She nods and pulls down a few books. We read in silence, snacking on Chinese food as we go. I am hungry and the food is edible. For some reason, edible is the best Chinese food gets in this town.

I consider bringing up lunch from the other day, but I remember the chocolates I meant as a gift. I feel a little embarrassed about that. Then I remember I gave them to another woman. I feel more embarrassed about that. Why did I do that? Circe was messing with my head, but I don't think magically. I sit here thinking myself in circles and not making much progress on my studies.

Eventually, I convince myself to just keep my mouth shut and work.

Emily is amazing. She rifles through books, cross references, and gives me a stack of resources in a fraction of the time it would have taken me. She clearly has a better understanding of a lot of this stuff than I do, which makes me wonder if she practices magic herself.

But she doesn't have the trademarks of a sorcerer. No occult tattoos that I can see. No ritual scars, and she doesn't have that creepy aura around her. There is a certain aura that attracts itself to people who work in magic a lot; it's off-putting. Emily doesn't have that, she just seems very knowledgeable, without any desire to pursue that knowledge for power.

Finally, exhausted, I push the books back and review the plan I've drawn up. My usual process on a project like this is I do an assessment. Then I write a project plan. The executive summary wraps up what I found, and what I am suggesting in very simple terms. Then there is a technical overview of exactly what will be implemented. Finally, there is an estimate of materials and labor.

This one is just a rough draft. I'll need to clean up the

wording, add diagrams, and write the executive summary. But the rough outline is there. It's a lot of work and it will cost JMBaptiste a lot of money to implement, but as the consultant, that's not my problem.

"I've got to clean up my plan and put a bow on it, but this is good," I say. "Thank you for all your help, Emily. I really, seriously, could not have done this without you. I should put you on the payroll."

"No, it was no problem! I had fun. It's interesting to see how you put all this stuff together," she says, smiling.

"Hardly," I say.

"Besides, if I didn't do this, I'd just sit around reading to my cats," Emily says.

"You have cats?" I ask. She doesn't seem like a cat person.

"No! I'm joking," she says. "Actually I have book club tonight. I'm a little late, but it's all good."

I nod. We sit there in silence for a moment.

"We are reading *The Meta-Wave* by Genevieve Gale," Emily blurts out, probably trying to fill the awkward silence with something. "My book club book this month. Have you read it?"

I surpringly have read *The Coming Meta-Wave: Rising Tide or Tsunami?* It's a fairly grim prediction of a coming merger of magic and technology and the potentially dire and calamitous results this could have for humanity.

"Yeah, actually I was on a panel with Genevieve Gale at a convention last year."

"Really? That's amazing. Was she cool? Tell me she was cool. If she wasn't cool, just say she was. Genevieve Gale is kind of my hero."

"Yeah, she was great. She was smart and funny. We solved a fake murder together."

"Was she as pretty as she is on the book jacket? I always wonder that like how glamoured is that glamour shot?"

"I guess," I say. She was pretty, or at least I don't remember her being unattractive. But I don't want to sound too enthusiastic about it. It's an awkward question to answer to someone you are interested in dating.

A voice in my head keeps telling me that if I am going to ask her out to dinner or something, this is a perfect opportunity. Here is your moment, Miles, quick before you make it weird again.

Okay, I tell myself, *I am going to do it, here goes.*

"Well thanks," I say. "Anyway, we should. Uh. Do this again sometime. And I should get home and type this up on the computer."

Yup, I'm a chicken shit, what can I say?

All of that internal fear, uncertainty, and doubt keeps telling me she's going to laugh in my face, and then I'm never going to be able to look her in the eye again.

"Yeah," she says, seeming amused. "Let's do this again."

"Okay, well, have a good night," I say sheepishly, gathering my things.

"Good night, Miles," she says, putting a few books away.

"And Emily, thanks again, really. I owe you one," I say.

"You can buy me dinner sometime," she says smiling.

"Yeah. I'd, um, I'd like that," I say, feeling probably ten times as nervous as I sound.

"How about Thursday? You can take me to Rochard and tell me about solving a fake murder with Genevieve Gale. Here is my number," she says, grinning. She's just named the second most expensive restaurant in town. I totally can't afford it. She scribbles a number on a little slip of paper and hands it to me.

"Thursday…" I start to say, Thursday is poker night. But you know what? Impulsivity for the win. "Yeah, Thursday sounds great. Rochard it is."

"Really?" she says. "I was kidding, but okay, Rochard. Pick me up at eight?"

"Um," I feel my face all flush. "Okay…where do you live?"

"Text me. I'll send you my address."

"Great," I say. As awkward and fumbling as I feel, this is still going better than the last time I asked a woman out on a date. Of course, technically Emily asked me out, which is probably why this is going better. I quickly text her so she has my number. A moment passes, and Emily looks up from what she's doing to see me still standing there like an idiot.

"I need to wrap up a few things here. But I'll see you Thursday!" she says happily.

"Great! Have fun at your book club," I say, waving and grinning like an idiot as I walk out to the street. What can I say, I'm suave.

She sends me her address before I've even gotten my car started.

Chapter Thirteen

The next morning, I get up and go for a run.

It's been a few days, but I need to maintain my physical fitness. I go for a six-mile run. My friends call me a little paranoid. I prefer to call it careful. I keep a simulacrum to protect myself from dark magic, even though I've never been the target of it. I keep a tent and sleeping bag in the back of my Jeep, just in case I get stranded somewhere. I keep a vial of pigs' blood in my fridge, just in case I need to do a little emergency hedge magic.

And I practice running like I'm being pursued by a werewolf, just in case I find myself in that exact situation.

I don't know if werewolves are even real, but it seems to me when you work in a job where you cross sorcerers, ask favors from dragons, find vampire assassins in your car and maybe go toe to toe with a Lamia, it's probably a good idea to practice running away from things that are faster than you.

I don't stick to trails; I go off the path. I jump logs and benches, and I climb fences. It's not parkour exactly. I don't have the kind of gymnastic talent to make that work. I mostly try to run as fast as I can and practice putting obstacles between me and someone that might pursue me. In addition to being good training for my paranoid fantasies, it's a very good workout. After an hour of that, I get home exhausted.

I shower, get dressed, dress Hank, and check my wards, whistling happily the whole time. Today is going to be a good day!

At about ten o'clock I e-mail my warding proposal to Abigail the Assistant. It's well put together, with a stellar executive summary. Comprehensive. I'm feeling proud.

I prance into my bedroom and confront Hank. The mannequin stares blankly back at me.

"Nailed it!" I say.

"Yeah, that's better than your usual kindergarten scrawl. You didn't even use crayons this time."

"Why are you such a dick?"

"You made me this way, bro."

I throw my hands in the air exasperated.

Technically my job is done for now. Technically until I hear back from Jean-Marie or Abigail, I don't have to do anything more on this job. Technically I don't even like Charles Whitman. But technically I also have a conscience, and even though I don't like him, I don't want to see him murdered.

Provide a plan, save a life. That's the Miles Ward guarantee.

I brew myself a travel mug of coffee and head down to JMBaptiste winery to check in on Whitman. He has been lying to me; he knows exactly what's going on. I suspect that admitting to whatever it is, would be admitting something to himself that he can't handle.

When I was in college, I needed to work a campus job to help pay for school, soI started working for the computer help desk. I'd talk staff and students through their day-to-day computer woes. One afternoon, I got a call from the school's Bursar. His personal printer wasn't working. After spending over an hour troubleshooting the issue, I had to go check out the printer itself. I hauled myself across campus to the

Bursar's office. As I approached the printer, the first thing I noticed was the strong smell of burnt coffee. I asked the Bursar if anyone had spilled coffee into the printer. He emphatically denied such an event had occurred.

When I opened the printer, there was a viscous black goo of boiled-down java coating the motherboard. I asked if he had any idea how coffee had gotten into the printer. He said no, that he had been here all morning and no coffee had been near the printer. He had an enormous mug on his desk with a representation of the caffeine molecule printed across the side. I roughly estimated that the amount of coffee in the printer would be about the same amount as this enormous mug held.

On his desk, next to the printer, I noticed a few cool but still fresh drips of coffee and noticed a relatively fresh coffee stain on his pants. I pressed the issue. Finally, once I had annoyed him to the point of near rage, he admitted that he had accidentally dumped his entire cup of coffee into the printer that morning—about six hours prior. There were no repercussions for the man. He controlled all of the college's money.

The only consequence was that the printer might, but probably not, have been saved if it had been addressed immediately. But it was instead ruined, and I wasted an entire afternoon. At no point was there ever a benefit to him to lie about this, and yet he did.

That experience has stuck with me to this day; the lies that we tell others are just the echoes of those that we tell ourselves. The Bursar thought himself an intelligent and responsible man, not the sort to accidentally and clumsily dump coffee on a printer. He lied to himself that he didn't spill the coffee. To me he was telling the truth, the truth he had created by lying to himself.

What lie is Whitman telling himself? What is it he is unable to confront?

I blow past the tasting room and go straight toward Whitman's office. I stroll through the short hallway and knock on the door of his office. He urges me inside, but the man who faces me is not the man I saw the day before.

He's haggard and sweaty, looking older than before. I'm about to ask if he's feeling okay, but he cuts me off.

"The ruby. It broke," he says, reaching down to his neck and holding up the chain. "It just exploded."

I look at the broken trinket. It takes my brain a moment to fully process what he's showing me. I did not expect this to happen when I gave it to him, even if I warned him of it.

"Shit," I finally say. "That's not good. Why didn't you call me?"

"I...I just forgot that's what I should do in the moment. I was so freaked out. Honestly, it scared the shit out of me when it happened, Mr. Ward. It got hot, and started buzzing, and then the ruby…it shattered into…well, into dust, with the most horrible sound." He's shaking and his words are running together. "I thought you were a charlatan, but what happened? That wasn't just a trick."

"No," I say, stepping close and squinting at the pendant. "I'm afraid it wasn't. That protective charm…whatever it stopped was very bad. Very powerful."

"I did what you said, I came straight here and hid in the circle that you drew," he says.

"I'm surprised you didn't erase it the second I left the room." I really am surprised.

"I wanted Mr. Baptiste to see the ridiculous efforts you were taking, hoping he'd fire you," he admits with a touch of unprecedented humility. "But no more of that. Help me, Mr. Ward."

"It's Miles," I say distantly. My mind is wandering.

"Right. Miles," he says quickly.

Crystals can trap and hold magic. A lot of defensive magic involves crystals as a result because with the right spell, you can trap the incoming magic and store it, like a battery. And like a battery, once the energy is stored, it no longer has a specific function. You can apply it somewhere else.

The amulet I gave him channeled magic energy into the ruby. The ruby was large enough, old enough, and high enough quality to store…well, a lot of energy. There are no measures of magical energy so far as I know. A little, some, a lot, too much: these are the only measures I've ever used. The size and purity of the crystal influence the volume of magic that can be contained, but at the end of the day, a crystal is a crystal. This is why circles of salt and the like are often used in wards.

Each grain of salt is a little crystal, and each can store a bit of magical energy. When a vessel has more energy than it can hold, that energy is released back into the universe…wildly. It has no shape or form, it just flows. Like electricity, the energy flows to ground; but in this case, ground isn't literal. It is more like returning to the ambient flow of magical energy in the Ley. It's in the ground, the air, and the water, pooling, ebbing, and flowing through everything.

Normally energy would trickle into the crystal and then as the crystal filled up, trickle back out, shapeless into the universe. In order to have shattered the crystal, it meant so much energy flowed in so fast that it didn't have the capacity to release any into the universe. Instead, the energy built up and, for lack of a better word, pressurized. Then when the crystal had exceeded its stress point, the energy burst out, destroying the crystal.

The amount of energy required to turn the gem to dust would be like it absorbing a bomb's explosion within his office. This quantity of magical energy could level a building if it was directed to do so.

This was something far beyond anything I've ever seen. Not the subtle, overly intricate spontaneous combustion spell that I was dealing with just yesterday. This was something very different.

"The good news is that whoever did this almost certainly believes that you are dead."

"How is that good news?" he asks.

"Because I think I know who did this and if we can keep them thinking you are dead for a while, maybe we can find a way to get them to stop trying."

"What's the bad news?"

"Very perceptive to know this good news came with bad news."

"Someone is trying to kill me; it can't all be good news."

"The bad news is that you are dealing with a top-notch pro, who is escalating their attempts. If she finds out this one didn't work, she already knows it's me that stopped it," I say.

He sighs. "I see."

"I need you to be honest with me."

"Fine, I'll be honest, I think you are an incompetent hack who is making things up as you go."

I ignore his quip and plow forward, hopefully pressure can keep this conversation on track.

"Tell me about The Red Door. I am almost certain that's got something to do with you being targeted."

"The Red Door," he says, pinching the bridge of his nose like he's suddenly fighting off a headache.

"I gamble. It's a problem, I can admit that now. I have an online support group," he says, clearly flustered. "I can admit that I have a problem *now*, but the Red Door was rock bottom. It's this place in the back of The Lantern, a dive bar on the other side of town, but you know that. I got invited to a very high-stakes game there. It was a bad idea. I knew it was at the time, but there's this voice in my head. You know, it tells me I can do it. I only need one big break, one score. Well, that voice was winning. I ended up there and I cashed out my retirement for buy-in at The Red Door."

He pauses and looks at me expectantly.

"Go on," I say, not sure what he's looking for, absolution probably, but that's not my job. Nor is it something I am interested in pursuing in my time off.

"Anyway, the first night was great, I made money. I mean a lot of money. Enough money."

"But…" I say.

"But…I went back, again and again, and I bet even more." He shakes his head, looking ashamed. "And before long, I lost it, all of it, everything I had won, my retirement, everything in my bank account, the change I had in my car and my couch cushions, everything. And more. I was in a hole so deep I could never get out."

I nod, just to show I'm paying attention.

"Out comes Ms. Redbrook. She's like the manager? The madame? I don't know, maybe the owner. I don't know. Anyway, she runs things The Lantern, on way or another. Ms. Redbrook makes me an offer, sort of a double-or-nothing. If I win, we call it even, no harm, no foul. But if I lose, I have to cut off my own arm and feed it to her. Raw. Like cut bits off and put them in her mouth like she's a baby or something."

"What?" I ask incredulously.

It's a horrifying idea. So horrifying it's ridiculous. But I also know from a ritual perspective, a magical perspective, someone freely and ritualistically sacrificing that much of their flesh and blood like that. Well, it's a lot of power.

"Yeah. I thought she was joking. But she wasn't."

"How do you know she wasn't joking?"

"She showed me to a room, and it had this special chair and saws and hatchets and things…not well cleaned. It was like a serial killer's lair. She was serious."

"What did you do?"

"Well…I mean what could I do? It was clear if I refused, I was going to get roughed up or worse. But it was obvious by that time, that the game was rigged, and I didn't want to have to cut off my arm. I excused myself to the bathroom and jumped out the window," he says, looking like he's about to throw up.

"Honestly, it seems like as good a move as any," I say, nodding nervously.

"But why are they doing this? Why not just kill me the easy way? My life has been like a horror movie ever since.

People creeping around my work, dead, eviscerated rats, there's been other stuff too." he says.

A floodgate is opening now that he's finally admitting this stuff.

"Horrible nightmares. Horrible, horrible nightmares. Things going missing from my home and my work. All my wine at home has turned to vinegar, and my milk curdles in the fridge," he says.

He seems almost ready to collapse.

"I think they want to use you as an example to show anyone else who might think of walking away exactly what happens to people that don't pay. Why didn't you go to the police?"

Whitman sighs. "I did."

"And?"

"And nothing, I went to the police and I filed a report. I got told they'd look into it and then nothing," Whitman says. "Though now she's running for mayor, so I think I am probably not the only one who she has on the books."

"Hmmm." This is bad. This is really bad.

"How do I get into the Red Door?"

"There is this token you have to give the doorman. I think I still have one here." He rifles through his desk for a moment.

After what seems like an infuriatingly long time to search a desk drawer, he pulls out a round disk about two inches in diameter and painted in alternating circles of black and white. He flips it to me across the room.

"Give that to the doorman, and he'll let you in."

"Okay, you stay in your circle. Don't answer the door. Don't answer the phone, keep your office locked, lights out, and pretend you aren't here. Sleep under your desk even."

"Right," he says. He seems pretty shaken and confused.

"I'll tell the front desk you are sick," I say. "Don't talk to anyone, Mr. Whitman. Seriously, no one."

"Okay," he says weakly, a broken man who will do whatever he's told.

"Have you slept at all?"

He shakes his head no.

"Seriously, man, why didn't you call me?"

"Because I don't like you."

I nod. "Fair enough. Well, try to get some rest now. Just vanish for the rest of the day, okay?"

Whitman nods and slides under his desk. I lock the door on my way out.

Chapter Fourteen

The Lantern is a sleazy little dive bar on the edge of town. It occupies one of the older buildings in Napa, the Soscol House, which dates back to the 1855. Its original location is now a large intersection where the freeway enters into town.

Back in the 1970s, when the highway was developed, they picked the building up off of its foundation and moved it a hundred yards to the west. The location features in many of the myths, legends and ghost stories of old Napa. It has stood there ever since, in a sort of no-man's land outside of town, off the freeway and in spitting distance of the sewage treatment plant.

It's been The Lantern ever since I moved to town, but that is just the most recent moniker for the roadhouse.

It's Wednesday evening when I park in front of The Lantern. There is a big, graveled parking lot surrounding the two-story building. It's painted off-white with a greenish-brown trim that reminds me of vomit. It still has that simple plank sided construction one thinks of when they think western town. You could imagine two men in a show-down at high noon on the deck that wraps around the front of the building.

I've been here once before when I had just moved to town.

I was looking to find "my" watering hole. I had a single drink, decided this was not it, and left. It took me a few weeks to decide that my watering hole was in fact my own apartment. But the fifteen minutes I spent at The Lantern have stuck with me ever since as the saddest, most depressing minutes I have spent in this city.

The patrons seemed largely there to drink themselves into sloppy oblivion. Few even made eye contact with each other. The staff were cold, distant, and suspicious looking. Every man in the place seemed to size me up like they wanted to fight. The three women seemed like they were estimating how much cash I carried on me. Thankfully, all seemed to find me lacking.

I open the front door. It has a little cut out in it that looks like a brass lantern, the old timey kind that a prospector might carry down into a mine blasted into the bedrock. The glass in the cutout is all smoked and beveled, so light comes out but you can't see through it. I open the door and a wave of smoke, both tobacco and vape smoke, washes over me.

It is illegal to smoke in bars and restaurants in California, because secondhand smoke might cause harm to the employees. The exception to this law is if the staff are all owners of the establishment and thus are all willingly subjecting themselves to the smoke.The Lantern is the only such establishment in town, and so it attracts all the people for whom smoking is a requisite part of drinking. It also means the employees, on paper at least, have a sort of stake in the business. I suspect this is an on-paper-only sort of arrangement, based on what I've heard about its proprietor.

The smoke hangs in a cloud that ends just about my chest level. I cough a little as I step in. The rancid smell of tobacco and a cloying fruity odor masks the herbal smell of marijuana coming from vape pens. Behind it all, I get a whiff of rancid beer and flatulence. The combination of smells makes bile rise in my throat.

I'm more of a micro-brew, fancy beer drinking type. But

they don't sell any of that here. They have an array of watery, urine colored American "beer", the kinds that all come in variations of a red-white-and/or-blue can. They have a variety of well drinks, using distilled spirits in one gallon plastic jugs. Finally, Jack, Jim, and their Russian friend

Stolichnaya constitute the "premium spirits" .

I order myself a pint of lawnmower beer and look around.

The Lantern itself quite large in floor plan and has a second story. Downtown you don't see places this big, but out here on the edge of town, there's not really any other buildings to contest for space with. The first floor is entirely devoted to the bar.

The bar itself is long, with two bartenders, one a bald middle-aged man who looks like he eats broken glass for a hobby and a tired aging woman who hides her thin, papery and prematurely aged skin by spackling makeup on with a putty knife. She wears an outfit that might have been considered sexy when she was a young woman, though fashion has long since moved on. I'm pretty sure tube tops and leg warmers aren't a thing anymore. Though I'm not exactly a fashionista, so I could be wrong.

There are numerous tables of different sizes, each with mismatched sets of stools and chairs around them. Entertainment comes down to a half dozen dart boards and another half dozen pool tables. Most of the clientele seems to be gulping down well-drinks and playing their favorite bar games with a complete lack of enthusiasm. At the far end of the bar, away from the entryway stands a huge, red velvet-paneled door. The fabric is old, worn, and dusty, but it is immense, loud, and unmissable.

Yet, it is as if the door has an aura around it, repulsing all patrons back at least twenty feet.

On a stool by the giant red door sits a man whose physique is built to match the impressive bulk of the door. A man so immense that I find myself wondering briefly if he's a man at all, not some sort of ogre guardian. I make a note to be careful; this is not as unlikely as it sounds considering the particulars of the situation.

I finish my malt beverage and throw down a couple of dollars on the bar. A tip. I take a deep breath, immediately regretting it as I gag on the mix of acrid and perfumy smoke that roils through the eaves. Steeling myself inwardly, I stroll over to The Red Door, trying to look casual.

As I approach, the doorman looks down his crooked, bulbous nose at me with a sneer. I casually pull the token that Whitman gave me out and dance it across my knuckles, vanish it into my palm, and then produce it to dance between my fingertips.

I once had the idea I'd be a stage magician and practiced a lot of palming and contact juggling. I never had the talent for the patter though and gave it up when I was still young. It probably looks to him like I'm showing off, but it's a nervous muscle-memory reaction I have anytime I hold a single coin in my hand. The same as I can't pick up a pencil without twirling it between my fingers.

I hold the token up. He squints at it, then nods and opens the door after taking the token. As I suspected, beyond the door a staircase climbs ominously into the darkness.

The walls of the stairwell are painted black.

The railings, black.

The stairs, black.

The carpet on the stairs, black.

The lights, black. That is the stairwell is lit with black lights.

"It's a little much, right?" I ask the doorman.

He shrugs, then scratches his cheek, and nods, eyebrows raised, forehead drawn, and head cocked slightly to one side. I take it to mean "fair enough," even though he still hasn't said a word. If he speaks, I bet he has a voice that sounds like Mickey Mouse, so he just stays quiet to be more intimidating. I laugh at the image. He glowers sternly at me, so I nod to him and start up the black stairwell that lays behind the Red Door.

The stairwell opens into a small vestibule with coat racks and an umbrella stand. I stop for a moment. It is awfully weird to have a coat rack and umbrella stand inside of an interior door. I decide after a minute that it's supposed to be ambience, giving the place an old-fashioned look. It's still odd.

The smoke isn't as thick here, and I take a deep breath. A wall extends out, making it so that I must turn a corner to exit the vestibule and enter the room beyond. As if to dispel any notions that I might not be walking into a den of evil, echoing around the corner is contemporary saxophone jazz. It's like the off-brand version of Kenny G. I imagine it's labelled Lenny B to avoid copyright infringement.

The sax solo calls out to me: "Abandon Hope All Ye Who Enter Here."

I take a moment to put on my game face and walk in.

The Red Door is done up to look like a very funky 1920s speakeasy. Red velvet drapery with gold rope trim, heavy brass lamps, and matching hardware hang on the walls. There is yet another bar on this second floor, directly opposite the entrance. This second bar is made of ornately carved mahogany with a brass rail around the base. It is serving a very different class of liquor than downstairs. There are a couple of young women in flapper dresses leaning against the bar looking bored. They must be the cocktail waitresses.

A dozen small card tables are spread out across the large room, but only one is occupied. Five men who look to be thirty to forty-something sit at the table. Each looks different but like they all came from the same fraternity. All are wearing shirts with the top two buttons unbuttoned, sleeves rolled up above the elbow. A pair of dark slacks accompany the ensemble. They all have short dark hair and all wear sunglasses. One is a little taller, another a little shorter, one kind of plump, but they must all shop at the same place.

It might be the light, but each of their faces has a sort of dry, impassive expression that makes it look like they are all wearing masks. It occurs to me that this isn't completely impossible either, depending on how loose a definition of "mask" you are willing to use. None of them react in any visible way to my entrance.

Dealing cards to them is a man dressed like a card dealer in a 1940s heist film. He's got a black silk vest over a crisp white shirt, which has gussets at the tops of the sleeves, black sleeve garters, and a little dealer's visor. My gaze draws his attention and he looks up at me with cold, distant, dead eyes that make me think of a shark. He assesses me and dismisses me in a single unsettling blink.

In the farthest, darkest corner are two figures at a table, one sits, one stands. They seem to be talking to each other in a very restrained debate. I immediately recognize one of them based on her long, graceful lines, notable height and her predatory eyes that I can make out through thirty feet of smoke and darkness: Circe. A lump rises in my throat; this woman makes me immensely uncomfortable. She's out of my league in basically every sense, and she knows how to appeal to my libido in a way that makes my brain turn off. I'm not expecting her here and I feel like someone is slowly turning my anxiety knob up to ten.

Circe stands near another woman, who is sitting at the table. She looks late middle age, a cloud of silvery white hair that instinct tells me is a wig. She is not tall but probably outweighs Circe. She is wearing a mass of gaudy clothes and jewelry, a loud red jacket, a busy patterned blouse, and a fountain of gold jewels, chains, pendants, and amulets that would cause me a long-term neck injury.

The two women see-me-see-them. They both smile. Circe's smile looks amused, almost on the verge of giggling; the expression doesn't extend to her eyes. The other woman's smile is entirely predatory.

Is this the smile a spider makes when it feels a fly get trapped in its web?

One of the cocktail waitresses pushes herself off the bar and starts walking toward me, visibly willing her face into a welcoming façade. I quickly skirt around the table toward Circe and the other woman in the corner. The cocktail waitress pursues me, but then Circe's companion, whom I am assuming is Lorelei Redbrook, shoos her way with her fingertips. The blood-red nails on those fingertips are entirely too long to be natural or functional. The cocktail waitress peels off and slouches her way back to the bar.

I walk up to the table where Circe and the other woman are. Circe is standing with one hand braced on a chair back, a cocktail in her hand. I can see from the level of the drink, the melted crumbs of ice and the large amounts of condensation dripping from the glass that it is untouched.

The other woman has a large goblet or chalice sitting in front of her, filled to the top with red wine. The open bottle sits on the table beside her.

"Good afternoon, ladies," I say in my best mid-Atlantic accent—which I'm not very good at, so I think it comes off sounding more of a cartoon imitation of an Irish accent than anything.

It's magically delicious.

"Lorelei, this is Miles Ward," Circe says to the other woman. "The spell-break I was telling you about."

"Miles," Circe says my name like she's talking dirty and makes eye contact with me. I wonder if this is all done intentionally or if that is how she always speaks. "This is Lorelei Redbrook."

Redbrook holds her hand out, palm down. It takes me a second to realize she expects me to kiss it. I have an instant to react, to define this relationship. Do I piss her off or placate her? Apparently, I take too long deciding and she retracts her hand looking peeved.

I guess I piss her off. No big surprise there. I smirk a little like this was my goal. In for a penny, in for a pound as they say.

"Ms. Circe. Ms. Redbrook," I say, my accent now sounds more mid-Western, possibly with an emphasis on the western.

When I was a kid, I could always get my dad to laugh by doing accents. I don't know why, but if he was on a rampage or freaking out, I could often break him out of it by putting on silly accents. When I feel uncomfortable or threatened, I often fall back to the goofy accents. It doesn't seem to amuse Circe or Redbrook as it did my dad, so I stop.

"Miles Ward, consulting Apotropaist. A ward on the home is worth two in the…um, bush," I say and slide my business card across the table to Lorelei Redbrook. She doesn't even glance down at it.

Circe quirks an eyebrow. I really need to figure out a catch phrase.

"Yes, I've heard all about you, Mr. Ward," she says, looking non-plussed. Her voice is high-pitched, grating, and gravelly. The voice of someone who pushes their voice from a natural tenor up to a falsetto, thinking it sounds more feminine. Her voice makes the hairs raise on the back of my neck and I grit my teeth with every diphthong.

"I'd like to say I have heard about you as well, Ms. Redbrook, but I'm afraid that just isn't true. I guess we run in different circles," I say, glancing pointedly around the room.

"Not a voter?" she says looking peeved. "You are here because of Mr. Charles Whitman, no? He's your client, and you're trying to keep him safe. Something like that?"

Apparently they know Whitman is still alive. This means they are either aware that the amulet stopped their spell, or they are not the ones that attacked Whitman.

I glance and see Circe give me a mischievous smirk. Behind Redbrook's back, Circe raises a single finger to her lips indicating silence. Or maybe Circe has been keeping Redbrook in the dark.

Interesting.

"Yes and no," I say. "He is not my client, but he works for my client, and I was hired to keep the winery he works at safe. He's like...what is the opposite of collateral damage?"

"Knight in shining armor, are you?" she says, smiling a hungry smile.

"Not how I'd describe myself. I prefer to think of myself as a thorough contractor, solving the problem I was hired for, solving the problems that got missed in the initial assessment," I say, smiling.

"Free advice, Mr. Ward?" Redbrook states this more than asks it, almost as if she added the question mark as an afterthought.

"Please," I say, knowing full well that I don't want to pay for anything here.

"Do the job you were hired for and walk away. Ms. Baros," Redbrook says, indicating Circe with a glance. Circe glowers at the use of this name, as she clearly didn't want me to know that for some reason. Redbrook notices Circe's expression and smiles a little. "Ms. Baros here tells me you have done an excellent job; you should be proud of yourself and call it quits."

"I do appreciate that advice, Ms. Redbrook."

"Please call me Lorelei."

"Great," I say, grabbing a chair and swinging it so the back is facing toward the table. I sit down, straddling it, arms crossed over the chair back, bringing my face down basically to Lorelei's level.

The chair I note with interest is well-made and heavy, exotic hardwood, teak, or mahogany, a quick glance around and all the chairs in the room are of the same manufacture. The furniture in the Red Door is a far cry from the mismatched field of dime store furniture downstairs.

"Lorelei. How do I get Charles Whitman off your books?"

"The same way you'd get anyone off any books. Pay his debt."

"You wanted him to cut off his arm and serve it to you, is that right?" I say. I don't expect the response she gives.

"His debt was a little over three million. So yes, I offered him that as an easy way out."

"I see," I say. When Whitman said he dug himself into a hole that he could never get out of, I never imagined a hole that big. "Not what I'd call easy."

"There were other offers," she says, smiling an unpleasant and obsequious smile. "Offers he found less palatable."

Circe stands quietly listening, her eyes dart back and forth between Redbrook and me like she's watching a ping pong match, waiting for one of the players to stop paying attention for a second so she can stab them with a knife. On the plus side, she doesn't seem to discriminate as to which participant she will take the opportunity to ambush.

"If I got you the three million…plus, that'd pay off his debt," I say, but we both know, that isn't going to happen.

"I'd let you pay off his debt in other ways, Mr. Ward," she says. She licks her lips, and I notice as she does that her teeth are all sharpened to points. She may be trying to be seductive, but it comes off as creepy and cannibalistic. She might also be actively anticipating eating my flesh. I don't know and frankly, I don't care to find out.

We are interrupted by a commotion at the card table behind us. It's not a commotion, but it is the first sound to break through the tepid saxophone stylings of Lenny B. The sound of a heavy hardwood chair being slid rapidly across the floor. I glance over, a man in the game has pushed his chair back hastily and is throwing his cards on the table. He turns and storms out silently.

"Another satisfied customer." Lorelei Redbrook chuckles. I ignore her quip and continue.

"That's a lot to unpack. Can I have time to think about your 'offer' to let me take on Mr. Whitman's debts?" I say, standing up, then I look over at Circe pointedly. "And while I do, muzzle your hounds."

Circe's eyes narrow, she feels slighted. That might not have been my best move. Lorelei looks immensely amused.

"Alright, this intrigues me. You have twenty-four hours to bring me the money…or agree to an alternative arrangement with me," she says. "Then I let the hounds off the leash."

"Very generous of you. I'll be back tomorrow with an answer." I stand up, fake a bow, and turn to walk away.

"Oh, and Mr. Ward," Lorelei says.

I turn my head to look over my shoulder.

"Yes?"

"She is not a hound. She's a kitten." Lorelei Redbrook turns to Circe. "You aren't producing results, kitten. You're fired. Kitten."

Redbrook emphasizes each time she repeats "kitten," Circe's face gets colder and more mask-like with each reiteration. Circe shrugs, her facial expression alone makes my blood run cold.

"You'll still pay full price," Circe says.

"Of course, dear, of course," Lorelei Redbrook says to Circe, her tone condescending. Then Redbrook turns back to me. "Tomorrow or the real hounds get let off their leashes."

I give her what I think is a nonchalant shrug and turn away. I am trying to look calm and collected but in reality, I am trying not to wet my pants. She's just implied that the blood-sucking sorcerer assassin I've been terrified of is the less-threatening option. I don't even know what she might have up her sleeve that trumps that, and I'd rather not find out.

Circe breezes by me as I start for the door again. She moves gracefully to the stairs, hips swaying, each step elegantly crossing to land on the opposite side of her body in a sort of crisscross. The motions look calculated and casual all at the same time, but still manage to carry her at my jogging speed. I slow my pace down and let her go ahead. Walking down the stairs next to her after that conversation would be awkward.

By the time I make it downstairs, through The Lantern, and into the bright sun of the parking lot, Circe is gone, vanished. This seems to be her style in departures. I walk across the parking lot toward my Jeep.

A man gets out of a pickup truck right as we lock eyes. He grabs something from a large cardboard box in the truck's bed and starts walking toward me. It's the guy who stormed out of the poker game upstairs. He's ditched the sunglasses and is wearing a worn trucker's hat now. He has unbuttoned his shirt all the way, revealing a white sleeveless undershirt beneath. In just a few minutes he has transformed from a mindless poker bro into a greasy-looking truck driver.

"Hey, kid," he says as he approaches me across the parking lot. "You got a minute?"

I pause and look at him, he looks like he's maybe forty years old, or a hard-ridden thirty-five. Either way hardly older than me and certainly not enough to call me kid. I see that what he has in his hand is a green truckers cap with the Knights of St. George logo on it. I was given a similar cap by one of these guys at MystiCon.

"I guess so. What's up?"

"You're that consulting Apotropaist right? Miles Ward," he says as much as asks.

"Depends on who's asking. I don't owe you money, do I?" I say, chuckling to myself.

"No, no, not like that. You know who that was you were talking to up there?"

"Lorelei Redbrook, don't know much about her," I say, trying to play my cards close to my chest until I know what his angle is.

"Yeah, that's right. You know what she is?"

"I'm sorry, you have me at a loss. I didn't catch your name."

"Right. Call me Alan," he says. "The word Lamia mean anything to you?"

"Hi, Alan. That Greek myth, right? The monster that eats children."

"That's right," he says, leaving the implication hanging there.

"What interest is that to you?"

"You ever heard of the Knights of Saint George?"

"Yeah, I saw the booth at a convention last year."

"I was there, saw your panel on that big corporate building you helped construct. Magical security is the next big thing. That was good. Then there was that magician guy…" he says, smiling.

"I was there. Are we reminiscing or are you going to get to the point?" I say, still not sure if he's going to attack me or hire me.

"Right, well," He gets a hushed and conspiratorial tone as he steps a little closer. "We are puttin' a hunt on the Lamia. But we are having a hard time getting an approach, as she's always surrounded by civilians. Pretty sure she's got monsters bodyguardin' her. And she's got all sorts of magic and stuff protecting her. She never comes out of that place."

I don't know what to say. The conversation feels a little like when you're walking through the park and a transient comes up and starts to talk to you. You might not bear them any ill will, but you just don't know what to say. I don't want to be in this conversation.

"Well, I saw you in there and I recognized you and it didn't seem like you were making any friends with her. So, I thought, you know, maybe you needed help. We need help, maybe we could, y'know, help each other," he says.

The longer he talks the more I get a hint of an Arkansas accent in his voice. Like as he's decompressing from his role as poker-bro, and I see more and more of the real him coming out.

"I'm more a loner than a joiner. You know?" I say.

"I'm not looking for you to join, just some quid-quo-pro. You're an expert at magical security. Maybe you could take down her protections, make it safer for us to do our business," he says.

"I don't know," I say. "I have a lot of moving parts and personal commitments to consider."

He holds up the trucker's cap and fetches a marker from

his back pocket. He writes something on the inside of the bill. "Well, think about it. Call me once you do," he says, shoving the hat into my hands.

I take it. There is a version of reality where I just work with these guys. It would be easy, to just hand off the responsibility to a band of vigilantes. But life has taught me that easy upfront usually means hard in the long run.

He winks, pats me on the shoulder, and stands there looking at me as I look down at the hat. He's written a phone number on it. There is a piece of glossy paper rolled up and stuffed into the crown of the hat. I take it out and unroll it. It is a bumper sticker, with the now-familiar Knights of Saint George logo and a poem or slogan printed on it.

I read it aloud back to him:

"Every monster led to slaughter.

Brings baby Jesus' laughter"

He grins at me. He thinks it's very droll.

"Slaughter and laughter don't rhyme," I say, looking at him more disgusted than confused.

"Well, they do on paper."

I look at him for a minute with my mouth agape, considering this. Then I shrug. He has a point. I put the bumper sticker back into the hat and fold the whole thing up then slide it into my shoulder bag.

"Heck yeah," he says as he turns to walk away.

I stand in the parking lot, watching him go. He gets to his truck, opens the door, and turns to wave once at me before climbing up the running board into the lifted truck. He fires it up; the engine is so loud that for half a second I think I might get a nosebleed from the vibrations. He revs the engine a couple of times and then roars out of the parking lot, leaving a rooster tail of gravel and a cloud of dust in his wake. As his tires hit the asphalt and squeal their way up the street, I take the hat out of my bag and glance at the number scrawled on the bill. I mentally file this under Plan Z. The plan I go to when I no longer care about the outcome, I just want something, anything to happen.

I can't help but wonder who the bigger monsters are. At least actual monsters understand how to rhyme.

Sitting in my car I notice that I have a message on my phone. It's from Chris Benson.

"FYI, Eric Walsh made bail this morning. Thought you'd want to know."

I message him back. "Thanks."

Eric Walsh. That's right, it was only a few days ago that he was slamming me into a metal staircase.

Well, he's the least of my worries at the moment.

Chapter Fifteen

I've got one day during which I need to:

•Get Whitman out of debt before Redbrook lets her "hounds" off their leashes.

•Keep myself from getting killed.

•And make my date with Emily.

I get into my car and start driving. I've made it halfway back to the city when I realize I am not driving anywhere specific. I need to think. The best first step to thinking is coffee, and the best coffee place is Soothsayer. So I adjust course to head downtown toward the coffee shop.

But I realize as I pull up in front, it's Wednesday, and Soothsayer is closed today. Two blocks away, a new place opened a couple of months ago called Charlton's. I still haven't been, so I walk there. It turns out Charlton's is also closed on Wednesdays.

"What the hell is with this town being closed on Wednesdays?" I say aloud to myself, standing alone on the street corner next to the empty parking lot.

"I'd guess because the tourists start arriving on Thursday or Friday and leave on Monday, so Tuesday and Wednesdays are 'slow' days? And even baristas need a weekend," a voice says behind me. It has a familiar, unplaceable accent. I jump out of my skin. It takes me a few beats before I compose myself enough to respond.

"Ms. Circe Baros, as I live and breathe," I say without turning around to look, I'm trying to sound like a southern belle, but it comes out sounding more Jamaican so I add in "Mon."

"Mr. Miles Ward," she says. She's close enough now that I feel her breath on the back of my neck, unlike the thing in my dreams, hers is warm. I turn around with a start.

"I thought you got fired," I say, stepping backward to give myself much-needed personal space.

"Yes, my business here is concluded. This is a vacation destination, you know? I thought I might go looking for a little…fun," she says, licking her lips.

"I'm not going to say I'm not tempted," I say. "Because I think we both know that's a lie. But I have pressing issues, hounds off leashes and all."

"Oh, that," she says, putting on a blatantly fake pout. "Well, if we are having fun together, then you're my friend and I could protect a friend."

"Do you normally undermine your former clients?" I ask.

"Only those who are special," she says. "And she's very special."

"What makes her special?" I ask.

"She makes the Hizarin look like an NGO," she says. When she sees my puzzled expression, she clarifies. "A mission-driven non-profit."

"You're saying she's the kind of monster that makes an order of emotionless and amoral magical assassins look like bleeding heart liberals?" I ask.

"We're not emotionless," she says. "But otherwise, yes, that's exactly what I am saying."

I shudder a little at the thought.

"You're suddenly being very chatty," I say.

"I like you, Miles. You intrigue me," she says. "I'd like to get to know you better, but if you stick with what you are doing, you will be dead in a day or so. That would be…inconvenient."

She says this like she's talking about a toy she just got for Christmas—one I knowshe will have forgotten about by New Year's Day.

"Yeah, I am not a fan of that outcome either," I say. "But I've got moves, you know."

"I bet you do," she says in a suggestive tone that makes my cheeks flush hot and my neck feel tingly. Again. She pauses for the statement to take full effect before continuing. "But yes, I would love to find out how you removed my curse so cleanly. I didn't think that was possible."

That's why she's interested in me. She still believes it was me that removed the curse, and she wants to know how I did it—presumably before she kills me so it never happens again.

I'll keep the little gem of truth as close to my chest as I can.

"I mean, what's she got that I can't handle?" I ask, I see her clever grin and immediately regret the question.

"Not as much as I've got that you can't handle." She winks. "However, in this case, she has millennia of experience, spells, magic, armed employees, and a host of Daunts at her disposal."

All good points and only one of them confuses me.

"A host of Daunts," I say, trying to sound in the know while wracking my brain for what she's talking about.

I have no idea what she's talking about.

"You have no idea what I am talking about," she states with a bell-like laugh. "You know the feeling you get when you are dreaming and there is something that is chasing you, but you can never see it? It's always right behind you, closing in on you. Waiting to pounce."

She emphasizes certain words and syllables: Dream, Chase, Behind, Pounce. The tone sounds aggressive and sexual. Each word heavy on the attack, but with a long almost moaning release. It seems to me, that she talks in this overly aggressive, sexual tone about everything. She's not even conscious that she does it. I'd bet she talks about tying her shoes like this.

In that, I see a small weakness that might be critical to keep in mind. She uses the constant aggressive flirtation as a defense mechanism, probably to keep people like me off balance and distracted from her actual intentions.

"Yeah," I say. "I've had dreams like that."

"The beings stalking you in the Dreaming are called Daunts because in the dream, that's what they feed on. The terror and frustration of failure, your insecurity, your shame, everything that daunts you," she says.

"Okay, I mean, I hate those dreams, but that doesn't sound bad," I say.

"Normally it wouldn't be. However, she has a bunch of them that she's pulled out of the dreaming, manifested in reality" she says. "They still feed on your insecurities, but in the real world, they do it by burrowing their proboscis into your brain cavity."

"Oh," I say, because what else is there to say?

"They are completely silent and invisible to the mortal eye. Human weapons have only a passing effect on them."

"If she's got these monsters, why'd she hire you to deal with Whitman?"

"As she said: They are hounds on a leash. I'm a kitten. Once she lets the hounds run wild, they'll get her prey and anything else that is nearby. Once they smell insecurity, who knows when they will stop. The Hizarin are precise, clinical, and subtle. The Daunts are going to be messy," she says this last phrase with a disgusted sneer on her face.

"How do I stop them?"

"I could stop them for you. Easily. I know tricks for dealing with dreams. You could say, I'm your dream girl," she says. "Come with me for a long weekend and I'll keep you safe."

"What about Whitman?"

"We could bring him along too if that's your taste, but you might find that difficult," she says with an impish grin.

"No, you know what I mean. No. Thank you Circe, you've been very helpful. Thank you for that. But I am going to have to pass on your most generous offer. Wait…why would I find that difficult?" I say, stuttering and stammering as she gets up close and her heady perfume subsumes my senses.

"He has, I am afraid, departed this mortal realm."

Oh right! Circe thinks Whitman is dead, but apparently she didn't tell Redbrook. I can't help but wonder what conversation I interrupted between Circe and Redbrook back at the Lantern. Did something make Circe turn on Redbrook all of a sudden?

"Oh," I say, trying to look shocked. Based on her expression, I am pretty sure I failed.

"You saved him again. You are full of surprises Miles Ward. Well, no matter, that contract has been terminated; he's not my problem anymore. But my offer still stands, you and me for a long weekend," she says with a sly grin and a wink.

"The answer is still no I am afraid."

Her facial expression becomes annoyed. She probably doesn't hear "no" a lot.

"Fine. Suit yourself. I'll look you up in Tulocay next time I'm in town," she says.

I roll my eyes to myself and sigh at her melodrama. Tulocay is the largest cemetery in Napa. I turn to walk back to my Jeep, take a couple of steps, then turn back to Circe to ask once more how I can get in touch with her. Having a Hizarin on speed dial really could be useful, but once again she has vanished by the time I turn around.

I have to learn that trick.

I climb into the driver's seat of my car and take a few deep breaths. After a moment, I notice a book on my passenger's seat. It's an old book, probably from the thirties or forties would be my guess. It has a heavy brownish-red leather cover and binding. In faded, chipped gold leaf the title is hand-painted on the spine. *Phantasmagoricon.*

I look around, seeing if anyone is watching who might have placed this here. The street is mostly empty. A young couple is walking on the next block, holding hands and drinking coffee from paper cups. I wonder where they got the coffee. I consider going to ask them but realize that I should stay on task.

I pick up the book and thumb through it. It's a handwritten guide to Dream-walking—to navigating dreams. There is an almost incomprehensible sort of index toward the back, listing topics and their associated page numbers. There might be an order to the index, but I can't tell what it is. I have to hunt around for a few minutes before I find "Daunts" on page 218. I flip to that page. I stand on the sidewalk next to my Jeep and skim through the section on Daunts.

It seems that Daunts would get their own whole chapter if the book were organized by chapter. Which it's not. But there is a rather large section on them with sketches and everything. Skimming the first paragraph tells me that Daunts are a type of Nightmare.

Nightmares, I am informed by a stilted footnote, are another category with a whole separate section in the book. As I close the book and place it on the passenger seat again, I notice a little slip of paper sticking out the top. Pulling it out, I realize it's a bookmark. Written on it in elegant and flourished handwritten letters it reads:

Thank you for the box of chocolates. Here is a little something to whet your appetite. Bon Appetit.

Xoxo, C.

This week is getting weirder and weirder.

I drive back to my apartment and stroll upstairs, carrying the heavy cloth-bound *Phantasmagoricon* under my arm. I change into sweats and a t-shirt, then I change Hank's outfit to match. I brew myself a pot of coffee, put it on the bedside table, and sit down on my bed.

The Phantasmagoricon is not an easy read. It is handwritten in a florid script. The narrative rambles, switching wildly between the first and second person. It is fluid in tense, filled with scrawled footnotes and sidebars. More than a couple of people have jotted notes in the margins or underlined phrases. The book has obviously changed hands many times.

When my pot of coffee runs out, I move from my bed to my desk. I brew myself a new pot and place it on one side of my laptop, with the *Phantasmagoricon* placed on the other. Returning to reading and drinking coffee straight from the pot, I jot notes down on my computer.

Daunts, according to the unnamed, unattributed author, are as Circe said: creatures that feed on your insecurities, your shame, your self-doubt. They exist in the Dreamtime, or Dreaming, or whatever you want to call it. To the normal slumbering visitor, while terrifying, they are kind of a symbiote, capable of consuming uncertainty, and allowing an experienced dreamer to emerge a better, more confident person when they awake.

In a dream pursued by a Daunt, there is not much you can do except run away or stay and let them feed.

To the Lucid Dreamer, the Dream-walker, they are an annoyance like mosquitoes. The book describes many methods by which the Lucid Dreamer can trap, confuse, and rebuke them. None of the methods make any particular sense to me.

However, the book clarifies that for those who find a way to physically transport themselves into the Dreamtime—or heaven forbid, bring a Daunt out of the Dreamtime—the creatures become are extraordinarily dangerous. They are essentially psychic bottom feeders in a dream, but given physical access, they become apex predators.

The book explains that between the Dreamtime and the world is a thing the author calls the Chimeric Veil, a sort of barrier that separates them. According to the book, only the Pneuma, the psychic energy that composes all living things, can normally cross from the real world into the Dreamtime. The Chimeric Veil sort of…stretches, for the lack of a better word, with the Pneuma.

The way the author describes it, it sounds almost like the veil extends and wraps around them, like pushing through a stretchy fabric, or maybe like a bubble that wraps around the Pneuma, protecting it. Through this Chimeric Veil, psychic energy can flow and allows the Daunt to feed but protects the Pneuma from direct exposure.

Lucid Dreamers are still protected by this Chimeric Veil, so have nothing to fear from the Daunt. But shaping dreams is hard when something is feeding on your energy, meaning they are kind of a pest.

If unprotected by the Chimeric Veil, the Daunt will, as intimated by Circe, burrow into the brain of a victim with a proboscis. This proboscis is very prominent if you can see them, and a Daunt can drain the victim of all psychic energy and consume the physical brain in the process.

The book describes a process in which a Lucid Dreamer can gather the Chimeric Veil around them while awake. The process refers to things like a cicerone, focii, reva fortikaĵo, vera vojo, and other concepts that I don't understand. It seems likely that the author might clarify these things in other chapters, but it'd take me weeks to get through the entire book and none of these words are referenced in the index.

Contextually, I intuit that cicerone is a sort of spirit guide or familiar. Focii is an object that a dreamer uses to anchor themselves in reality—a sort of object that tethers the Pneuma to reality. Lucid Dreamers can create persistent constructs in dreams that they can use ritualistically. That part was harder to follow, but reva fortikaĵo and vera vojo seem to be such constructs, built for a specific purpose. A purpose that eludes me.

Dawn light breaks through my window, and I blink bleary-eyed. I hadn't intended to be up-all night reading. More frustrating still is that while this has been interesting, it hasn't helped much. I know a way I could theoretically protect myself from a pack of Daunts made manifest *if* I were a Lucid Dreamer, which I'm not; and if I knew what all these terms in the book meant, which I don't. But I will find out.

Based on my reading, I believe an exclusive circle would hold them off for a while. The book seems to imply that dreams are made of magic. Or maybe that magic is made of dreams. It wasn't entirely clear. I would probably dismiss this theory entirely, but Circe gave me the book. Whatever problems I have with Circe, I can't deny her immense magical knowledge. If she wanted me dead, she must have far more direct methods at her disposal than disinformation. Right?

I think that I could probably set up a series of barriers to keep them at bay, almost indefinitely. But I read that Daunts are invisible, tireless, unaging, and patient.

Daunts it seems are ironically dauntless.

If I were to protect Whitman and myself with a circle, we would still have to step out of it someday and we wouldn't have any way of knowing if we'd have our brains devoured on the spot. From what Circe said, it sounds like with nothing else to do, the Daunts might just go on a brain-eating spree across Napa.

The best solution would be convincing Redbrook to not let these "Hounds" of hers out of their cage at all. But that means dealing with Lorelei Redbrook. Everything I've heard about her makes me think I cannot trust her even if she gives her word. I don't want to make a deal with her of any variety. She definitely eats people and probably eats babies. The world would be better off without her.

I could try to take Redbrook out, but there are a lot of problems with that. The first and probably most significant is that I'm not a killer. The second is, even if I wanted to, I don't know how to kill her. It might be as easy as the Knights of Saint George seem to think it is…? But somehow, I doubt that.

Finally, I don't know what her pet Daunts would do if she

died. Do they go back to the Dreamtime? Are they stuck here but tethered? Do they just get to run free across the world invisibly eating brains? I'm not willing to find out the hard way.

I check my clock. I have about twelve hours to figure out a plan before she unleashes her monsters on me.

I pour myself a bowl of cold cereal and eat it joylessly with milk. I'm overtired now, feeling that bleary-eyed sickness that overcomes you when you've been up all night and sunlight hits you and you realize how much sleep you've lost.

"Twelve hours to either: come up with three million dollars to buy Whitman out of his debts; or take on his debts myself, which involves at least having my arm eaten, probably worse; or take out Lorelei Redbrook. Frankly, I am not excited about my options, and I am not really excited about my odds," I explain to Hank around a mouthful of Cheerios.

"Why not just let the tool bag die? He made his bed, why do you need to sleep in it?"

"You wouldn't understand. You're just a lump of silicone."

"Ouch, Miles. Hitting below the belt. Wouldn't understand, or you don't want to admit it?"

"I don't have time for this."

"You aren't Dad, and Whitman is not me."

"You're not Henry," I say, raising my voice. "You're not my brother!"

Blood is pounding in my head, and I have tunnel vision.

"But you named me after him."

"I don't have time for this."

"Saving Whitman won't change your childhood, Miles."

"I don't have time for this!"

I slam my half-empty cereal bowl into the sink. It shatters, spraying milk up the backsplash. I leave it for now; I'll clean it up later. I get into the shower and stand in the hot water, letting it run over my body for a long time. Eventually, I calm down and dry off. I return to my room to get dressed. I stop to stare at Hank, but he surprisingly stays quiet for now.

I get dressed. Black boxers. Comfortable blue jeans. A black t-shirt with a magic circle I drew printed on it. Black athletic socks. A green, hooded Oakland A's sweatshirt. I take extra care in dressing Hank today in the exact same outfit. If there was ever a day I would need his help, it would be today. I stand next to him with a mirror and examine our outfits to make sure they are a perfect match.

"Twinsies!" Hanks says.

"Shut up," I growl.

I grab another cup of coffee on my way out the door. I unlock my car door and then realize I left the *Phantasmagoricon* in the house. Leaving my coffee cup sitting on top of the Jeep, I run back for the book.

When I return, I swear the coffee mug handle is turned the opposite way from where I left it. Maybe not. I didn't sleep much, maybe I am just tired and getting paranoid. I'm probably paranoid.

No, I'm definitely paranoid. I dump the coffee out in the hedge beside my apartment.

Nothing wrong with paranoia.

Chapter Sixteen

I'm feeling shaken, tired, and out of sorts. I start driving and then without intention find myself at Soothsayers. It's as if there is a magnet pulling me toward caffeine. If there is a day I am going to need coffee, this is it.

"Miles!" Jesse says enthusiastically as I enter.

"Jesse!" I say, trying to sound equally enthusiastic, but I just sound tired.

"You look like shit, man, nothing personal," he says with a tone of concern. He sizes me up. "Not sleeping much?"

"It was a bad night, I'll take a double…triple…can you just give me like a bucket of espresso?" I ask.

He looks skeptical.

"Sure, but don't overdo it, man," he says.

"Hey, Jesse, who's that guy who comes in here. He's always talking 'Tibet Man' this and 'Dude…Tantric' that, and 'Amigo…Lucid Dreaming' the other thing?" I ask.

"Oh, Russ," Jesse says chuckling. "You gotta mean Russ."

"Yeah, that's the guy. I don't know him other than the couple of times we've chatted here. Do you know where I could find him?" I ask. This Russ guy is someone else who seems to run in similar circles to me, but he's intense and has very esoteric opinions on basically everything.

"He's an artist or a musician or something like that, I don't know if he's got a day job," Jesse says. "He usually comes in on Thursdays. He hasn't been in yet."

"Could you do me a favor and give him my card if you see him today?" I ask, pulling out a business card and handing it to Jesse. "Tell him…well it's a very time-dependent issue. I need his help, and I am willing to pay."

This Russ guy, weird and intense though he may be is the only person I've met who claims to be able to Dream-walk. It's a long shot that he can help me with this, but I'm short on options. Hopefully, he's not full of it. If I am going to figure out how to deal with Redbrook's Daunts, I am going to need help.

I could try Goldsmith, but he's unreliable to begin with and I've already seen him this week. He doesn't like frequent visits. Maybe if I get really desperate, I'll try Goldsmith. This leaves Russ as the best shot in town I know of. Hopefully, he's willing and able to help.

"Yeah, sure. Just so you know, he's kinda flaky, so if it's time-dependent…" Jesse says, sounding a little uncertain.

"Thanks, Jesse. This is important, like life-or-death important."

"No problem, Miles," he says, giving me an awkward thumbs up. He clearly thinks I am a little loopy, but I don't care, it's probably true at this point.

I tip him very well before saying goodbye and jogging back to my Jeep. As if the seconds I shave off with my hustling are going to change anything.

The drive across town to JMBaptiste seems interminable. I feel like I hit every light and get caught behind every slow-moving car. I am fighting off the road-rage demon by the time I park. I take a moment and sit in the car, staring out the window at a hill covered in rows of grape vines. The wind blows, sending little ripples or waves through the vines. It's peaceful. I take a moment and just stare, catch my breath, and center myself. It really is beautiful here.

I get out of the car and walk into the tasting room. The staff seems to have already accepted me as a normal part of the day and ignore me. I walk straight to Whitman's office unhindered, unacknowledged, and I assume unwanted.

I knock.

"It's Miles," I say through the door.

He answers the door looking haggard. Clearly, he has gotten even less sleep than me. He hasn't changed his clothes since I last saw him. I realize a little sheepishly that I told him to stay safe and didn't tell him that I got us a 24-hour reprieve on his torment. That was an oversight. Or perhaps my way of unconsciously trying to punish him for being a jerk.

"Good news, Mr. Whitman," I tell him as I slip into a seat across his desk from him. "We have a temporary reprieve from your assassination!"

He looks at me with hope in his manic, sleep-deprived eyes.

"Really?" he asks.

"Yes. Bad news, it's only till about six tonight," I say.

His face falls.

"That's not a lot of time," he says.

"It's time for you to get a shower and a nap. I've got a plan. I'm working on the details," I say, starting to feel jittery as the excessive amount of caffeine I've ingested hits my bloodstream.

"What's the plan?" he asks.

"We are going to get a hippy to banish a pack of dream monsters, and then I am going to dispel the magical protections on The Lantern and hope that's enough to get Redbrook to back off. It may end up that we help an ancient order of dragon slayers to kill a local political figure who possibly also eats children, but that's plan Z," I say.

I sound ridiculous, even to myself.

This does not elicit the look of confidence and relief in Whitman that I was hoping for.

"You have no fucking idea what you are doing," he says, a manic giggle creeping into his voice.

"Of course, I do."

"No. You're a fucking lunatic. I told Mr. Baptiste that hiring you was a waste of time."

"Woulda, coulda, shoulda. This is your mess, not Mr. Baptiste's. So here we are. You're in this. I'm in this. You won't admit it, but you know what you are up against. We're in this hot-mess together."

He starts to laugh, it's not an amused or entertained laughter. It's manic barks of I-think-I-must-be-dreaming-because-I-can't-cope-if-this-is-real laughter.

"Go get a shower, a nice meal, and take a nap. I'll pick you up here at five," I say once his laughter subsides.

"Um, alright, but..." he starts to speak, his voice still cracking with mania as he comes to stand beside me. My phone starts ringing, so I raise a single finger between us, interrupting him. The number is local, so I am hoping it is Russ.

"Miles Ward Speaking, Consulting Apotropaist. You get cursed, we get it reversed," I answer. Whitman is standing uncomfortably close now, I try to twist my back to him, but he doesn't take the hint.

"Hi, Miles!" Emily says. This must be her home phone or something because I have both her mobile and Grape Reads numbers in my contacts and this isn't either.

"Oh. Hi, Emily," I answer back, my voice sounds disappointed and embarrassed, and I mentally kick myself.

Smooth Miles, real smooth.

"Am I interrupting something?" she asks.

"No. I mean yes. I mean, kind of, sorry, it's a crazy day and I didn't get a lot of sleep last night."

"Oh, do you need to cancel for tonight?"

Shit! Shit! Shit!

That's right. I have dinner with Emily tonight. I do a little quick calculus in my head. Okay, it's more like simple arithmetic, but I didn't sleep last night so it feels like calculus. If Russ can figure out where the Daunts are beforehand and trap them, and then meet with Redbrook at say 5:30. Then I, let's say I take an hour…and a half to figure out how to deal with Redbrook and Whitman's debt. That's 7:00. So yeah, I can be free by eight o'clock. I've got this. My arithmetic ends up leaving me more confused than I started, but I can do this.

"Are you making a date?" Whitman tries to interrupt. I put a hand over the phone.

"Shush," I say.

"Is that an appropriate use of your time, you know with your brilliant plan and all?" he says.

"Shhh," I say.

"Excuse me?" Emily says on the other end of the phone.

"No, not you. You can talk," I stammer.

"Oh, may I?" Emily says, her tone sounds amused, but I think it's to hide actual annoyance.

"Sorry, I'm just meeting with a client," I say into the phone.

"Can we deal with the pressing issue here? Someone wants to eat my fucking face!" Whitman says.

"Will you shut up?" I say covering the receiver with my hand.

"Excuse me?" Emily says.

"No, not you, my client."

"Do you talk to all your clients like that?" Emily says.

"Just the pro-bono ones."

"I'll show you pro-bono," Whitman says.

"Okay," Emily says. "I think I should let you go now."

Her tone does not sound impressed.

"Great! I'll see you at seven," I say.

"Eight," Emily says.

"Eight," Whitman echoes in my other ear. I'm glad to know he can hear both sides of my conversation.

"Right," I say, "eight."

My phone vibrates and another local number is calling me.

"Alright then. I'm looking forward to seeing..." Emily starts.

"Awesome, sorry, I have to take this. Hold on, I'll be right back," I interrupt. I attempt to press the hold and answer button, but I fat-finger and press the button that hangs up on Emily and answers the other call.

"Shit!" I say into the phone.

"Huh?" a nasally male voice says on the other end of the line.

"Jackass," Whitman mutters.

"I mean, hello?" I say into the phone.

"I'm going home," Whitman says, with an exasperated tone. He turns and heads toward the door. He says something else at the door, but I am too focused on my phone call to hear it.

"Hey, Miles, man, this is Russ. Russ Russo? Jesse at the coffee shop gave me your card and said it was...y'know...like a matter of life..." Russ then pauses dramatically and finishes with emphasis, "and death."

His name is Russ Russo?

"Yes, Russ Russo! Thank you for calling me! Listen, this is going to sound weird, so I'm just going to lay it all out there and if you can or will help, then great, and if not, I understand. There is a potential element of danger, and I want to be upfront about that. I have a client, who owes money to a Lamia that wants to eat his face, or actually his arm. But I think you get the point. Anyway, she has these Daunts, these dream creatures, that she can sick on people like attack dogs. I want to track them down and trap them, or banish them, or whatever, to get them out of the picture. This is so she can't use them, and I have a book that can help me do that, but I need a Lucid Dreamer, which I am not, but you said you are, so maybe you can help, oh, and the Lamia is Lorelei Redbrook. Also I can pay you," I blurt out.

I am sleep deprived, over-caffeinated and babbling almost incoherently. I feel disconnected from my body like I am watching another coffee-fueled idiot speed talk into the phone.

"Woah. Woah. Slow down there. Man. Yeah, I'm…like… in," Russ doesn't talk in a way that inspires confidence, he sounds like he's trying to be The Dude from *The Big Lebowski*.

"Really?"

"Yeah, I was 'in' at Lorelei Redbrook. Hell with her man, she's like, toxic. Also, like corporeal Daunts, those are, y'know, a real drag," he says, maybe he's more going for Tommy Chong.

"You're familiar?"

"Yeah, man, she's got signs like all over town, and she keeps saying the most not-dope shit in the paper."

"No, no, I mean you are familiar with Daunts?" I ask, sounding more exasperated than I probably should.

"Yeah. Yeah, man. They're like the flies of the Dreamtime buddy. But out here, no bueno," he says. I'm unsure which stoner icon he's channeling, but I just got a hint of Pauly Shore.

"Great. Can we meet somewhere?" I ask.

"Sure, can you meet me back at Soothsayer? That's where I am. I'm using their phone."

"Why?" I ask authentically curious.

"I don't have a mobile. Man, that's just a way for the government to listen to your conversations and track your location and stuff like that. Man."

"I see," I say, glad to know I'm not the only weirdo now in this mess. "Okay, I'll be there in…ten minutes? I'll see you in ten minutes."

"Cool, I'll see you then. Oh, and also Miles, could I like get a ride home when we're done?"

"Yeah, of course," I say.

"Sweet. My license got suspended, so I've been hoofin' it."

Chapter Seventeen

It's a short trip back to town. Most would just take a quick jaunt down the Silverado trail. However, I have a shortcut I take that skirts a small road that goes between two vineyards. It's rarely traveled and out of sight of everything. I like it because it avoids tourist traffic and all the erratic, crazy driving that brings.

It's the perfect place for an ambush. That is what the paranoid part of my brain tells me a couple of seconds after a truck collides with me out of the blue. My Wrangler goes spinning off the road in an instant.

My world becomes a tumbling, whirling mass of breaking glass, and screeching metal, muffled through the star-inducing barrier of an airbag smashing me back into my seat.

There's a moment of chaos and panic in my head. Maybe I blacked out, or maybe I just couldn't see with the airbag in my face. I fight and kick my way out of the Jeep, which is laying on its side, crushed grape vines beneath it.

I roll out of the Jeep, expecting to make a smooth landing on the ground. But I don't; my legs are shaky and I fall to my knees. On the ground in front of me, covered in and surrounded by broken safety-glass cubes, is the *Phantasmagoricon*. I look at it bleary-eyed for a second and then glance up to the road. Two men are getting out of a truck. The truck's front bumper is crushed, and its headlights smashed.

The first man I don't recognize; he's young and well-dressed and muscular. He looks like a professional boxer.

The other man I do recognize. He too is young, well-dressed, and muscular, though he lacks the trained confidence of his companion. It's Eric Walsh, the stalker whom I helped deal with just a few days ago. But today, it seems like years ago. He's holding a baseball bat in one hand. His friend is holding a tire iron.

"Motherfucker!" Eric points his baseball bat at me. "We are gonna beat you till you have to wear a colostomy bag."

I blink at him. Chris texted me that this guy was out of jail, but I didn't think he'd track me down. I look down at the book. I shake my head. I grab the book and dazed, push myself to my feet.

I'm shaky, so I have to brace myself on the Jeep. I sneak a glance at my vehicle. The passenger side door is crushed, the roll-cage served its purpose, but I can see it is slightly bent. I think the frame on the left side might also be damaged. I sigh and then remember that two men are coming for me. I turn to see they are stalking toward me, taking their time for dramatic effort, because they want me scared.

"See Eric, the thing about that is…" I say loudly, on the borderline of yelling.

Then I turn and run, drunkenly at first. Adrenaline and muscle memory kick in as I get going. I tear into the vineyard, as fast as I can. I briefly pat myself on the back for all the years I spent training for just this moment. Then I catch my shin on the support wire of one of the vine trellises. I stumble briefly, screaming profanity, then lift my knees and keep running. Less focus on the self-congratulating Miles, and more focus on running.

"Fuck!" I hear Eric yell, and then I can hear the two give chase.

The thing about running in vineyard trellises is that once

you are in a row, you pretty much have to go in a straight line. There aren't a lot of breaks. They are narrow, with vines and leaves everywhere. The ground is level, and this vineyard has kept the grass well-trimmed between the rows, so it is pretty easy running. But it is all running in a straight line.

Unless you have a long metal object in your hands, which keeps hitting on the posts, the vines, and the trellis wires—which thankfully I don't have, but my two pursuers do. I'm better at distance than speed, and this seems to be working in my favor in this circumstance. I glance back and it looks like these two both are faster than me in the short haul. For some reason, they fell into a line with Eric in front and the other man right behind him. This is to my benefit, having one of them try to get ahead of me in a parallel trellis would be the smarter tactic.

Thankfully smart doesn't seem to be the threat here.

I make it about twenty yards and there is a break. I quickly cut hard left and travel up the column between the rows of trellis. I glance back just as I see them turn the corner, and I cut hard right into the next row . My zig-zag maneuver gains me more distance. They start to gain on me in the dead sprint, but their relative bulk slows them down on the turns.

I glance back as I push forward. This guy Eric is muscular, but I don't think he gets his cardio in and he's flagging. I slow to a jog when I see Eric sucking in air a row behind me. His friend doesn't seem to be winded, but he's stuck behind Eric on the narrow path. I get the sense that the other guy is just a follower, as he doesn't seem too worked up by the delay. I head up onto Big Ranch Road, jog across the road, and down into a gully.

After I make a few hundred yards in the gully, I pop up on the other side of it. I skirt between two fenced yards and make it out onto a residential street. I am pretty sure I lost them. I look around and get my bearings. My poker night buddy, Alistair, lives a few blocks away. I start walking in that direction, clutching the large book under one arm.

I hear a fire truck's siren back toward where I wrecked my Jeep. Someone must have noticed. Normally I would go straight to the police. However, with my current timeline, that's going to lose me hours I can't afford.

Alistair's house is a decent-sized, two-story house. I don't know what style to describe it: maybe inflated California ranch? It's probably three thousand square feet, with an in-ground pool and a trampoline in their backyard. Their neighborhood is one of the more upper-middle-class neighborhoods in Napa. A little suburban snapshot, so, so far from my own life.

I knock on the door to Alistair's house. It's late morning on a Thursday, but it sounds like most of Alistair's sessions are done online these days. I know he works from home three days a week, but since I don't know his schedule, I'm hoping today is one of those days.

Jon, Alistair's husband, answers the door. I've only met him a couple of times, but I get the impression that Jon does not care for me. Jon's family is from Puerto Rico, but he was born and raised somewhere in New England. He has short curly black hair with the beginning of salt and pepper dotting about it. He's wearing glasses and a bathrobe. His hair is still damp from the shower.

"Hi, Miles. You look like shit," Jon says.

"Thanks, Jon, I wrecked my car and then got chased all the way here by men with baseball bats," I say, sounding sarcastic despite actually telling the truth.

"Jesus." Jon points at my arm. "You're bleeding. Get in here."

I'm glad to know that while Jon doesn't like me, he still respects me enough as a human being not to let me bleed out on his front stoop. He ushers me in, guides me to a chair, and sits me down.

"Sit down. Let me get something to clean that up," Jon says bustling off.

I look down at my arm, which I must have cut in the

wreck. Or maybe I caught it on a trellis running in the vineyard. The last ten minutes have been a blur. I look closer at the cut. It's superficial, and kind of messy, but nothing too concerning in my completely uninformed opinion. I've had my tetanus shots.

"Ali! Your tatted, sarcastic, broke-ass friend is down here bleeding," Jon yells up the stairwell.

"Megan?" Alistair calls back.

"No, the other one," Jon hollers.

"Buckley?" Alistair's voice echoes down the stairs.

"No, the wizard. You have too many sarcastic, broke-ass friends, Ali," Jon calls back over his shoulder as he returns to me with a bottle of iodine, cotton balls, and a bandage. He starts cleaning the wound up and bandaging it.

"Thanks," I say.

"Somebody gotta stitch his loser friends back together," Jon says. "And you know it's not him, because he can't stand the sight of blood."

Jon laughs at his own joke as he finishes up. I recall now that he happens to be a nurse.

Alistair comes down the stairs as if on cue.

"Hey, Miles. What happened to you?" he asks incredulously.

"It's kind of a long story, but long and short, a couple of guys attacked me, kind of out of the blue. But I'm sort of under a time crunch for work," I say.

"Jesus. Have you called the police?" Alistair asks.

"Yes," I say. It's a lie and I immediately feel defensive about it. It's not really a lie, because I will call the police. If I call the police there will be standing around for a long time, there will be questions, and there will be paperwork. The police won't acknowledge invisible brain-eating monsters, let alone be able to do anything about them. I will call them as soon as I've dealt with that, so it's just an issue of chronology, right?

"Oh good. What did they say?" Alistair asks.

"I'm going to stop by and fill out a report later."

"Oh," he says, his brow furrowed with open skepticism. "Okay."

"I was hoping to ask you for a favor."

"What do you need?"

"I need a ride to Soothsayer; I have to meet a guy there…" I glance at my phone. "Like three minutes ago."

"Aren't there men trying to kill you?" Jon asks, as he finishes cleaning and bandaging my arm.

"Well, I don't know if killing is their goal. Anyway, I lost them. I think," I say, "If you can't, I can call for a ride or something."

"No, it's just a few minutes away. I'll give you a ride," Alistair says, picking his car keys up off of the counter.

"Ali, don't get involved in this," Jon stage whispers to Alistair. I think this is literally why Jon doesn't like me. He's afraid that being friends with me is going to get Alistair dragged into weird cult stuff with axe-wielding murderers.

"I'm just giving him a ride to the coffee shop. That's it," Alistair says, putting a soothing hand on Jon's shoulder and kissing him.

"Okay. But then you have to get back to work."

"Don't you have to get to work?" Alistair asks back.

"Yes," Jon huffs. "I need to change."

"Thank you again!" I say to Jon as he hustles up the stairs.

"You want to thank me, keep my man out of your Harry Potter bullshit," Jon says and storms upstairs.

"Well, at least I don't have to guess what he thinks of me."

"He's just worried. You get in an inordinate amount of trouble, Miles," Alistair says, laughing. "Come on."

We head out the door and get into Alistair's car. It's an older Prius. Blue. There is a car seat in the back, and cereal ground into the rugs. I sit down on something hard and pull it out from under me. It is a small plastic robot.

"Sorry about that. Kids," Alistair half-heartedly apologizes. Alistair starts the car up and we drive a minute in silence.

"What have you gotten yourself into?" Alistair asks. I get the sense that saying he wasn't interested was just for Jon's benefit.

I explain it to him at high level, skipping the more personal details. Namely, the vampy sorceress, the blood in my fridge, and Jeff's status as the Anointed one.

"So, your plan is to send these monsters back to the dream world they came from, and fight the mayor in the underground card room at the back of a dive bar?" Alistair asks. He looks like he's trying not to laugh.

"Mayoral Candidate, and I'm not fighting anyone," I emphasize. "But when you put it that way…."

"Lorelei Redbrook, even if she's not a baby-eating monster, is awful," Alistair says.

"Yes, definitely," I agree.

We ride in silence for a bit.

"I feel like I should offer to help," Alistair says as we are pulling up in front of Soothsayer.

"You are helping."

"I mean, I feel like I should help more. You and Jeff did a field trip into 'The Weird World of Miles Ward.' I feel like I should join. We've been friends for a while, and I've been kind of dismissive of what you do."

"This part is pretty dangerous," I say. "Besides, Jon would murder me."

"That's true. Well, if you need anything else, let me know. I don't know how much of the mumbo-jumbo I buy, but if any of that is even metaphorically true, I want to help."

"You help plenty, but thanks, I'll let you know," I say, opening the door.

"Miles," Alistair says. "Be careful."

I smile. "I'm always careful."

"Yeah, that's what I'm worried about."

Chapter Eighteen

I turn and head into Soothsayer. Russ is sitting on a bench by the door, holding an empty insulated steel coffee cup and looking agitated.

"Sorry," I say as I arrive. "I had car trouble."

"No problem, man. All good amigo," Russ says.

"Can I buy you a cup of coffee or something?" I ask him.

"Yeah, a cup of chamomile tea would be stellar," he says, his agitation seeming to melt away with the word chamomile.

I order Russ's herbal tea and another cup of coffee for myself. I also grab two muffins on a whim. A few minutes later, I return to the table.

"Can we walk and talk?"

"Sure, man, sure," Russ says.

We head out the door and walk down the streets. I look at all the Bradford Pear trees the city planted; they're all in bloom. The smell is entirely unpleasant and gives me terrible hay fever. I sneeze and mutter darkly to myself about them and take a gulp of coffee.

"You know what this is?" I hand the *Phantasmagoricon* to Russ.

"Shit, man, a *Phantasmagoricon*. I haven't seen one of those in years. These things crack me up," Russ says, he draws out all of his A's in a way that makes me impatient.

"How so?"

"Like every wanna-be emo, angsty, broody dream walker type has written one of these," he laughs.

"What do you mean?"

"Oh, well, so there's this like story, that there was this guy. Different versions of the stories give different dates. Some say like the 1880s, others say the 1920s or whatever. Anyhoo... always, you know, before anyone alive was born. The story goes that this guy studied the Dreaming, and he wrote the most accurate guide to dreaming, Dream-walking, Lucid Dreaming, or whatever that was ever written, and he called it the *Phantasmagoricon*, right? But it's like a myth. Every version of his name is different, or where he lived is different, or whatever. Sometimes it's a chick, not a dude, but you know, the tales we tell. Anyway. So, everybody who comes along and thinks they know a thing or two like writes one right? But it's mostly bunk," he says.

"Did you write one?"

Russ laughs.

"Yeah, man, when I was like twenty-three or something, I did. It was dumb. Like really dumb. You know what it's like when you're a kid though; you think you know everything."

Russ looks the book over while we walk. Then he stops.

"Though, if the real thing did exist," he says thoughtfully, "this could be it. Where'd you get this?"

"A vampire left it on the passenger's seat of my car?" I say, trying to sound sure of myself.

"Right on," Russ says without a hint of sarcasm.

"Anyway, that describes a process by which one can protect themselves from Daunts or any creature from the Dreamtime. It also talks about how to trap or banish them. But I don't understand it and don't have time to read the whole thing. So, I was hoping you could help me."

"And these Daunts like, what's their deal?" Russ asks.

“As I understand it, they have been summoned from the Dreamtime and trapped here.”

“Dreamtime, I like that, like the Aboriginal Australian thing. We always say Dreaming, but you know, whatever. Dreamtime. I’ll use that,” he says.

“So, Daunts, summoned to the real world?” I say. Russ is easily side-tracked.

Russ winces. “Yeah, that’s bad news. Could get super dangerous.”

“I understand. If you could even explain to me how to do it,” I say.

“Are you a Lucid Dreamer? Can you wake yourself in the Dreaming, man?”

“Wake yourself in the Dreaming?”

“Yeah, you know where you realize that you are dreaming and you, like, awaken, but stay asleep. Still dreaming, but you aren’t just along for the ride anymore.”

“No,” I say, the idea itself seems a little confusing to me.

“Well then, that’s going to be tough for you. I mean you could learn, but it takes time,” Russ says, nodding to himself.

“Unfortunately, I don’t have time.”

“Listen, I’ll do it for you if you give me the book,” Russ says.

I think quietly for a minute.“Okay, but I want to copy it first. I can just take pictures of all of the pages. It’ll be quick.”

“Sure,” Russ says. “That sounds fair.”

“Okay, so we need to track down and banish these Daunts.”

“When do you want to do this?”

“Um. Now?”

“Now! Hah.” Russ laughs, but then he sees my expression. “Oh, you are serious. I’m going to need time to prep, gather materials, you know.”

“What kind of materials do you need?”

It takes him a minute and me taking notes on my phone,

but he gets me a list, mostly crystals and incense, and herbs and things.

"What's all this for?" I ask. "Aren't you just going to sleep?"

"Yeah, man, but you want to like ritually prepare. Make magic barriers. You need to create a space where your body is safe and where you are tethered to reality. You go too far, too deep, man…you can get lost. Rip Van Winkle style, you dig?"

"Sure," I say, but I'm not following.

"And I'm gonna need some peyote," Russ concludes.

"Peyote? Where the fuck am I going to find that on short notice?" I ask incredulously. But honestly, I wouldn't even know where to find that with lots of notice.

Russ shrugs.

"Doesn't have to be peyote, but like anything psychoactive and powerful. I know a guy who might have a little something."

I jot down that information too.

"Okay, so you are going to prep, and I will get you all of this stuff?"

"Yeah, meet me at my place," Russ says and then gives me his address. It's in the old town neighborhood, which surprises me. I'm not sure where I imagined him living, but he lives much closer and more "on the grid" than I expected.

"Can I get that ride?" Russ asks.

"Yeah, my car is right over…" I start to say, but then I realize my car is wrecked in a vineyard on the other side of town. "You know what? Let me call you a ride, I don't have my car here. I forgot, it is in the shop or at least soon to be."

"You know what dude? Don't sweat it, I can hoof it. See you on the flip side." He waves and starts off toward Old Town.

"See you then," I say. I sigh and stand on the street corner for a minute, just breathing and trying to pretend this isn't becoming my weirdest week ever.

My phone rings, and I see it is Chris Benson calling. This is going to complicate things.

"Hello. Miles Ward, you spell em, we quell em," I answer.

"That was disappointing," Chris mutters quietly on the other end of the line.

"Good morning, Mr.Ward. This is Officer Christopher Benson calling," he adds, sounding louder and more formal. This must be about my Jeep.

"Yes, and a most illustrious day to you, Officer Benson," I say, trying to sound formal.

"I am calling because we found an abandoned vehicle registered to you. It has been in an accident," he says. He doesn't seem to think I'm funny today.

"Yeah. So. Chris. Here's the thing: I got run off the road by that Walsh guy you texted me about. He had a buddy with him. I ran, but I'm sort of on a job that's very time-dependent…very. I was going to call once I got all this dealt with…"

He's quiet for a second. I can hear movement, like he's rearranging so whoever he's near cannot overhear as well.

"Okay, Miles. I assume this is related to all your weird stuff?" he asks.

"Yeah, the weirdest stuff, honestly."

"I'll cover for you, but you cannot make a habit of this. It already looks weird that I insisted that I be the one to call you. Can you come down to the station in the morning to make a report and give us a statement?" he asks.

"Yeah, I can do that."

"Okay, I'm putting my ass on the line here, so don't forget."

"Of course," I say. "Thanks."

"Yeah, no problem. Let me know if there's anything else I can help you with."

"Not right now but thank you for this. It is literally a matter of life and death, of the sort that the police aren't equipped to deal with."

"Be safe. See you tomorrow," he says and hangs up.

Chapter Nineteen

I put a request in for a ride-share. Then I stand on the street corner, leaning against a concrete wall, staring at my phone, lost in thought. I notice after a bit that a motorcycle has pulled up on the curb near me and is sitting idling.

The rider is wearing a helmet with the darkened visor down, despite that I recognize her in her skintight black motorcycle leathers.

Circe.

She pops the visor of her helmet up for a dramatic reveal of her fox-colored eyes. Taking her helmet off, she flourishes her hair so the wind catches it. Pink blossoms blow off a nearby tree and swirl in a cloud around her. The sun reflects in a nearby window surrounding her in an aura of light. There is magic at work, but I have no idea how or even why she's doing it.

"Nice trick, Try-Hard. What are you doing here?" I say. Circe still scares me, but she is really laying it on thick, and I am just too tired and terrified to deal with it.

"Getting a cup of coffee."

"Bullshit."

"What? A girl can't get a 'cuppa at your favorite place without it being suspicious?"

"Yeah, that's what I'm saying."

"Okay, you caught me. I just wanted to check in on my favorite consulting apotropaist."

"Your favorite."

"What, a girl can't just be interested in a guy?"

"I don't buy it," I say skeptically. "What's the game?"

"You're gonna die if you go after Redbrook," she says bluntly.

"And you're concerned about that because…?"

She just shrugs.

"Why should I trust you?" I ask.

"You shouldn't."

"Great. You haven't clarified anything."

"You are entirely too suspicious of the wrong things," she scolds me.

"I don't think I am suspicious enough," I respond, turning to walk up the street.

"Fine," she says. "You undid my curse, which I didn't think that was possible. I want to know how."

"And I'm not going to tell you."

"Not now, but someday you'll realize that I'm not the bad guy, then you'll tell me."

"What have you got to offer?"

"I can tell you how to defeat Redbrook."

"Well, I think I've got a pretty good plan for that already," I say. I don't want to depend on Circe if I can avoid it. I do have a plan; it isn't a lie. I've recruited a Dream-walker, and… okay, I don't have much of a plan.

"What? You're going to run in, banish her Daunts and defeat her with a stand-up comedy routine?"

"I have a couple of killer jokes."

"You know she cannot be killed by mortal weapons? Guns, knives, swords. Not going to work. Maybe an explosion big enough to obliterate her and the entire building she was in. Something nuclear would do the trick. You have anything like that?"

"Obviously not. So, you're offering to take her out for me?"

"You couldn't afford me," she laughs.

"Okay, what then?"

"I can give you information, I can even help you take down her defenses," she says, "but there has to be quid-quo-pro."

"I don't think so."

She shrugs and pulls her helmet back on. I don't trust Circe as far as I could throw her. Considering how out of sorts the thought of putting my hands on the athletic curves of her hips to pick her up makes me…anyway, I couldn't throw her very far at all. But I'm way out of my depth here. And this is her day job. I'll deal with the consequences later. I wave my hands at her to stop.

"Okay, Okay. What can we do to help each other?"

"You could start by telling me how you lifted my curse."

"That's not gonna happen. It seems like that's my one bargaining chip, and if I let that go what use am I to you?"

She smiles and shrugs. "Fair."

"That leaves us in an impasse."

"No, no. You'll just owe me a favor in the future," she says with a wicked grin on her face.

I consider this for a moment. I don't know this woman at all, but what I do know of her is not good. She is not the sort of person that I want to owe a favor. On the other hand, if I don't do something about Redbrook, I'm going to end up dead or at least maimed; Whitman probably isn't going to make it either. I'm not seeing a lot of options at the moment.

"Fine. But no killing, no enslaving, enthralling, or victimizing people, and I'm not telling you how I broke your curse."

She rolls her eyes and says, "Very well. If you don't pay up—"

"You'll kill me. I got it."

"Alright then. What you need to understand about Redbrook is she isn't and never was human. But she isn't immortal either, at least not exactly. She has used magic to make herself more powerful and prolong her life. She's spent centuries consuming the lives and blood of others. She's gained immense power, much of which she captures in her hearth? Is that the right word?" Circe says.

"In her hearth? What does that mean?"

"There are lots of ways of storing magical power. Some store it in crystals, or wands or staves, or other objects. The objects are designed to channel magic into a specific form or effect. Others store the power in their bodies," she says, and with the last part, she gestures her hand down her long, lithe frame.

"She stores it in The Lantern. It's a labyrinth of effects and designs. She has a great deal of power; she has spent decades building it up. It's her hearth, her nest, her lair. That's the word I was looking for: lair," Circe says.

Lair seems like a very fitting choice to describe The Lantern.

"She's basically unstoppable while she's in it, as she's had decades to build up her protections there. If you walk in there to fight, she'll just kill you. You have to dispel her rituals, and destroy her protections. Once her lair is gone, she's vulnerable. Even if you don't kill her, breaking down her lair, the magics she has built will set her back enough that she will have to focus energy on that and not on her other plans."

"And you know how to dispel it? And what do you mean other plans?"

"Miles, I thought *you'd* know how to defuse it—seeing as how that seems to be your specialty."

"All I need to do is undo all of the enchantments and spells set on the building and she'll be powerless to stop me?"

"Something like that. It doesn't have to be all of them, just enough to weaken the structure and make her vulnerable. She'll be too terrified to focus on you. You'll make a powerful enemy, but it will take her time to be able to get back at you."

"Well, that's great, thanks for that," I say sarcastically.

"I'll help you of course."

I'm not excited by her offer to help, but I don't see that I have a lot of choices. I'm swimming with the sharks. Circe is one of the sharks. It could be very beneficial to have her on my team, but if I forget what I'm dealing with, even for a second, it could end very poorly for me.

"And what did you mean about her other plans?"

"I don't know the specifics, I just have a general idea, based on bits I've heard here and there," she says, looking amused.

"And?"

Circe seems to dislike parting with information. She prefers hinting about it, dangling it out there like a worm on a hook.

"She wants to run this valley. She wants to make it a haven for all of her kind, a place where the awful monsters come to vacation."

"Not much of a change if you ask me. Aren't you in her target demographic?" I ask.

"Miles, that's unfair," she says, jutting her lower lip out to make a pouty face that doesn't look upset. "The Hizarin serve a purpose. Sometimes that purpose is bloody and dark, but it is a purpose nonetheless. We prevent any one faction from becoming too powerful. And that's why we've been watching Redbrook."

"Alright," I say, feeling suspicious. "How does Whitman tie into her wanting to run The Valley?"

"She's making a show of power in hiring me and sending out Daunts; it's all to impress a certain category of people. Showing she can murder people, torture them and bring suffering, intimidate those that might cross her. At the same time, she's showing others that she can protect them and their way of life. All without consequence. She's ambitious."

"Killing Whitman is a dog whistle."

She looks a little confused by this. Circe isn't too modern in her vocabulary. Another tidbit I file away for later.

"It's an expression, for little things people say and do, that are code to call to other people of a like mind."

She nods in affirmation.

I sigh.

"And that is why the attempted move into the political arena. It makes sense, though it seems strangely out in the open."

"Out in the open is the new direction of the Dominium Doloris."

"The Dominion of…hurt? Pain. The Dominion of Pain. What's that?" I say, struggling to dig up the Latin classes I took back in college.

"It's an organization of powerful sorcerers, and for the lack of a better word, monsters. They have a not-so-secret secret agenda to influence politics to their benefit."

"The Illuminati."

"Something like that, yes. They have always existed, in one form or another, at least as long as recorded history, but in recent years they have become radicalized," she says.

"What do you mean?"

"Their agenda is less quiet. It's less about gaining power behind the scenes, and it's become more about demonstrating their superiority. They are less and less in the shadows. Nowadays they want all the boogeymen out of the closets and all the boggarts out from under the beds."

"Sounds right up the Hizarin's alley."

"No. We are an ascetic order; we have no political ambitions. Mastering magic is our goal. Assassination is just a way to pay the bills. We remain neutral in all matters, equally hirable by all sides. That is how we keep a balance," Circe clarifies.

"Ethical murderers. You must be proud," I say sarcastically.

"I am," Circe says. Every time I start to think this woman is human at heart, she disappoints me.

"Fine, I'll owe you a favor. Let's go. First, I need to get a things for my Lucid Dreamer. Can you give me a ride?" I say.

"Sure," she says with a flirty tone. She pulls a helmet out of one of her saddlebags. It is black and has a large pentacle on the back, matching hers. She tosses it to me.

"Safety first!" she says glibly. I catch the helmet and put it on. I climb on the back of her bike.

"Tienda Magia. Do you know where it is?"

"I do," she says. "Now wrap your arms around my waist. Come on, Miles, you can hold me a little tighter than that. Tighter."

I wrap my arms around her waist tightly, feeling her pressed into my chest. She smells like spices and lavender.

"Oh, Tiger!" she says loudly and provocatively.

I see a passerby give us a sidelong glance just as we zip away.

Chapter Twenty

I'm feeling very uncomfortable pressed this close to her, my arms clasped around her waist. Part of me is excited, but part of me is terrified. Feeling self-conscious, I relax my grip on her waist.

That's a mistake.

She suddenly hits the accelerator and roars down the street, leaving a black mark and a cloud of acrid smoke behind her. I barely manage to stay on the back of the bike. Now I'm nothing but terrified. What seems like three seconds and three blocks later as we are squealing around a corner through a red light, surrounded by an angry chorus of car horns.

I'm pretty sure I am going to soil my pants.

I can't tell if she's just trying to impress me or if she always drives like this. I suspect it's a little of both.

Tienda Magia is a little store in a building located off the aptly named Industrial Way. It has an industrial kitchen-for-hire on one side, a gym on the other, and is directly across from one of the great mysteries of town: The Paper Animal House. That's what I call it anyway. While it has no signs or indications as to what might be housed there, so I call it the Paper Animal House. A place that seems eternally closed.

Through its wide glass doors, one can see a small zoo's worth of life-sized papier-mâché animals. Giraffes, elephants, rhinos, oxen, and all sorts of other exotic animals rendered in painted paper. It's been there for years.

Tienda Magia is another, lesser mystery. They sell crystals, incense, oils, herbs, tarot cards, bones, teeth, and other oddments. A really, truly bizarre array of goods, many useful in magical rituals. Other goods are more useful in confidence scams to take money away from the grieving and lost.

The clientele, so far as I can tell, consists mainly of me, a couple of Bruja types that are into Santeria, and the emo kids from the local high schools and college. Somehow, despite Napa real estate prices, Tienda Magia stays in business. Tienda Magia and the Paper Animal House are two of the Seven Wonders of Napa in my book. That is, I wonder how the hell they stay open in a city like this.

The same woman sits behind the counter every time I'm here. She never says a word, and she never helps me. Anything I want at Tienda Magia I have to find on my own. The first time I came in and asked her where something was in English, she said in Spanish that she didn't understand English. When I repeated my question in the broken, pathetic Spanish I do speak, she responded in another language. I think it was Quechua, but I don't know. I don't speak Quechua. It could have been Navajo for all I know. I got the point. She doesn't want to talk to me.

I quickly gather up all of the items on Russ' shopping list. When I get to the counter, Circe is having a quiet conversation with the woman at the register. She laughs out loud at something the woman murmurs to her.

"She is delightfully wicked," Circe says to me as I heap my purchases on the counter.

"I bet she is," I say, eyeing the woman. She smiles at me, her teeth I notice for the first time are mostly silver crowns.

I pay for all of the stuff and walk out without another word. I glance at my phone.

"Shit!" I say. I forgot that I had called for a ride-share, which was now waiting for me at the coffee shop. Oh well, I'll get charged for the ride anyway. Stupid.

"Where to next, hot pants?" Circe asks me.

"They are only hot because I wet them," I say. "You drive like a maniac."

"That's the nicest thing you've ever said to me," Circe says, climbing back onto her bike.

Reluctantly I climb on the back once more. The most blissful thing about abject terror is that your mind usually blocks it out and the memories fade quickly. That's what I'll spend the rest of my life telling myself when I wake up from recurring nightmares of this motorcycle ride.

We pull up to Russ's house after another ride from hell. I can only describe it as a barrage of hippy-dippy stuff. It's a single-story ranch tucked in a small side street of old town. Incongruous with its surrounding homes, it is painted bright purple. Wire and glass mobiles are hanging from almost all the branches of almost all of the many trees that dot the front yard. Lawn gnomes and stone Buddhas festoon the overgrown lawn, like ceremonial cairns. The front door has a giant rainbow heart painted on it. The wooden side gate stands open and I can see into the backyard—which is choked with arbors and benches, all with hand-done tile work on them. I can see a dome of blankets I recognize as a sort of backyard sweat lodge. Hammocks hang between trees in the backyard like giant cobwebs.

Russ appears seemingly from out of nowhere.

"Hey! You made it!" He eyes Circe and observes her in three stages. The first pass is the pervy old man pass. His facial expression changes as there is something about her that makes him connect the dots. He reassesses her in potential threat mode. Having confirmed this fear, he goes for a third assessment, which I imagine is him trying to remember if he left any valuables out and if his living will is up to date.

Russ is holding the *Phantasmagoricon* in his arms.

"You gave him the book?" Circe asks me, eyes like daggers.

"This is Russ. He's a Lucid Dreamer and he can make far more use of it in this situation than I," I say flatly.

I shift my attention back to Russ.

"Russ, this is Circe. She's Hizarin, if that means anything to you."

"Explains a lot. Order of all-female, magic-vampire-assassins. Origins in the twelfth century. Read a lot about them on Mon-Anon."

"Mon-Anon? You read that trash?" I ask.

"Mon-Anon is a conspiracy board for kooks and nuts who follow monster sightings. Bigfoot runs the UN, lizard people are in congress, that sort of stupidity? Why would you believe anything you read there? And we aren't vampires," Circe says through clenched teeth.

"You drink blood," Russ says.

Circe's glower, while not confirmation, isn't a denial.

"You live for like what? Hundreds of years," Russ says.

"Only the truly skilled," Circe retorts.

"And I am guessing that you don't like garlic," Russ says.

"That's just a personal preference, not a requirement of being Hizarin," Circe grumbles.

"I rest my case," Russ says.

"We are alive; none of us are undead," Circe says.

I interrupt before this turns to bloodshed. "What say we get working on this? Circe is going to help us."

Russ shrugs, whatever his concerns may have been, his sniping with Circe has allowed him to move on. Or maybe he's just that laid-back.

"Okay. C'mon," Russ says as he leads us into his backyard.

The yard isn't that big, but it's been overgrown and thoroughly landscaped to make traversing it seem like a much bigger ordeal than it should be. We wind a narrow path through manicured shrubs, past benches and sundials, buddha statues, and succulent gardens until we come to a little clearing. There is an outdoor daybed in the middle, surrounded by incense holders and the like.

I hand Russ a large paper bag containing all of the stuff from his list. He rifles through it, setting crystals down, and filling braziers with incense. He gets to the bottom of the bag and looks at me.

"Where's the peyote?" he asks. "To try to get in the mind state I need in the timeframe you want, I'm going to need that now."

"Shit!" I say. In all the motorcycle riding, near death, semi-erotic shenanigans, I forgot the peyote.

"Here," Circe says, producing a small vial from a pocket. This is a bit of a mystery as her clothing is too tight to conceal anything, including this little vial.

"What's this?" Russ asks.

"It'll do the job. It's a tincture of mescaline and hashish oil and a selection of herbs. My own recipe," Circe says with a wink.

Russ looks skeptical, but eventually shrugs and takes the vial from her. He's clearly from an older generation that doesn't feel paranoid that anyone would give you bad drugs. I give him an alarmed look, but he either doesn't see it or is ignoring it.

"Okay, so what do you need now?" I ask skeptically.

"Now I enter the Dreaming and I find these Daunts you're looking for. I know how to drag them back into the Dreaming and trap them, thanks to my new book," Russ says, patting the *Phantasmagoricon.*

Circe raises a critical eyebrow at me. I ignore her.

"You get on to the rest of it. I've got this, dude," Russ says, then he ushers me closer. Circe rolls her eyes, but I get close.

"Are you sure you want to get involved with this chick, man? We don't know each other well, but I can tell she's no bueno, dude," Russ whispers to me.

"Yeah, I know. But she knows more about…well, all of this than I do," I whisper back.

"As long as you know what you're doing, man."

"Pretty sure I don't, but I have to do something."

"That's what makes it heroic. Fightin' the Man! I mean the proverbial man. I know Lorelei Redbrook is a woman," Russ says loudly.

Circe snorts a sound of derision. I can't tell if it's at the gender fumbling or the idea of heroism.

"Down with the proverbial man, Russ! I'll text you when I'm going to meet Redbrook," I say.

"Righteous, dude," he says. "But I'll probably be asleep."

I GIVE HIM A THUMBS UP, then Circe and I walk to her bike together. I look at my phone, it's 4:30 in the afternoon already. Where the hell did my day go?

"Okay, I have about an hour to get back to Lorelei. Can you drop me off at JMBaptiste? I'll get Whitman and you can do your thing. Wait, what exactly are you going to do?" I ask.

"I'll deal with her guards, clear the place out, and keep her distracted. You just dispel her wards."

"Okay. You sure this is going to work?"

Circe just nods as I get on the back of the bike. I am looking forward to when I'm not riding on this thing again. Circe rides like she can't die, and I don't know, maybe she can't. However, I am certain that I am not afforded the same luxury.

We make it to the JMBaptiste winery, violating numerous laws of both the state and physics. Circe drops me off and, before I can turn around, is showering the front door of the winery with gravel as she peels out of the parking lot.

I sigh and turn my face up to the late afternoon sun. I'm briefly on an adrenaline high, but by the time the growl of Circe's motorcycle has faded into nothing, the exhaustion catches back up with me. I turn and sullenly march toward the front door.

Chapter Twenty-One

I walk into the winery and head straight to Whitman's office. I knock on the door, but I am met with silence. The window is also dark. I have an instant of panic, thinking perhaps Redbrook sent someone to finish the job after all. I try the door and discover it is unlocked. I open the door and go inside. I look behind the desk, under the desk, and in the small storage closet in the corner.

No Whitman.

I return to the tasting room and ask the server if Whitman is around. I'm told Whitman left a while ago, around the time when I visited this morning. Damn it! I forgot that he said he was going home while I was talking to Russ earlier. I subvocalize a string of expletives, then out loud I thank the server and step outside to call Whitman.

The phone rings and rings, I'm almost certain it is about to go to voicemail when Whitman answers. He doesn't sound good.

"Herlo!" he says. He sounds like he's trying to imitate Robin Williams imitating Julia Childs.

"Mr. Whitman, it's Miles Ward."

"Shit. Sorry, I'm playing hooky from work-y today!" he slurs.

"Are you drunk?"

"I'm somewhere between shit-faced and blacking out," he says earnestly.

"Great…"

"I figured I was gonna die. Tonight. So I might as well drink all the good stuff I've been saving for a specific…a pecial. Especial. For an occasion," he says. I can hear him slurping wine to punctuate his sentence.

"I mean, what more sp…what more occasion could there be?" he declares drunkenly.

"Well. You're not driving. Where do you live?"

He mutters an address. I have to get him to repeat it three times before I can make out his words. I don't recognize the street.

"Alright," I say. "Stay put, I'll come by to get you."

"I'm just gonna finish this bottle then," he slurs.

"Sure, that sounds healthy. We will take your car," I sigh. "But I'm driving."

He's murmuring incoherently when I hang up. No sooner do I hang up and start to look up Whitman's address than another call comes in. I answer immediately when I see it's Jeff.

"Hey, Jeff, what's up?"

"I have a little surprise for you."

"I'm not sure now is the best time," I say, I probably sound pretty stressed and frantic.

"What's going on?" he asks, concerned.

I bring him up to speed on what's going on as quickly as possible while trying to figure out how I am going to get to Whitman's.

"I have something that will interest you. It's pretty cool. Can you come by my work?"

"I will as soon as I can, okay?"

"Of course."

"Thanks, Jeff. I'll see you soon…ish," I say and then hang up.

I look up Whitman's address. It's not too far away, but on surface streets, there is a lot of zig-zagging and doubling back to get there from here. However, I notice it's just off the river trail, if I head down Big Ranch Road, cross Trancas to the trail, and then jump the fence, it will shave quite a bit of time off the trip.

I start walking toward the road and I notice that the winery has an automated bike rental out front. Perfect. I tap my credit card and pull a bike out of the rack. I race there as fast as I can on the bike. I'm not used to biking, so despite not being in terrible shape, I am puffing and sweating by the time I reach the fence behind Whitman's condo complex.

I lift the rented bike over the fence and drop it. It's only a little drop. I wince as the bike clatters and bangs onto the ground. I jump and lift myself over the fence. I roll the bike two doors up to Whitman's condo. In the driveway is a slightly older BMW with the door open. I quickly stow the rented bike behind the side gate of his unit and go to check out the car.

Whitman is in the passenger seat, passed out cold, but he had the presence of mind to put his car keys in the ignition first. I didn't see that coming.

I have to adjust the seat around as Whitman is a bit taller than me. He also apparently prefers driving in a near-supine position. Once I have the seat fully adjusted, I begin to drive to the outskirts of town and The Lantern. I'm just getting to the freeway when I remember Jeff's call. So, I get off the freeway after one exit and loop back north. I don't have a ton of time for this, but Jeff seemed certain I would want whatever his "surprise" is.

I call Jeff on the way to let him know that I will be there, but I don't have a lot of time. Jeff is waiting in the parking lot when I arrive. He hands me a paper bag and explains its contents to me. I thank him and take off. Inside is a spray bottle of clear liquid. I slide it into my pocket. If it's even half of what Jeff says it is, I am sure glad I made this detour.

When we get to The Lantern, the parking lot is basically

empty, which seems improbable for 6:03 on a Thursday evening. It takes me a few minutes of prodding before I can get Whitman up and on his feet. His presence at this point seems a formality, but I would hate for this whole thing to go sideways on account of formalities.

I have to put an arm under Whitman's shoulder and all but carry him with me into The Lantern. He's incoherent and staggering. He bears some of his weight, but if I let go of Whitman he would just fall into a drunken heap on the ground. He smells bad, I don't think he's showered in days and his breath smells like a stale wine barrel. I have to half kick the door open to get in while guiding the drunken man.

As I turn the corner into the room, I feel like I'm in a cowboy movie, walking into the saloon before a gunfight.

It's probably more accurate than I would like, so I push the thought from my mind.

Chapter Twenty-Two

The Lantern is empty. There are no bartenders, no patrons, no staff, and the doorman isn't sitting by the Red Door. It's what Circe said she'd do, but it's still a little ominous.

"You know what, Miles?" Whitman slurs in my ear. "I love you, man. No really, I know I've been a hard-ass, but you are a good guy."

"And you are very drunk," I say as we make our way across the bar.

I clumsily heave open The Red Door. Whitman and I climb our way up the black-carpeted stairs to the second floor. He is slurring my praises into my ear and showering me with spittle the whole way.

We turn the corner into the card room. Lorelei Redbrook sits at a table in the center of the room, holding a pocket watch conspicuously. There are four cocktail waitresses there too. However, they no longer look haggard and harassed; they look vigilant and on edge. I sure hope that Russ is holding up his end; otherwise, this is going to get ugly.

Lorelei Redbrook clucks her tongue and wags a corpulent finger at us.

"You boys are five minutes late, and I do not abide by tardiness," she taunts. She's enjoying this.

We sit down across the table from her. I have to help Whitman into his seat, and he slumps over face down on the table the instant he sits. By the time I sit next to him, he's asleep.

"What is it going to be Mr. Ward?" she says, smiling, her filed teeth looking particularly menacing in the ambient gloom. She must have a way of hiding them, I can't imagine the look going over well in a candidate debate.

"I'll take Whitman's debt. But he's out. Completely. You just forget he exists."

"That's delightful," Lorelei says.

"The problem is, I don't trust you. What sort of assurance do I have that you leave him alone? How do I know you'll hold up your end of this bargain?"

"I offer a blood pact," she says boldly, seeming almost insulted that I might doubt her.

"A blood pact," I say. I have no idea what that is. I mean, obviously I know it's a pact, an oath or agreement—one that's probably signed in blood. But other than being a melodramatic effect for cinematic storytelling, I don't know why this should be an assurance. That doesn't stop me from faking it though.

"A pact ritually signed in our mingled blood means mutually assured destruction if the pact is broken. We welch, we destroy the pact, the curse destroys us both. It's old magic, some of the oldest," she says, sneering.

Maybe I'm not faking it as well as I thought.

"A blood pact. Let's do this," I say, but a voice in the back of my brain is screaming to *run, run away!* I really should listen to that voice more. But not today, today it is being drowned out by a voice that boldly tells me: *"You've got this, Miles! You've got a plan here, disable her minions. Disable her lair and wards and she's powerless."*

Signing a blood pact wasn't part of the plan, but a good plan often requires improvisation to make it work. She produces a knife and cuts herself on the back of the forearm and pools a little blood into a small glass bowl. She slides the bowl to me. I notice her blood isn't red, it's a bluish purple so dark it's almost black. I produce a small pocket knife from my courier bag and do the same. Then I use the tip of my knife to swirl the blood together. Lorelei produces a quill—an old-timey one, not a modern pen attached to a feather—dips it into the impromptu inkwell, and writes:

"I, Lamia, vow that Charles Whitman shall come to no harm directly or indirectly by my hand and that I shall leave him to his Fate. I shall abide by all verbal agreements and pacts made with Miles Ward."

She has tight, neat, and entirely archaic handwriting. I also notice she signs it Lamia, not Lorelei Redbrook.

While she writes, I slowly wipe my blood over my forearm tattoos, activating my bond with Hank. This seems like as good a time as any to try out my simulacrum. A selection of the sigils I have tattooed on me always act as a sort of low-level protection in and of themselves, warding my body against magic. Since blood always flows through vessels in the skin around the tattoos, they are always sort of active.

However, putting blood on like this, for lack of a better word, primes the linkage between Hank and me. Theoretically allowing a much greater amount of energy to flow from me to the simulacrum.

Redbrook doesn't seem to notice, or if she does, she doesn't seem to care. I lean forward take the quill from her, and write:

"I, Miles Henry Ward, accept all of the debts as I understand them owed by Mr. Charles Whitman to Lamia aka Lorelei Redbrook and shall arrange compensation to her for all such debts as she has previously disclosed to me."

Henry isn't my middle name, but I think signing the Simulacrum's name in there will help in redirecting this spell to him.

She then murmurs a phrase in a language that isn't English. It might be ancient Greek; it has that sort of singsongy quality to it. I repeat it, as best I can. She grimaces in disgust at my enunciation but otherwise says nothing. As we finish, I feel a sort of queasy shaking feeling. It's a feeling that took me years to associate with being targeted with a hex, magic settling into my body. The feeling passes quickly.

"Excellent. That is done," she says. She has perspiration on her brow and looks a little paler if that's possible and queasy herself. So, whatever this blood pact is, it took a toll on her as well. She slides the paper so that it sits on the table between us.

Interesting.

As I watch her, it seems like the magic took an even bigger toll on her than me. The pale, sweaty look isn't fading like it is for me. This makes me think the simulacrum is working.

"Now on to business," Lorelei Redbrook says eagerly.

"No, I want to see him safely off before we talk," I say firmly. This was part of my plan.

"Ugh," she groans. "Very well."

I call for a ride. We sit in silence for the twenty minutes it takes for a car to arrive. When it does, I escort Whitman down to it. I explain to Raul, the driver, that he needs to get home safely. Raul gives me a thumbs up and they head off.

I stand in front of The Lantern and watch them go. I pause to ponder the irony if I bound my soul to a Lamia to save the guy and something bad happens to him on his drunken way home. I usually love irony, but I'm not so fond of this version.

As I turn to head back in, I notice the intricate runes carved into the lintel and head of the door. I examine them for a moment, they are complex, a web, just like Circe said. Break a couple of strands and the whole thing unravels.

My original plan was to go old school, to take a magic marker and change the runes around. This could work, but it's not reliable. Thankfully I've upped my game in the last hour.

I pull Jeff's spray bottle out of my pocket and spray the runes around the door. Then I walk back inside. The bar inside is still empty, and I notice that there are magical glyphs incorporated into most of the structure and decor. Sigils carved into support beams, incorporated into the artwork. I spray them all as I walk by. The smell of acetic acid begins to overpower the smells of stale cigarettes and beer.

I get into the black stairwell leading up to the card room, I can't see runes in here, but with the lighting and everything, it would be hard. I spray it all as I go, using about half of Jeff's bottle on my way back up to the card room.

I sashay around the corner at the top of the stairs and into the card room. I am trying to look casual and unconcerned. This is as much to quiet my concern as trying to throw Redbrook off a little. It seems my casual and unconcerned look isn't working as well as I hoped.

"Okay, Redbrook. We've blood pact'ed. Mr. Whitman is off and away. What do you want from me?"

She laughs.

"Direct. I like it," she says in her high pitched, screeching voice.

"It seems like at this point, there is no point in us beating around the bush."

"I want you to work for us, Mr. Ward."

This was not what I was expecting.

"Who is 'us' exactly?" I ask though I have a suspicion that I know the answer. The answer still confuses the hell out of me, but I think I know.

"The Dominium Doloris," she says.

There it is.

"The Masters of Pain," I say. I finally dig up a more fluid translation from my head. "Yeah, that sounds like the employer I want to work under."

"I would forgive all of your debts, and you'd be paid and paid well."

"That's what this was all about? Getting me to work for you? This is a very elaborate scheme just to get me on the payroll."

"No, no, you weren't in my plans until you walked in that door yesterday. I was just going to make an example out of Whitman, so those other jokers knew what I was about. But when you walked in my door, I thought 'Whew, Miles Ward, now that'd be a feather in my cap'," she explains.

"I don't follow. I mean, 'thorn in my side' I've been called, but 'feather in my cap'? I don't think so. I'm nobody."

"Not to the Dominium," she says. "You are a rockstar, exactly the kind of fresh blood we are looking for."

"Yeah, sorry I still don't follow," I say, and that's the truth.

"The Syzmek Building. Genius!" she exclaims.

I'm still confused. I look at her for a moment blankly.

"Ah," she sighs. "Not as much vision as I hoped. You see, Miles. Can I call you Miles?"

I nod, my brain racing to try to figure out what her game is.

"Miles, when I was young, your kind would bring their firstborn children as sacrifices to me. To placate me. To please me. I didn't have to hide in the shadows! I didn't have to change my name or my face. I didn't have to hide among you. I was free! We were free! But your kind grew powerful. You found ways to chase us into the dark, to force us all into hiding. You took our freedom."

It strikes me how it seems it is always the most entitled that yell loudest about their loss of freedom.

"Magic! Ugh! But magic is fading, it's slowly been leaving our world for centuries. We want our lives back, our freedom back. We have been working for decades to come out of the shadows. We want the world to know that Monsters exist. We want them to know that we exist. We want to take our place as celebrities, as captains of industry, and as Rulers of the World. The balance restored. The hunters will no more be the hunted. We've been hiding for too long, and now is the time. The world is ready to accept anything!" she rants and raves.

"Okay. I get that, social media has broken down a lot of peoples' grip on what is and isn't real, and now the fringe stuff is more acceptable. But still…" I say, still not sure where this is going, "is it ready for Pandora's Box to open?"

"Yes, and you have done it, Miles! You have undone the latch on that box. You have bridged the divide. You've even made it fashionable for corporations to use magic," she says, excited.

"No, I mean companies have been doing mystical feng shui for years, longer than I've been alive," I retort.

"Yes, individuals have incorporated little bits of mysticism and magic into their professional lives. But you. *You.* You integrated it into a major corporate building, you brought it to scale, you got it in magazines. You are an innovator. The day you hired on to the Syzmek building project, you made history!"

"Syzmek hired me, they were going to do all of that anyway."

"Oh, I know you aren't the real innovator. You aren't the idea guy, but you are a name and a face we can work with, and you are a good story, Miles. Sign up with us and you'll go far."

"I'm a scam artist and a con man if you believe the internet."

"It depends on where on the Internet you look. There are places where you are regarded as a hero, an innovator," she says. "And that's who we want, someone with the brazen audacity to pitch a major corporation on this stuff and the boldness to follow through. We can make you a star. We can make you immortal."

"And what if I say no?"

"Then you owe me three point one million dollars as of twenty minutes ago. Mr. Whitman, I am afraid, was not a very good gambler and was easily influenced."

"Influenced?" I say with surprise, the kind of surprise that immediately dispels itself and is replaced by mental self-flagellation. Of course, he was influenced; Lorelei Redbrook isn't going to play a fair game.

She laughs.

I try to remember the runes I did see in my head, a bunch of focal stuff, very basic redirections, and—

"Everyone here is under a spell. There's a compulsion curse on the whole building. A compulsion of…recklessness," I say.

Of course. If you are going to run a bar and an underground gambling operation, what better way to make it successful than to put a curse that compels everyone inside to take risks, that shaves away a little bit of their inhibitions, that quiets the voice in peoples head that says no.

"Good eye! Something like that, yes," she responds, looking giddy.

"That's why I signed that blood pact, even though I knew it was a bad idea. I'm being magically compelled to recklessness. In hindsight, it's so obvious."

"Yes, it means I get more bar fights, thefts, and the like, but it sure is good for business," she says gleefully.

The smell of vinegar and nail polish remover wafting up from downstairs has become quite strong now.

"But I am feeling less reckless now."

"Not that it will help you much," she says, showing her full mouth of sharpened teeth. She has more teeth than a normal person.

I sigh and rub the bridge of my nose, trying to think for a second. I am feeling less reckless, the plan must be working, and her spells, her lair is fading. I need to find a way to undo that pact. I look to the center of the table where it was when I went to take Whitman down stairs.

"Okay," I say. "What did you do with the blood pact?"

I indicate the center of the table where the paper signed in both of our blood had been sitting.

Lorelei looks at the table in front of her. I give her a questioning look. The blood pact isn't there. I assumed she'd stored it when I went to put Whitman in the car. But the expression on her face says that isn't true.

"Tsk. Tsk," a sultry voice in the corner says.

Appearing out of the shadows is Circe. She's ditched the skintight motorcycle leathers for a skintight black cloth suit with a triangle cut out for her cleavage and completely bare midriff. She has lots of pockets and flexible split-toed cloth boots. The outfit is complete with the purple bikini sewn on the outside, and her hair done up into an improbable topknot. She looks like a kunoichi straight from an anime.

Circe is holding the blood-pact in one hand.

"*You,*" Lorelei hisses between her teeth. Lorelei makes a motion with her hand. The four cocktail waitresses all hiss, their necks and limbs contorting unnaturally as they crouch to pounce. They suddenly look like marionettes, heads bent at odd angles. Limbs moving in directions they weren't meant to. All to a chorus of popping cartilage and creaking bones.

The waitresses charge, but Circe simply waves her hand and speaks a short incantation in a language I don't understand. The four waitresses fall to the ground, like puppets whose strings have been cut. They hit with a dull, dead weight on the ground, four successive thuds.

"How can you do that?" Lorelei shrieks at her. "You should not be able to cast like that here."

Circe laughs. "Somebody broke your wards," she says in a high-pitched, mocking voice.

Both of them both look at me—Circe amused and Lorelei with rage in her eyes.

"How?" Lorelei demands in a strangled howl.

"Magicians never tell their secrets," I say.

Circe smiles. "Still not giving up your tricks, I see.""Why are you doing this?" Lorelei demands, looking first at me and then at Circe.

"The Hizarin knows about your plan to go public. We can't have that. We exist in the dark. We work in the dark. We make money on the mystery, if you make it so everyone knows, then our business gets harder. So, when you die, the Dominium Doloris will hopefully get the message," Circe says.

Lorelei cackles; that's the best sound I can use to describe it. A horrible laugh like a stereotypical, green-skinned witch with a pointed hat. I think I can hear the sobs of children echoing in her awful, awful laugh.

"You can't kill me. No mortal magic can kill me," Redbrook exclaims.

"Mortal magic cannot. But your magic can," Circe says, holding up the blood pact.

Lorelei's smug expression fades to understanding and then to horror.

"But that will kill him as well," Redbrook says, indicating me.

Now it's my turn to look horrified.

"You're going to kill me?"

"Sorry Miles. You're cute, but it would never work out between us," Circe says, producing a palmed lighter in her other hand. She begins chanting and weeping blood from her eyes and nose. There is a high-pitched yelp of horror that I realize after a second came from my mouth.

Lorelei's face distorts, her teeth seem more pronounced and her eyes bulge. She looks now like the monster that I've been led to believe she is.

I pull the spray bottle out of my pocket and spray a heavy cloud between us as Circe lights the paper on fire. My skin feels hot, and I start to noticeably sweat. The tattoos on my arms that link me to Hank start to itch and then burn. I fall to my knees. Circe keeps chanting.

Lorelei Redbrook is smoking, and I don't mean a cigarette. A plume of smoke is coming up from her hair. An instant later I see that, as I suspected, her hair is a wig. She casts it aside, and it flops onto the floor like an exhausted Pomeranian. Her makeup has burned away and now she no longer looks human at all but like a corpulent, bactrian, child-eating monster.

I would scream at the sight of Redbrook's now inhuman, hunched, bloated, and blistering form, but I am already screaming from the burning pain in my skin, my bones, and my stomach. I'd run madly from the room to escape the great toad-like thing on the other side of the table from me, but my muscles feel like they are on fire and my legs don't seem to work.

Lorelei Redbrook thrashes and howls. I look up at Circe, and she's holding the last bit of burning paper. The look on her face is grim; she is covered in blood, and it seems to be sweating out her pores now.

"I really am sorry, Miles," she says. "This was the only way to get rid of her. And you. You are too much of a liability. Everything she said is correct, you are outing the magical community. You are like a kindergartener who learns how to play with matches, trying to teach all the other kids. It's just not safe, I'm afraid. Goodbye."

The pain is horrible; but then as the paper vanishes, I feel something snap. I can feel the link to Hank break. Poor, poor Hank. He's provided all the protection he can.

Thanks, buddy.

I spray the water bottle all over myself, and it cools the burning. A bit.

And then the pain subsides, and I feel the panic draining out of my mind. I can think clearly again. Relatively clearly anyway.

I understand that Redbrook and I ritually bound ourselves together with the blood pact. I also understand that Circe used the blood pact to channel energy into both of us. However, I don't know where she drew enough heat energy to incinerate two people from. Maybe the lighter itself is enchanted. Or maybe this is just what the pact did when broken.

I look over at Lorelei on the ground, unmoving. Her body is just a charred heap now with a few tendrils of noxious smoke rising from it. A horrible stench has filled the room—a mix of smoke, charred flesh, vinegar, and acetone. Circe seems unfazed by this, but she is staring at me in awe.

"You continue to amaze me, Miles," she says, her mouth ajar. "How are you still alive? This is impossible."

"Not for The Blethspa Amah," I say. I mean I have no idea what it means, and frankly, I assume it is gibberish, but it's also true. If not for Jeff's spray, I don't think I would have survived. I push myself to my feet and try to stand tall and confident. It hurts too much to succeed at either.

"*You* are the Blethspa Amah?" she asks, her mouth agape, the look on her face is one of awe with a touch of horror.

I may have made a tactical error in saying that, but it's too late now. I am going to have to stick with my bluff. I am assuming she is the one that tattoos Jeff and dragged him into all this in the first place. I can't get poor Jeff onto her radar again.

"What'd you think I was just some slacker Napkin?" I say with as much bravado as I can muster.

"No, no, it makes perfect sense. It's just that the Blethspa Amah is a myth. Or I thought it was a myth," she answers, biting her lower lip in thought. Self-doubt looks incongruous on her face.

"Alright, well I'll just be on my way then, shall I?" I say, backing my way toward the door.

"No. I don't think so. I can't kill you; you are too valuable. But I think I am going to take you with me," she says, offhanded as you might say to a goldfish at the pet store that you decided to buy on a whim.

I've wondered why Circe is so open about her plans and motivations and I think that's it. She views me as a cute and entertaining pet that she'll just flush down the toilet if I turn up dead in the tank one day.

"Cool," I say. "Cool, cool. I'll just go sit over there and wait till you are ready to go?"

Okay Miles, new plan. I wait for her to look away for a second and then run. But you know what they say about the best-laid plans.

Chapter Twenty-Three

From outside, a chorus of car horns, one of which is playing "Dixie," suddenly floods the room with light.

I look over at Circe quizzically; she looks back at me and shrugs. Surprise has put an unspoken temporary truce on the table. We both turn and look out the window. The building is semi-circled by a dozen pickup trucks, all with the headlights facing toward The Lantern. It's hard to see past the lights, but there are twenty or so silhouettes of men standing between and in the beds of the trucks. Many of the silhouettes seem to have rifles.

"The Knights of St. George," I say as I slowly do the math in my head.

I imagine Circe is doing the same. Bullets damage with kinetic energy. One could block them with magic, but it would take an equal and opposite amount of energy to do so. That many guns firing that many bullets would run through whatever energy reserves Circe has left very fast.

"My job here is done. You should run," she says.

I start to ask where I should run exactly, but that is when the reports of automatic weapons begin. Circe jumps into the shadows and just vanishes again. I don't know how she does that, and I'm only a little jealous. Why didn't she take me with her? Jerk.

Windows are shattering and wood is splintering, all while there is a cacophony of muzzle flashes and rifle reports from outside. The world is turning to hell around me. The southwest corner of the building has no parking lot and so hopefully no gunmen. I run in that direction. There is an unbroken window there, and my plan is to jump through it.

I imagine myself looking like an action hero crashing through the window, flying through the air in a shower of flame and broken glass as the building explodes behind me. But when I get there, I find myself hastily opening the window and looking out. There is a tree not too far from the window. I can probably reach it. The gunfire continues, though there are occasional lulls as they reload. I sit on the window ledge ready to jump.

I'm going to jump.

Any second now. I will leave the safety of this bullet-riddled building to leap and grab onto that tree. I'm sure I won't fall short. I'm sure I won't miss and plummet to the ground and break my neck. My chances are much better with the tree than with the hail of bullets.

I'm going to jump. Like right now. Jump.

But I don't.

I sit paralyzed, crouched on the edge of the windowsill until the shooting stops, and I can hear a dozen trucks doing donuts in the driveway and then roaring off, one particularly obnoxious truck's horn is still playing Dixie as it goes.

Unwilling to go out the front door, even though it's silent now, I find a fire escape and climb down. I can hear sirens in the distance as I get to Whitman's car in the parking lot. Its windows have been smashed out and it too has been riddled with bullet holes. The same with the three other cars in the lot.

I don't want to be the lone witness to this fiasco. I dash across the street and find a culvert there. I duck into it only a moment before I can see the red and blue glow of the first police car drive by. I crouch down and scurry through the culvert as quickly as I can.

It's dark in there. But I don't dare produce a light. It smells, but I don't dare make a sound, not even the retching sound my throat wants to make. I move forward, groping through wet, disgusting things in the dark. At first, it feels like I am making amazing time, scurrying through this culvert, but as the feet stretch on it feels slower and slower and longer and longer. I glance back and there is nothing but darkness; I look forward, darkness.

The complete absence of light is something few of us see in the modern world. There's almost always something glowing or pulsing or reminding us that it is there plugged into the wall. This true, pitch black: it's unnerving. Lacking visual stimuli, my brain starts to create its own narrative of what's happening.

Imagined monsters lurk in the darkness. I can feel panic and claustrophobia building in my chest. I push it down and tell myself over and over in my head that I'll get out soon. And it will be light and the air will be fresh and all the monsters will be behind me.

It feels like I have been slogging on bruised knees through putrid muck in the dark for hours when I emerge out the other side. My legs are soaked to my knees in foul brown sludge, and my hands are covered in it. I'm scraped up and bruised all over from the hard metal tube. I stand and shake my sore limbs out as I look around.

I'm in a stand of high grass just below the freeway. I jog a dozen yards, stumbling through the overgrown vegetation and mud, and eventually come to a road. It's a side road in one of the industrial parks on the edge of town. I must be just west of the crusher statue on the south side of town. I've never been in this area before. I cross the road, to a stand of trees, and I sit down there to catch my breath.

"Well, that didn't go according to plan. Not that I had

much of a plan, but that wasn't it," I say aloud to no one in particular.

I lean against the tree. It's a species of willow. It's large, but the branches are long and narrow, going up high, but then have little leaf-covered tendrils hanging down in a wide canopy. Underneath is a little open area around the trunk. I sit down on the loamy ground with my back to the gnarled trunk.

I just need to rest for a minute.

What would I do without Jeff's magic spray bottle? I'd be dead, that's what. Good old Jeff.

Suddenly Jeff is there looking at me.

"Class, do you remember when we read about acetobacter?" Jeff asks.

I blink at him. What the hell is Jeff doing here? Why are we in Mr. Slokum's biology classroom? Why am I in nothing but my underwear?

I'm sitting at a desk. It's got a metal frame that attaches to a wooden back seat. The desktop is a slab of vinyl composite with a wood grain texture laminated on top. The surface has been heavily carved on. I don't look down to see what they say, but I can feel the etchings on the surface with my fingers. I slouch down in my seat and pull my biology book up in front of me to cover my bare skin.

Jeff is standing in the front of the class, like a lecturing high school teacher. He is holding a brown paper bag in one hand.

"Today we will perform a series of experiments in which we will attempt to isolate Acetobacter Magusficedula. The papers on your desk describe our experimental procedure, controls, and expected outcomes," Jeff continues to lecture.

I raise my hand.

"Mr. Ward." He points to me.

"What is going on, Jeff?" I ask.

"Please call me Mr. Reba. Acetobacter Magusficedula is a rare bacterium that I have discovered. It has the unique ability to consume magical energy. When exposed to a field of raw magical energy, such as that created inside an inclusive magic circle, the Acetobacter Magusficedula begins to reproduce at a geometric rate. The greater the concentration of magic, the faster they reproduce. Much like yeast might in a sugar-rich environment."

"Oh," I say. I am clearly confused.

"We will be experimenting with the size of the circle and quantities of blood. Finally, having demonstrated growth of the Acetobacter Magusficedula strain, we will attempt to inoculate an agar sample and isolate the strain. The intention of today's experiment will be to create a spray containing Acetobacter Magusficedula," Jeff explains.

"For what purpose?" I blurt out.

"Please, Mr. Ward, hands."

I raise my hand in the air and wave it around frantically.

"Yes, Mr. Ward?" he says, putting his hand to his forehead and sighing as he speaks.

"For what purpose?"

"To make a spray that will consume magic, and clean it away like a disinfecting spray. Such a concoction might be useful? Yes?"

I nod stupidly.

He opens the mysterious paper bag in his hand and pulls out a plastic spray bottle full of an almost clear liquid. He tosses it to me. As I catch it, I see that there is a faint pinkish tinge to the concoction.

"Wow, thanks."

"Miles, you're in trouble"

"What?"

"You're asleep and people are coming for you," Russ says.

It's no longer Jeff talking to me, it's Russ. I look around and realize I am no longer in a classroom. I'm on a battlefield with blood and bodies everywhere. I can see enormous house-sized standards flying in the distance and hear the din of battle, the clashing of swords, cries of pain, and the distant bellow of horns. But I don't see any combatants nearby.

"Wait, Russ…?" I am confused again.

"Yeah, dude. You're asleep. I'm in your dream, but you need to wake up, man," Russ says, he is wearing an intricate leather outfit, in browns and greens and an archer's cap. He has a bow slung from his shoulder and a quiver on his back. At his side is a huge mastiff.

"I'm asleep? But I was just talking to Jeff."

"Just dreaming, dude. Listen, I trapped the Daunts like you asked. Then I was like, I should keep an eye on that Miles guy, because he's gonna get into deep shit. Anyway, you're like asleep under a tree, a willow, I think. There are like two dudes are searching for you now. They are close."

"Okay, but how are you here? What is going on?"

"Oh, well the problem with Dream-walking like this is that I am kinda, like, stuck here until the drugs wear off. And whew let me tell you, amigo, whatever your friend gave me I'm not sure it's gonna wear off anytime soon."

"My friend?"

"Like the Hizarin. Man."

"She's not my friend. Don't trust her. She tried to kill me"

"I never trusted that chica, dude. Not surprised. Still, you're dreaming when you need to be movin'. You got to wake up now, man."

Wake Up.

Wake Up.

Chapter Twenty-Four

Movement 438 of the Ballad of Sir 'Rusty' Russeo the Russet Ranger of Russoshire, by Russell Russo

Early eve I consumed the tincture of the dark sorceress.
Then door I found and then door through I, dancing spritely, leapt.
And so, I pierced chimeric veil, and hail!
I awoke and rose from my aspen bower.
Up Korotrapki I did loft, mine weapon of power.
Crafted in forgotten days from the bows of great Yggdrasil.
Up my quiver, ever-full gift of the sprites of N'drazil.
Then girded fine in links mythyreal, I rose to face my quest.
And from my reva fortikajo I then traveled west,
With my most intrepid heart.
On vera vojo, I took up my horn
and blew to summon true,
Virĉevalo, my faithful hound,
who I would send to pursue.
"Virĉevalo!"
Said I.
"There is a beast so foul.
That we hunt in this dream,
That we hunt so long, too long to tell

Daunts that daunted me before
Whom mock and taunt and daunt me more
To send my soul to fly, and fell,
straighter than the straightest arrow.
Down down, straight to hell.
I now seek these, self-same for my new friend.
So, to the gloaming we wind and wend."
Virĉevalo raised his nose to the air
and inhaled deep once more there.
Twice, a roar
a third time before,
he scented his prey so fell
and with that let out a baying howl.
And lead on toward our quarry's smell.
In gloaming dusk Virĉevalo charged
and I took foot to chase.
Over creek and through green glen,
up high hill we raced
and then.
River forded and mountain climbed,
When day turned to night.
At long last we came to Tyr Hausteur where
Then I was destined to fight.
There dwelled the lost dreamer foul.
A warren of defenses.
There in the fetid loamy light,
a labyrinth to destroy my senses.
Army foul,
lost ancient haunts came to fight before.
Virĉevalo and I stood,
intrepid as the eldritch knights of yore.
A nightmare storm fell upon us then,
my heart it pounded quicker
when the smoke cleared in the end,
it was I that was the victor.
Through hall and door, through passage beyond

I swept and charged and stride
and soon to foul dreamer's throne room dark,
I did heroically arrive.
We battled high, we battled low,
we battled long and blow to blow
Until lost was Virĉevalo,
and to the earth my tears did flow.
Friend, I shall see you in the next world.
Then my nemesis I did strike and cleave.
His onslaught had no reprieve.
As finally I stood, toe to toe,
with my ancient and hated foe.
There I drew back my bow
I sought to land the final blow,
but he to waking world did go.
So, climb I did, from ground to high,
until my crown did touch the sky
And in that nightmare dreamers tower lie,
To north to south to west, east I looked sly
And in a shrouded bower, why
My compatriot lain fatigued, perhaps soon to die.
As to his place yon villains fly,
through the muck and mire.
To him I traveled and, in his shoe, I found a hidden way.
Into his tread I tread and slipped and crawled and hope and pray
but not before I raised my hands to shield eyes
from the sights that I might see that lies
In the thoughts of one so young, horny and alone.
In his mind though all I found,
A conversation to confound.
And so, into his dream I went
to finally bring it to an end.
"Wake my friend!"
I did call. "Wake and do not die!"
But my friend, he did not hear me cry.
And so his Reva Fortikaĵo I did siege,

With subterfuge then I did seize,
The keys of his ethereal sentries.
And I found myself a way,
that I might gain my entry.
Call then I did, times in number twelve.
So that through his dreams I then might delve.
There in twilight I did see,
the demons there did abound before me
through vine and hill and darkened alley
those Daunts did flee before me,
Their canine cadavers I did pursue.
With ancient bow, I did strike true.
But those Daunts that day, they did fight,
like no Daunts ever fought before with such might.
From my arrows they did not fall,
into my dream-ed flesh they slashed and tore,
For you see that they bore
armor there made of dream
from their mouths they spat forth streams
Of flame in gout and burning beams.
I battled hard as ages past,
but soon 'twas sure to be my last
when those baying sounds did blast
Approaching in upon me fast
echoing over glen and over dale.
Hope approached like an eastbound gale.
As to my side Virĉevalo flew,
now resuscitated
and in his mouth, he held to me,
An enchanted treasure bladed free.
The ancient blade that severed earth
from the land of dream
there was no thing it could not cut as
it hummed and shined and gleamed.
Sonĝoklingo, I did wield
on that fateful day

and severed hard the tethers marred
That bound the beasts to stay,
Thus, bonds severed they did to dream revert
and before me they did cower.
For then they did behold
Songôklingo's awesome power.
Unincepted, I did go
Searching high and searching low
and to him I did speak
and so, it was he woke
before the night ran bleak.
Across the realm the faeries came,
and the exalted Sidhe
and puck and goblin to come to join
in the grand party.
Revel then did all the creatures
With their sultry exquisite features,
until once more 'twas time to wake
before the first sunbeams.

Chapter Twenty-Five

Wake Up!

My eyes snap open.

I fell asleep under the tree. Apparently having a sorceress try to burn me from the inside out took a lot out of me. Maybe it was the sewer crawling. Maybe it was the biking across town or getting run off the road and chased through a vineyard. Maybe it was because I didn't sleep last night.

Actually, thinking about it now, I am not sure how I didn't spontaneously fall asleep earlier. Man, I could use a cup of coffee.

I was dreaming about the crazy magic-eating spray that Jeff gave me right before I came out here. I am certain it saved my life. I look around, remembering what Russ told me in my dream.

People are looking for me. I glance out between the boughs of the tree; it takes me a minute scanning the darkness, but I can see them. They are getting closer. Two men. One of their outlines and movement I recognize even from his silhouette.

Eric Walsh. Again. What the hell?

The other must be his friend who wrecked my Jeep with

him. How the hell did they find me? There must be magic involved; there's no other explanation.

I can see Eric stumbling along in the dark, walking more slowly behind his friend. The other, however, walks unerringly across the field on the other side of the street. Like a bloodhound, he traces the exact route I took to get to my current location.

I pull a crystal out of my mud-crusted courier bag and hold it between my thumb and index finger. I take a deep breath and center myself. Aura reading is unreliable at best. It's kind of like meteorology. You use a method to make a prediction. The prediction may or may not be true and will probably be a gradation of both. No matter what, if you tell your prediction to anyone, you will be some percent wrong, which usually in the human mind, just means wrong. I go to aura reading as a sort of last resort.

The problem with aura reading is that most people have basically normal, neutral auras. They ebb and flow based on moods, state of mind, health, and a million other potential factors.

You might look at a person's aura and see a tie-dye of colors blending and mixing. Then you might see a black shadow hanging around them, as they think about something that makes them sad, but it fades the instant they get distracted. A normal aura is constantly moving, shifting, and changing as the person does. It's hard to read. Meaning and significance are contextual depending on the individual as well as the observer.

In most cases just reading facial expressions is a more useful and reliable way of gathering information about someone.

I learned to read auras when I was a kid; my new-age, grifter dad taught me how. It has minimal uses and I don't do it very often. As a result, I am not particularly good at it, and still have to use a crystal to help me focus…or rather unfocus on the subject. This is a little bit of an embarrassing thing for me to admit. Most people with any experience at all can just read auras without the proverbial training wheels.

The only reason I keep the crystal on me—the only reason I ever consider resorting to this particular tool—is because much like meteorology, aura reading is highly accurate when things have gone very wrong.

Much like it is easy to accurately predict a hurricane as the 100-mile-an-hour winds and rain rip the shutters off your home, it's easy to tell when a normal, fluctuating, multifaceted human's aura is wrong.

This man with Eric has an aura that is wrong. Very wrong. A flat, uniform gray. No movement. No ebb. No flow. A single thin red strand leaving the nape of his neck and trailing off into the night somewhere behind him. This is not what a human aura looks like. Or at least this isn't the aura of a normal, healthy human.

This is the aura of the enthralled.

This is one of the areas of magic that I know quite a bit about. It is possible through magic, by using a constant, sustained barrage of antipathetic energy to drain someone of their free will. It takes months, years sometimes to subvert one's ability to think and turn them into little more than a mindless robot.

It is an intimate, personal, and abominable magic.

This is one of the most horrifying uses of magic there is. It is also, sadly, a pretty common use. Most people that do this are sloppy and it doesn't last long. They simply don't maintain the onslaught for long enough, and the human brain or maybe the soul is surprisingly resilient. If it's done skillfully and maintained long enough, though, it can reduce a person to little more than an automaton, subverting their will forever.

Like my friend Shelly in college.

And that is what had happened to this man. I can tell by the clean-edged lines of his almost perfectly uniform aura that this man is controlled by a pro; there is almost nothing remaining of the individual. I note as well that they have used magic to modify him, make him faster, stronger, have better eyesight and sense of smell.

Different cultures and traditions call such victims many different things. Everything about him—mind, body, and if you accept that sort of thing, soul—has been carefully altered, crafted, and tweaked to fulfill the purpose of another.

When I first learned about the enthralled, I came to know them as Fetch. It's an old term. I'm not sure where it comes from. Maybe Mean Girls. Eric's friend is the victim of an expert's touch. Stories of zombies, ghouls, ghasts, or other undead horrors are often based on the Fetch, as they might as well be the walking dead.

I think of a Fetch as an "it"; this is not to demean the person that it was, but more to recognize that what is chasing me, what is trying to kill me, isn't human anymore. It had its humanity taken away from it, its identity effaced, its goals, hopes, and dreams all destroyed.

Now all that is left is the flesh and bone vessel. Used like a toy. Like a puppet. It's disgusting, but I might be in a situation where I have to hurt it or worse. I still respect the person that was, even if I don't respect the thing that is.

Disassociation makes dealing with it easier.

I have only a minute or so before the Fetch gets to me, with Eric close behind it. I glance briefly at Eric's aura. He appears fundamentally normal and human, though I note there is a blackish-red, oozy-looking stuff on the edges of his aura. He has probably attempted to alter himself with magic and this black-red ooze is the fallout from that effort, a sort of decay on his being. If he keeps up with the amateur work, he could do real damage to himself.

I take a canister of salt out of my messenger bag and hastily make a circle around the area beneath the trees. I fumble for a piece of chalk as I see the Fetch perk up. Getting a whiff of me, it charges. I hastily chalk a symbol on a root on the inside of the circle. I call this sigil the Duck-Shield, because I think it looks kind of like a duck outline on a shield.

It is the quickest and sloppiest way of preventing energy from flowing into the circle. I scrape open the wound on the back of my arm where I cut it before. It hurts like hell. I smear a bit of the blood on the sigil and chant my incantation.

I'm interrupted as the Fetch blindsides me and shoves me to the ground. It pulls an immense knife out of a sheath it wears on its back under its shirt and begins to lower itself toward me like a predator about to pounce.

I finish my incantation. It freezes, like it's stopped in time, but only for an instant. Then it collapses to the ground in a heap. I grab it by the shoulders and guide it to the ground, so it doesn't break the boundary of my exclusive circle. While it won't last long, the circle prevents energy from flowing in—the very energy that is being used to control the Fetch like a puppet. If I could still see its aura, I'd see that red strand I saw before severed, cutting off the control-line between it and its creator.

As I said, unfortunately, this isn't my first time dealing with this sort of thing. I scramble to my feet as Eric bursts into the stand of trees. I take off running. I can hear him yelling at the Fetch behind me.

"Get up! Get him! What the hell, man?" Eric yells.

The delay gives me a little bit of a head start before Eric curses and begins chasing me.

He is faster than me, but I've got a head start and more endurance. I hope it's enough. I run down the street and turn hard right on the sidewalk around an old industrial building. I glance back and Eric is still chasing me. In fact, he's regained the ground he lost yelling at the Fetch.

I turn another corner and another. I have no idea where I am. I've been in this area maybe twice to go to the DMV. This just isn't a part of town that I'm familiar with. The small side road I am on leads to a larger road, and I turn left. Eric's still behind me, but we seem to have fallen into a jogging contest at this point. I have maybe a thirty-foot lead.

Ahead of me is a large chain link fence. There is a big sign warning me of all of the hazards I will encounter beyond and that I should keep out. I don't have more than an instant to weigh my choices and I sprint toward the fence and leap.

I grab on and scurry up as fast as I can. I can hear Eric hit the fence and an instant later I feel the impact. The fence lurches suddenly and I almost get launched off. I can feel him batting and scrabbling at my feet as I vault to the other side and land roughly on the ground, falling and scraping my already cut and bruised hands and knees as I catch myself.

The asphalt on the other side of the fence is bedazzled with broken glass. It cuts into my flesh as I push myself back to my feet.

I bite down a yelp and glance over to see Eric begin climbing the fence. I look around and spot a piece of rusted metal, I think it might once have been a signpost.

I grab the rusty shaft and turn. Eric is just getting to the top of the fence, and I hurl it up at him like a javelin. It hits him in the arm, not doing much damage but he loses his grip with the arm and his legs slip, leaving him hanging at the top of the far side of the fence by one hand.

Waiting for him to recover would be foolish, so I turn and run as fast as I can into the darkness. I've never been out here, but I know where I am now. It's called the Napa Pipes.

Once upon a time, a huge industrial pipe factory was here. It closed at some point, but the ground remained all toxic with lead and mercury and who knows what else. For years, the city has been trying to clean it up to use the space for residential and commercial construction. However, for some reason, it has never come to pass.

The Pipes are dark and desolate, a huge swath of concrete dotted with rows of crumbled foundations of buildings long gone and the rusted husks of the industrial buildings that remain. A few huge old loading cranes stand rusted by a dry canal, in the darkness, they look like looming ancient, fossilized skeletons of great robotic dinosaurs. The concrete is weather-worn and cracked, and a carpet of weeds zig-zags its way across the ground like leafy lightning. It's quiet and the only sound I can hear over my ragged breathing and pounding heart is the constant low din of distant road traffic.

My best thinking is always done while running, so I run, pumping my arms and legs, occasionally tripping on detritus in the darkness.

The only person I know of who might be skilled enough to have destroyed that poor man and turned him into that Fetch is Circe. Lorelei Redbrook might have been capable, but as far as I know, she's dead—which sort of rules her out.

If it was Circe, what is her relationship with Eric Walsh? Is that new or did that exist when I dealt with Eric's creepy stalking awhile back? That would mean everything Circe has done is even more personal than she's let on. It also means that Eric had wanted to get caught.

All her sudden moments of inexplicable openness and honesty could simply be smoke and mirrors to distract me from the truth. Not that this is the first time I've suspected this, however, this makes it more probable. But this all seems so intricate and complex; I just don't know.

There is a lot that I just don't know.

There is an immense metal structure ahead of me. It looks like an old warehouse or hangar. It's all iron struts sided with rusted corrugated metal sheets. I dash toward it and duck inside. I quickly find an old rusted-out steel drum and hide behind it, crouching down and trying to catch my breath. I try not to think about what might be stored inside the drum.

It isn't long before I can hear Eric's heavy footsteps and labored breathing fill the building. I can tell by the cadence of his walk that he's limping a bit now. He must have twisted his ankle or something. I try to time my breath with his so that he can't hear me over his own wheezing.

As I get my breathing under control, I can hear something else. Voices perhaps, at the far end of the warehouse. There must be a small homeless camp in this structure we are in. It breaks my heart that here, amid all this wealth and affluence of The Valley, vast encampments of homeless exist.

I hear Eric start in that direction.

I wait a moment before peeking out. His silhouette is backlit by the faint ambient light filtering in through holes and openings in the tin roof. I wait until he's far enough away and I move low and quietly back out the way I came in.

I find a stand of large weeds that's grown up through the asphalt, and I duck down into it to give me cover while I think about what to do next.

There are raised voices inside the metal building. Eric is hassling whoever is in there, but it doesn't sound like violence is occurring—at least not yet. I have to pee, and this seems like my only shot, so I trot across the broken asphalt to one of the rusted-out old loaders. I stand with my back to it and relieve myself into a dried-up old canal. I look out across the river to the west. A huge marsh extends from here to the freeway, with the river running through the middle. The expanse is covered with reeds and cattails. There is a kind of muddy sulfurous smell, that comes with drying mud and tidal muck.

On the far side, I can see a huge stand of eucalyptus silhouetted in the twinkling lights of cars on the freeway. Despite the smell and the perilous moment, there is a sort of beauty to it. No matter what is happening here and now, the world is still happening, it's still moving on. People are still going places and doing things.

In my mind's eye, I look down on myself, urinating behind a rusted-out crane, covered in mud, admiring traffic. All while I am being hunted down by vampires, monsters, and angry frat boys.

Life is strange.

I finish my business and map out my next move.

I am tired. I am sore. I am hungry. I need to get out of here.

I could go back the way I came, but that leaves me stranded out on the edge of town and nearer The Lantern. If

I make my way north along the river, it will bring me to Kennedy Park, and from there I can take the River Trail downtown.

Even though I don't know where I am going between here and the park, I'll have to take that risk. I start across the asphalt and come to a concrete berm. As I am about to jump over it, I feel my phone vibrate in my pocket. I quickly take it out and glance at it.

The call is from Emily. For the first time, I realize: It's late. It's nine o'clock. I missed our date by an hour. I consider answering the phone, but that seems like a good way of getting myself killed.

I slide it back into my pocket and act like I never saw anything.

Tomorrow, I know, I'll be sad that I missed the date. Currently, I am too terrified for that little detail to affect me too much. It turns out to be a good thing that I stopped to check my phone. I look over the berm I was about to jump over and see a long drop, probably twenty or thirty feet into a huge cistern. It's hard to tell exactly how far in the dark, and it is hard to tell if the reflection at the bottom is standing water, or river water, or just a slick sheen, or something else. In any case, I am very glad I didn't jump into it.

I skirt around the cistern and make my way across the asphalt, weaving in and out of weeds, old rusted folding chairs, coffee cans, broken bottles, and other less identifiable refuse. I get to another chain link fence. Climbing could get me spotted, so I look for another way around.

A brief scan up and down the fence reveals a place where it has been pulled up, making an easy passage through. I turn to look back and I can see movement coming across the asphalt, unerringly toward me. That's not Eric, it's moving too fast and too certainly in the dark. That's the Fetch, it's been freed from my magical trap, which means Circe, or whoever is controlling it, is not far behind.

I can outrun Eric; I can't outrun the Fetch. A Fetch doesn't care if they tear muscles or break bones in pursuit. A Fetch doesn't care about anything.

Crap.

I duck under the fence and find a trail that runs along the riverbank just beyond. I start down the trail as fast as I can in the dark. Which isn't remotely fast enough. I come to a split in the trail I can barely make it out in the moonlight. To the right, I can hear voices and banter—probably another encampment.

I don't want to lead these monsters to anyone else, so I turn left along the riverbank.

Chapter Twenty-Six

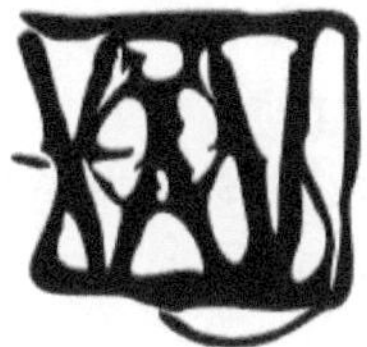

Back in college, Hale and his little 'club,' our forays into dark magic. I saw first hand what this sort of magic can do to a person, what it did to Shelly. While these memories fill me with guilt and regret, in moments like this those experiences are useful.

There is quite literally nothing that I am more prepared to deal with than a Fetch, at least in a magical sense.

I can hear the sound of chain link being torn away from steel fence posts behind me. I can hear the Fetch's heavy footsteps in the mud. The wet squelching plodding sounds move toward me. It's gained a lot of ground in a short time., though I still have a lead of twenty yards or so. I am guessing I have probably thirty seconds to a minute tops before it catches up with me.

There's not enough time to make another circle. That would be the best way of dealing with it—cutting off the magical flow that gives it direction and intention. Without that, it's just a lobotomized person.

But I do have one more trick up my sleeve.

I charge up off the muddy riverbank trail and come out onto an open paved trail at the end of Kennedy Park. I can see the darkened baseball field just down the hill below me and hear the Fetch charging through the underbrush toward me. I find a spot in the circle of light cast down by a buzzing sodium light pole above me.

I pull Jeff's spray bottle out from my pocket and shake it, there's only a tiny bit of liquid left in the bottle, and I can smell the vinegary scent even from the distance I hold it at. I hope that it still works. Rummaging around in my bag, I produce a small hand mirror.

The Fetch clears the brush and charges toward me, face emotionless, with an immense knife brandished in its left hand.

I take a deep breath, willing the terror down. I hold the mirror up at the Fetch's eye level. As it charges, I have to bob and weave the mirror around trying to catch its attention. A few feet and half a second before I am slaughtered like a pig, the Fetch sees itself in the mirror.

No matter how thoroughly the mind is erased by magic, there are still shards, tiny vestiges, that remain. Shattered slivers of the original person, like little, tiny bits of glass you can't ever sweep completely off the floor, and years later you still find under the stove or behind the refrigerator.

Self-recognition is the common thing that remains in all Fetches I've encountered. A Fetch that sees its reflection often gets confused. It doesn't break the control over it or stop them for long, but it slows them down; they tend to stop and stare at themselves for a while until the sorcerer controlling them focuses more energy on control.

With Shelly, it would break Hale's control for three to five minutes or so. If Circe is responsible for this as I suspect, she is a far superior sorcerer to Hale. It stands to reason that I have less time than that.

But I don't need much time. I don't hesitate. As soon as the Fetch stops, I begin dousing it with Jeff's concoction of magic-eating bacteria.

I still can't believe that's a thing.

Once I've sprayed all that's left onto the Fetch's now-glistening head and shoulders, I shove the bottle back in my jacket pocket and pull out my crystal. I stare at the aura of the Fetch.

The Fetch still has that grey, staccato aura with the thin red line leading off into the darkness. But now I can see another aura, a cloud really. It has a purplish color that almost defies description or categorization, it's sort of iridescent. But the aura is filtering and flitting away, dissipating ineffectively.

That must be Jeff's magic-eating bacteria. But the magic is too diffuse, it needs a higher concentration to get going.

"Here, take it," I say, holding the mirror out to the Fetch.

It grabs the mirror and pulls it close to its face staring intently into its reflected eyes.

I wasn't sure if that would work, but I'm thankful that it did. I quickly pull out the salt and make a circle around the Fetch, then chalk inside and outside of the salt as quickly as I can.

Sadly, I have plenty of open, oozy wounds at this point from which I can get blood to activate the circle.

I step back and re-examine the Fetch's aura. The red control line is broken, dangling at the edge of the circle. The purplish cloud is now coalescing around the red line and growing rapidly. As I watch, the red line fades and dissipates.

And then something I didn't expect happens. The purplish cloud begins consuming the hard lines at the edges of the gray aura. The Fetch's aura quickly loses its rigid, structured form and becomes the sort of amorphous flow that a normal person would have. The color is still a flat, monotonous grey, but I think I can see a faint glimmer of light in the center.

I watch dumbstruck. Jeff's concoction might actually cure this Fetch.

It will certainly take time, but he might just be able to heal. However, my bafflement is interrupted by the sounds of someone else slogging and cursing their way up the muddy trail on the riverbank. I recognize the voice immediately.

It's Eric Walsh.

There is part of me that wants to leave this Fetch, this poor man, and run. It would be the easy choice, or as easy as any choice I have right now. But if I leave him here, who knows what might happen to him? He might get re-enthralled.

He might just get killed to dispose of the evidence. Leaving doesn't feel like the right thing to do, but if I stay Walsh might kill us both.

I stand on the asphalt looking from the shimmering downtown lights reflected on the water, back to the Fetch, or former Fetch standing looking lost and dazed staring into a small mirror beneath the bright sodium lights. It only takes me a second to come to a conclusion, but it seems like hours knowing that Eric Walsh is tromping toward me with probable intent to beat me to death.

This time there's no Chris Benson nearby to save me.

I DUCK behind a shrub just out of the circle of light cast by the lamps above. I crouch down and my hand bumps a large rock, which I pick up. It's one of those tense moments when your blood is pounding in your ears and your breath sounds like deafening gusts of wind blowing through your head. In these moments it is hard to grasp time. Seconds drag on for what seems like minutes, but minutes pass between heartbeats.

I don't know how long I am sitting crouched in the shadows, rock in hand, tensed and ready to strike. It seems like a lifetime in an instant and Eric comes barging up the muddy path from the riverbank. He's huffing and cursing and stomping mud off his shoes.

"Hey, buddy," he exclaims as he starts walking toward the dazed and afflicted man standing in the middle of the path. When he doesn't receive a response, he walks closer and taps the man on the shoulder.

"Hey, buddy," Eric repeats.

I take this moment to move. I charge across the asphalt, into the circle of light, and pounce on Eric. Pounce on him like a guinea pig pouncing on a mountain lion. He hears me coming and partially turns by the time I get to him. In my mind, I have an idea I should say something pithy, but it only comes out as a strangled grunt.

This isn't the clean surprise attack I wanted.

To my advantage, I have a large rock to aid in the assault. To his advantage, it seems fairly obvious that this isn't his first time getting hit in the head with a rock. He sees that he is not going to stop the blow completely, so he turns his head into the blow taking it on the forehead.

While one shouldn't try to get hit in the head, if you have to get hit in the head, this does seem the better option. If he instinctively shied away, he would take it on the temple, which would be far more likely fatal.

At the same time as turns his head, he brings his right arm up toward my gut. Not a punch so much as a straight-armed shove. This forces me back a bit and while it doesn't prevent the blow to his head entirely, it does soften it some.

I hit him in the head and the rock splits in my hand; there must have been a flaw or fissure through it. I can feel the shards cut into my skin. His rising arm catches me in the gut, I get that sick feeling like I might make a mess in my pants and rock back on my heels. Eric is dazed, I can see he's trying to focus on me, but he can't see.

Blood is starting to trickle from cuts on his forehead where the rock shattered. I charge again and catch him in the mid-torso, throwing him on the ground. We tumble in a chaotic jumble for a minute.

If I survive this night, I'll probably tell my friends about a graceful dance I did around while he flailed at me with his hulking lumbering meat clubs. And the truth is, maybe that won't be a lie. But at this moment, I have no idea what is happening or what just happened.

It is all chaos and pain and adrenaline and then I am lying on the ground huffing and puffing and considerably more bruised than I was a moment ago, and Eric Walsh is on the ground next to me. He's not moving. I sit up and look at him. I'm gasping for air, huffing and puffing and sweaty and hurting all over.

"Eric," I say.

No response. I crawl over to him and feel for a pulse. He's alive. I look at him beneath the harsh glow of the sodium lights above. He's got a big bruise on the side of his head, and an oozy cut on his forehead.

It looks like in addition to the blow from my rock, he got hit on the head again while we were scuffling on the ground. I should get him help, but I don't want to be caught here right now.

I pat his pockets and find his phone. I take it out, and when the facial recognition passcode comes up, I hold it in front of his face. I dial 911 and put the phone on speaker on his chest. I can hear the operator's tiny tinny voice from the speaker as I walk over to the stupefied ex-Fetch a few feet away.

"Come on," I say. His face lifts and tracks me.

"Come on!" I say and take his hand; he follows me. I'm not sure where I am going to take him. I am not qualified to deal with this and I'm not sure who is qualified to deal with this sort of thing.

No, I do know exactly who is qualified to deal with this sort of thing and I know exactly where to take him. But I don't think they're going to like it. Alistair. He used to work at the State Hospital. He's got a degree…in something to do with mental illness. His husband is a nurse. And Alistair did say he wanted to help.

Have you ever been woken up at 1:00 AM by a beaten and battered poker night buddy who is leading a zombified stranger to your house?

Alistair has. Well, *now* he has.

And the only explanation I gave him:

"I'll explain later."

Only, in Alistair's case, this is probably not the weirdest

thing that's ever happened to him. He is in private practice now, but I know at the hospital he saw stuff that even *I* would think is off the rails.

I put the Fetch on Alistair's doorstep and ring the doorbell. A few minutes later, a bleary-eyed Alistair answers the door.

"Miles, what's going on?" Alistair asks, holding his robe shut.

"Remember how you said you wanted to help? This guy needs help. I'll explain later," I blurt out and start to move down the stairs.

"Miles! Miles! Come back. Miles? What the hell man! Miles!" Alistair demands.

"Sorry, there's a lot going on. I will explain tomorrow. Hopefully. I'm really sorry, I didn't know where else to go," I call, jogging backward up his street.

Then I turn and run.

Faintly, as I turn the corner and run off into the darkness, I swear I can hear Jon say, "I told you this would happen."

Chapter Twenty-Seven

I don't really know why I am running at this point. I don't really know where I am going, or what I am doing. I wander street to street the four or five miles toward my apartment.

I look like hell. I'm battered, bruised, cut, covered in blood and mud and who knows what else. I wind my way down less trafficked streets and avoid streetlights and parking lots. At a point, I realize that less traffic seems to mean no traffic.

This slowly goes from being convenient to being suspicious, to being worrying.

The streets are deserted. I take out my phone and immediately see that there is an alert message from the County Sheriff's Department. The city is under lockdown after a massive shooting. I'm shocked and horrified.

A massive shooting in my town? Who would do such a thing?

It takes me a minute to realize that this is about what happened at The Lantern. Now I definitely don't want to be spotted on the streets looking like this.

There is a creek nearby that I think comes out close to my apartment building. I slide my way down into the creek bed and make my way through it. The creek is almost always dry these days, so it's pretty easy to traverse, even in the dark. I use my phone's light to help me navigate over the rocks and branches that I encounter.

It is after three in the morning when I stagger up the stairs to my apartment. Bruised. Battered. Sore. Muddy. Let's be honest, smelly, I am very smelly. Exhausted beyond belief I pull my way up the last half dozen stairs and who is standing on the landing waiting for me?

Circe.

Shit.

She's leaning against my door, one leg propped up behind her, arms crossed. It looks casual, impatient, but provocative. I wonder how many different poses she tried before she settled on this one.

She has swapped out her kunoichi outfit for a red dress and high heels, she looks like she's just walked out of grifting at an upscale bar. She seems to wear more outfits in one day than I own.

She looks upset but I can't tell if it is because I'm still alive, how long she was waiting, or if it is out of concern for my well-being. I'm certain it's one of the first two.

"I'm tired, and I just want to go to bed," I say.

"I can help you with that," she suggests in her usual tone.

"Gonna pass, Circe," I say.

She faux pouts. "You don't like me?"

"I don't know you, Circe, and I don't trust you. You tried to kill me back at The Lantern and you sent a Fetch and that meathead Eric Walsh after me."

"I did try to kill you. The Lamia exposed a weakness by making that Blood Pact. Strike while the iron is hot, waste no advantage, you know. But I didn't send those two after you." She sounds sincere. Based on the time I've spent with her now, she's probably very good at sounding sincere about anything if it helps her agenda.

"Then who? This was professional work. You killed Redbrook, so…who else in town could do this?"

"My partner."

"Your partner…?"

"Yes, the Hizarin always work in pairs," Circe explains.

How did I not know that Hizarin work in pairs? That answers so many of the small questions I had, about the timing of events and the amount of power required to curse Whitman, while also hexing the whole winery.

"She doesn't believe you are the Blethspa Amah. She thinks you are a liability. I think if she did believe it, she would have taken greater efforts. She didn't tell me she was going to send her thralls after you."

Circe laughs a high-pitched tinkling laugh; it is very practiced and doesn't have a hint of actual mirth to it.

"What's funny?" I ask.

"Usually I'm the 'rash' one and Morgan's the 'planner'," Circe says.

"I fail to see the humor."

She shrugs, playing with the fabric of her dress.

"You'd have to know us better."

"Pass. How'd Eric Walsh get involved in this?"

"That's kind of Morgan's go-to. Find a dumb guy with a grudge and manipulate him into bad decisions, make him dependent on her, and slowly drain his will and turn him into a thrall."

"I see."

I feel like that's been Circe's approach to me as well.

"So how do I keep Morgan and maybe you from killing me? At least for tonight?" I ask.

"I'll talk to her. Even Morgan Le Fey will listen to reason," she says and then winks at me.

"Circe and Morgan Le Fey? Do the Hizarin all take the names of famous witches and wizards?" I ask.

"How do you know we *aren't* those famous witches?" she asks coyly.

"Because that would be too campy. Improbable. Ridiculous."

She furrows her brow and glowers like a toddler on the verge of throwing a fit.

"And it's just witches. There are no male members of the Hizarin," she says.

"Really? I did not know that," I say, surprised that apparently Russ knows what he is talking about. I add this to a list of possibly confirmed facts I know about the Hizarin.

Then after a moment I ask, "Why not?"

"Interested in signing up? Men have tried, but they just never seem to have the grit and skill to make it."

"Oh, is it like a moon cycle, blood thing?" I ask. I'd read that because of the whole willing blood sacrifice, women have a monthly boost in magical power.

She glowers at me, looking offended, but again I can't tell what is genuine and what is intentional manipulation.

"No. And that's offensive. It's not completely untrue, but it's not the reason. Men just don't put in the time or attention to detail. They are obsessed with bringing more power, not carefully manipulating bit by bit. They lack the patience, control, and grit to do it right. Men usually go in for big and loud and burn themselves up in the process. Often literally."

She runs a finger around the door frame of my apartment appraisingly. She stops to examine the glyphs I've placed there.

"See, sloppy. Crude. Hastily built. But they still work. You're still alive. That must be the advantage of being the chosen one. I can teach you. I can make you the greatest sorcerer of our time. Just imagine…the Blethspa Amah becomes the first male member of the Hizarin," she says.

"I'm going to pass. I don't even really know what the Blethspa Amah is," I say. "I'm in over my head, and I just want to get to bed."

She narrows her eyes.

"How do you know you are the Blethspa Amah if you don't know what that is?" she asks suspiciously.

"I kind of got ambushed with the information by a

prophet. I didn't get much detail," I say, and it's not a lie. Not technically.

"Who is this prophet?"

"I am not at liberty to say."

She glowers at me. I see an expression pass her face, a little clenching of the jaw, a slight curling of the upper lip. I read that expression to say, 'I can make you talk.' But it passes quickly.

"Hmph," she snorts. "The Blethspa Amah means something like 'The Unweaver' in Suphis, the alleged ancient language of the dragons. It's all kind of magical boogeyman stuff, honestly."

"Boogeyman stuff?"

"Yeah, the Blethspa Amah will rise and destroy all your spells and undo everything and make the world a mundane place without magic or monsters, blah blah. Until tonight I didn't believe any of it."

"I see, but now you believe?"

"Believe the whole myth? No. Believe that there is something there? It makes more sense than you just 'somehow' broke my curse on Charles Whitman; you 'somehow' stopped my bone-hex on him; and that you just 'somehow' shirked off a blood pact. You shouldn't be here. You should be burned from the inside out like Redbrook."

"Goodnight, Circe," I say trying to push my way past her.

"What no goodnight kiss, Miles?" she asks flirtatiously, but it's words only. Her face is a mask of irritation bordering on rage.

I push past her and unlock my door. She tries to look casual about it, but she is very careful not to cross the boundary of any of my wards.

Professional paranoia? Or are my exclusive wards preventing her?

Food for thought.

"If you change your mind, Miles, I'll train you. It will be

fun. There are so many things we could do together…" she says as I close the door in her very pretty, very inviting face.

"Rude," I can hear her muffled voice from the other side of the door.

I stagger into my bathroom and throw my filthy clothes in the corner and climb into the shower. I'm not usually a leave-my-clothes-on-the-floor kind of guy but I'm just too tired to care.

After I soak for too long in the shower, I walk into my room.

My heart sinks when I realize…there's Hank.

He's partially melted, hunched over, there is a dried pool of blood on the floor around his feet. I'd put a small vial of my blood inside the mannequin, right where the heart would be. It helps with the sympathetic link between creator and simulacrum. Hank is a broken, melted mess.

"Sorry, Hank," I say.

"It's what I'm here for," he says, sounding disturbingly like Eeyore.

Chapter Twenty-Eight

I take a step up the escalator.

There are people in the way, faceless people who are little more than moving obstacles to me. I need to get to the top fast, I know I need to, but I can't remember why.

"Excuse me," I say. "Pardon me. Comin' through. On your left!"

I push my way to the top of the escalator. I look back down, and I know I need to move, there is somewhere I have to be. I look at the huge, vaulted atrium, large wide-leafed palms sway in enormous planters, and the sun filters in through immense skylights. I look up one side of the gallery, then the other. I have an overwhelming sense of urgency. There are hundreds of stores and doors and shops here. There is one I need to get to, but which one?

I have a note in my hand.

Right, the note.

I hold the note up to read it, but as I unfurl it in my sweaty palms. I remember I have to hurry. I have to keep moving. I can't stop. I start to run down the long gallery, trying to read the note as I go, but the handwriting is blurry, and I can't hold it still enough while running.

A woman is standing in front of a shop, and she has a little cart with free samples on it.

"Miles," she says. "Miles, in here."

I look at her and shake my head.

"I have to go," I say.

"No Miles," she says again, but I force myself to run off, and she's left talking to her sample cart.

I push through a group of teenagers that is blocking the way. They shove and push me, and I stagger and spin. I get disoriented, the dozen teenagers become thirty. Thirty teenagers become a hundred. A hundred become a whole sea of them. They push and prod me until I fall into a store.

Pillow Warehouse. Rows and rows of shelves, stacked with pillows of every shape and size—couch pillows, bed pillows, down pillows, cotton pillows, animal-shaped pillows, Japanese body pillows shaped like manga girls—flood my vision. I walk down row after row looking at pillows.

I pick up a human-sized pillow that looks like me.

"Sorry Hank," I say to the pillow as I drag it along with me.

"No problem, Miles," the pillow says.

"You can't talk. You're a pillow," I say.

"Miles, it's me. Russ," the pillow says suddenly.

"Oh, hi Russ? When did you become a pillow?" I ask and look back at the pillow, which now as I look at it no longer looks like me, but Russ.

"I'm not a pillow, Miles. You're dreaming."

"Oh, that makes more sense," I say. "Why are you here?"

"Well, that stuff your girlfriend gave me…."

"She's not my girlfriend. I don't think she's even my friend."

"Whatever. Anyway, it was pretty potent. I am still stuck here, man, so I thought I would check in on you."

"Great."

"Dude, those Daunts you had me banish?" he says. "They are after you again in the Dream. They keep stalking around you like wolves, man, like wolves."

"Harmless," I say. "You want a churro? We should go to the food court and get a churro."

"No! No Churros, man. Daunts. Remember? Yes, sort of they are harmless, but something is different. They are acting weird."

"Aren't I protected by that veil thingy?" I say through a haze, I feel

almost drunk. Talking and following the conversation is taking as much focus as I can muster. My mind keeps wandering back to churros.

"I need you to be lucid, Miles, I am going to need you to awaken in the dream."

"I can't do that."

"You can. The fact that you are talking to me at all shows me you can do it. You are doing it, man."

"How? I just snap my fingers? Is there a magic word?" My voice is warped and slurring like I'm drunk and talking through a broken speaker. I start shouting things at random. "Hocus Pocus! Abracadabra!"

"Oh, don't say that! That word is originally an invocation to Abraxas, a sort of demon god thing," Russ says. "You don't want to summon that shit into your dreams."

I stare at him and then start thinking about that churro in the mall food court again. I find myself singing:

"Sweet.
"Crunchy…on the outside.
"Chewy…on the inside.
"Cinnamon-y."

"Miles! "Stay with me, man. You need to find, like a door. There will be a door somewhere it doesn't belong, and you have to open it and go through. You will want to look at it, man, but it won't make sense. Going through it will be like the hardest thing you ever have to do. Like no matter how close you get it will always seem a few steps away. You'll get distracted, dude, things will come up to try to tempt you away. It will seem like impossible, man, but you gotta go through, okay?" Russ sounds very sharp, especially for Russ.

"Sure pillow-Russ. Sure. But how do I know you are Russ looking like a pillow and not Circe looking like a Russ-shaped pillow? Or a Daunt looking like Circe looking like a Russ-shaped pillow?"

The pillow shrugs at me.

"I don't know, amigo. Find the door."

That sounds like a Russ answer. I walk hand-in-hand with a man-sized pillow shaped like a man I barely know through this mall. Endless, ever-twisting atriums go on and on. I pass places selling things both predictable and bizarre. The House of Cards sells nothing but playing cards of every type, branded with characters from famous tv shows, and cartoons, celebrity cards, joke cards, theme cards, cards with birds, cards with animals, dinosaurs, space, sushi cards, cards with hot peppers on them.

I see a deck of cards in the window labeled "18+ Girls of the Hizarin" and I turn into the store to buy it, but the Russ-pillow grabs me by the shoulder.

"I wouldn't go in there."

I shrug and continue walking.

"Ooh, look! That must be the place." I point to a storefront with a sign reading 'The Door Store'. Inside are rows and rows, stacks and stacks of doors.

"No, this will be somewhere you don't expect it. That's too predictable, you'll get lost in there. Maybe forever."

We walk and walk, continuing to pass weirder and weirder storefronts.

The sense I have of being pursued, that I need to get somewhere soon or there will be consequences grows constantly. I begin to tire and stop and hang my head dejected.

"The Daunts are closing in, Miles, man. As I said, there are things different about those ones, something's been done to them. They aren't normal dude," Russ says.

I blink as I am hanging my head looking at my feet. There is a door on the top of my shoe like it has been sewn onto the toe.

"That's weird," I say and lean over to open the door. As I am about to open it, I can hear someone pounding on it from the other side.

"Who is it?" I say in a sing-song voice.

"Just open the door, man!"

The pounding increases in intensity…and—

I wake up, lying in my bed sweating slightly.

There is a pounding on my front door and a familiar voice, loud and urgent.

"Miles," it calls.

Chapter Twenty-Nine

I roll out of bed and land with a *thud* on the floor.

Left knee and ball of foot on the ground, the right knee bent with my foot flat on the ground. In my mind this is a superhero pose; in reality, I probably look like someone who is too beaten and battered to stand.

I reflect for a moment that that is probably what superheroes would actually look like a day after battling giant robots and aliens.

I stagger out of my bedroom and grab my bathrobe off the back of the door as I go. I pull it on. The pounding on the door continues.

"Miles!" It's Chris Benson's voice, which is why it sounds so familiar. I walk like Frankenstein's monster to the door and open it.

"Good morning, Chris. What's up?" I ask, with difficulty. He's in uniform. "Or is it Officer Benson this morning?"

"It's Chris for the moment, but I am going to have to talk to you as Officer Benson in a sec. Miles, *please* tell me you weren't at The Lantern last night," he says, sounding a little frantic.

"Uhhh…" I stammer, avoiding lying through incoherence is one of my tricks.

"Miles, last night. This is a cluster-F, Miles. They are calling it a terrorist attack, politically motivated. It's making national news. There are feds. There's National Guard. You want to be a thousand miles away from this, Miles," he insists.

"Why do you think I'd have something to do with that?" I ask, genuinely curious.

"Come on Miles. The thing with your car yesterday…plus Eric Walsh was found about a mile away from The Lantern out by the park. He's in the hospital but when he wakes up, he's a suspect in last night's debacle."

"I don't think he'll say anything about me," I say more confidently than I feel.

"Miles, I know you well enough to know that if you weren't involved, you have an idea about what's going on. Either way, you gotta steer clear of this."

"Okay, I get it. I had nothing to do with any of the stuff you are talking about. I promise," I say. Which is true, as I had nothing to do with the Knights of Saint George's attack. I was just a bystander.

"Good. You don't need to come into the station to make a statement about the car. I can just take one quickly and file it. Pretty much all hands are on last night's spree."

"Spree?"

"Yeah, it started at The Lantern, and that was the worst of it. But they drove around and shot up a bunch of other places."

"Okay, well my statement is that Eric Walsh guy and another guy drove me off the road and tried to beat me with baseball bats. I ran and hid."

"That's not great. Do you know the other guy?" Chris asks, pulling out a notebook and jotting something down.

"No, never seen him before."

"What did he look like?" Chris asks, putting on his Officer Benson facade.

"Big white guy, fit, athletic, hard, like a boxer," I say. "I didn't get a good look at him, because I was too busy running for my life."

This is also technically true. At the time they ran me off the road, I didn't get a good look at him.

"Why didn't you call the police then?"

"I was hiding from them and by the time I got out, Napa was a war zone?" I say more questioning if that was the right answer than actually making a statement.

"That makes sense," Chris says.

"Okay. So now off the record, Miles, what the hell happened last night?"

"It is complicated. I'm not sure the ins and outs of it all. But the carnage last night, that's the Knights of Saint George. I'm pretty sure anyways," I say. I beckon him inside and close the door.

"The Knights of Saint George? I've never heard of them."

"One second," I say and go back to my room. I fish around in all the crap on the top of my dresser and dig up the hat I got the other night. I bring it back to Chris.

"Here, one of these guys approached me outside The Lantern a couple of days ago."

His face looks grim as he looks at the bumper sticker.

"Laughter and slaughter don't rhyme," he says.

"I know, right?" I say.

I can't help but notice his eyes go wide with surprise and recognition when he sees the Knights of Saint George logo, the stylized image of the dragon slayer. He didn't seem to react to the name, but he's certainly seen their logo before.

"These guys are monster hunters?" he asks, with a kind of sick look of recognition lingering on his face.

"Yeah, kind of like human supremacists? They are pretty radical and violent. And for some reason, it seems like there are a lot of them."

"Great. Do you know any more about them? Anything I can use?"

"Not other than that hat and bumping into them last year briefly at a MystiCon. It's a magic convention. That's pretty much it. I guess I saw a couple of them downtown a few days ago," I say. "I've tried to avoid them. They aren't my people."

"I'll bring this in as an anonymous tip." He waves the hat. "I need to get going now, Miles. It's a mess out there. Stay home and stay inside. There's a city-wide lockdown order."

"Still?" I ask.

"Still. It's bad, Miles, really bad," Chris says as he turns toward the door.

"Okay, I'll stay home today. Thanks, Chris."

"Thank you, Miles," he says, waving the hat as he lets himself out.

I sigh, lock and deadbolt my door, and sit back on my bed. I sigh and pick up my phone. Four missed calls. Two from Alistair, two from Emily. *Shit, Emily.* I didn't make our date. I'd kick myself, but my legs are too sore to lift that high.

I listen to Alistair's messages first.

"What the hell, Miles? I know I said I wanted to help, but what the hell? You just drop a catatonic man off at my house in the middle of the night and run? Miles, call me back." He sounds pissed.

I listen to the second message from Alistair.

"I just got an alert on my phone, Miles. What is going on? There's a terrorist attack or something and you are out running around the streets on foot? Call me back." He now sounds more concerned than pissed.

In the background, I can hear Jon saying, "We know you're involved, Miles."

"Miles, seriously, be safe man. Call me," Alistair repeats, concerned.

"Don't die, Miles. I want to kill you myself!" I can hear Jon calling in the background. He doesn't like me, and he really makes no qualms about letting me know. It must be a nurse trait, not having any time for bullshit. Alistair's message ends.

I sit staring at the two messages from Emily. The first one is from 6:00 PM last night, right about the time the mess at the Lantern was starting.

"Hi, Miles." Emily's voice sounds chirpy. "Ren said they saw you driving around town on a motorcycle with "biker-barbie?" Their words, not mine. I don't need to be jealous, do I? Hey, I was wondering if you wanted to pick me up early and we could grab a drink at that new tiki-lounge downtown before we go to dinner? Call me."

She sounds happy and good-humored, so that's good. I see the next message is from about 8:00 PM.

"Oh my god, Miles, I assume you aren't coming, based on the alerts I am getting and reading on the news sites. I hope you are okay." She sounds scared. She pauses for a second.

"Call me. Seriously," she says, sounding very concerned. Then she hangs up.

I check my text messages. I have dozens, numerous alerts from the County Sheriff's office, Jeff and Mike texting to see if I am okay and several follow up texts from Emily asking me to call her. I sit back on my bed and dial Emily.

She answers on the second ring.

"Miles," she says.

"Good morning!" I say trying to sound upbeat, but I can tell my voice sounds tired and strained.

"Are you okay?"

"Nothing that a couple of days in an ice bath won't fix."

"So you were involved."

"Why does everyone keep assuming that? I don't even own a gun!"

"Miles…" she says, her tone sounds like she's scolding a child.

"I mean, yes and no. I was present, but uninvolved in the stuff on the news. I had a whole different series of problems."

"And biker barbie? This has something to do with the woman Ren saw you with?"

"Hizarin," I say. "She's Hizarin."

"Oh," Emily says. As I suspected she would, Emily knows exactly what I am talking about. She always seems to.

"It got messy and then the Knights of Saint George showed up."

"Those monster hunter nuts? They seemed kind of obnoxious but harmless to me," she says, sounding skeptical.

"Turns out they are obnoxious *and* heavily armed."

"You just happened to be at a dive bar with a sexy Hizarin when a band of well-armed psychos showed up and blew up the place," she says, clearly not impressed.

"Well, it's more of an underground card room and Lamia's mystic lair. But otherwise, yeah that pretty much sums it up. And yes, I hear how it sounds," I say.

There is a long quiet moment. I can tell she's thinking, and I just let her.

"Well, I am glad you are okay," she says. "I was scared when you didn't call back and I saw all the text alerts and posts about the shootings."

"Thanks. I am glad you are okay too."

"Well, I didn't leave the house," she says. I can hear the judgment in her voice.

"Rain check on last night until maybe the world isn't blowing up?"

"I don't know, Miles. I need to think about it. I like you, I do, but honestly, I am not sure I need all that in my life. You know? I feel like every time something bad goes down, you are in the middle of it."

"Oh," I say.

"Magical assassins? Lamia? Terrorist attacks. It's a lot."

"It is. That's fair," I say, my voice quieting.

"I need time to think. Can we talk more later?" she says.

"Yeah, of course," I say. I'm a little disappointed, but we are still friends for the time being, which is good.

We hang up. I go over to Hank and look at him. I spend a few minutes lifting his arms and trying to see if I can't piece my simulacrum back together. Eventually, I decide that he is a lost cause.

I disassemble him and put him in a plastic bag and slide him into the back of my closet. I'll have to dispose of him properly. I don't want any pieces left that someone could use to figure out the specific spells, wards, and rituals I used when I made him.

I get out my laptop and go to the vendor's site that I ordered the mannequin portion of Hank from originally. It was expensive. When I first made him, I wasn't sure it would work or if it would even be a useful tool. I worried I'd wasted thousands of dollars on a weird piece of room decor. Now, though, I have no problem ordering a new one. Hank was well worth the investment, five stars. My biggest regret is naming him, because now I feel a little bad that he's gone. I order a new one right away, but it will be weeks before I'll have that safety net back.

I make a checklist in my head.

The JMBaptiste Winery is protected, Whitman is safe, and Redbrook is out of the picture.

My date with Emily is off for the time being, and Circe seems like she's not planning to kill me—at least for the moment. My last real concern is Circe's partner, who has been identified as Morgan Le Fey.

Circe said she would take care of it, but I just don't know if I can trust her when it comes to, well, anything. The wise money would be to try to take care of this myself.

Circe and/or Morgan have been either engineering or following my exploits. It's far too suspicious that Eric Walsh got involved. I cannot accept that as a coincidence. Circe also knew to find me at Soothsayer, which is also too coincidental to accept. I have to assume I've been being followed for at least a few days and they know all of my usual haunts.

. . .

EVERYTHING I KNOW about the Hizarin is from rumors or the little bits that Circe herself has told me, and I have no reason to believe any of it. But if rumor and legend are true, then the Hizarin consider the contract their bond.

Once a Hizarin takes a contract to kill, only two things will stop them from completing their contract: the death of the Hizarin themselves or the client calls off the contract—like Lorelei Redbrook effectively did with Whitman.

Also, if rumor and legend are to be believed, the Hizarin only kill on contract, never for personal gain or revenge. If both of those are true, then I should be in the clear. Obviously, if Circe thinks she needs to deal with Morgan, then one of those isn't true.

Or there is a separate contract that has been put out on me.

This means that either Circe intends to help Morgan kill me, or Circe intends to kill Morgan herself. The former makes more sense, except that if that was the case, Circe could easily have killed me last night.

"No," Hank says, his voice muffled by the bag and the closet door. *"She might have been out of magic juice."*

"Except," I retort, "she could have just knifed me or shot me. She said it herself, they only use magic if it is necessary and there are lots of other ways to finish a contract."

"Okay," Hank mutters from the closet, *"but what if taking down the world's greatest consulting Apotropaist with magic* was *the contract?"*

"You're just flattering me now, I don't know about world's greatest," I say with over-acted, feigned modesty. "That might make sense, but I honestly think she is more interested in the Blethspa Amah thing than she is in a contract. She also didn't say it was a contract, it sounded like Morgan had a personal beef."

"Then if she thinks Morgan is violating Hizarin protocol to kill a potentially valuable asset, maybe she would kill Morgan."

There are a lot of assumptions there, but I conclude that this is the only scenario that I can work with.

If Circe is lying and both she and Morgan are out to kill me, I don't think I stand a chance either way, but I think I would already be dead. I have no way of getting in touch with Circe and no idea where, or what, or who Morgan might be.

And especially how she might come at me.

I am stuck at home, at least for today. Even though I'm not afraid of some alleged terrorist group—likely consisting of some monster hunters—I really just need to recharge and devise my next steps. Preparing to deal with another ancient—probably vampire—magical assassin is much harder than one might expect. Especially because I've already used up a lot of the tools in my toolbox.

Chapter Thirty

I scratch my head. The man Morgan turned into a Fetch. I broke the bond of control, but there would still be a residual link between him and Morgan. Something I can track.

Probably.

Maybe.

Circe would almost certainly know how to do this, but I have no way to contact her, and I don't trust her. The only other person I know and trust who might have an idea of how to track someone with that kind of magic is Emily.

I call Emily back. She answers on the fourth ring, and I start talking before she even has a chance to speak.

"Hey, Em, I am wondering if you can help me with a tracking spell?"

"Hi, Mom. Now's not a great time," Emily says.

"What? It's me, Miles."

"Yeah, I'm busy. I have a friend visiting, Mom. Can I call you back later? Great. Bye," Emily says and hangs up.

I sit there staring at my phone. It takes my brain a minute to process the call. There is someone at her house, and she's trying to let me know. I'm still trying to work through what might be going on when my phone rings. It is Emily calling back. I answer quickly.

"Hello?" I say.

"Hi Miles, it's Emily!" she says in a chipper voice.

"Hi, Emily, are you okay?"

"Yeah, I'm great. I was hoping you could come over. I am, um, you know…like a little worked up over everything going on, and I could use some company," she says, sounding very sincere.

She is a really good actor.

"Okay. I think I hear you. Are you in danger?"

"Yes! That would be great, bring a bottle of wine. We can put on some music. You know."

"Hizarin?"

"Probably. We could probably do that."

"Should I come over now?" I ask.

"Yeah, that's what I am saying, but be careful. I hear things are crazy out there. I wouldn't want you to get caught in a police checkpoint or a speed trap or something."

"I understand. I'll come as soon as I can."

"Hurry and be careful," she says.

We hang up. She was slipping a lot of hints into our conversation, but I honestly don't know if I would have picked up on them if not for the confusing call right before that. Morgan or maybe Circe—or worst-case scenario, both are at Emily's house, and it is definitely a trap.

Part of me wants to charge over to Emily's and kick in the door like a valiant white knight. But then I'd promptly get torn apart by curses and hexes like a paper doll. Or maybe just shot. Discretion as they say is the better part of valor.

I need a plan.

I need the perfect counter-spell.

I need someone that can unmake magic.

I need the Blethspa Amah.

It rubs me the wrong way. It's an internal frustration that I would never express to anyone but Hank and my therapist—and I haven't seen him in years, and Hank's as good as dead. I am jealous of Jeff. I was jealous of Jeff *before* the whole chosen-one-thing.

He's better at poker than me, he's a better guitar player than me, he knows more about science than me, and he juggles better than me.

The one thing I had was the whole apotropaism thing, and it turns out he's the chosen one and better than me at that too!

But he's also my friend, and I don't want to drag him into this mess. I don't see a lot of options and I don't have a lot of time. I am just going to take care of this myself, no need to involve Jeff. And I don't have a car. I should probably follow up on that.

I wrestle my bicycle off of my balcony, where it doesn't quite fit, through my apartment which is a little narrow, and down the stairs, clanging and cursing the whole way to the street.

I sit on the curb, straddling my bicycle. I look up the street, which is empty. I look down the street. Empty. Just like my brain. I'm sore and tired and out of ideas. Just charging over to Emily's isn't a good plan. I have no good next steps. I sigh and push my bike back up to my balcony and lock it.

Then I call Jeff.

"Hey, Miles. What did you do?" he asks, sounding half-amused but half-incredulous.

"I was catastrophe adjacent, but I didn't do anything. Listen, Jeff, I don't have a lot of time, there is someone in trouble and I think only I…that only we can help them."

"This sounds familiar. Didn't we just help someone that only we could help?"

"Yeah, this is new and ultimately a side effect of helping Whitman."

"See how that turned out?"

"If this is a plea for me to go to the police, I should point out that any call they respond to right now is going to be responded to with SWAT, and they won't know what they are getting into. There are hostages involved."

"Is this your call to make?" Jeff asks somberly.

"We are more informed and prepared to deal with this than anybody. Us, Jeff. This is your call too. You're the Blethspa Amah, after all."

I can hear him take a deep sighing breath on the other end of the line. He is quiet for a moment. I let him think.

"Okay. What do you need?" he asks. That's one of the many things about Jeff I like; he is always ready to step up to any task.

"Do you have any more of your acetobacter formulae stuff?"

"Yeah, I've been experimenting with it a bit more. It's interesting, you can sort of measure the amount of magical energy built up somewhere by the growth. If you start to smell acetone, that means it is a lot of magic, and the bacteria are kind of going nuts."

"Yeah, I noticed that. Why does it make that acetone smell? When that stuff started cooking it smelled like nail polish remover."

"It's one of the byproducts the bacteria make if they go too long and consume too much. It's what puts the aceto in acetobacter," he says.

"That is interesting, but I have another question. What if you injected these bacteria into a person?"

"I don't know, but I can't imagine anything good. A small dose, maybe nothing? A larger dose might make them sick. That's more a question for a medical doctor."

"But what if their blood was full of magic?"

"With the Acetobacter Magusficedula's rate of reproduction in a high-energy environment? Well, that could be horrifying, to be honest," he says.

"Acetobacter Magusficedula?"

"Yeah, that is what I named it, the magic-eating species. It means basically, 'magic eating acetobacter'," he says.

"Okay," I say, thinking. He continues to explain.

"Acetobacter Magusficedula consume magical energy. In a

normal environment, the ambient levels of energy just sort of sustain them, they are there, but they don't proliferate. But if given a place where the energy pools, they reproduce very fast. If that environment has other nutrients for them to absorb, like in wine, that proliferation becomes geometric. So, in someone's bloodstream, with an ample supply of magic and nutrients, it would turn acetic fast—in minutes, most likely. That would be a horrible way to go."

"If we injected it into something, that'd work?"

"If you wanted to murder a magical creature in a cruel, horrible way, yeah I'd say that would work," he says. "Do you have a plan?"

"No. I'm working on that. Can you pick me up and bring your concoction?"

"Well we are under a lockdown order, but if it's a matter of life and death? I can try."

"It is a matter of life and death."

"Okay, I'll be right over," Jeff says.

We hang up. I have no idea where to get a hypodermic needle, especially not when my entire town is on lockdown. Then it occurs to me. Mike is diabetic. He has to pull out a needle and inject himself almost every poker game. I call him.

"Hello, Miles," Mike answers.

"Hey, Mike."

"Crazy, crazy times, right?" Mike says.

"Yeah…about that."

"Miles. You know you need to call about normal stuff sometimes, right?"

"I know, Mike. I know I keep asking for favors, but this is like a life-or-death favor."

"What do you need now?" he says, sounding resigned.

"I owe you like six favors, man. Whatever you need, whenever, call me, okay?" I say. "But right now is a needle, like something I can inject something with. You know something I can put my own…payload, is that the right word? Anyway to put fluid into."

"I," he starts, then pauses to laugh. "Man Miles, it's never safe or normal with you, is it?"

"I guess not," I say sheepishly.

"Yeah, I can give you something. Do I want to know what this is all about?"

"I'm happy to tell you all about it, but, no. I don't think you are going to like it or believe it."

"You are probably right. Just come by. No questions asked."

"Thanks, Mike. I owe you one," I say.

"Yes, you do. Oh, and Miles—"

"Yeah?"

"You need to call about normal stuff."

"Yeah."

Chapter Thirty-One

I hastily prepare for today's adventure. I grab my courier bag, which is still filthy from last night's escapades. I shake off as much of the dried mud into the trashcan as I can. I snatch another pint of Goldschlager from my cabinet and shove it into my bag.

I don't know what I am doing but getting all my go-to tools together seems wise. I close and lock my door and dash downstairs where I pace around the parking lot till Jeff arrives and picks me up.

"Any trouble getting here?" I ask.

"Nope, just had to lie to the cops and say I was going to tend to my elderly mother," Jeff says with a hint of sarcasm.

"Good?"

"Where to, boss?"

"Mike's place."

"Mike's?"

"He's going to give me a needle."

Jeff grunts, clearly not comfortable with this solution. Truth be told, I'm not excited about it either. I just don't see any other options. It's only a short drive to Mike's house, and thankfully we aren't stopped by any police on our way over.

Mike is standing on his lawn in sweats and a t-shirt. He is

holding a paper bag, which he walks up and hands to me through Jeff's passenger window. He doesn't say a word or even make eye contact.

I take the bag from him and mutter my thanks. Mike doesn't acknowledge me; he just walks back into his house. I can see his kid's eyes and noses peeking through the blinds watching us.

Jeff drives away. Once we are down the block, I take the needle out and carefully fill it with Jeff's concoction. I cap the now-filled hypodermic and slide it into my pocket. I look back through my messages and find Emily's address, which I relay to Jeff.

THE FIRST EIGHT minutes are eerily quiet. Neither of us talks. The radio doesn't play, and Jeff's car doesn't make a sound. Finally, I break the silence a few blocks from Emily's.

"Jeff, you should just drop me off and let me do this. I don't think you should be near this."

"Why not?" he asks, seeming authentically confused. "It's not like you have any more obligation to deal with this stuff than I do."

"You aren't wrong, but here is the thing. I found out a tiny bit more about what that Blethspa Amah thing is. Or what people think it is. It's a sort of prophesied person that can like undo magic? Well, it turns out that at least one evil-blood-sorceress-magic-assassin thinks that I am the Blethspa Amah. I think they have pretty bad stuff in mind for the Blethspa Amah. I feel like it is to our advantage to keep them misinformed. Keeping you away from this will help. Also, right now, they have one bargaining chip over me with Emily; I worry that you might get grabbed as a bargaining chip as well," I say in a rush.

"Why is everyone so excited about this Blethspa Amah thing? It's something an old crazy guy who may or may not be a dragon told us."

"Yes, but then I used your concoction to do exactly what the Blethspa Amah is prophesied to do. I guess."

"Oh. Yeah," Jeff says, realizing the truth and gravity of the situation.

"Anyway, true or not, someone grabbed Emily as bait."

"Why did they grab this Emily lady?"

"I think they've been following me, spying on me. They seem to know Emily and I are friends and so are using her as bait. This is mostly speculation though."

Jeff thinks about it for a minute.

"Okay…but I am just going to park down the block. Send a 911 text if you need help and if I don't hear from you in fifteen minutes, I am coming in," Jeff says.

"Fifteen minutes. Okay," I say and slip out of the car. I am worried that it already has taken too long, and that they might have already hurt Emily.

He pulls away casually. I stop on the corner and try to clear my mind. After taking a deep breath, and I walk toward Emily's front door. I have never been to her place before, but it's a cute little ranch on the north side of town. She has an older grey Honda Accord sitting in the driveway, which I don't recall ever seeing before. She usually bikes to work from what I recall. The house itself is painted light gray with dark gray trim and has a sort of rock garden in the front, planted with a bunch of flowering succulents.

I knock on the door, but the action pushes it open slightly, revealing that it is neither locked nor latched.

No, this doesn't feel like a trap at all, I think to myself.

"Hello?" I call out.

"In here," Emily calls back.

I scratch open one of the many scabs on my arm and run the blood over my forearm tattoos, activating the warding runes. They aren't as powerful or as useful without Hank, and they won't last long or hold up to much, but they are better than nothing—at least I hope. I pull the needle out of my pocket and palm it.

I walk down a short hallway into a living room with a relatively high ceiling. Whatever attic this space might have had was removed to make a high vaulted ceiling. It looks weird and incongruous with the rest of the house and makes the room echo in a weird and kind of creepy way.

Emily is sitting on a burgundy loveseat on one side of the room, hands crossed on an open book in her lap. She's wearing flannel pajamas, her hair is unbrushed, and she isn't wearing any makeup. I didn't realize she normally wore makeup; I guess she goes for a more subtle look. Now seeing her without it, its usual presence becomes obvious to me. I find her as beautiful as ever, even still.

She looks at me and her eyes dart quickly to my right. I cannot help but notice that her seat is surrounded by a series of runes drawn on the floor in black marker. It is an intricate and concise inclusive circle. She is under the effect of a spell, but I don't have time to figure out what it does.

Suddenly I hear chanting from a corner to my right. I cannot quite see the source of the chanting from my vantage point. I feel my heart start to race and palpate. I twist my head far to my right.

Standing there is a woman I have never seen before. Or have I? She looks vaguely familiar, but I can't place her.

Where Circe has dark copper-colored skin, naturally dark hair, and dark eyes, this woman has pale skin, the palest blue eyes, and hair so dark that it must be dyed. Where Circe is tall, lithe, and athletic, this woman is average height, voluptuous, and full-figured. While at the superficial level they seem polar opposites, this woman has the same confident grace that Circe has, the same practiced and absolute certainty of action.

She continues chanting. My muscles freeze. I'm paralyzed. Terror begins to rise in my throat. Maybe this was a terrible idea. As the rigor sets into all my muscles, I am pretty certain that I am going to die.

The pale woman walks toward me, ethereal like a ghost.

Morgan.

I am assuming that's who she is anyways. She holds a knife up toward my throat and continues chanting, my muscles feel somehow bound to the words, like each silence between syllables they begin to relax, but not enough to move before the next syllable causes them to painfully tighten again.

So, this is how ends the entirely mediocre life of Miles Ward. This was not how I had it planned. I am going to have my throat cut by this woman. Then she'll probably kill Emily and in fifteen minutes, if Morgan Le Fey is still here, she'll kill Jeff.

My big hope now is that she just leaves once I am dead.

She is so close now I can feel her chanting breath on my ear. I am quaking and quivering, trying to fight against the paralyzing charm she has me under. I am very painfully unsuccessful. She holds the knife against my throat, close enough I can feel the cold steel pressed against my neck.

"You are not the Blethspa Amah," she says matter-of-factly. "The Blethspa Amah would not be taken by such a simple hex"

She also has an accent I'm not familiar with, very northern European sounding, Scandinavian or maybe Icelandic?

"I'm pretty new to all of this," I whisper. It's a struggle to do even that.

"You are but a babe in a world of giants," she whispers back. She's put on a different accent; she now sounds English.

"Y'all won't grow old in this game now, y'hear?" she finishes in a very bad southern accent.

Is she making fun of me and my bad accent habit?

She makes eye contact with me and winks with her pale, pigment-less eyes.

It comes to me in a flash, I remember her now. She was one of the Brits at JMBaptiste. She asked me for directions in front of the liquor store. I'm pretty sure I've seen her browsing books at Grape Reads. I've seen her in a half dozen other places, I am positive now. She's been following me at least since that first day I went to JMBaptiste.

How did I miss that? I'll blame magic.

My eyes scan the room. There is a dark corner that lies away from the windows, on a wall shared with the garage. The darkness in that corner is too dark, it's too black to exist in this well-lit room. I see movement quavering in the darkness. Stepping out of the shadows in a blur and immediately chanting, blood dripping from her hands, comes Circe.

Morgan starts at the motion and nicks the front of my throat. Thank goodness she doesn't hit an artery, but I can feel the blood trickling down into my shirt. I plunge backward.

You'd think from reading books or watching movies that seeing two expert sorcerers duel with magic would be a big flashy affair with lightning and fire and ice flying everywhere. But that isn't the reality, at least not in this case. Their motions, their words go back and forth in a sort of call and response.

Like a very intricate, arcane, and bloody game of rock-paper-scissors.

Maybe as Circe indicated male wizards tend to do bigger, showier, and less efficient stuff like fire and lightning? There's none of that here. Watching Circe and Morgan fight is both horrifying and dull at the same time.

They stand about ten feet apart, making a constant stream of hand gestures and chants in a language or maybe languages that I don't understand. At least two different languages. Morgan starts using my blood on the knife to catalyze her spells, but when it isn't enough, she puts cuts on her arms.

Circe doesn't seem to be cutting herself, but blood begins weeping from her eyes, ears, and mouth. It is a horror show, and I find myself torn between wanting to look away and being glued to the scene—almost like when you drive by a car crash.

I watch dumbfounded for a moment.

It is hard to tell what exactly is going on in the battle. I get the immediate sense that Circe is losing. She looks tired and, in that exhaustion, somehow suddenly more human. She's done a lot today, magically speaking, and that has to take a toll on even the most skilled sorcerer.

Fighting with magic like they are doing requires preparation; the spells are built in advance ritually. They are stored to be catalyzed and triggered later. The number and complexity of spells they are using would have taken years to prepare. This is an investment for each of them. I do not understand the motive for either of them to commit so much, there is more going on here than I understand.

I feel the rigor in my limbs begin lifting as Morgan is no longer focusing her magic on me.

Circe begins side-stepping between motions, not looking where she is going, and continuing her onslaught of offensive and defensive magic. Her movements bring her so that she stands next to Emily.

Circe kicks Emily hard.

I'm a little shocked that she went out of her way to attack Emily like that, but then I realize her goal is to push Emily out of the circle she is trapped in.

This is an even bigger surprise move on Circe's part. Emily hits the floor and sprawls half out of the circle. Suddenly she starts moving, freed from the paralytic hex Morgan had cast on her.

Emily leaps to her feet as soon as they will carry her and runs off around a partition wall.

I don't blame her for fleeing. It is probably the wise move, but I hoped she'd at least try to drag me with her. Nevertheless, I don't have time to dwell on her motivations; this is a moment for action. My limbs are slowly moving again, albeit they are stiff and tingle like I have been laying on them wrong.

I'm torn: Do I stab Morgan with the needle? If I stab her

and it works how Jeff says, I will kill her. Or it could simply not work, and I will just draw Morgan's attention.

My thoughts are interrupted when Emily comes dashing back around the corner holding a large cast iron frying pan. I have a dumb moment where I am not certain what she's going to do with it. I blink, astonished.

She cocks the big piece of iron back with both hands like a baseball bat, ready to club Morgan.

Emily swings.

Morgan sees Emily coming. With blood dripping from her arms, she makes a quick series of signs with her left hand while she continues to engage Circe with her right.

I am stunned, Morgan is casting multiple spells at the same time.

Now is when I'm truly starting to realize the extent of which I am out of my league.

Just for an instant Morgan's figure blurs ever so slightly. Emily's frying pan seems to go right through her. Then with one claw-like hand, Morgan grabs Emily's arm on the backswing.

Morgan hurls Emily like a rag doll at Circe.

Emily crashes into Circe and they fall to the ground in a heap.

The pale woman stands over the two other women cackling and begins a new chant. Her voice deepens, it seems to take on an unnatural reverb. The energy in the room is ominous, it feels like her voice is sucking the light out of the room as shadows draw and pool over the windows.

I realize that this is her magical coup de grace, and my indecision melts away. I charge forward, slipping the cap off of the hypodermic needle as I do, and stab her square in the back. I hammer down hard on the plunger with my thumb.

She never sees it coming.

She doesn't get the chance to blur out of the way.

She screams, loses her focus, and stops chanting.

The light seems to return to the room. The next minute

seems to go by in slow motion as Morgan turns and looks at me horrified. She wildly claws at the thing stuck in her back, screaming. But it's too late.

As I watch, her smooth pale skin begins to wrinkle and dark liver spots begin to appear around her face. By the time she has turned and lurched toward me, she is no longer a voluptuous young woman but a hunched old lady of excessive years. Her clothes suddenly hang loose and baggy on her frame. Her wrinkled face is contorted with rage.

"What have you done?" she screams—her voice a ghastly rendition of what it once was.

She lunges at me, but the supernatural grace is gone.

Now she's just a very old woman with cuts on her arms and a bloody knife in her hand. I easily step aside and slap the knife from her hand. She falls to the ground sobbing.

Emily and Circe make their way toward me in a flash.

"What did you do?" Emily exclaims.

"You stole her magic," Circe looks at me wide-eyed, terrified and confused. Confused by her terror I expect. I don't think she has been afraid of anything in a long time.

"I didn't know if that was going to work," I say.

"Why didn't you do that sooner?" Emily exclaims, walking over and slapping my chest, sounding annoyed.

"I thought it might kill her. I didn't want to do that if I didn't have to."

"No. No," Circe exclaims, distraught. "You did something worse than kill her."

Circe's wide-eyed, frantic tone communicates to me that I am the only true monster she has ever encountered.

For the first time that I've seen, the vampy seductress facade falls completely. She walks over and picks the old woman up from the floor, looping her hands under Morgan's armpits and picking her up like a child.

Her eyes stay locked on me, the way one's eyes would stay locked on a jaguar crouching in the corner. Circe is using

Morgan's decrepit body as a shield, holding her up between us.

Circe is afraid of me.

"What are you doing?" I ask.

"I'll take care of her." Circe backs toward the corner she came out of. She doesn't look as tall or intimidating any more. "Come on, Morgan."

Circe mutters a phrase, and darkness pools in the corner once more. Hefting Morgan onto her shoulder, she leaps into the darkness. They both vanish silently as the shadows fade and the room returns to normal.

There is a long moment of silence, the only sound that can be heard is the ticking of an old-fashioned clock that hangs on the wall.

Emily breaks the silence.

"T-thanks for coming in with a plan. I thought when she forced me to call you, that you'd just come charging in and get us both killed. But you had a secret weapon, impressive. Two secret weapons if you count the giant vampire-ninja lady."

"Yeah…" I say with feigned confidence.

"What was all that about? Why did that woman do all this to get to you? Why did the other one save you? What is going on, Miles?"

Emily rapid fires questions at me. Her pupils have dilated to consume most of her brown eyes like two little singularities in her head. She's talking very fast and in a slightly higher timbre than usual, I can barely follow what she's saying. She waves and shakes her hands in a blur of constant motions.

She's excited? Frightened? Exhilarated?

"They are both Hizarin, and they seem to think I am the Blethspa Amah, a sort of prophesied chosen one. But to be clear, I am not."

"You sure you aren't?" she asks.

Emily has an amazing poker face. I expect to see either a look of confusion or recognition on her face. She has either heard this phrase before or it will be gibberish. But there is no indication on her face either way. For the first time since I met her, I am suspicious of Emily.

"Positive."

"Okay, so what's so special about this Belt spa ama anyway?" she asks, overtly butchering the pronunciation, making it sounds like an intentional mistake. This is the first time I've ever dropped a magical reference that Emily didn't already know. Does Emily know more about this stuff than she's letting on?

She opens a small closet and produces disinfecting spray, which she begins applying to the blood that's splattered all over the floor from the battle.

"It's like someone who's prophesied to be able to undo any spell or…something? I don't know, it's all pretty vague."

"Isn't that what you just did?"

"Well yes, but not really. I mean, I didn't make the thing that did it. I just stabbed her."

"Then who did?"

"Someone who wishes to remain anonymous. You know, in case Circe didn't leave and is just hiding in a shadow or something?"

Emily thinks about this for a moment and nods. She rights a table that was knocked over in the scuffle.

"Why is one trying to kill you and the other saves you if they think you are this chosen one?"

"Circe wanted me to become her apprentice or something."

"Her apprentice…more like her boy toy," Emily says mirthfully. I can feel my ears burning. Emily must notice my embarrassed expression because she stops snickering and falls silent. She gets a mop from the closet and begins cleaning up.

"Don't want this stuff to stain, but maybe it's too late," she says dejectedly, looking at the blood stains already setting on her furniture.

"The other one was afraid I might take her powers away

or something and felt I might be a big threat to them and their organization. Can I help?"

"There is some stain remover on the second shelf down in the closet. I can't say I'm used to scrubbing blood from my floors though. Anyway, she wasn't wrong…you did take away her powers."

"I just don't get why Circe ended up saving Morgan at the end."

"Protecting Hizarin secrets, I'd bet," Emily says.

"What do you mean?"

We continue to talk and clean. The cleaning seems to be helping Emily stay calm.

"Both of them have spells woven into their bodies, lots of them, right? I mean you saw that magical duel. If she left the old woman's body, you could figure out how those spells worked. If I was going to guess, I'd say she was cleaning up. It's what I'd do. You know, if I was a vampire-assassin-sorceress or whatever," Emily says.

I nod. We clean in awkward silence for a moment.

I pull my phone out and quickly text Jeff, letting him know that I am fine and asking him to just wait for me to come out.

"I have a friend waiting down the block to give me a ride. I should probably go."

"I really don't want to be here right now, not after that. I have a lot to process," she says. "It would just feel wrong to stay here."

"Of course. You can come with me I guess, back to my place?" I say. I mean it completely innocently, but partway through my sentence I realize it could be construed as a come-on, which feels inappropriate at this moment. In conclusion, I fumble out, "I mean, we can drop you off somewhere else too…or whatever."

Emily honestly seems to consider. "If you could drop me off at the bookstore. I'll be safe there and just get the cataloging done that I am behind on. Something to distract my mind after all that," she says.

"Yeah, of course. No problem." I'm feeling both relieved and a little rejected at the same time.

Emily excuses herself to change quickly. I stand in her living room looking at the hastily cleaned space. It's still a mess but now looks more like the aftermath of a wild party than a bloody battle. Emily returns a moment later and we walk out the front door. Emily closes and locks it behind her.

"Hey, Miles?" Emily stops on her front porch.

"Yeah?" I say, stopping and turning to face her.

"We had plans last night. You didn't make that and things were going on. I get that. But then all this, magic assassins, paralysis spells, and being held captive…" she says.

"Yeah, I get it."

"Is this normal for you?" she asks, seeming concerned. "I just…like I said earlier, I don't know if I want to get caught up in this business if it's always going to be like this."

"This isn't like a daily thing; this is a little beyond normal. But this isn't my first time getting roughed up on a job," I say. I see where this is going, and I could try to spin this in my favor, but I want to be upfront and honest. "And the way things are looking, I don't think that is going to change anytime soon, with this Blethspa Amah business and everything else."

She nods and looks thoughtful, eyes downcast, lips pursed. Maybe a little bit sad.

"Yeah. That was kind of what I thought. What you do seems interesting. Exciting even. On paper, anyways. But I don't want to do that again. And if that's the kind of thing that happens after not having our first date, I just don't think we are going to work," she says.

I nod solemnly. "That's fair."

"We can still be bookstore friends?" she asks.

"Bookstore friends it is."

She smiles. "Bookstore friends."

I nod and then lead her down the block to Jeff's car.

"Jeff," I say as I open the front door and hold it open for Emily. "This is Emily. Emily this is my friend Jeff."

Emily slides into the front seat.

"Hi, Jeff."

"Hi, Emily, good to meet you," Jeff says as I get in the back seat.

"This is a nice car," Emily says admiringly.

Jeff and Emily start talking on the drive to the bookstore, and I find myself immediately feeling like the third wheel. There is even an exchange of numbers as we near the shop. I knew Emily for more than a year before she gave me her number.

Of course, Jeff actually asked for it.

My jealousy of Jeff begins to grow, he's better at everything than me, has a nicer car than me, and is better at talking to women than me.

Yay.

I am uncharacteristically relieved when Emily gets out and makes her way into the bookstore. I climb into the front seat next to Jeff.

"That went well. Do you want to go get lunch?"

"The town is under lockdown, remember?" Jeff asks.

"Oh yeah. That's too bad. I could use a sandwich and a cup of coffee."

Chapter Thirty-Two

I turn down a street named after a tree in my new Crosstrek. My Jeep didn't make it. The damage it took just wasn't worth the amount it would cost to repair. After a ridiculous amount of paperwork and time on the phone with the insurance company, I bid my old Wrangler a fond farewell as it was towed away to the scrapyard.

I wanted to have a Viking funeral for it, but it turns out burning a car at sea is both expensive and illegal.

I considered buying another Wrangler, but it just wouldn't be the same. I settled on the slightly more grown-up, but still off-road capable Subaru. It has less character, but at least I've got a reliable vehicle for the first time in my life.

I may never stop making payments on it, but it's totally worth it.

I park down the street from Russ' house. It seems like street parking near anyone's place is impossible these days; every parking spot on every road has cars occupying them. I have to walk a block and a half back up the street and around the corner to get to his house.

I stump on up to the front door and go to ring Russ' doorbell. Then I notice a little paper notice 'Doorbell doesn't work, please knock.'

"Okay," I sigh to myself and give a hearty knock on the door. I wait a few minutes humming to myself tunelessly when the door opens. There is Russ, he's wearing old patched-up corduroy slacks, a Guatemalan shirt, and leather sandals, the kind my father used to call 'Scootin' Jesus Slippers:' just a couple of thongs on a leather sole.

"Hey, Miles," he says. "Like how are you, dude? You made it through the gauntlet and like survived!"

"Hi, Russ. Yeah, we made it," I say. "I wanted to come by and say thank you, seriously. I don't know what I'd have done without your help the other night."

"No problem, like no problem, my man," he says. "I, you know, just want to help and all."

"I brought you this," I say, and I give him a package. It has old Frank Zappa vinyl that was my fathers in it. I'm only guessing that this will be up Russ' alley, but it feels like an educated guess.

He holds the package up. He can't see inside, but it doesn't take psychic powers to recognize the size and shape.

"Albums, man, vinyl is the best. All this new digital stuff, it just lacks the soul, you know?"

I don't, and I don't agree with this particular nostalgic sentiment, but I'm not going to make a scene over it.

"Yeah."

"Oh, hey, do you want your book back, man?" Russ asks, he sounds a lot like Tommy Chong at the moment.

"No, as I said, you can keep it. I just wanted to get pictures of the whole thing. I can do that now, if that works for you?"

"Yeah, man. And thanks for it, it's actually really interesting. I've learned a thing or two already."

"That's great," I say as I follow him into his house.

If the outside of his house looks eccentric, the inside of his house is even more surprising. It has all the beaded curtains, wall tapestries, and the portraits of Timothy Leary that I expected. But the surprise is: it's clean. Immaculately so.

Possibly the cleanest, tidiest hippy house I have ever seen in my life.

And I've seen my fair share of hippy houses in my life.

"Come on, it's back here in the study." He leads me down a short hallway and into a room. The room is filled with books. A glance at the shelves reveals a wide array of topics, from philosophy to environmental science, new age mysticism to trashy romance novels.

Interesting.

Sitting on a desk, laying open is the *Phantasmagoricon*. Next to it lays a notebook full of notes written in concise, neat handwriting. Russ continues to defy my expectations.

He motions me to the desk.

"Yeah, go for it, man. Can I get you tea or something?"

"Yes please, that would be nice," I say as I flip the book to the first page and take my phone out.

"You want Manuka honey in that?"

"Um, sure," I say. I have no idea what that means. Russ either picks up on that, or is so used to explaining it he does out of habit.

"It's made from bees that pollinate the Manuka bush in New Zealand, man. It has all these great anti-microbial healing properties, man. Good stuff. Real good stuff."

"Sounds great."

He wanders off while I begin to carefully photograph each page. I'm about thirty pages in when he returns and puts a mug of steaming green tea down next to me.

"Thank you."

"No problem, man," he says and sips his own tea. Then while I continue photographing, he opens up the package I gave him.

"Woah, old Zappa albums. These are original prints, man; they could be worth something to a collector. You sure you want to give them away?"

"Yeah, no problem, Russ. If you like them, I want you to have them."

"Cool. Cool. Thanks, dude."

He puts an album on a turntable in the corner of the room.

"Here, I'll get us some mood music," he says, drawing out the double 'o'.

I don't mind Frank Zappa per se, just nothing I'd listen to on my own. I also don't own a turntable; I listen to everything on my phone. So really if Russ enjoys them, all the better.

"So, Miles, man…."

"Yeah?" I say as I turn the page and take another photo.

"You are photographing that whole thing. Are you interested in Dream-walking?"

"Yeah actually, I kind of am. I feel like there's a lot I could learn there."

"Yeah, man, it's like, woah. There's a whole other world to explore, like literally."

"That's what it seems like."

"Sooo…I could, you know, like, teach you and stuff."

"That would be great, but you know, I don't want to impose."

"No, no imposition, man. It's great to like, have someone who, you know, takes it seriously. I could use an apprentice, dude."

"Alright. Well. I don't know, when do we start?"

"Well, while you're here I can talk you through the basics and then you can try it at home and we can like touch base, you know?"

"Okay. I have questions."

"Shoot, man."

"That concoction that Circe gave you: do you have to take drugs to lucid dream? To dream walk?"

"Oh, no, no, man, you don't. In fact, it's best if you can do it without…but that's like hard, you know, when you have timelines or you wanna go like deep and hard, and all that shit. Going deep fast, sometimes a little pharmaceutical assistance is required."

"Ah," I say, kind of understanding.

"When you came to me, there was like time and it's hard to get in the right head space for something like that I need a little something-something sometimes. Or if like, I want to stay in for a long time or something. I'm not saying this right. Um. Like the Daunts, you don't want to be partially done dealing with them and like wake up, it'd go bad. In a situation like that you wanna be in till your done, you dig." he says.

Then he ponders for a moment and continues.

"Imagine that the world is like, you know, the world. And we impose free will, time and space, and all of those illusions onto the world. And the dream is like its reflection, its shadow, but like, also it. It's like part of reality and not part of it. Inside the dream, time and space, and all that, you know they don't exist as those illusions get stripped away. Well, when normal people enter the dream, it's like an amusement park ride, right?"

I nod encouragingly. I'm not sure I know what he's talking about though.

"You sit on it, and you see what it has to offer, pieces of existence from everywhere and every-when. Just sit there, and the ride takes you through it. It can be scary or exciting or fun, but it's safe and then you wake up and you are back in reality. You get off the ride."

I'm so lost.

"Your mind imposes things like time and space and agency on the experience, afterward right? Sometimes it can be hard to let go of all those illusions we cling to without a little nudge off the cliff, you dig?" He pauses to see if I am with him.

I think about what he has said for a minute before responding.

"So, in a normal dream, you are just along for the ride, and it's confusing, but your brain makes a story out of it when you wake up. That sort of reconciles it with your experiences, and that's the 'dream' you tell people about. But sometimes you need the drugs to let go of your attachments and get off the ride?" I say, I'm trying to follow but his metaphor is a little confusing.

"Yeah, that's pretty much that in a nutshell. So now, a Lucid Dreamer is like in the gondola on the amusement park ride, but they can like, get out. And they can walk around and look at the exhibits and even see some of how it works. They can walk back and look at things they already saw and really examine them. They can even go and get into other people's gondolas and shit, right? When they wake up, they can sort of…" he pauses and stares out the window for a moment.

"Hey, check out that bird, man, I think it's a barn swallow."

I look out the window and see the bird he is talking about perched on a branch near his window.

"That's cool. So you were saying, when a Lucid Dreamer wakes up from the…gondola," I try to nudge him back on track.

"Oh right. Um. Gondola. Lucid. Wake up. Oh, yeah. Um, I don't know, they like craft the narrative of what they experience as a conscious effort, not an unconscious one. Cause like the real dream; it can't be explained in terms that make sense in reality, man, so you have to make the sense for it. Dig? You gotta make a context in which to explain it. A metaphor. To impose will and time and space and all that. Like that barn swallow there."

I nod. I thought I was following his logic, up until the barn swallow.

"I guess that makes sense," I say, though I think that's a lie. I think I understand what he means, but I'm not certain. My brain isn't ready for more.

"Okay, so a true Dream Walker though, there's like lots of names, but you know like a master of dreams? They can open the 'employees only' door hidden in the corner of the ride, and they can walk back behind the scenes. They can see how it all works, shape it, change the ride, right, man? They can turn it backward, they can walk to other rides, see? Where other people are dreaming and they can, you know, add stuff to the other rides. They can take things off of one ride and put them somewhere else, or even put them in storage.

Anyway, finding the employees-only door can be hard, it's usually somewhere they don't want you to see it, right? The drugs, they are like bringing a flashlight, man. Sometimes you just need a little put-me-down, man. See what I did there, it's like a pick-me-up, but it's for sleeping?"

I give him a polite half-hearted chuckle. This was confusing enough without puns that require explanation.

"And that's how you got into my dream and how you got rid of the Daunts?"

"Yeah, man. And it's how I put a wall up around your dreams to keep those Daunts out, 'cause man, they are still after you. I've never seen anything like it."

"That's unsettling. Thanks for that. I guess. See, this is why I need to learn this stuff."

"You remember I talked to you about a door, man?" he says. "I mean a door-comma-man, not a doorman."

He laughs to himself.

"Yeah, it was in my shoe," I say.

"Sometimes they are in weird places, sometimes they are in obvious places, sometimes they are hidden. But they are in places you will want to look but will always find a reason not to look. I call them the Ambivalent Doors because you will always be of two minds about wherever they are, and they will never be in a place you'd expect. In a nightmare, they are usually wherever seems like the scariest to go, and in other dreams, they are like somewhere kind of uncomfortable or something? Like a juice bar. Like, who wants to go to a bar for juice?"

I start to chuckle, but stifle it when I see he isn't being ironic.

"Anyway, wherever is scariest or weirdest or most embarrassing, that's where they are. So, the trick is, that when you are in a dream, and you have that instant where you think to yourself 'Am I dreaming?' you say, 'Hell yeah I am!' and you break the flow of the dream. If you are being chased, you stop and don't run, if you are in school, in nothing but your underwear, you take 'em off, you know? You gotta get off the ride first. Once you get off the ride, you find the door. You open it and go through. And there you are."

"That sounds pretty easy."

He laughs.

"It's not, man. You'll try a hundred times before you find the door. You'll try a thousand times before you make it through."

"Okay, so that's where I start, trying to be aware that I am dreaming, and then breaking it and looking for the door."

"Yeah, man," he says.

"I've heard that one can physically enter the Dreaming, is that true?"

"I've never done it; I've heard it's true. That book…" he motions to the *Phantasmagoricon*, "it's got a section about that. Anyway, everything and everyone says it is super dangerous to do and super-super hard. Big rituals, lots of prep, both in the real world and the Dreamtime."

I ponder, there is something I suspect, and I am hoping Russ can confirm or refute this for me.

"If someone could physically enter and exist, more or less at will, could they effectively teleport? Like jump in and out of shadows sort of thing?"

"Yeah, I mean usually it takes magic circles and like big rituals, but like if someone got real good at it? Or found some kind of trick? They could use it to travel. Again, it'd be super dangerous. Because physically in the Dreamtime you don't have the chimeric veil protecting you from stuff, Daunts go from being annoying pests to horrifying monsters that'll eat your face. And there's worse, oh man, my dude, so much worse."

"Thanks, that helps."

"No problem, dude. And that's all like a way simplified version, we will talk the more existential stuff later."

Great.

"I spend my nights practicing that, and I avoid trying to physically enter the dream and—"

"I think we make weekly check-ins on progress; you know once you are feeling more comfortable, we can like plan some in the dream meet-ups to like, you know, get hands-on experience or whatever."

I've pretty much finished photographing all of the pages and have drunk half of my tea at this point.

"Sounds great. Thank you again, Russ."

"No problemo, Miles. So, what, I'll see you again next week? Same Bat Time, Same Bat Channel?"

I'm pretty sure he means here at this time next week. I check my calendar on my phone.

"Sounds good, Russ. Sounds good."

He gives me a high five, we say goodbye, and I head home, my head frankly spinning from everything he's just unloaded on me.

Chapter Thirty-Three

Is it the truth that defines us? Or is it the lies that we tell ourselves that define our perceptions of ourselves? Is it the lies we tell others that define their perceptions of us? And in the intersection between the two that we ourselves become defined? Is it this great internetwork of lies and self-deception that collaboratively define reality?

Or is there an ultimate, unchanging truth that exists outside of our experiences that defines it? If all the façade was taken down, the veneer stripped off and the cold, hard face of this external truth was all that remained, would we exist at all?

These are the thoughts going through my head as I stand on Alistair's porch, proverbial hat in hand, debating if I should ring the doorbell or not.

Might as well get this over with.

I push the button. It takes about two minutes before Alistair answers the door. He's wearing a collared shirt, a tie, pajama pants, and fuzzy pink bunny slippers—the attire of someone who spends their entire day as a talking head on video calls.

"Hi Alistair," I say sheepishly, standing on his front porch.

This is the third time I have come by, but the previous two times I kept driving when I saw that Alistair's snarky husband

Jon's car was there. I don't want to deal with Jon's heckling right now.

"Hi Miles," Alistair says, crossing his arms as a frown plasters his face.

"Hey, so, I'm sorry about dropping a random guy on your doorstep in the middle of the night. And I am sorry it has been almost a week and I'm just getting around to talking to you about it. I slept for the entire first day and a half."

"Miles. The other night, shit was going down. I get that, and honestly, Jon and I are better equipped to deal with that than most. I get that. I'm fine with friends coming by at any hour if they are in trouble. Any kind of trouble. What I don't appreciate is you running off without a word."

"No…I understand. A lot was going on, and most of it was dangerous. The more I stuck around, the more it felt like I'd drag you in. I didn't want to drag you in."

This is true, but it's not the whole truth. The truth is I just didn't want to answer questions, I just wanted to hand my problem off and go to sleep.

"But you did. You dragged us right into the middle of it," Alistair responds. "I cannot tell you how much explaining I've had to do."

Alistair uses his hands to motion around the whole city.

"All that shit that went on the other night. We have been asked a lot of questions. Do you have any idea how much relationship collateral it cost me to convince Jon to keep your name out of it?" he says, but I can see his crankiness fading.

"I mean I can guess, but no, obviously I don't know. Jon doesn't like me, does he?"

"You might not believe it, but Jon is constantly impressed with you."

"Really?" I ask, confused.

"Impressed with your ability to piss him off, he's usually pretty levelheaded. Nothing gets him worked up, but you do," Alistair finishes.

"Oh," I say, feeling a bit dejected.

"No, that's impressive. You're the only person who pisses him off more than me. Honestly, I get a little jealous."

"Oh?" I say, not knowing if I should be flattered or not.

"Anyway, that catatonic guy, you left on my doorstep in the small hours of the morning…" Alistair changes topics.

"Yeah?"

"Super interesting. His name is Lawrence Metz. He was an up-and-coming MMA fighter, then one day he just stopped showing up to his training and stuff. Vanished. Missing persons, back of milk carton kind of thing. His family is offering up a big cash reward for information leading to his return."

"Really?"

"Yeah."

"My leaving him on your doorstep is getting you a bunch of cash?" I ask incredulously.

"Yes, technically. But Jon and I already agreed that we would be donating any reward to charity. Jon felt that something helping with mental illness was appropriate."

"Like to help Mr. Metz?"

"No. Jon specifically was hoping we could get you into the program," Alistair says, laughing.

"Hah. Hah," I say without mirth.

There is a long awkward silence. Finally, Alistair breaks it.

"What happened to that guy anyway? Like how'd you end up bringing him to my doorstep?"

"I don't think you would believe me," I say. "The truth is crazy even by my standards. I'm not sure I believe the story myself, and I was there. I know you don't really buy into my occupation."

"Honestly, I don't. But after just a couple of hours with Mr. Metz, I'd like to hear your version," Alistair says with honest curiosity in his voice.

"Okay. I don't know the full details. But a very powerful, very old sorceress turned him into a Fetch," I say. Seeing the blank look on Alistair's face, I clarify, "A thrall. She basically lobotomized him with magic and made him like a living zombie that she could control. Just enough left of his brain to hear and follow orders, but no real will or self-motivation. Up until the other night, I thought that once they were that far gone, it was like over-over. But Jeff's concoction—"

I see Alistair's face when I mention Jeff and I see his glower.

"You dragged Jeff into this?"

"No. No! Not really. He helped me out with lab work only and it turns out he's good at this stuff. I made sure he wasn't getting chased by vampires and child-eating monsters. He wasn't around for that part," I blurt out to try to cover.

Alistair always seems a little jealous of Jeff—I guess that's something we have in common. The single, childless life seems to have a secret draw for Alistair. Jeff is the epitome of that lifestyle. I, on the other hand, am also single and childless, but show up on Alistair's doorstep battered and covered in mud in the small hours of the morning to remind him how sideways the single and childless lifestyle can go.

"Child-eating monsters?" Alistair raises an eyebrow.

"Yeah. But don't worry, it's dead. Killed by a magical vampire assassin," I say, and he raises a single eyebrow in skepticism. "Yeah, I know how it sounds."

"Well. I'm glad you are okay. I'm glad Jeff's okay. I am glad we got Mr. Metz into a program where he can get help, and I am glad that one child-eating monster—whether real or imaginary—is no longer in this world," Alistair says.

"Anyway, I just came by to apologize. I know I probably could have handled that better, but I hadn't slept in days and I was under duress."

"Apology accepted. You should probably not come by while Jon is home for a while," he says, pausing as he looks around and chuckles. "I notice you waited till he was picking the kids up from school to stop by."

"He doesn't pull any punches."

"No, he does not," Alistair agrees. "On that note, you should probably get going, he'll be back soon."

"Yeah. See you at poker night?"

"See you at poker night."

I wave at him as I walk back to my car; he waves back and smiles. I can tell from his casual manner that he has forgiven me for leaving a living zombie on his doorstep in the middle of the night. A week ago, we were just poker night buddies, but I feel like now we might be friends.

I get back into my car and start the engine. I am only a few blocks away when my phone rings. I answer it on a wireless headset.

"Miles Ward speaking. Wards raised; monsters braised. Affordable prices," I say as I answer.

"Hey, Miles, it's Jeff. If your prices are affordable you need to raise them, and the braising thing doesn't flow well."

"Hey, Jeff, how's it going?" I say. "Thanks for your help the other day."

"You're welcome."

"What's going on?" I ask. Jeff doesn't usually call me in the middle of the day.

"So, about Emily…?" he says, sounding awkward. I'm pretty sure I know what's next.

"Yeah, Emily is great."

"Yeah, I think so too. Anyway, she and I made a date for later this week, and I couldn't help but feel like you were interested in her and—"

"I like Emily and I was interested in her, but she made it clear that she didn't want to get caught up in all my shenanigans."

"So, you're okay if I date her?"

"Not my place to be okay or not. You two get to make your own decisions. It's not like she and I have an actual history together or anything," I say, blowing out a breath. I am still a little disappointed that Emily changed her mind, but I understand.

It's not like my having a little crush on her entitles me to anything in her or Jeff's life.

"I get that. It's just me, nothing to do with her. I want to make sure that you and I will be cool if I do."

"We're always cool, Jeff. Always cool. Though, you should come clean with her about the whole anointed-one thing. She deserves to know up front, if she doesn't want to get involved in the danger and excitement. There is potential there. If nothing else, it's pretty weird."

"I was planning to. Anyway, I need to get back to work. I'll see you a poker night?"

"Definitely. Ciao," I say, releasing any feelings I had for Emily for the time being back into the universe.

I hang up and keep driving. I roll the windows down. I turn down a lane, vineyards stretch out in every direction. The grape leaves are just starting to turn. Soon they will be a blaze in yellows, reds, and oranges and I can smell the first hints of the sweet funky smell of wine must on a gust of cool air.

For a moment, I feel at peace with the world.

Did you enjoy this story?

Miles Wards next adventure:

Blood, Wine, Magic: Book 2

Charred-Donnay

Will soon be available for pre-order. Find it at https://www.justingodey.com/blood-wine-magic/books

Want to stay in touch? Join my newsletter at https://www.justingodey.com/newsletter

www.ingramcontent.com/pod-product-compliance
Lightning Source LLC
Chambersburg PA
CBHW020929310726
48980CB00007B/696/J

* 9 7 9 8 9 9 9 9 5 3 8 0 3 *